R L Martin

THE WINE AND THE MUSIC

WILLIAM E. BARRETT

The Wine and the Music

BOOK ONE

PORTRAIT OF A CELIBATE

BOOK TWO

PORTRAIT OF A WOMAN

BOOK THREE

TOMORROW AND TOMORROW

Doubleday & Company, Inc.
GARDEN CITY, NEW YORK

TO
CHRISTINE
FOR WHOM ALL OF
THE BOOKS ARE WRITTEN

BOOK ONE

Portrait of a Celibate

– I –

He was thirty-two years old and he was dedicated to chastity by a vow of celibacy. He had accepted celibacy as essential to his way of life. That acceptance did not make sexual deprivation easier to bear, of course, but it did provide him with a hard core of resistance to the sexual lures. He had learned in the seminary a series of rationalizations about women and he had cultivated a habit of detachment which affected his relationship with men almost as much as that with women. He did not know that this was so; it had never occurred to him. He said that he liked people, and he did, but he did not know any individual person well. He came to focus swiftly when confronted with human trouble, grief or difficulty, and his emotions were immediately involved; but his involvement was of the moment. He advised, consoled, shared a worry or helped another human being to meet an emergency; but once a crisis was past, when he had done what he could, he forgot, or dismissed, or moved on. He could permit many people access to his life, but the pattern of that life in terms of time, habit and facility would not sustain them; they came and they went away. He was a lonely man but he did not think of himself as unhappy, or as in need of anything that was essential to him. He was a devout man, a warm and generous man, a man with a quiet sense of humor and with no trace of a halo. He lived along the surface of things with other creatures and, without realizing that he did so, avoided both the heights and the depths.

His name was Gregory Lind. He was a Roman Catholic priest.

5

Father Lind was one of three priests serving Saint Anselm's parish. He was the only priest assigned to hear Friday afternoon confessions and there had been many Fridays. He had not enjoyed any of them. A man was penned in a dark little box for hours and voices came through a screen to him, out of darkness into darkness. The Friday afternoon voices would be those of children and of old women, seldom of anyone else. The confessions would be incredibly alike. Occasionally a child would surprise a man, but an old woman? Never.

It was dark in the church, shadow dark. The huge stained-glass windows were dimly lighted by the winter sunlight and it was too early for artificial light. Two candles burned on the altar and the red sanctuary lamp glowed. High on either side of the altar there were kneeling angels with folded wings. In this light they were visible only as silhouettes and the wings seemed taller than the angels. Father Lind knelt on the lowest of the three altar steps. The one priestly function which he disliked more than any other was the hearing of confessions. He offered up his prayer, as he always did, that he would not fail anyone who came into his confessional today, that he would be able to serve the will of God, not condoning evil but compassionate to human weakness. He prayed, sincerely, finding the words that he wanted, not reciting to a formula.

Behind him a foot tripped against a kneeler, the sound echoing hollowly. Someone coughed and there was a click of rosary beads. He was aware of the sounds, aware that there were people in the church, and yet he was alone; kneeling in the presence of God.

He did not know precisely when he ceased to be solitary. He was in mid-prayer when she came; a face floating before the tabernacle. His prayer faltered, then picked up again as he willed his mind to ignore the distraction. It was a familiar distraction. She came to him in similar fashion when he was reading a newspaper, when he was reading his office or eating his lunch, driving an automobile or drifting on the edge of sleep. It was ridiculous. He was thirty-two years old, and he should be, if he wasn't, after nearly eight years of priesthood, in sufficient command of himself that he could block out such fantasies.

The girl was nothing to him, a teacher in the adult education night school where he served humbly himself. Her name was Pamela Gibson. She was a Protestant and, someone had told him, divorced. He had had only brief, polite, formal conversation with her. He did not know her at all. It was preposterous that he should remember her, think of her, see her face through his prayers; utterly preposterous. She was not even a good show in the remembering. He had not, actually, seen her in many poses or watched her do many things; so

6

his imagination had little material with which to work. In these annoying visions she did, over and over again, the few things that he had seen her do.

It was an obsession, he supposed. But why? She wasn't beautiful, not memorable in any way. Her face was an inverted triangle with the chin as the apex. There was not much shape to her mouth and her lipstick was too red. He did not know the color of her eyes but her hair, he supposed, would be called auburn, a dark, coppery shade of red. She was not very tall and she was thin. Her body looked angular and she had a striding walk, awkward. She was not a friendly girl. She kept people at a distance.

Father Lind made the sign of the Cross. His prayer had been ruined. There was no sense or point in saying that Pamela Gibson had ruined it. She did not know anything about his prayers. She probably would not enter a Catholic church under any circumstance. The ruining of the prayer had occurred in the mind of the man who prayed. That is what he would tell another human being in the confessional and that is what he had to tell himself. He stood for a moment, facing the church, and it seemed to him that he could see her striding down the aisle, an impatient young woman with no time to waste. He decided that he did not like her. That was the proper exorcism, and an honest one. He did not like her.

He walked down the side aisle, a tall young man in a Roman collar and a black cassock. He heard his penitents rising hastily from the pews. They would be finding places for themselves in line behind those who were already waiting. He did not look at them. He never looked at the people who were outside of his confessional. They would be coming into the box and he preferred to know them merely as voices, as souls in trouble, not as individuals with whom he shared simple greetings, friendly exchanges of conversation. The social value of the confessional was low.

He seated himself on the straight wooden chair between the two windows. He faced the door by which he had entered, a closed door now, sealing him in. He stretched out his right hand and opened one of the windows by sliding back the solid wood panel. There was a fine meshed screen across the aperture and beyond that there was darkness. A voice came to him, pitched low and slightly hushed, a woman's voice:

"Bless me, Father, for I have sinned. I confess to Almighty God."

His afternoon had begun. Father Lind listened patiently to a familiarly innocuous recital of petty faults, spoke a few words of admonition, imposed a penance and granted absolution. He closed the panel and opened the one on his left.

There were quite a few people, a steady flow. With the fifth or sixth penitent, Pamela Gibson entered the box with him. He was seeing her face in the darkness as he had seen it at the altar. He said a "Hail Mary," refusing to think about the girl, closing his mind against the vision of her. There was a boy in the left-hand box, a boy with a childish voice that had occasional deep tones in it.

"I had dirty thoughts, Father. Seven times."

Some boys said "impure thoughts" and others, like this one, said "dirty thoughts." It made no difference; they were the same thoughts under one label or another. Girls were less frank about accusing themselves in that department and when they did there was a lot of circumlocution about it, a lot of evading the issue. Such mathematical precision as "seven times" when applied to thoughts was fascinating. That was the confessional requirement, of course; the sin and the number of times committed. The confessor lectured a sinner sternly about the holding of such thoughts, commanding him to resolutely dismiss them as soon as they appeared. The confessor knew, of course, that the penitent would be back with the same confession, but he had to spur him to fight because indulgence in sex thoughts and fancies and mental pictures were bad for him, weakening his moral fiber, paving the way for greater sin.

Father Lind spoke solemnly, sternly to the sinner beyond the grille and, even as he did so, he was fighting his own battle against a thought, the projection of a girl's image from his mind to a suspended screen. There was nothing "impure" or "dirty" in his thoughts of Pamela Gibson, nothing sinful about seeing her face in the church or anywhere else; but, to be fair, a man had to see the similarity of situations. His thought of her was distracting him from his work. Why didn't he banish the thought of her as he told these youngsters to banish their thoughts?

There was a straight run of little girls in the confessional now; the most stereotyped of all sinners, mouthing small offenses in a manner that proclaimed them big, seeming to take pride in transgression but remaining good children, very good children. Father Lind's attention wandered away from them.

Pamela Gibson was not the first woman who had claimed a place in his mind without consulting him. From time to time he was impressed with some one woman out of the many, attracted by her eyes, the way she held her head, or some combination of qualities. It was inevitable, of course; he was a man as well as a priest. He never did

8

anything about any of the women and they faded from his mind after a short stay. Pamela Gibson did not fade. She definitely did not fade. Not today, at any rate. Ultimately she, too, would disappear, certainly. A priest had no room for women in his life.

The voices droned or pattered or stuttered, dropped low, climbed high. The window panels clicked as they slid back, thudded gently as they closed. The afternoon ran itself out, the penitents became more widely spaced and then they ceased to come. Father Lind rose. His left leg felt stiff and he worked it back and forth before he stepped out into the church. His shoulders felt stiff too, and he wanted to stretch, but one didn't. He walked up the aisle and knelt again to pray. He did not see Pamela Gibson but he could feel her presence like a hovering ghost. He made the sign of the Cross, the sign-off of prayer, and walked through the sacristy.

A hovering ghost! He thought of that phrase with which he had mentally described his impression to himself. It amused him. She would not like being that. She would not, he was certain, like it at all.

Outside, it was snowing. The flakes were large, floating lazily down. The air was gentle. Father Lind went indoors again reluctantly. The rectory was warm, stuffy as he had known that it would be. The lower hall was dark and there was no sign of life in the pastor's domain to the left of the hall. Father Schafer was dining out. Father Guyton would not be in, either. He had dinner at his mother's house on Friday night. Mrs. Wagner, the housekeeper, would not put much of her mind into cooking tonight with only one man to eat what she cooked. Father Lind hesitated with one foot on the bottom step of the stairs. It would be pleasant to dine out, in some clean, cheerful place. He put his hand in his pocket and shook his head. The budget wouldn't carry it.

His room was on the second floor, a rather large room with a bay window. His bed was a narrow affair with a hard mattress. He had two chairs, one of them comfortable, and a small table for his typewriter. His dresser was bearing the years bravely but without beauty. Apart from that, there was little to command attention: a crucifix above his bed, a night stand which held his alarm clock and which would, doubtless, hold medicine if he ever needed it, a group of photographs on one wall. The pictures were of his family: his father, mother, three sisters and a brother. His father was dead. He had portraits of his three brothers-in-law and his sister-in-law but he had never had them framed.

Gregory Lind had been a long, lean, rangy individual through all of his career but, of late, he had been picking up weight. He felt that he should take off at least five pounds and it might be a salutary thing to

9

take off ten. He stripped to his underwear and lifted his light barbell without joy. He hated solitary exercise and he would not indulge in it if he did not hate even more fervently the idea of a bulging belt line. His belt line did not actually bulge but it was beginning to convex a bit where once it had consistently concaved.

He worked silently, grimly, for fifteen minutes, then laid the bells aside. He showered and did a quick runover with his electric razor. He was dressed again, just settling his shoulders into the trim black coat, when the hand bell rang at the foot of the stairs. Mrs. Wagner rang her bell for supper even if there was only one priest in the house, and the one priest knew exactly when she would ring it. Father Lind went slowly down the stairs. The rectory seemed particularly empty tonight, spookily so, but on its best nights it was not a companionable place.

The dining room had probably been quite elegant at one time, but the green draperies were faded to a dull tone now and the gold figures looked almost brown. The carpet, too, had been green and gold but the colors had been dimmed under the pressure of many feet; long ago feet, Gregory Lind thought, feet that were gone before he came. From the east wall and the west wall, two former pastors of Saint Anselm's looked at each other with a marked lack of cordiality. They had been done when oil paintings of prominent personages were the vogue. There had been pastors since who were not represented in the house by so much as a snapshot. At the far end of the room there was a television set. It was seldom that anyone turned it on. Neither Father Guyton, the other priest in the house, nor Father Lind, owned a set but it was a bother, somehow, to come downstairs to this one and the room was a gloomy, depressing setting if one sought entertainment. The pastor had his own TV in his suite.

Mrs. Wagner served Father Lind's dinner silently. It was a plain omelet, a limp-looking salad and two slices of bread. Mrs. Wagner was a relative of the pastor's and she did not exert herself unduly when Father Schafer was not home. Her attitude toward Father Lind was forever reserved. She treated him, after nearly three years, like a visitor in the rectory. So, too, for that matter, did the pastor. Father Lind could understand that, or at least partly understand it.

Gregory Lind had been the editor of the seminary newspaper while he was preparing for the priesthood. He had ended his seminary career about halfway down on the scholastic ladder but on the top as a writer. When he was ordained, the bishop had assigned him to the diocesan paper, the *Catholic Star*, as associate editor and had coupled the appointment with a priestly assignment to the cathedral where his duties were light. He had five years there and he would, probably, have remained at the cathedral if Father Schafer had not laid siege to the bishop, demanding another assistant. The bishop gave him Gregory Lind and Father Schafer was enraged.

"A part-time priest!" he said. "What good will he be to me? Let him work at his paper and stay at the cathedral where they never know how many priests they have anyway."

Such minor dramas happened behind the scenes of Roman Catholic administration, and the minor dramas resulted in major changes for human beings in terms of their living. Father Lind had been comfortable in the cathedral rectory and he had lived well; but he did not miss the cathedral greatly. It had never offered him a genuine priestly opportunity. The pastor had accepted the fact that this priest belonged to the newspaper and he had interfered little with a newspaper priest's life. The pastor of Saint Anselm's was another matter. He did not seem to have any respect for the newspaper or for its priest. There were days and nights when Father Lind sympathized with him and considered him justified in his attitude. Making an editor out of a priest seemed to do violence to the purpose for which he was ordained. He was very likely to end up as a mediocre priest and as a mediocre editor.

"Morbid thought!" he said aloud. "How many brilliant priests does one know? On a newspaper or off one?"

He ate his omelet slowly. Usually, when he had his breakfast, lunch or dinner alone, which was often, he read a book or a newspaper for companionship: tonight, he did not feel like reading. He thought about his day, about his experience in the church. He could think of Pamela Gibson now without conjuring up images. She did not float before him, nor move like a presence in the room: he could think about her as he would think of anyone else.

Pamela Gibson was a girl in her mid-twenties, a teacher in a project to which he dedicated all of the time that he could spare. He did not know her very well and he rarely had any reason to confer with her. She had never shown either interest in him nor liking for him; she had never made the simple, harmless, flirtatious gestures which women, even nuns, make when a priest comes on the scene. There was no reason, absolutely no reason, why he should remember her, why she should disturb his prayers at the altar.

He turned her over in his mind as an interesting problem, a riddle without an immediate answer. There was sex, of course, as the obvious cliché explanation, but it did not explain. His emotions were not, in any way, involved. As a male, he was quite aware of females in the

11

world. Some of them were more attractive than others, some more memorable. There had been some women during his seven-plus years as a priest whom he had liked, whom he had looked forward to seeing from time to time, including one nun who had taught at Cathedral School during the time he was stationed there. The awareness of certain individual women out of the mass was as far as he had ever gone. He was a dedicated man, a conditioned man, who had faced and accepted long ago the fact that there were human associations, human experiences, that were not for him.

He rose from the table, vaguely dissatisfied with this quiet house that was his home. The pastor and Father Guyton would be hearing the Friday night confessions and they would come back to the rectory before going to the church. Father Lind did not want, particularly, to see them and he had work of his own to do. Friday was one of his nights at the project.

– II –

Culverton was an old city and it climbed away from the river on a series of low, jagged hills. It had a population of 186,972 and it had grown away from its beginnings through a sequence of semi-suburban developments. The original town had been established by German immigrants who built solid houses, raised large families and established themselves in trades, in business, in industry and in banking. The descendants of those settlers still dominated the town. Some of the descendants lived in houses that were sixty to a hundred and twenty years old. The oldest houses, with many that were built later, were in Saint Anselm's parish and the inhabitants gave the parish its strong conservative coloration. Only those who were by nature conservative stayed in the old town; the others moved out to create new neighborhoods, new patterns of living.

North of the parish was the one-time Irish section which no longer housed people with Irish names. Half of this section was attached to lower downtown, the inevitable Skid Row, the other half had been taken over by Spanish Americans who were oddly misplaced in a river city of the Midwest. Labor contractors had brought the Spanish Americans from the Southwest to labor in the fields west of Culverton, and some of them had stayed, no longer working in farm country, badly adjusted to city living and to city jobs. These people were exploited,

12

more or less, by politicians and they were resentful of their precarious position in the community, seemingly unwilling or unable to leave it.

The Spanish Americans were Father Gregory Lind's concern, his own parishioners. More than a third of them were, geographically, in Saint Anselm's parish although few of them sought it as a church. Saint Cajetan's, the city's one Spanish church, was small and poor, badly equipped to take care of those legitimately on its lists, overloaded when asked to take any of those beyond its boundaries. Father Schafer, pastor of Saint Anselm's, had no knowledge of Saint Cajetan's problems and no interest in Spanish Americans.

"These people have a church of their own," he said, "and they'll be happier among their own kind."

There was no malice in Father Schafer. He was, actually, under his bluff exterior, a kind-hearted man, but his attitude toward Spanish Americans was the popular attitude in Culverton. Spanish Americans did not blend easily into the community pattern and honest citizens believed that what did not blend was better off in a community of its own. Father Lind, with two jobs, neither of which fulfilled him as a priest, spoke Spanish rather well and he made these people his own. He had, of course, first cleared with his pastor.

"Do what you like, provided you do not neglect the little work you're called upon to do around here," Father Schafer said impatiently. "But do not commit me, or the parish, to any activity with these people. None!"

Father Lind had opened a campaign with stories and editorials in the *Catholic Star*. The Spanish American community needed adult education more than did any other segment of the population. Young people and old, they were shocking in their lack of skills; pitifully handicapped, many of them, by their lack of English.

Saint Bridget's school building was in the Spanish American sector, idle and boarded up, only superficially vandalized. Saint Bridget's Church had burned in 1963 and when the Bishop decided against rebuilding in a deteriorating neighborhood, the school had closed. Father Lind took it over. The morning paper helped him with daily publicity over a period of weeks and money flowed in to him. Qualified teachers and instructors who could speak Spanish volunteered their services. Equipment came from many sources. One of those sources had taught the priest a lesson in fund raising.

He visited the office of the district superintendent of a medium-large airline.

"We need a shop in our project," he said. "I don't know what a shop

13

needs in the way of equipment but our people are good with their hands. They can learn hand skills."

"How much do you need?"

"I don't know." Father Lind hesitated, then plunged. "Could you spare us a hundred dollars?"

The airline man laughed. "Father," he said, "you can't buy a decent screwdriver for a hundred dollars. Let me look into that shop idea of yours."

The "shop idea," with an airline subsidy, soon filled the basement of the school building and Father Lind understood only vaguely what went on there. He had no mechanical skills.

Originally, Father Lind had planned to dedicate the project to "Our Lady of Guadalupe" but he revised his plan out of deference to the many Protestants and Jews who helped him generously. He called the school "Guadalupe House." The Spanish Americans knew what he meant and everyone else seemed to like the name.

Once the school became a reality, Father Lind faded into the background, taking no credit for it, leaving its direction to trained educators. He assumed neither title nor authority. He had an office to which he came on free evenings. He was a chaplain of sorts, an adviser, morale builder, troubleshooter. His job was one of subtle definition and it demanded much of him.

He came to Guadalupe House out of the snow, with the Friday afternoon confessions and the omelet dinner behind him. There was a hum about the place, voices from different rooms that blended, and a heavier sound that was a compound of machine shop noises downstairs and the pound of feet on passageways. The typing class was halfway down the main ground floor hall and Father Lind was tempted to look in on it, for no particular reason save his curiosity. He was not certain that Pamela Gibson looked as he remembered her. He shook his head. It made no difference, no difference at all.

There were two boys waiting for him in his office; Juan Archuleta, seventeen, and Arturo Monso, nineteen. They were high school dropouts who had had an idea that they wanted to be carpenters. They had been working in the carpenter shop, learning the rudiments, and now they no longer wanted to be carpenters. They were going to quit, definitely, but the man said they must first tell the padre, so they were here. They sat tensely in their chairs, prepared for argument. Father Lind leaned back comfortably in his own chair.

"O.K.," he said. "What was it that you did not like in the carpenter shop?"

"We did not like it."

14

He nodded. This was an old story. The average Spanish American had an inferiority complex deeply rooted in his personality. He tackled study, a job, a course of instruction, anything at all, bravely; then, as soon as it became difficult, when it called on him for effort, he quit. Many of these boys had left jobs they could have held because they did not believe in themselves, in their own ability.

"Do you boys know how to ride a bicycle?" Father Lind asked.

"Yes."

"But, of course. Well, tell me something. When I was learning to ride, I fell off a number of times, fell over in the street. Did that happen to you?"

Juan Archuleta leaned forward. "*Sí*. It happened."

"You kept trying and you learned. So did I. Now we can both ride bicycles."

"*Sí*." Juan's teeth flashed. They were very white teeth. He was a young Spanish American who had conquered a difficulty. This Anglo priest was aware of it. It was a bond between them. Arturo Monso sat frowning.

"I did not fall from that bike when I learned," he said bluntly.

"Oh. That is interesting. You had a talent then for the bicycle. You did not know you had the talent till you tried, of course. Juan and I did not have the talent so we had to learn slowly."

He had their attention. It was the same with everything, Father Lind said, plumbing or electrical work or carpentry. Some men had a talent and learned easily. Other men had to work harder but they learned, too. Carpentry was an interesting trade. A man did many kinds of jobs and he was well paid. There was a lot of building and probably always would be. All the babies one saw would grow up and need houses in which to live. Yes. The priest spoke simply, chatting with a couple of friends. He did not mention the fact that Saint Joseph was a carpenter. The boys knew that and they were expecting him to mention it. One could do, or say, the obvious thing with Spanish Americans but one could not do or say the *expected* obvious thing; one lost them if one did. Father Lind sensed the time to break off discussion. It would not do to reach the point of advocacy or argument. He swung his chair around and took two white cards from the alphabetical file behind him. The steel drawers of the cabinet clicked decisively when he closed them. He had the cards in his hand.

"I've enjoyed this chat," he said. "Very much. I am sorry that you boys are leaving us. Please sign your names on the cards and I'll check you out."

He laid the cards down and neither boy reached for the pen that

15

he extended. Juan Archuleta raised his eyes after looking at his card. "I have changed my intention," he said.

Arturo Monso was slower. He sat, frowning, then rose abruptly, almost violent in the simple act of rising from the chair. "I am thinking about this," he said. "I have maybe a talent for the carpenter."

"*Bueno.* I am happy that you boys are staying. Come in once in a while and have a talk with me."

Father Lind smiled, shook hands and watched them go down the corridor. He did not know whether they would make it or not but there was a chance. If he had opposed their intention of quitting he would have involved their pride and they would have taken no backward step from their position; if he had overwhelmed them with reasonable argument, superior to their own, he would have made them feel inferior and they would have been beyond his reach. Such knowledge as he had of Spanish Americans had not come easily. The priest role in relation to them was more difficult yet. Their background, and the lack of understanding with which the Anglo confronted them, had made them a secretive, oblique-dealing people. They were disliked, mistrusted, feared. Father Lind could not quarrel with that. On the record, they deserved to be. Still, he liked them and he had a strange faith in them.

He crossed the room to the file and put the cards away. When he turned around, *she* was standing in the doorway. There was a young man with her whom he remembered but could not identify.

"May we have a few minutes?" she asked.

Her voice was soft, low, pleasant. She did not address him as "Father" and had never addressed him as "Father." That was the Protestant in her, he supposed, but Protestants all over town, and Jews, called him "Father." It was a kind of title that went with priesthood. She was not as tall as he remembered. He was still not certain about her eyes. They were probably gray.

"Of course," he said. "What can I do for you?"

He indicated the chairs which faced him across the desk and Pamela Gibson seated herself. She was wearing a suit, tweed, rusty brown color. The young man remained standing. He was perhaps twenty: a handsome young man with pale smooth skin and intense dark eyes, not a tall youth, five feet seven or eight.

"I am the problem," he said. "I have lost the parole. I must go to the walls."

"How? Tell me about it."

"The police, they say that I took a bicycle that is not mine. They say I am a thief."

"Did you—and are you?"

16

"*Sí.*"

The young man's features were a mask. He had already accepted disaster. Father Lind turned memo pages in his mind and found his name. It was Raimundo Baca.

"Raimundo," he said gently, "where do you live?"

"Holder Street, 517."

"That's pretty far away. Let's see. About twenty blocks."

"Twenty-two."

"You walked here to the school."

"*Sí.*"

The issue lay stark and unadorned in the room. A boy who walked twenty-two blocks to a night school obviously had no resources. The weather was cold now and there would be colder weather ahead, snow and more snow. The boy was Spanish American with a simple, direct mind. He needed transportation badly and he took it. He stole it. He was already on probation, so there had been another offense before this one. At least one other offense; probably more than one. The priest leaned toward him.

"You come here to night school. Do you have a job in the daytime, Raimundo?"

"Yes. I am a laborer. I work in the streets for Culverton Gas."

The boy was still on his feet, standing straight, with that odd quality of the better Spanish apparent in him, their capacity for appearing clean in whatever they wore, and no matter what they did.

"What do you plan to do about this bicycle problem?" Father Lind asked.

The boy's expression did not change. "I can do nothing. The police have taken the bicycle. I have lost the parole. When I see the judge tomorrow I will go back to the walls."

Pamela Gibson had been sitting quietly. Father Lind had felt the intent concentration of her eyes and had seen her face in glimpses, a face almost as well controlled as the boy's. When she spoke, the sound of her soft voice was startling.

"Raimundo," she said. "Will you wait outside for a few minutes? I want to talk about you."

"*Sí.*"

A wide smile broke the tense mask of the boy's face. He nodded his head, jerkily, to the priest and walked out into the corridor.

"I did not want to embarrass him," Pamela Gibson said. "He is a good boy. I don't care if he stole a dozen bicycles; he is a good boy. I don't know one thing about his home background. I imagine that it is terrible, but that is none of my business. I've got to take my pupils for what they are with me. I can't go further than that. Going that far with Raimundo, he's tops. I want to do something for him."

"Like what?"

"I don't know who to call or who to see, but I don't want him to go back to that dirty prison that he calls the walls."

"Did he tell you that it is a dirty prison?"

"He didn't tell me anything. I didn't know he'd been in prison till this thing about the bicycle came up. All I know is that he wants to be something. He's taking both shorthand and typing from me. He hasn't a typewriter at home on which to practice. I offered to rent one for him because he works hard. He wouldn't let me do it. He said that someone would steal it."

The girl spread her hands wide. It was a gesture of helplessness. There was a softness in her face and Father Lind wondered why he thought of her as angular. Her mouth was odd. The upper and lower lips seemed duplicates of each other. Her lipstick was too flamingly, vividly red but she didn't seem to be wearing any other make-up. Her eyes were compelling. He still did not know what color they were.

There was a picture of a boy in the room, too, although the boy was gone. Raimundo wanted to be something. He worked at his courses and he impressed his teacher. He walked twenty-two blocks to the night school and, presumably, another twenty-two to get home. He worked at a hard, tiring job during the day. There were probably many things wrong with him to balance the things that were right but, even when one discounted him, he looked like the kind of boy for whom Guadalupe House had been created.

"I'll see what I can do," Father Lind said. "I probably can't get an answer tonight. I'll let you know when I get a decision; either way."

Pamela Gibson rose. She looked at the man but he had an idea that she did not see him. She was suddenly aloof, withdrawn.

"That will be kind of you," she said.

She was gone and two young men from the automobile body shop came in. They believed that they were working too hard, learning too little. It took time to discuss their difficulties and to lead them into a voluntary return to classes. When they left, Father Lind called Sergeant Regan, downtown police, a man he had bothered often. The sergeant was out so he left his name and number. The evening continued to flow through his small office. A swaggering young Latino came in, his bravado covering badly a case of nerves. He was married and he had four children but he had not stayed on his own reservation. There was a girl and she was pregnant. He did not know what to do about her.

18

"You are a student here?" Father Lind said.

"Yes. I am in the body shop. I learn to put the paint on automobiles, to straighten the dent. It is good work."

"Yes it is. What do you do all day?"

"I work in a filling station. It is very similar."

Father Lind nodded. It was a marvel to him that a man could work all day, go to school at night, live with a wife and four children and still find time to get into trouble with a girl.

"You have committed an offense against God," he said sternly, "and against your wife, your children and this girl."

The young man hung his head. "*Sí.*"

"I have no sympathy with you. You deserve to be hurt, but I do not want any more people hurt with you. Give me the girl's name and I'll talk to her. I'll try to have her taken care of with the baby."

There was indescribable relief in the man's eyes. Father Lind made a rough, sweeping gesture with his right hand.

"As for you," he said, "you go to Confession and after that, stick close to your wife."

"*Sí.*"

It was an hour before Sergeant Regan returned his call. The priest related the story of Raimundo Baca in crisp sentences. The sergeant grunted.

"A bicycle is a step down in the world for him," he said. "I can remember when he used to joy ride autos."

"I wouldn't know. Is his record bad?"

"Not too bad. He did a jolt for car theft and made parole. We haven't had him in here lately, as far as I know—not till this bicycle thing."

"He's been going to school at Guadalupe House. We would like to keep him. Wouldn't you rather have him here with us than taking a postgraduate course in crime at the pen?"

"I would. But he can't go around picking up bikes on the side."

"He won't. We'll work on him."

"O.K. Do that. God knows I can't blame these kids half the time for the things they do. I'll bury this bike thing and I'll talk to Baca's parole officer. We'll give him another free ride."

"Thanks. I'll do something for you someday."

Sergeant Regan laughed. "Say a prayer for me. A cop needs prayers, believe me."

Father Lind replaced the receiver slowly. He was glad that Raimundo Baca was going to have another chance. It couldn't stop there. He would have to do a little work himself. Raimundo might be up against more than he could handle. His problem seemed to be, always, transportation.

19

The school had quieted down in the time that had elapsed. There was life and movement and noise still in the basement shop but the first floor classrooms were dark with the exception of the speech room. Old Doc Chavez presided there, helping bilingual people to improve their speech in two languages. His students never wanted to go home. He was accused of running a club.

Father Lind walked down the corridor, although it was obvious that there was no point in what he was doing. The typing room and the short-hand room and the English room were all dark. Pamela Gibson had gone home without learning the result of his appeal in Raimundo's behalf. Raimundo had gone home, too. He walked back to his office. Raimundo's home address was in the file, with no telephone number. It was too late to go there, to a strange neighborhood that was probably on the tough side. He opened the telephone book.

There were a number of Gibsons listed but no Pamela. She would live probably with one of these Gibsons but perhaps not. The names on the page spelled out for the priest the extent of his ignorance, or his non-knowledge, where the girl was concerned. The Gibsons were an old family in Culverton, a prominent family. He did not know if the story that Pamela had been divorced was true, whether she had become a Gibson through marriage or had been a Gibson and reverted to her own name after the divorce.

He knew nothing about her but he felt oddly cheated that he was not able to report to her on his conversation with Sergeant Regan. He put the phone book away and snapped out the office light.

"What difference does it make?" he said.

– III –

Saturday was a busy day at the *Catholic Star*. Father Gregory Lind said the six A.M. Mass at Saint Anselm's, had his breakfast in the rectory and was working at the paper before eight. He was lord of all he surveyed, arbiter of the news and ruler over those who dispensed it. He could play up any angle of Catholic news, foreign or domestic, assigning prominence to whatever he willed. He could headline a strike at a Catholic college, the departure of an angry prior from his monastery, the decision of a prominent local nun to ask dispensation from her vows. He had several hair-raising dispatches from the church in the Netherlands, some of which had been around the office for weeks.

20

He had all of these stories, among many others, and an issue of a paper was made up of stories, wasn't it?

He could do whatever he liked until Father Peter Coyle, the editor, strolled in. If he indulged his own tastes, exercised his own judgment, rated the news as he saw news, Father Coyle would toss his effort into the wastebasket and they would start all over.

Father Lind went to work, indulging in no vain dreams of glory. The newspaper would be as it had always been; the chronicler of minor events, a prime ignorer of the time in which it existed, crossing no swords and tilting no lances at man or beast or windmill. The art of creating such a paper lay in placing undue dramatic emphasis upon the obvious, in playing up personal names, in attacking only the old, safe, established enemies and in seeking no new challengers to tranquillity. There were Catholic papers which met both event and opinion with reasonable courage, but the *Catholic Star* was not one of them. None of Father Lind's attempts to escape from it into parish work had won any serious attention from the Chancery office.

"His Excellency is happy with you where you are," he was told. "If he wanted you elsewhere he would move you."

Ordinary priests, when they held gripe sessions among themselves, had few good things to say about the bishop, or the Chancery staff. They were private soldiers looking upward at the brass, resentful of the forces that moved them, placed them, set their lives and their talents into channels not of their own desire or choosing. Gregory Lind, who had done some of that kind of griping himself, did not believe that all of it was justified, or fair; but there were evils. This newspaper was one of the evils and, yet, he had to admit that it had given him a creative outlet and that there had been moments of great pride, moments of triumph. His record on the paper had not been a blank; among other things, the *Catholic Star* had called into being the admirable Guadalupe House. A man, in his inward or outward griping, usually held to a narrow view.

Father Peter Coyle, the editor, came in at ten-thirty, a tall, lean, rather stoop-shouldered priest who wore large glasses with brown plastic rings. He entered the offices cheerfully and he scattered cheerfulness around the premises. He was a friendly man, a popular man, a good priest. He sat at his desk with the air of a man assuming heavy responsibility but he would not work hard at the desk; he had men under him who were hired to work hard and he never confused his own mission. He was tact and diplomacy and the spreader of oil on troubled waters, a mender of nets and a preserver of the illusions of other men. There was humor in him and he had a good time in being precisely what he was. It was difficult to know if he cherished any illusions of his own; about himself, the paper, anything at all; he probably did not.

Father Lind allowed him time to confer with his secretary and to make half a dozen phone calls, then he entered the sanctum. Father Coyle greeted him with a friendly wave and reached for the telephone. "I'll be with you in a minute, Greg," he said. He always did that. Father Lind sat patiently through a phone conversation that couldn't have meant less. Father Coyle cradled the receiver.

"That was Jimmy Price," he said. "The mayor is going to put all of the Negro pacification activity under him. Jimmy's a good man. The bishop wants us to give him any help he wants. We can't have riots breaking out. It's the old stitch in time."

"Fine. In the meantime, we've got a minority of our own in the parish that needs a little attention. Our Spanish Americans—"

Father Coyle was shaking his head. "No good, Greg. No good. No one is interested. The Spanish don't swing any weight. Not anywhere. We got Guadalupe House for them. That's the package."

"It's not enough. I don't begrudge the Negroes anything but they are off my beat. The Latinos won't march—not the ones we have here anyway. They know that people would laugh at them. They are proud. They couldn't take it."

Father Coyle's head was still shaking. He had a wide mouth and a broad nose. His eyes behind the glasses were wise eyes. "We're not supposed to create the action, Greg," he said. "You and I have a newspaper to bring out every week. We go where the action is."

"I know, Pete. And that means whatever we make it mean. I've got an idea." Father Lind leaned across the editor's desk. "Most of the Spanish Americans are Catholics, our people. They don't work at it much except in their own way. Their own way makes a lot of sense. I'm beginning to understand it. Never mind. The point is, they are very poor, lower per capita income than the Negro. When they get into trouble, maybe a priest gets them out a time or two. He doesn't do anything to keep them out. They go to prison and they serve time and how do they make a living when they are released? If we talk a lot of them into attending a feast day Mass, fill the church with them, that's a big deal. We're a success. We don't know where they go after the Mass. It doesn't do them any good. They need help. What I would like to see is a convict sodality, and a parole society, something in which we could get these guys together, the ones in trouble. We could help them and they could help each other. We'd have to put ourselves into it and a lot of money—"

Father Coyle rocked back in his chair. "Are you out of your mind?"

"Not painfully so."

"No? Well look! Do you believe for one minute that the bishop would let anyone dramatize the fact that the prisons are full of Catholics? You're crazier than you suspect. A sodality! Good Lord! You'd be shouting to the world, look at all the ex-cons we've got!"

"We've got them. Maybe trying to cut down the number is better than making a secret out of it."

Father Coyle laughed. "I always liked Newman's statement that we arrive at certitude by accumulated probabilities. You, Greg, are starting to accumulate *im*probabilities. I don't know where it will take you but, in the meantime, let's work with the bishop and the mayor and my friend, Jimmy Price; shall we?"

Discussions with Father Peter Coyle always ended like that. He did not waste much time on ideas opposed to his own. Back at his own desk Father Lind could see his own mistakes. His timing had been poor and he had tossed his idea off half-baked. He had not thought the idea through or dressed it up. He hadn't given himself time to do so. The idea had been born of last night's experience with Raimundo Baca.

"So I had to go charging in with it," he said. "Well, it's still a good idea."

He had a busy desk. His phone rang constantly and members of the staff came to him with their problems or their complaints or, occasionally, an account of something funny that had happened down the news line. The staff of the *Star* was a good staff, earnest young laymen, with, perhaps, more than their share of idealism. Father Lind knew them well on the job but he did not know them as people. They were married, most of them, with lives to live away from the paper. They came from a wide range of parishes but nobody on the *Star* except Gregory Lind himself lived in Saint Anselm's.

It was dark when the priest called it a day and nearly everyone had left before he did. The cold had moved in with the dark and last night's snow was solidly frozen on rooftops and in alleyways. He drove home on slick pavement and, once again, he was the only priest in the house. The pastor was simply "out" and Father Guyton who was responsible for sick calls, had left a number at which he could be reached. Father Lind was cold and he wanted to relax with someone, talk a little and then have an interesting meal.

Mrs. Wagner served stew which was left over from noon when Father Lind had not been home. It was better than eggs but the table was cheerless and he did not feel like reading. It was the dead, hard cold that made everything seem dismal, he told himself. A good snowstorm would clear the woofits away. Last night's snow had been a minor affair.

23

He drank his coffee and the other priests had not come in, so he went over to the church. He was early but there were always some early penitents.

The vision of Pamela Gibson came to him again as he settled into the box. He had not thought of her all day and now, suddenly, here she was. She wasn't looking at him. She was walking and her walk was, once again, the long, striding walk that looked awkward. She was angular, not attractive at all. His thought moved through the vision and he wondered if she was worrying about Raimundo. He did not know how to call her and probably she was without any idea of how to call him. There was no reason why she should associate him with Saint Anselm's or with the *Star;* it was quite possible that she had never heard of either Saint Anselm's or the *Star.* That was a thought that would bruise Pete Coyle if he knew about it.

The first penitent came into the box and the evening had started. Saturday night produced tough sinners occasionally but not too many of them in a nice quiet old parish like Saint Anselm's. It was, too, a night in January and most of the hardcases had come in to make their peace before Christmas. This was a quiet night. There were lulls, periods when he flicked on his light and tried to read his office. In those intervals, he was most sharply aware of Pamela Gibson. It was strange that he still saw her as angular, graceless, unattractive. She had not seemed so last night and he recalled making a mental remark to that effect; but he could not remember how she had looked. Even when he put effort into it he could not summon a vision of her as she looked when she sat facing him, talking about Raimundo.

Pamela Gibson did not disturb him tonight. He could dismiss her when a penitent entered the box; when he summoned the thought of her again, he assured himself that he did so because the idea amused him. The Raimundo Baca affair was, of course, a worry. She had been concerned and he had not been able to tell her that Raimundo would have another chance. He could not avoid thinking of her in that connection. She came and went in his mind during the long hours. Finally, all of the confessions had been heard and he went up to the altar where he thanked God for using him as His deputy and for permitting him to serve as he did. His solitary prayers were sincere prayers and they had meaning for him, as the great dark mass of the altar had meaning for him and the great solemn hush of the church.

He remembered when he reached his room that he had neglected his exercises before dinner. He groaned inwardly. The idea of exercise was repugnant at this hour but there was no arguing with the fact that to be effective an exercise program had to be consistently followed.

He was stripped to his underwear, contending with the barbells when the door of his room opened. Father Guyton entered without knocking, coming to a wide-eyed halt when halfway through the door.

"Glory!" he said. "I heard all the thumping and I thought you were being attacked by thugs."

"A lot of good you'd be if I were! A skinny specimen like you!"

Father Lind sat up, the bar across his legs. Father Thomas Guyton leaned against the door frame, amused and making no effort to conceal his amusement. He was medium tall, slender, with blond hair that was receding fast from the area above and behind his forehead. He was normally a bland, cynical young man and the follies of the world seemed to delight him.

"Nobody ever looks at a priest below the collar," he said. "Nobody knows whether he has muscles or not. Why the hardware routine?"

"Waistline trouble. A premature pot."

"Pots are symbols of maturity, perhaps of wisdom." Tom Guyton laughed softly. "But never mind. Have fun. When you are free, drop over to the room. I have a bottle. Delayed Christmas present. I can't seem to drink alone."

"I have the same problem. I'll be over."

"Fine."

Tom Guyton went, whistling, down the hall. Gregory Lind slipped into slacks and a sports shirt. He was mildly surprised at the younger priest's invitation. They had worked harmoniously together, but they had never had much in common and their leisure periods, because of the way they divided parish duties, seldom coincided. There was little about this rectory that encouraged sociability. Laymen, by orders of Father Schafer, were not allowed above the first floor under any circumstances and the two priests who lived upstairs were required to report the names of their guests to the pastor if they invited priests from other parishes. It was simpler to go out.

There was a bottle on the table in Tom Guyton's room, a bucket of ice and several splits of soda. The priest waved his hand.

"*Violà*," he said. "Admire the ice, please. It was the difficult ingredient."

"I can imagine."

The room was even simpler in its furnishings than Gregory Lind's although it had a portable stereo and records in comparison with the Lind portable FM set. There was a high, narrow bed, a bedside table on which the telephone rested, a dresser, a small desk and a straight chair, two overstuffed chairs which were showing their age. Above the bed, inevitably, there was a crucifix; on the opposite wall there was a

Yale pennant, blue with white letters, its grim-jawed bulldog frowning down upon the room.

"How did Old Eli get into your life?" Gregory Lind asked.

"Salvation Army store. I found it and it delighted me. Still does. Mix your own drink. You know your strength; I don't."

"Thanks."

Gregory took water in his drink rather than soda. There was wry humor in the Yale pennant and he liked it, but there was a certain awkwardness between this young priest and himself. In this diocese a young priest had hard liquor forbidden to him for three years after his ordination, but the breech was honored and not the rule. Gregory Lind's generation, nearly eight years ago, had obeyed that prohibition to the day but the seminaries had been turning out a different breed of cat since about 1960. He did not have a sense of commonality with anyone who came out in the sixties. The old norms did not hold any more. He sat in one of the overstuffed chairs, facing the other man. Tom Guyton had narrow eyes.

"You are probably wondering why I invited you over," he said.

"To share your present."

"Of course. That is just a prop. You know that. Actually, I want to ask you something. You're on the paper. You know every pastor in town and all the esteemed monsignori. You probably know where skeletons are hid and bodies are buried. Okay." Tom Guyton took a deep swallow. "How do I get out of this dry dark parish?"

"You don't."

"Why not?"

"Your pastor would have to consent to a transfer. He won't. He does not like upset or change. What's the matter with this parish?"

"Lord! You know what's the matter. It's old and German and it hasn't any parish activities except Holy Name and the Altar and Rosary. It hasn't any young people or any young ideas. The young people get out of it as soon as they can. There isn't anything to do that means anything."

"What do you want to do? March in some movement and carry a placard?"

"Sure. It would be a change, a break in monotony, an experience. But this is Culverton. No marching."

"No. Our Negro districts seem pretty quiet. We do have Spanish Americans in this parish that seems so tame to you."

"I know. That's your beat. Tell me about them."

Tom Guyton sat deep in his chair. Gregory Lind, to his own surprise, accepted the invitation to talk about Spanish Americans. He spoke of

Raimundo Baca and he outlined his idea of a church-sponsored society that would offer a man direction, companionship, a sense of goals and some practical assistance when he came out of prison, or while he was sweating out a parole. Peter Coyle had waved the idea out of the window. Tom Guyton looked solemn. He rose and poured himself another drink.

"A select society of jailbirds might make the idea of jail even more respectable than it already is, Greg," he said. "If a man's friends, relatives or neighbors were in your society, the man would want to be in it, too, wouldn't he? I'd hate to be the chaplain."

"Maybe you're right."

Gregory Lind let his own idea drop with a dull thud. He would have to put more thought into it. There was a job to be done and the Church, at least in Culverton, was looking the other way. Tom Guyton was turning his glass around in his hand, his eyes fixed on it. Obviously, he, too, was willing to let the idea drop. There was something else on his mind.

"Another thing," he said. "I'd like your help on it. There's a girl, a woman. Hell, I don't know. I've never seen her. She comes into my confessional. She's there practically every time I draw the job. I'm not even certain that she's a Catholic. All she wants to do is tell me a lot of lurid sex stuff, experiences of hers or slime out of her imagination. She's full of details, damn dirty details."

"You don't have to listen to her."

"I know. I've had the book on it. I've been on the job two years. Long enough to have had this kind of stuff before. This is the first one I haven't been able to handle. She keeps wanting to meet me outside the box. I've reached the point where I hate to leave the confessional. I expect her to be outside, ready to ambush me."

Greg Lind nodded. This, of course, was the real reason for the invitation tonight. One always had to lead up to these things. Father Guyton probably wanted to escape from Saint Anselm's parish, wanted devoutly to escape; but the other situation was the urgent one.

"You'll probably have that problem as long as you're a priest, Tom," he said. "We all do. There are some women with fixations on priests. Usually they are Catholics; not always. Almost invariably they are married women, living with their husbands. They are dangerous as hell. If an incident happens, nobody will believe that the woman made the pass."

Tom Guyton's eyes were fixed intently now on the older priest's face. "So, what do I do next?"

"Invite her over to the rectory. Be damned sure that I'm there, or the pastor; preferably the pastor. Alert us in advance. None of these women can stand up to two priests."

"What if she doesn't come?"

"She probably won't. The invitation will scare her. If it doesn't, if she keeps after you, we have another step. Let's try the rectory invitation first."

"I will." Tom Guyton took a swallow of his drink. "It helps just to have someone else in it with me."

"I know."

Father Gregory Lind did know. He had been assigned to the cathedral when he was fresh from the seminary. Cathedral priests were an elite corps, smoothly mannered, eloquent, sharp in appearance. Gregory Lind had considered himself below the standard; not there on his own merits but simply because his seminary reputation as a writer had earned him a post on the *Catholic Star*. The cathedral had given him early experience with the women who haunt young priests. He had discovered, too, and with youthful horror, that there were women capable of setting up fraudulent sick calls to entrap a priest. He sighed now, remembering, feeling a bit old.

"I'm glad we did this, Tom," he said. "Let's do it again. Soon. My room."

"Good. And thanks."

They shook hands and Gregory crossed the hall to his own room. He was feeling lazy, relaxed, with no pressing problem of his own. The other man, he thought, was going to have some bad hours before he became an old priest. They all did.

–IV–

Six o'clock Mass on Sunday morning was, in Gregory Lind's estimation, man's closest approach to pure worship. Outside of the church it was still dark and the air that one breathed was hard, cold, heavy with the frost that had blown off the river in the night; inside the church, icy fingers of draft moved, touching the huddled figures in the pews. There were not many people at six o'clock Mass but the people who were present had come because they wanted to be there; not because they were afraid to stay away. They were poor, for the most part, the early worshipers, and they were not youngsters. Father Lind was their priest. He said the first Mass of the day every Sunday. He also said the seven-thirty Mass and helped to distribute communion at the eight-thirty and the nine-thirty which were the pastor's Masses. Father Guyton had the late sleepers at eleven and at twelve. The nine-thirty was High Mass, sung by Father Schafer who did not sing nearly so well as either of his assistants.

The Mass, early or late, was the one reality of his priesthood that had never disappointed Father Lind. There was a magnificent solemnity in it, a slow march of ritual to the awesome climax. He felt very close to God in the saying of his Mass, never closer than at six when he shared it with the faithful of the early day. They were slow to accept the dialog Mass, these six o'clock Catholics, and their mumbled responses were more obedient than devout. They had liked the Latin Mass better, in God's soft silence, before Vatican II changed it, and so had their priest; but they were in the minority. At the later Masses, any Sunday, there would be happy extroverts who loved the Mass in English and who gloried in bellowing out the loud, clear tones of the responses.

Seven-thirty Mass was almost if not quite, like six. Gregory Lind considered himself fortunate that the early assignments were his. He assisted at two of the later Masses, in a minor role, and then he was free. Occasionally, he had a child to baptize, but that was a rarity. The baptismal font belonged, as a rule, to Father Schafer or, in lesser degree, Father Guyton. Tom Guyton also drew the assignment of counting the day's collection money and of packaging it for the bank. That was the low task of the day, one of the lowest tasks of priesthood. A man could not love a job like that.

It was nearly eleven when Gregory Lind left the rectory. The sky was still heavy with cloud and the air had ice in it, but there was no wind. Footsteps created fantastically loud echoes and an automobile had difficulty with climbing starts on hilly streets. Father Lind drove to 517 Holder Street, the address which Raimundo Baca had given him. He had difficulty in finding it. The street had been named honestly. A gas holder, shaped like an immense tumbler, dominated the neighborhood and all of the streets were forced to swing in arcs to go around it. Holder Street was the closest street to the structure and 517 was three blocks beyond the holder, one of a shabby block of row houses. The street was dirty and the sidewalk paving was broken at intervals. There were beer cans in the gutter, a number of cars parked along the curb.

Gregory Lind rang the bell at 517 and there was a long delay before the door was opened, timidly, just a crack, by a small, dark-haired girl of eleven or twelve. Her eyes widened when she saw the Roman collar.

She took a backward step, opening the door wide. There was no hall-way. Pamela Gibson was standing in the center of a low-ceilinged, cluttered room. She had evidently been talking to, or with, a short, thin woman whose features were frozen into the Spanish mask which Father Lind knew so well.

"Hello," Pamela Gibson said. "Maybe you are just in time. I don't know. This is where Raimundo lives but nobody will admit that he even exists."

Father Lind looked beyond her to the older woman whose eyes gave him no recognition. He had seen the woman in church. Not too many Spanish Americans came to Saint Anselm's. He did not know that she was Raimundo's mother, but it seemed a safe assumption.

"Mrs. Baca," he said in Spanish, "we are friends of Raimundo. We would like to talk to him. We have good news for him."

The mask held for a matter of seconds and then broke up. The woman's lips trembled. "It is about the parole, Father?"

"Yes. I did not know if he told you. He will be all right. He has an-other chance."

There was a belief common among Anglos that being arrested meant nothing to "the Spanish," that it was an accepted commonplace. Mrs. Baca's eyes leaked tears. She was wearing her mask again but the tears ran over it.

"I am glad," she said. "I am happy. He is a good son to me."

"Yes. I'm sure he is. Miss Gibson is his teacher. I know him well, too. Do you know where he is?"

The dark eyes did not acknowledge the teacher by even a glance. The woman shook her head. "He lives here, doesn't he?" the priest said.

"He is here sometimes. Sometimes no."

The statement was reluctantly made and said nothing. Gregory Lind understood that. The Latinos were great talkers but only about matters of no importance; they were equally great protectors of all information about themselves and their own kind. They hated to answer questions, even simple questions.

"Thank you, Mrs. Baca," he said. "Tell him to call me please. I am Father Lind."

"Sí."

She had known who he was, of course, from the moment she saw him. Gregory Lind followed Pamela Gibson through the door. She moved swiftly, gracefully, her head high. She was wearing a heavy coat, deep brown in color, and a brown hat that was vaguely military in style. She was aware, as he was, of the row houses across the street, duplicates of the ones at their backs. There were people at most of the windows, watching them. Her shoulders contracted.

"Ugh!" she said. "I hate to be stared at. I want to talk to you. Let's sit in my car."

She took acquiescence for granted, moving to the door of a small blue car. Gregory Lind hesitated only a moment or two then followed her, walking around the car to the passenger's door. He was thinking that the Spanish Americans, crowded into these mass shelters, had no privacy themselves and would not understand another person's desire for privacy; they would assume a different explanation for two people seeking shelter in a car. "Well, I'll give no scandal," he thought. "I won't be in that car long."

Pamela Gibson sat, half turned, in the seat, one gloved hand, her left, on the wheel. She had level eyes and there was inquiry in them; but when she spoke she did not ask, she stated.

"I did not speak to that woman in Spanish, as you did. Stupid of me. My Spanish is better than yours."

Gregory Lind laughed. "I'm certain that it is."

"Tell me about Raimundo."

"I looked for you on Friday night. You were gone. I didn't know which Gibson in the phone book was you."

"Nice of you to try."

"I knew that you were concerned about him. He'll be all right. A police sergeant named Regan is fixing him up for another chance. One more. If he slips again, he's gone."

The girl stared through the windshield, frowning slightly. "It's so far from here to school," she said. "And so damned cold. He's been walking it. Two ways. No wonder he stole a bike. He works all day besides going to school."

"I know."

She turned her head, meeting his eyes. Her face looked small. The emphatic lipstick distorted her features, or seemed to do so.

"I'm going to buy him a bicycle," she said.

"I wouldn't."

"Why not? I can afford it."

"No matter. It throws things out of balance. There are sadder stories around here than Raimundo, people with a rougher home life than he has, and greater handicaps. Some of the other people would believe that he got a bicycle because he called attention to himself by stealing one." Gregory Lind spread his hands. "You are not exactly rewarding virtue, you know, if you buy him a bike."

31

"I am. He's a good kid. Worth saving. But I don't give a damn about virtue. That kid needs a bike. That's all that is important."

"I still wouldn't do it."

She lifted her chin and he knew that she would do whatever she wanted to do. When she lifted her chin, or set it, her features appeared angular and she lost her softness. There was line in her face, however. An artist could define it. He wasn't certain if she would be classed as a beautiful woman or not. Her beauty seemed to come and go, like the scent she wore. The scent was light, very faint, pleasant. He had been aware of it when he entered the car. It disappeared and came back.

"I appreciate your getting the parole fixed," she said. "You didn't do it for me, of course. You did it for him. It's something I wanted, so I appreciate it."

Gregory Lind was suddenly amused. "Do you always explain yourself like that?" he said.

"Was I explaining myself? Yes. I guess so. No. I don't always do it. Not to people who don't need the explanation. I guess maybe you better go. The audience over in the gallery will be thinking you are one of Boccaccio's Monks."

"I'm afraid you're right." He opened the door. "I am glad that I found you. I wanted you to know about Raimundo."

She smiled at him and he had not seen her smile before. Her face lighted up. She had lovely teeth, large, even, lined in a short, perfect arc.

"Men have been glad to find me for more interesting reasons," she said, "but Raimundo will do."

She waved her hand in a careless farewell as her foot pressed the starter. He stood in the street and watched her drive away, aware once again of the staring Latinos but not caring much.

She would, of course, receive many compliments from men, he thought. He must have seemed awkward but he hadn't been trying to pass compliments. She wouldn't, perhaps, realize that.

He was walking around his car to the driver's side when the girl from Raimundo's house ran out to the curb. She stopped before she reached him and stood, swaying, off balance, suddenly self-conscious.

"Ma—my mother wants to talk with you," she said.

Father Lind reentered the house. Mrs. Baca was standing in the middle of the room. She was still a young woman, probably no more than forty, but her figure had thickened and the years had marked her face with lines.

"I have a worry for Raimundo, Father," she said. "There is a girl. You do not know that?"

"I didn't know."

"It is the right thing. Maybe. He is of the age. He needs a woman. He cannot afford it. He makes a little money only on the job. He goes to the school. Me, and his sisters, we must have help from him."

Father Lind gestured toward a chair, inviting her to be seated in her own home. He chose another chair, facing her. "Let me get this straight," he said. "You need financial help from Raimundo? Where is his father?"

"Who knows?"

"You do not work?"

"Sometimes."

"How about relief? Does the city help you?"

"No. There is a crackdown."

Father Lind nodded. There had been a number of relief scandals in Culverton and the lists had been pruned. He suspected that Mrs. Baca was still being helped, not as much as she would like. In diverse ways, subtle and complicated, Raimundo was being enveloped in a web of responsibility. His own decency and concern for others would fasten him securely in that web; but if he revolted, broke loose, ran away as his father had done, he would be doing his bit as so many men had done, toward the creation of a slum in which other people would have to live.

"If Raimundo and his girl love each other," Father Lind said, "it would be best for them to be married. It will not be easy but other young people have difficulties, too. Certainly, I do not want him in trouble with a girl after this bicycle thing. I don't want him to get the girl in trouble; neither do you."

"I am a good Catholic."

The mask was back on Mrs. Baca's face and he could read nothing in it. He knew though, looking at her, that, despite the good Catholic claim, she would rather have Raimundo living in sin than married. She was looking at her own realities and there was little of the spirit in them.

"I'll talk to Raimundo," he said. "In the meantime, say a prayer of thanksgiving that he is still on his parole."

"*Sí.*"

She slipped off her chair to kneel on the floor. There was a priest in her house and she wanted his blessing before he left it. This was one of the Catholic customs that was rapidly slipping into the realm of old things, ancient practices, sentimental pieties. Father Lind blessed her, and he added a prayer to the blessing as he walked to his car.

Raimundo was a young man of problems, all young men were, of

33

course. They moved one way or they moved another; the problems became less burdensome, or more complicated, or practically insoluble. A young man could be helped, but not greatly; the decisions which shaped his course were made within himself. A priest saw so many patterns repeated, helpless to change them even when they were sad patterns.

"Let's hope Raimundo works out okay," he said. "He hasn't got too much going for him."

He spoke aloud, to himself, or to his car. He often did that, part of a way of life, perhaps, in which some prayers were always to be articulated, or, more likely, a habit of his loneliness.

The streets on the south side of town were slick and the day did not warm. Gregory Lind drove to his sister's house on South Garfield. This was a part of his Sunday that was fixed and unchangeable. His mother, who lived with his sister, Janet, expected him.

She was sitting in a huge overstuffed chair beside an open fire in the living room. Cecilia Lind had been a small and dainty woman and, although she had grown stout with the years, she still liked her furniture oversized, reducing herself to tininess again. She was sixty-three and since her husband's death in 1961, she had accepted the fact that she was an old woman, making no attempt to be anything else. Physically sound, she was still a dependent, dramatizing the dependency.

Cecilia Lind held out her arms when her son entered the room. He crossed to her, dropped to one knee and kissed her. She held him tightly, her fingers pressing into his flesh, then released him and lowered her head, bringing her hands up, clasped. As Mrs. Baca had wanted his blessing, so his mother wanted it, but his mother did not kneel. He stood over her and blessed her.

"It has been a long time since I saw you, son," she said. "They must be keeping you very busy."

It was a stock statement. She made it every week. His reply, although he had tried many times to vary it, was a stock reply. He told her of his week, not the actual week and its realities but the fantasy week which consisted of things she liked to hear; the simplicities, the sentimentalities, the legendary incidents of priestly life which had small relationship to actuality. It pleased her to hear what she expected to hear and he hurt no one in pleasing her.

Janet, his sister, had vanished after admitting him. That, too, was customary. It was a half hour before he was able to seek her. She was in the kitchen. Janet had been a lovely girl, sparked from within by some force that lighted her. She still had that spark. Her face was round and her chin firm. She had dark eyes. She was thirty-one and she had

34

three children. Gregory thought that she was more attractive than she had ever been, but he wished sometimes that she was less belligerent. It would never have occurred to her to ask for his blessing.

"You are looking fit, as always," she said.

"I am. You're looking in top form yourself."

She ignored that. "You lead the Life of Riley," she said. "If men were smart, they'd all be priests."

"The pay is bad. So is the cooking."

"You do all right. Anyway, you'll get a first class meal today, even if I say so. But one thing!"

"Yes?"

"If *she* opens up with you about Joe, cool her down. She's given him a bad week and he's the most patient guy alive. He shouldn't have to put up with it. One of these days I'm going to straighten her out."

"Count ten first."

"Hah. If you had any idea how often I count ten. Go and say hello to Joe. He's hiding out in the game room."

Gregory Lind went downstairs to the game room. His brother-in-law, Joe Booker, was a thin, quiet, soft-spoken man with a love of sports and a sense of humor. Gregory's visiting time with him was always short, family pressure being as it was; but he was certain that he would have a good time with Joe if they could share ball games, card games, anything at all. He did not, of course, have time to share those things with anyone. The priest's "Life of Riley" had a few drawbacks, a few shortcomings. Joe Booker turned off the television set.

"How are you, Father?" he said. "You had a cold trip out, didn't you?"

"Cold enough. All the traffic signals were working."

"Good for them."

Joe was in the traffic engineering office of the city, second in command, and he worked in the weird mathematics of timing and synchronizing lights, among other things. Gregory did not understand Joe's work at all, so they usually talked along the surface. They talked generalities now for five minutes and it was time for Gregory to go upstairs again. If Joe had been having a bad week with Cecilia Lind, he did not mention it. Gregory did not hear any of Joe's complaints; they never came up.

The house was warm, fragrant with the odors of roasting lamb and trimmings. The Bookers had three children; a boy of nine, two girls of seven and five. They, too, knew the rules. When Father, their uncle, came to visit, they were last on the calling list. He visited with them, probably, he thought, overdoing his friendliness because he didn't know them too well. He did not know the wants, hopes, disappointments

35

locked up inside of them so his conversation did not really touch them. It was time, after a few minutes, to return to his mother; then it was time for dinner. His afternoon was neatly parceled into segments of time and it never seemed to him on a Sunday that he had any control over the parceling.

On alternate Sundays, Gregory Lind took his mother out to dinner and that, although it had its special difficulties, was preferable to dinner at Janet's. The trouble with the home dinner was his mother's open animosity toward Joe Booker, which often included Janet. She complained sweetly, and with a professed resignation about her health, her restricted life and her present surroundings; particularly her present surroundings. There were faults and deficiencies in the house which she had to endure, noises in the neighborhood, neighbors of dubious character. She came around ultimately, and inevitably, to the appalling number of deaths in traffic accidents, the dangerous streets, the fact that nothing was done to protect human beings from the menace of incompetent planning.

Gregory Lind always tried to divert this line of conversation, embarrassed for his brother-in-law who accepted it all stolidly, making no comment. Cecilia Lind could not be disputed. Her son regarded her with astonishment. He knew now, looking back, that she had always been like this under a surface of very real sweetness and gentleness. Those around her had always been reminded of any faults she noticed, any neglect she felt, but she had never had a target like her son-in-law. She hated him, probably because he had taken her daughter from her; and she fought her environment because she was living in another woman's house.

Gregory Lind could understand all of that, and sympathize with it, but he could do nothing about it, either of correction or of relief. The chances were good that he would have gone along seeing only the lovely qualities he had always associated with his mother, if Joe Booker had been less patient. Joe Booker had his wife's mother in his home, a disruptive force, a responsibility, a care, a flicker of verbal whips. He accepted the situation in which he found himself, neither walking out nor lashing back. Gregory found himself in Joe Booker's corner, seeing his mother all too clearly and wishing that he did not have to see her as he did.

They left the table and his mother was pulling at his arm. This, too, was in pattern. Janet recognized it as he did, urging her husband to return to the game room and drafting her two older children as kitchen police. Gregory was left in the living room with his mother who did not, seemingly, recognize the effort that had been made on her behalf.

36

"I thought they would never give us a minute to ourselves," she said. "I am at the end of my rope, son, the very end of my resources. You have no idea what I put up with in this house. It is not my nature to complain but it is all that I can do sometimes to hold myself in check. The things that I could tell you! But they would only upset you. Tell me, is there any word of your getting a parish of your own?"

"None at all, I'm afraid."

"And why not? Can't you speak up to them? You are eight years a priest. It's high time you had your own parish."

Gregory had tried vainly, on many of the Sundays, to explain why he could not hope for a parish. He was half newspaperman and half priest, holding no high rank as either. His mother never followed his explanation, no matter how simply he phrased it. He wondered sometimes if she was senile and, in charity, hoped that she was; but she was an alert woman, a keen-minded woman who knew what was happening in the world around her, who clouded only the issues affecting herself.

"I could stand what I am enduring," she said, "if I thought that I could come into your rectory as your housekeeper. I would take good care of you. It's a dream of mine, son, a dream I have held a long, long time—"

She was looking into his face and there were tears misting her eyes. This was very real to her. He could feel the reality. She had two other married daughters in addition to Janet; Agnes in California and Anne in Pennsylvania. She had a son, Bart, whose wife, Barbara, did not get along with Janet. Her family, in one way or another, was a disappointment to her but her personal hope or ambition, involved none of them except Gregory. She wanted to be a priest's housekeeper, *her* priest's housekeeper. He looked at her, embarrassed by his helplessness. He had failed her, too, by not being the kind of priest who cleaves through to the mark, one of the early year pastors. As matters stood, and as they looked into the dim future, her ambition would never be fulfilled. He had no chance at a pastorship, and probably none of the qualifications. He hugged her close to him, desperately sorry for her.

"You just say your prayers," he said, "and I'll say mine. We'll see what comes about."

All of the Sundays ended like this, or in ways similar. He felt like a hypocrite through most of the day and a liar by inference at the end. He was relieved when he finally put on his topcoat and walked out into a rising wind; relieved, yet feeling guilty because of that relief.

The thought of Pamela Gibson came to him as he opened the car door. He could see her clearly in his mind as she stood in the middle of the untidy Baca living room. He could see the brown coat, the brown military-style hat, the scarf that was looped with seeming carelessness beneath her chin, the small brown bag she carried. The bag had a clasp that was shaped like an eagle in flight. He would have sworn that he had noticed neither scarf nor bag in the morning, but they were clear in his memory now. She was an attractive girl, perhaps a pretty girl, much different in an indefinable way than she appeared at the school. There was a breeziness, an informality about her that he had not expected. He liked it.

He had no right to think about her. She was nothing to him. He turned on the car radio to distract his mind.

–V–

Father Gregory Lind hung his vestments in the closet after the six o'clock Mass, said good-bye to the altar boy and put on his overcoat. He was starting out of the church when one of his morning regulars, Jim Bergen, raced across the sidewalk.

"Father," he said, "come quickly. There has been a bad accident."

"Lead on!"

The two men ran to Bergen's car. The morning was still dark and there were icicles on the eaves of buildings, thin, hard patches of ice on the sidewalk and out on the street.

"This car came off the River Highway, right through the railing," Jim Bergen said. "On its nose in the street. I'd just left the church after Mass."

There was shock in his voice but he drove fast. They could hear the siren of an ambulance some distance behind them when they came within sight of the revolving light on top of a police car. There was a small crowd around a savagely wrecked automobile, a policeman keeping cars moving, another policeman standing beside the wreck. There was a mound covered by a soiled cloth. Gregory Lind's Roman collar was his passport through to the standing policeman. The man touched his fingers to his cap.

"He isn't a pleasant sight to see, Father."

"No matter. I'll have to see him."

"I know that."

The policeman bent over and lifted the sheet. There was a great deal of blood. There was a thick layer of ice in the early morning shadow of

38

the freeway. The blood had melted patterns in the ice, lines and blobs and patches. The man's body was hunched, misshapen. It was difficult to see his face because his head was twisted over his shoulder. It had been almost severed from his body.

"Thrown out of the car, he was," the policeman said. "We'd have needed torches to get him if he wasn't."

Father Lind turned the head with a touch of his fingers. He knew this boy, Carl Oberwitte. No more than eighteen. Old Saint Anselm family. He knelt there in the street, just clear of the blood, and prayed. He pronounced conditional absolution over the body. Behind him the ambulance crew wheeled in but they gave him time when the policeman told them that there was nothing they could do. Gregory Lind rose. He was feeling ill and he could not think of that.

"I know his family," he said. "I'll have to tell them. Somebody has to do it."

"It's usually our job," the policeman said.

"Do you want it?"

"No. We'll be glad if you do it, Father."

"I'll do it. They'll be taking him to the morgue, I suppose."

"That's right. Will you identify him, Father?"

"Certainly. He's Carl Oberwitte. His father is Oscar Oberwitte. They live at 1001 Paskert Avenue, maybe 1003 or 1005. It's the corner house."

He stood for a couple of seconds, watching as the policeman wrote the identification into his notebook, then turned away. Jim Bergen walked to the car with him.

"I don't envy you your job, Father," he said. "It will go hard with the Oberwittes. Their only son! It will be better for them to hear it from you than from a cop."

They drove in silence to the rectory. Father Lind was not certain that he would be better than a policeman at breaking bad news, but he should certainly be of more help to the people who had to accept that news. They stopped in front of the rectory and he left Jim Bergen with a brief "thank you." He was already concentrated on the task ahead of him.

Halfway to the garage he stopped. He remembered suddenly that he was not an individual, free to accept a task or to reject it, he was a unit in a large organization, a minor member of a small organization. Father Schafer had reserved for himself all the sick calls, most of the priestly responsibilities, for the old families in the parish. The Oberwittes were an old family, one of the oldest. Reluctantly, he changed course and

39

entered the rectory. The change of course was a bow to authority. A priest made many such bows.

Father Schafer was crossing the hallway as he entered the door. The pastor would have passed him with a curt "good morning" but Father Lind blocked his way.

"A minute, Father," he said. "I have to talk to you."

"Not now. See me at ten."

"I have to see you now. Young Carl Oberwitte is dead."

Father Schafer stiffened. "Come into my study," he said.

The pastor was fairly tall, a solidly built man. He had heavy features, a long straight nose, thin lips. He walked around the desk in his study.

"Let me have it," he said.

"He went through the guard rail on the River Highway. He was thrown out of the car. Killed instantly. He hit on Korst Street. I identified him."

Father Schafer passed his hand over his head. His eyes were bleak. "My God!" he said. "What a terrible thing that is! That poor family."

He had not seated himself behind the desk although some dictation of habit had taken him there. He moved swiftly now toward his wardrobe.

"I will go up there immediately." He hesitated a moment, half turned, as a thought struck him. "What was he doing on the River Highway, do you know?"

"No. No idea."

A thought hung there between the two priests. A young man of Carl Oberwitte's type seldom started out at six forty-five A.M.; he was more likely to be coming home. Carl had been something of a problem in many ways.

The pastor put on his coat. His face was set in grim lines. He and Father Lind went out together but he waved the younger priest on to the garage alone.

"I'll walk," he said.

As he drove to the offices of the *Catholic Star*, Gregory Lind marveled that this, these few words exchanged, was his closest personal approach to his pastor in nearly three years. He was no longer thinking of himself as a man bowing to authority. He had had a glimpse, a brief glimpse, into Father Schafer's parishioner relationship that he had not had before. He had sensed, too, a deep emotional current in the man of which he had never been aware. The pastor had always seemed cold to him, a stern, withdrawn executive figure.

The *Catholic Star* on any Monday morning was a busy place. This morning there was an early pile-up of paper on the Lind desk, and the telephone was ringing when he entered his office. Father Peter Coyle was in Miami, Florida, away from the ice and snow, attending some very important minor convention. The *Catholic Star,* with, of course, the full line of reservations and taboos, was all Father Lind's. One of the memos on the desk was from Father Coyle himself.

"Greg," Father Coyle had written, "here is an idea that came to me tonight. We should take note of the fact that women, young and old, are ignoring the rule that they should have their heads covered when they enter the church. It is very noticeable. Some priests are taking individual action. A pastor in Kansas City has announced in his parish bulletin that he will refuse communion to women with uncovered heads. I suggest a three-week campaign in the *Star.* Open it with an editorial. Close it with another. Have someone—I suggest Leo—interview pastors. You will know which ones. This, I feel is important. Get on it right away. Don't wait till I return. It's your idea now."

Pete—

Gregory Lind grimaced. He placed the memo under the small clock on his desk. It could not, unfortunately, be ignored. He ran through the flashes from the wire services. Priests in various cities were experimenting with the liturgy. Some of them were saying Masses in homes and apartments, consecrating ordinary bread and wine. Two of them were in trouble with their bishops. A priest of a respected order had just married a nun, "attempted marriage" was, of course, the approved phrase. A priest had been suspended by his bishop after his third unauthorized journey outside his state to participate in race protest marches. A priest on the faculty of an Eastern university had written an article on the Eucharist which was interpreted as a denial of Christ's divinity.

The pile of stories which an acting editor could not use in the *Star* was a thick pile—and Pete Coyle wanted a lusty campaign to put mantillas back on the heads of ladies in church!

The telephone rang. Dan Tierney, who ran the church goods house downtown, wanted to know why the *Catholic Star* was "letting our Lady down." There was no Marian emphasis in the paper, no effort being made to encourage the saying of the rosary. It developed in the course of the telephone conversation that Mr. Tierney had a store full of rosaries and no one was buying them. He hadn't sold a statue of the Madonna in months. The saints weren't selling either. Some fool in Rome, taking old saints out of the calendar, had shaken public confidence in saints.

Greg Lind said that he would see what he could do about the rosary, but he doubted that he could do much about the saints. He had felt pretty badly himself when they ruled Barbara out of her halo. He liked Barbara, even as an ex-saint.

There were local stories; bazaars, bingo, parties, rummage sales. A girl from the Polish parish, north on the river, Saint Stanislaus, was going away to be a Franciscan nun. She would have her picture in the paper. A girl who had left the Lorettines and who came home last week would not even be mentioned.

The phone rang again. This was Monsignor Kevin Hurley of the Chancery office, speaking for the bishop. He had a clear, cold voice and the assurance of authority. Father Lind knew him well, had seen him often during the cathedral years, but the monsignor indulged in no personal pleasantries.

"His Excellency is concerned at the many discourses on celibacy, written or spoken, which are wide of the mark," he said. "It is not an open question. We are a celibate clergy. Priests have been forbidden to wed since 1123. There has been no change and no evidence that any change is considered possible. The Church is standing firm in this celibacy matter. His Excellency wants you to say so, and to keep repeating it. You can devote the lead editorial to the subject this week?"

"It is close to the deadline, but yes. Yes. We can do it."

"Fine. I shall assure His Excellency that you are supporting him."

Monsignor Hurley hung up his receiver decisively. Father Gregory Lind took the Coyle memo on female head covering from under the clock and placed it in the drawer of his desk.

There was an editorial to write. It would not be easy but it was a subject that a man could get his teeth into. Gregory Lind cleared his desk of the routine, went to lunch alone, and came back to his typewriter.

He believed in a celibate priesthood. Celibacy was not easy; it was, in fact, one of the most difficult paths that a man could walk in life. For that very reason, a man walking it was closer to God. He offered up a sacrifice at the very moment when he asked for the powers and the privileges of the priesthood. There was no questioning the depth and the profundity of that sacrifice. In renouncing the family that he might have had, the priest freed himself to serve God wholeheartedly and to serve the people to whom he was assigned; he had no divided loyalties.

Not all priests agreed with him, Father Lind knew. Many of them believed that celibacy was one thing and that a vocation to the priesthood was another; that a man to whom the idea of celibacy was intolerable might still have a genuine desire to be a priest; a true vocation.

It was interesting, it was challenging and it was difficult. Father Lind wrote paragraphs and pages that he threw away. He wadded paper and tossed it at the wastebasket, placed a fresh sheet in the typewriter and tried again. It was so easy to be stuffy, to be above the battle, to ignore the realities that men faced when they took the vow. He did not want that approach. He did not want to tell men what to do; he wanted to praise them because of what they did.

The afternoon vanished. When he read over his final copy, not quite satisfied but convinced that he could do no better, the night had moved in. He discovered when he left the Star Building that the weather was decidedly unfriendly. There was a stiff wind and the low temperature had dropped lower. The gloomy old rectory with the dim glow behind the fan light was a welcome sight.

He had barely cleared the front door when Mrs. Wagner was coming toward him, waving a slip of paper. "Ah, I'm happy you've come in," she said. "There's a sick call and nobody here. The pastor's at the Oberwittes, God help them, and Father Guyton went to the hospital. That poor soul with the broken hip!"

"Who? Who has a broken hip?"

"Mrs. Dahlen. Poor soul. Fell on the ice. She'll probably not live through it."

Father Lind winced. He remembered Mrs. Dahlen very well. She was one of his regulars at six o'clock Mass. He did not know how old she was, but she was thin and frail and cheerful. He wished that, if he had to have a sick call tonight, he could have gone to her.

"What about the other?" he said.

Mrs. Wagner waved the slip of paper.

"Mrs. Robert Dillon. Nadine Dillon, and no Saint's name that! 1465 Kaylor Street. One of those river places. I don't know anybody down there. Father Guyton's been to see her a few times. Very bad, she is . . ."

Gregory Lind took the slip of paper. He stopped in the church for the Sacred Host. He always felt particularly solemn, carrying it, unable to think of anything else. He drove carefully and there was fog in the low section along the river. Kaylor Street was west of the River Highway, the near side to him, and it consisted of apartment houses set in rows. Mrs. Wagner had dismissed the area contemptuously, but it was better than she had indicated. It was new, clean, constructed on the cleared area after the building of the freeway. The apartments would be all alike, of course, but inhabited by young people who would not give that a thought.

He found 1465 in the middle of the block. The Dillons lived on the second floor. A thin young man opened the door. He was pale and he looked as though he needed sleep. He looked, too, as though he had been crying.

"I am Father Lind," Gregory said. "Father Guyton was away from the rectory. Is there anything you want to tell me before I see her?"

"Oh, yes. She's very sick. The doctor says . . . well, no hope, he says . . . She doesn't want to die. She's frightened. I don't know what to do for her."

Father Lind nodded. "Let us put her in the hands of God," he said. "They are gentle hands."

He was taking the girl's Catholicism for granted. Father Guyton had been here more than once. He would have checked anything that had to be checked. As he moved toward the bedroom behind the young man, Father Lind could see the table covered with a white cloth. There was a small pitcher of water and a single candle. Someone had known what to provide.

There was an older woman standing beside the bed. She stepped back and moved across the room when the priest entered. He looked down at the girl.

She looked like a child. Her hair was light gold and her eyes a delicate blue. She had a touch of make-up on her cheeks but the skin under the make-up was pale. She was terrified when she saw the priest.

"Bobby," she called. "Bobby! Please. Tell him to go. I don't want to die."

"I didn't come here to frighten you," Gregory Lind said softly. "Please don't be frightened. Please let me talk to you."

She ignored him, continuing to call for "Bobby." Her husband, who had withdrawn when the priest entered the room, returned. His eyes asked a question at the priest, who nodded in reply. There was no reason why he could not stay. There would be no confession.

"I am not going to ask you for any details," Father Lind said to her. "Just think for a moment. You are sorry for your sins, aren't you, all of your sins, because they offend God?"

The girl turned her head away from him, directing her thin, childlike voice toward her husband. There was desperation in her voice. "Bobby," she said, "if you love me, you'll get me another doctor. Please. Get me a doctor to make me well, Bobby."

"I'll try, Naydee," he said. "I'll try. But talk to the priest first. His name is Father Lind, Naydee."

44

"I don't care. I don't care. Please, Bobby, make him go away. Don't let me die, Bobby. Don't!"

She turned her head and looked at Father Gregory Lind. Her eyes were suddenly dull. Her lips puckered and moisture bubbled on them. "Don't!" she said.

Her body stiffened and relaxed. Her breath was a long sigh. She was gone as the flame of a candle goes; instantly.

Father Lind knelt beside the bed. He gave her the general absolution and not until he started to pray did the young man realize that she was dead. He threw himself across the bed and the woman who had been standing against the wall came over and gripped him by the shoulders. Another woman came in behind the priest and went out again. He could hear her talking on the phone in another room.

Father Lind stayed for an hour. He talked to Robert Dillon and he encouraged him to talk. The young man was desperately in need of sleep. He did not manage words well. At intervals he stopped, put his head in his hands and wept. Nadine Dillon had been twenty-two. She had left two children, four and three. It seemed incredible. She had seemed such a child herself. Gregory Lind was oppressed with a sense of failure. He had been of no use to her in those last minutes of her life. He had not reassured her. He had not lighted her on the way that she had to go.

People came and went; the doctor, the man from the mortuary, relatives, friends. Father Lind went to the church when he left and then to the rectory. Father Guyton had not returned but Mrs. Wagner came to the front of the house when she heard the door open. Father Lind told her of the girl's death. Mrs. Wagner might be indifferent to the needs of priests committed to her care, but she was conscientious about parishioners.

"May she rest in peace," she said. "I didn't know the woman but it is a pity to go so young, and leaving a husband and children. Can I fix you a bit of supper, Father?"

Such friendly proffers were rare in Saint Anselm's rectory but Father Lind shook his head.

"No, thank you," he said. "I have to go to Guadalupe House."

– VI –

The wind raced down the river and its flank patrols roared over the chimneys of town, or down the deep canyons of streets. Ice rode on the wind and the street lights were dim. There was little traffic and the occasional motorcar moved slowly. A white mist hung between the street and the windows of Guadalupe House. Gregory Lind did not believe that there would be many students in the place. He was mistaken in that.

Every classroom and shop in the school was functioning. There were three young men waiting for the priest in his office, despite the fact that he was late; so late that the classes were using up their last half hour. Two of the young men were discouraged and ready to drop out of their courses. Father Lind marveled at the strength of a discouragement which would bring a man out on a night like this, bring him out to announce that he was quitting.

He maneuvered both of the young men into trying for a while longer, as he usually did with such cases; the third young man was a different matter. He had a problem that was becoming common, a problem that Father Lind had faced only a few nights ago, that he had faced often.

This one was a short, thick-bodied man in his middle twenties. He had a small mustache on a broad lip. His lids drooped over his eyes. His name was Juan Lucero.

"Father," he said, "it is told to me that the Church says now that the abortion is O.K. I have to know of this."

"It is not O.K., and it never will be O.K. Get that out of your head! Abortion is murder. Now, why do you have to know of this?"

"There is a girl. She needs it."

"Your child?"

"She says."

"You probably know whether it is or not. Is it?"

"I think maybe so. Could be. I will not marry her."

"You don't love her?"

The young man grinned. "It is not love."

"It isn't funny either. You got this girl in trouble and now you want to walk out on her and let her handle it."

"No. I told you how it is. I want an abortion. I will pay for it. I am a Catholic. She is a Catholic. A man says it is O.K. now with the Church."

"Well, the man was wrong. So, now what do you do?"

Juan Lucero shrugged slightly. He looked at the priest and there was neither emotion nor intelligence in his face, merely patience. He had no answer to offer so he was willing to wait.

"You should marry this girl and give the child a name. It may be a boy. Your son."

"I do not want this. I will not marry her."

"Well, I don't have a shotgun. The girl must give birth to that baby.

46

She *must,* you understand. I can arrange that she has care, hospitalization and the rest of it. Now about the baby. Will you contribute to its support?"

"No. I cannot do this."

Father Lind appreciated an honest answer and did not argue with it. A Spanish American, even with a skill, was at the bottom of the wage scales, at the top of the layoff lists. He had a worse time with unions than the Negro. If he was saddled with a financial obligation that he could not meet, he ran away; not out of cowardice but for the simple reason that he had no answer to his problem.

"If the mother is willing to release the child for adoption, you will not object?"

Something about the question, or in the idea that it suggested to the man, amused him. It was a temporary amusement that showed in his face, that flickered over his lips; there for an instant and gone.

"I do not object. No."

The priest took a pad from his desk. "I will talk to this girl," he said, "if you will give me her name and address."

"*Sí.* You will not talk to her mother?"

"No. I'll talk to the girl."

"*Bueno.*"

The man wrote a name and address on the priest's pad. He stood before the desk, all expression erased from his face. "Father," he said. "I thank you for this."

He was gone then and Father Gregory Lind looked at the paper on which the young man had written. That "thank you" had been eloquent. One read Spanish Americans between the lines, always, in the few words rather than the many. There was never a way of undoing what had been done, and when there was a baby on the way and no marriage, there was no perfect answer to the problem. One did what one could.

The interview had taken time. The school was closing. Most of the classes were already dark. Father Lind crossed his office to the door and looked down the corridor. The typing section was dark and he experienced a sense of disappointment which he did not attempt to define. He turned back to the office, put on his hat and coat, then turned off the light.

At the front door he met Pamela Gibson. She was coming back into the building. "I need a phone," she said. "Are any of them still connected?"

"Why do you need a phone?"

"My car won't start. Battery quit. I want to call the three A's."

"They'll have a lot of calls tonight. You might have to wait an hour. Why can't I take you home?"

"Because it's out of your way."

"That doesn't matter. I hate to leave your car in the lot, though. Guadalupe House is respected and it has been let alone, still?"

"I'll chance it. It's too cold for thieves. If you want a passenger, you've got one."

"*Bueno.*"

They went out together into the swooping wind which came now in swift spurts; dropping off into deceptively quiet lulls and picking up again with fury. The Lind car was equipped to meet weather; snow tires, anti-freeze, heater. It belonged to the *Catholic Star* and was equipped by the *Star*, but, in effect, it was solely Father Lind's. It was silver gray which certainly had more dash than did the ecclesiastical black. He was very proud of it.

"I'm sorry," he said. "I don't know where you live."

"How could you? It is 751 Steuben Drive."

Pamela Gibson relaxed in the front seat beside him while he started the engine and turned on the defroster. The glass was gray white with frost, opaque rather than transparent. "It is an apartment house," the girl said, "only three apartments. You couldn't find my telephone number. It's unlisted, silent, verboten."

"You sound mysterious."

"I'm not. Not very."

Gregory Lind got out to clear the rear window. When he came back, the windshield was clean. He drove carefully. It had just occurred to him that he could win headlines in the paper by driving into an accident with a feminine member of the Gibson clan. His objective, Steuben Drive, was on the high line of the second hill, one of the nicer neighborhoods. The houses were old, stylishly old without shabbiness. Most of them had been broken up into apartments because the day of the big family home was nearly over; but there were no rooming houses, no cheap, modernistic conversions. Number 751 was mid-block; a straight, narrow three story house that was shaded by two enormous trees, bare now but undoubtedly impressive when in leaf. Gregory parked only two doors away from the entrance.

"That was nice," Pamela said. "Much more comfortable than driving it myself. For a reward I can offer a highball or something and a fire to drink beside."

Gregory had walked around his car to help her out. He hesitated and she moved swiftly into his hesitation. "I know you are a priest," she said. "I have no designs on you."

48

"It wouldn't ever occur to me that you had."

"All right. Come on up."

She walked ahead of him. There was pride in the way she walked, or, perhaps, arrogance. Her apartment was on the second floor; it was, in fact, the entire second floor. They ascended on a curving white staircase. Pamela unlocked her door. There was a small foyer.

"First door on your left is the guest closet, second door the guest lavatory. I'll be back immediately."

She vanished through a middle door. Gregory hung his hat and coat in the closet. He did not have any waiting. Pamela was wearing a dark blue suit with a red diagonal across the upper half. Her hair was softly curled, her mouth vividly red.

"What do you drink?" she said. "I can't mix a decent martini."

"I can't drink one, either. When it's available I drink Scotch. With water."

"Good man. So do I."

She led the way into a long living room. "Fire is laid in the fireplace," she said. "Touch a match to it while I pour the drinks."

He looked at the room with appreciation. It had soft cream walls and high ceilings. The furniture was distributed so artfully that it looked casually haphazard. There were two short, oversized couches flanking the fireplace, with other chairs at a distance. A walnut stereo-television cabinet faced the fireplace from the opposite wall. Above the cabinet there was a painting with a narrow, almost-non-existent frame. A Spanish dancer in greens and reds danced against a stark black background. She was reflected in the mirror above the fireplace mantel.

"Nice," he said.

The paper and kindling flamed instantly from the one match. There were two small split logs and some other pieces. Gregory sat in the small couch on his left. He was looking through an arch at the far end of the room. There was a credenza with two swan lamps at either end of it, the white, swooning figure of a dancer between them. From this distance the dancer appeared to be ivory. There were bookcases against the far wall, big cases with many books.

"Nice fire."

Pamela was back. He rose and took the tray from her. She had mixed the drinks but she had put a bucket of ice and napkins on the tray. They sat on facing couches with their drinks. Pamela had flicked out all the lights in the room except one when she returned to it. The fire sang contentedly, glad perhaps that it was fire and not water, its flame dancing, its shadows moving on the cream walls. Music came softly as from a distance, the Mendelssohn *Violin Concerto*. Gregory dipped his glass toward the apparent source of sound.

"The music," he said, "yours?"

"In a sense, yes. It's FM. When I have someone to talk with, I like music two rooms away."

"I never heard it put that way before. It sounds like a good prescription."

"It is."

She was relaxed, one leg drawn up under her, facing the fire, her drink in her hand. The flickering light softened the lines of her jaw, the strong line of cheekbone. Her hair, reflecting, had a definite tone of red.

"When I don't feel like talking myself," she said, "I am a good listener. This is one of those rare nights when I don't feel like talking."

He laughed. "I can't talk either. This perfect fire, this excellent Scotch, this beautiful room, and soft music; it is all beyond anything I could have dreamed, much less anticipated."

"You mentioned everything except me. I'm here, too. Never mind. That is probably the priest of it, overlooking the woman as a matter of principle. You know, I've never talked to a priest before, never in my life."

"Do you feel a lack?"

"A little. I'm curious. How does one become a priest? Why? Wait! Hold it! First, your name. It doesn't sound like a priest's name."

"A great many priests' names do not sound like priests' names. There's a Father Zywolewski in Chicago. But O.K. I can't take the Linds back any further than my grandfather. He came to Wisconsin from Sweden and he was a Catholic when he came. My father met my mother in Mankato, Minnesota. She was only half Swede. I was born in Chillicothe, Ohio." He spread his hands. "The complete story of a priest named Lind. The name was probably Lindquist in the beginning."

"Your mother. Only half Swede." The girl drank from her glass. "What was the other half?"

"Irish."

"Oh. That's where the priest came from."

"Maybe. A little. There's more to it than that."

"Of course. What is it? What puts the priest in a man?"

"God."

"Ooops! I should say, 'of course.' I can't. It was the wrong question. You know what I was trying to ask. Tell me. Your way."

He took a swallow of his Scotch, liking the bite of it. "I couldn't make you understand," he said.

"You might. But never mind. We drank that Scotch pretty fast. Shows we needed it. I'll fix another."

"I shouldn't. I should go home. But it is a lovely Scotch." He handed her his glass. "I was told once that the drink one *needs* is the drink he should never take."

"Not so. People tell other people the damnedest nonsense."

He watched her as she walked away from him and he wondered how he had ever formed the impression that she strode, that she was awkward; she moved easily, floatingly, gracefully. She seemed tall and he knew that that was an illusion. He thought about her question.

One could not tell anyone, much less an unbeliever, why one became a priest. So much of the reality of it was wrapped up in the vaporous, partly forgotten stuff of one's youth; the loving of quiet, lonely visits to the church, the awareness of God, the habit of looking at everything in nature as something created. One couldn't explore a thousand memories, or describe the process of evolving faith or explain even to oneself that sense of being different, of having been created to serve the spiritual need of others. Something was in one and it unfolded. How could one discuss that?

"Make this one stretch a little. I never send a guest home with three drinks in him unless he's had dinner after them."

Pamela handed him his second drink and he tipped his glass toward her. "Right," he said. "And it's your turn to talk."

"No. I told you that I'm on a rare silent night. Almost silent, that is; silent for me. I still want to know what makes a priest. Here's another way. Tell me what you did today, all of it."

"All of it?" He watched the flames. They were not so exuberant now, not leaping so high. The room was comfortably warm and he was warm inside. It was difficult to pursue reality across a frosty day.

"I said my Mass at six," he said. "There was an auto accident. A young man drove off the River Highway. I reached him a few minutes after he died."

"Carl Oberwitte," the girl said softly.

"Yes. You knew him?"

"Slightly. He was younger. I know the family. Not well. Sorry. I interrupted."

Gregory took a swallow of his drink. It was not surprising, in a town like Culverton, if a person with money knew other people who had money.

"There was that," he said. "I was going to notify the family but my pastor, Father Schafer, is a friend of theirs, so I told him."

He was aware of the girl's eyes fixed intently upon his face. He still did not know their color. "I'm talking on and on," he thought. "Why don't I shut up?" The words pushed forward out of some depth of his consciousness.

"I went to the *Catholic Star*," he said. "I have a number of jobs down there so I'm only a part priest in a parish. When the editor is out of town, I'm the editor, in my fashion."

"You write. I didn't know."

"Today I wrote an editorial on celibacy."

"Not in favor of it!"

"Certainly, in favor of it. For priests, that is."

"How could you? It's unnatural. It's inhuman! Terrible! For priests! For anybody!"

"No. It's a way of living. One dedicates himself to God that way. He sacrifices the things that would distract him. He can serve people better because he is not serving a family."

"He goes far away from people if he shuns human experience."

"There is a balance. He has experience that they can never have."

The girl drank. She shook her head. "Strange," she said. "I can't imagine a man doing that to himself deliberately. I never gave it a thought. I just assumed that, of course, priests have a sex life; that they just keep it out of sight. Talking to you, listening to you, I'm not sure. You register. There's a lot of sincerity in you, a lot of something else. Suddenly I can't believe you have a hidden sex life."

He laughed because he felt uncomfortable. "I haven't," he said. "And that's that. An end to Scotch and time I was going home."

He rose and the girl rose with him. "Oh, no," she said. "There was so much I wanted to ask you. And no matter how I talk, I seldom have anyone in, someone to just talk, and no men. It's been a creepy day. I wanted to hear someone talk. You don't know."

"About loneliness, you mean?"

She raised her head, looked at him, looked away. "Yes. I guess you do. Well, look. I haven't even talked about Raimundo. I meant to do that. Let me half break a rule. Let me fix you a half drink. You'll be all right, won't you? You haven't had much. You can drive O.K.?"

This was sophist argument. He knew that he should go. He marveled that he had not given Raimundo a thought. He had wanted to ask her about Raimundo. The idea of another drink had charm. He shook his shoulders. He was feeling fine.

"All right," he said. "Thanks. And don't worry about the driving. There's practically no one on the streets and I always drive carefully."

"Good," she said. "Put another small log on that silly fire while I bartend."

The flames were dancing happily again by the time she returned. The music, two rooms away, was not too lively, something he remembered vaguely but could not identify. Pamela Gibson handed him his drink. He tasted it and it tasted like a full drink. He was, perversely, glad of that. No use wasting one's time on halves of anything.

"About Raimundo," he said, "I haven't seen him."

"Neither have I. He didn't come to class tonight. It's the first night he's missed." She paused, looking at her glass. "My fault, maybe. I may have made a mistake. I acted against your advice."

"You bought him a bicycle."

"Yes. I had to do it. That is, I felt I had to do it. It's the same thing. I didn't try to pick out one for him. I just ordered it and told the store I'd pay for whatever he selected. They were going to find him and tell him. I didn't make a big production out of it. I'd just as soon stay out of it. I just wanted him to have it."

She was talking freely now, without awareness of it. Some of her words blurred slightly but she made sense. She was concerned about Raimundo.

"The bicycle probably didn't have anything to do with his missing tonight," Gregory said. "That was a wicked wind."

"I hope it didn't. Oh, yes. Another thing I wanted to ask you. It impressed me, made me curious. I became aware of you. You didn't know I was in the school. But you licked a problem I had. The boys told me you did, making fun of me, and they said you didn't use religion or anything like that."

"What problem?"

"Using dirty language in class. I hated it but I tried not to make an issue. I really tried. But it seemed so unnecessary, so pointless, so immature and unclean."

Gregory laughed. "It's the way they think. They grew up from babies speaking three languages; Spanish, English, Dirty. I don't like it a bit better than you do."

"But what did you do?"

"Nothing. I just said that I knew I was in a slum when I saw bottles in the street, and beer cans, and yards full of trash and I said that I felt that my office was a slum when people threw a lot of dirty words around in it. I said that I wouldn't try to stop a man from throwing a beer can in the street, or breaking a bottle, but I wouldn't respect him when he did it."

"That's all?"

"That's all. I probably repeated that several times in one way or another. They stopped dumping verbal beer cans in my office."

53

"It's improved in my classroom, too. I ignore it when they slip."

"*Bueno*. They'll slip often."

The girl drank from her glass. "I'm feeling sober again," she said. "I was whirling for a while."

"False dawn," he said.

He did not want to get up and go. He was enjoying the warmth, the stimulation, the conversation, the companionship, particularly the companionship. This girl had surprised him. He liked exchanging opinions with her. The conversation had probably been anything but brilliant and the chances were that neither one of them would remember much of it tomorrow. No matter. He had never sat in a beautiful room like this with anyone else, talking freely with no end to serve, no job to do, no purpose save the talking itself. He could not risk spoiling a memorable experience by stretching it too far. Everything had to end. He rose from the chair, startled that, for a moment, he seemed to sway. The girl rose, too, and she, perhaps, felt as he did, that an invisible clock was striking somewhere.

"I've never had a more pleasant evening," he said.

She laughed. "You probably do all right. But thank you. I enjoyed it, too. Tremendously."

She walked ahead of him to the foyer and he was sharply aware of her walking. She held herself straight and she moved with grace. She did not seem tall now. She was small beside him and he was not quite six feet. He got his hat and coat from the closet. She helped him with his coat and when he turned, he was looking into her eyes. She stood there, not moving at all, and he was aware of her in every nerve of his body. She was so close and the night was so still. She smiled.

"Good night," she said gently.

The moment was over. He echoed her good night and then he was going down the white staircase. In his car, driving into the wind from the heights of Steuben Drive, he laughed aloud. It had been a wonderful evening. Some people would be scandalized if they knew that he had been sitting in a girl's apartment, drinking Scotch. It wasn't discreet, of course, but nothing ontoward had happened, nothing at all. He laughed again.

She wanted to hear about his day, the entire day. He had not got halfway through it. He would have liked her opinion on the youth who would not marry the girl. It made no difference. It had been a wonderful evening.

The rectory was quiet normally when Father Lind came in after saying the six o'clock Mass, so quiet that it seemed uninhabited. On Tuesday morning, Father Schafer had his door open and he came out into the hall when he heard his assistant enter.

"Good morning, Father Lind," he said. "You were out late last night."

"I am afraid that I was. I was visiting friends and I did not notice the time."

"Oh, yes. Well, that's no matter. Your affair. I mentioned it only because I tried to find you. I wanted to thank you for handling that accident as you did. The Oberwittes, all of them, are friends of mine. A fine family."

"I know."

"Well, anyway, some young priests would have gone pell-mell over there, carrying the bad news. That wouldn't have done. Not at all."

Father Schafer was smoking his pipe. He obviously found this conversation difficult just as, obviously, he felt that he must speak. When he put his pipe in his mouth he bit hard on the mouthpiece; when he held it in his hand he gestured with it. He had a strong face. Gregory Lind had always considered it a cold face. There was nothing cold about the man now. He drew on his pipe, then shook his head.

"Fred Oberwitte, the uncle, is coming down from Anchorage, Alaska," he said, "so I've set the rosary for seven-thirty Wednesday night. I'm asking you and Father Guyton to be present out of respect for the family. I would like to have you at the altar with me on Thursday morning, too, but it will not be necessary that you go to the cemetery."

"Thank you," Father Lind said.

The pastor turned away and Gregory Lind walked into the dining room for his breakfast. He was thinking of how narrowly that decision of his yesterday had been balanced. He had very nearly qualified as one of those young men who go pell-mell over to deliver bad news. He had very nearly gone to the Oberwitte house and the pastor was right; it would have been a mistake. They needed their old friend at that moment. He thought, too, of how swift he had been with an unnecessary lie in telling the pastor that he had been visiting "friends" last night; a minor matter, of course, but unnecessary. He did not know why he had done it.

Mrs. Wagner brought him one of the pastor's characteristic memos before he finished his breakfast. The mortuary had been informed that Father Lind would say the rosary tonight, Tuesday, for Mrs. Robert Dillon and that he would sing the requiem on Wednesday at ten.

The week was beginning to look pinched. It had too many tasks in it already. He would be editing the paper all week. Father Peter Coyle was going to stop for meetings in Washington at the National Catholic Welfare Conference headquarters on his way back from Miami. He would also have two or three days in New York. His trip, ultimately, would be a hell of a bore to everyone but himself.

Father Lind went briefly to his room and Father Guyton knocked on the door before he got away. The young priest was in a subdued mood, lacking his normal exuberance.

"I thought that you would want to know," he said. "Your friend, Mrs. Dahlen, died in her sleep last night."

Father Lind had one arm in the sleeve of his coat. He stood while the coat dangled, making no effort to find a sleeve with his other arm. "May God be good to her," he said. "She was a lovely little woman."

"Yes. She was. She liked you. She told me that she always went to your Mass. I was sorry that I drew the call when she was hurt. You should have had it."

"No matter, that. I'm certain that you took good care of her. You'll handle the rosary and the Mass, of course."

"I guess so. I'm going to speak to the pastor now."

Father Guyton went noisily down the stairs. Father Lind found the other sleeve to his coat, shrugged into the garment and put on his hat. Out of doors, it was a bleak morning. The wind had moved east and the hard, still cold had settled down on Culverton. Alone in his car, he was able to think of his morning. The pastor's attempt at friendliness had been a surprise and the man's difficulty in expressing himself had been oddly appealing. The death of Mrs. Dahlen had been a shock and should not have been; she had lived a full span of years. He shook his head.

Despite the consolations they offered from the pulpit, priests did not find death a welcome visitor. They might confidently voice the belief that God had called a departed soul to heaven, but there was still a feeling of loss when a regular parishioner died, a diminution of the parish itself. One did not grow callous to tragedy on a human

56

material plane even when one spoke in terms of spiritual triumph; one knew the survivors.

He pulled into the *Catholic Star* parking lot and casual thought stopped there. Problems were awaiting him on his desk inside, in the unopened mail, in the phone calls that were to be. Roger Bailey, one of the many sub-editors, was waiting to tell him that two key people were ill with the flu, or at least bad colds. What should he do about it? Well, one didn't do anything about it; one carried on, one way or another. There were three memos which Father Coyle had mailed from Miami, each of them marked urgent and none of them worth a moment's thought. The priest in Gregory Lind went out somewhere, back to church or off to some springtime babbling brook; his other self took over and tried to cope with the day. Many hours later, after the dark came down, he looked at the clock on the wall and his priesthood came back to him. He had barely time for a quick hamburger before he was due at the mortuary to lead a rosary.

There were two bouquets of flowers, small bouquets, behind the coffin of Nadine Dillon. There were only eight or ten people in the mortuary when Father Lind walked down the aisle. He stood beside the open coffin for a few seconds remembering her as she had been. She was frail, and pretty in death. She looked so very young and she had so few friends and she had not wanted to die. Her funeral would be so poor, so minimum in everything, and her husband, probably, could not afford the little that she would have. He made the sign of the Cross and he hoped, as he knelt beside the body, that she was happy with the eternity she had found.

His voice went up, offering the prayers of the rosary, and behind him the other voices rose and fell in the responses. "May she rest in peace, O Lord, and may perpetual light shine upon her."

The Church said its farewell to her on the following morning. Father Lind said the Mass and he blessed the casket and he drove to the cemetery. There were two other cars in the small procession. When the earth had claimed her, he offered what consolation he could to Robert Dillon, her husband, the "Bobby" of her last cry, and to her parents, knowing that nothing he could say would have the slightest meaning. He felt extraordinarily close to these people in the cold, cheerless cemetery, close to them in his own emotions, in their need of something that was beyond his power to give, in the sharing of brave, sad prayers. It was, of course, a moment of time. He might not ever see any of these people again and if he did there would be no bond, no closeness, no emotional association. A priest lived too many

57

poignant moments in the lives of other people; he could not live any of them over again.

He drove downtown and the paper absorbed him; his thought, his energy, his various skills with human beings. On the staff of the paper itself, and outside of it, in letters and phone calls and personal visits, one dealt with people, forever with people. Sentences, paragraphs and pages were seemingly the secondary things in the people-dominated day and yet, oddly enough, they were all that tangibly remained when the day was over.

Night meant another rosary and the Oberwitte rosary was not a small one. The Oberwitte family was an important family in the community, a family of long tradition, of influence, of moderate wealth. Saint Anselm's was a large, old-fashioned church and the people who came to offer their prayers with, and for, the family filled most of the pews. Carl Oberwitte's coffin was closed. The three priests of the parish knelt beside it and Father Schafer led the rosary. The answering voices rolled in waves of sound, rising and falling waves that broke abruptly, gathered strength and rolled again.

"Hail, Mary, full of grace, the Lord is with Thee; blessed art Thou amongst women, and blessed is the fruit of thy womb, Jesus."

The pastor's deep baritone voice sent the prayer forth and the tide of voices behind him rolled prayer back; "Holy Mary, Mother of God, pray for us sinners, now and at the hour of our death. Amen."

There were five decades in a rosary, fifty Hail Mary's; the effect could be one of tiring monotony or of dramatic repetition. Father Schafer set the key of supplication. He was praying before the throne of God for the soul of a sinner, and he had all of those people in the church praying with him. Father Lind, responding with the others, felt the power of that leading voice. Father Schafer, perhaps, was what a priest should be, a dweller in a community which included the living and the dead, a man of God living among his friends, sharing joy and sorrow with them.

The rosary ended and the crowd moved slowly out of the church. Father Schafer visited with various members of the Oberwitte family. Fathers Lind and Guyton left the church together.

"I have some liquor left and I could do with a drink. Have one with me?" Father Guyton said.

Gregory Lind shook his head regretfully. "I have to hurry down to Guadalupe House. Sorry. I could do with a drink, too."

He wondered about that, about Tom Guyton's feeling and his own, the feeling of people in the church. Few of those who knew him, he imagined, had any real liking for Carl Oberwitte. Altogether apart from their feeling for the family, few people would be moved by his death. A young man who was driving over ninety miles an hour on a city freeway when he lost control of his car was not trying desperately to live. Life, and the leaving of it, seemed without meaning if one met it solely on a physical plane.

It was late when he reached Guadalupe House, as it so often was; nearly eight-thirty. The school evening ended at nine on Wednesdays. He parked his car and walked briskly toward the entrance. It was damned cold. A figure moved out of the deep shadow.

"Padre, I must talk with you."

A thin line of light from a school window fell across Raimundo Baca's face. Raimundo was shaking with the cold. "I have wait a long time," he said.

"You shouldn't wait out here. Come on in."

"No. I cannot. There are people in your office who wait for you. I must talk private."

"Must you? All right. Let's try my car as an office."

Father Lind fought down his feeling of impatience. He wanted to go inside, to see whoever waited for him, to thank Pamela Gibson for the other night, with an apology for staying so late. He led the way to his car, opened the door for Raimundo, then seated himself behind the wheel.

"Let me have it," he said.

"It is hard to tell you simple what is in my mind, Padre."

"Tell it complicated, then. Any way you want. What's troubling you?"

"The teacher, Miss Gibson, she has made an order for a bicycle. I am supposed to have this bicycle."

"I know. She likes you. She thought you needed it."

"I cannot take it."

"O.K. You know best. Give it back."

"She would not understand."

"She would understand if you explained how you felt about it. Why can't you take it?"

"There is a girl, Padre. She is Ysabel Jaramillo. She has a good job in the office of the Gas Company. I would marry her but it is not possible. We are saving money for an automobile. That is maybe possible for us, the automobile. A bicycle would not be right."

"You mean that two of you couldn't ride it?"

"Sí."

"Miss Gibson would understand that."

"I cannot tell her."

Raimundo sat hunched forward in the seat. He was still shaking with

59

cold. Father Lind felt his impatience rising again. There were more grave problems than this. If Raimundo couldn't use a bicycle, he didn't have to take it. His constant problem was transportation. Pamela Gibson might be willing to contribute toward the automobile if he didn't accept the bicycle. That, however, could not be suggested. That idea had to come, if it came, from her.

"If you meet an understanding person who likes you, Raimundo," he said, "you can tell her anything. How about this girl of yours? I don't know her. Can I help you there?"

"No. She is very pretty. Very fine. I have no money. I must give money to my mother. Always I must give her money."

"Money is difficult stuff. If your mother needs help, you must help her. Miss Gibson says you are a good student. If you finish your course here, you can get a better job and make more money."

"I do not go to the course. I cannot explain to Miss Gibson about the bicycle."

"Do you want me to explain the matter to her?"

"Sí."

Raimundo held out a crumpled sheet of paper. This, Father Lind supposed, was the bicycle purchase order. "If I do this for you, will you go back to your class and work hard?" he said.

Raimundo did not answer immediately. He seemed to be drawn unhappily into himself, hugging himself. "It is an embarrassment," he said.

"Nonsense. There will be nothing to embarrass you. You walk right in and say good evening and go to work. If Miss Gibson wants to say anything to you, she'll say it. Remember that she is your friend."

The car beside Father Lind, on the left, pulled out of parking. He had been aware for several minutes of cars leaving. That meant that classes were over. He would have to be getting in or he would see nobody. He laid his hand on Raimundo's shoulder.

"I have to go now, Raimundo," he said. "Do what I told you. And be patient about that girl. You are young. You can wait a while. I'll say a prayer for you."

Raimundo's thank-you was mumbled. Father Lind slid out of the car on his own side and strode toward the building, hurrying. He was too late. The shorthand-and-typing section was dark and there was no one waiting in his office. He went slowly back to his car and Raimundo was gone.

"I could, at least, have offered him a ride," he said.

He drove back to the rectory, dissatisfied with the evening and dissatisfied with himself. The pastor's suite was dark. He climbed the stairs, hoping that Tom Guyton would still be up. He would welcome that proffered drink now and welcome even more the opportunity for conversation, the passing of ideas back and forth with someone of his own world; sound ideas or idiotic ones, it would not matter.

There was no line of light under the Guyton door.

In his bed, with the lights out, Gregory Lind lay on his back, staring up at a ceiling that he could not see. He had been of no aid to Raimundo who had waited in the cold to talk to him. He had not gone, step by reflective step, into the matter of the automobile, the rejection of the bicycle, or the matter of the girl. He had made a mistake that he should have been too wise to make. He had accepted the confidence of a Spanish American, a sharing of the deeply personal, without treating the privilege with respect. He had been impatient with Raimundo, or with the time that Raimundo was taking, and the impatience had wiped out everything else.

His mind moved relentlessly on. The reason for his impatience lay in the fact that his primary interest in Guadalupe House tonight had not been the helping of those who needed help; without putting the hope in words, even to himself, he had hoped that he would see Pamela Gibson.

"Absurd," he said. "Ridiculously absurd! She is nothing to me and she can never be anything to me. I have to put her out of my silly mind."

– VIII –

The Mass for Carl Oberwitte drew another large crowd to the church, the Mass for Mrs. Dahlen had only a few, mostly old people. Life at the rectory resumed its slow, even pace and there were no new alarms, no serious illnesses in the parish. Lent was looming over the ecclesiastical horizon, only a few weeks away.

Thursday was deadline day for the *Catholic Star* and Friday was a light day. Father Lind called on the girl friend of Juan Lucero. She was home alone and had been watching television. She wore shabby, dirty slacks and a brown shirt. Her hair was long, untidy, but her face was clean. She had a round face and wide, brown eyes. She might have been eighteen but she was probably younger. She did not seem surprised to see the priest. The room in which he talked to her was one of a three or four room apartment in a shabby block, just across the boundary line of Saint Anselm's parish.

"I know about your problem," Father Lind said. "Juan Lucero came to me. I told him that there could be no abortion—absolutely not. Did he tell you that?"

"Yes. I do not care. I did not want it."

"Good for you."

He felt friendly toward the girl where he had been reserved and watchful. She immediately let him down.

"The abortion is dangerous," she said.

"Yes. About the baby. Will you keep it?"

"No. I am not married."

"You did not think of that when you got into this situation."

"I cannot have a baby."

"You will have. I can arrange for you to be taken care of. There is an order of nuns out of town. You will do light work in exchange for care. If you cannot keep your baby, or will not, you may surrender it for adoption."

"They will not tell my mother?"

"It is difficult to keep things from mothers. Why don't you tell her?"

"I cannot do this. I will go to these nuns. When do I go?"

"I'll have to arrange it. I'll let you know." The priest rose. "You will be getting a better break than you deserve. Say your prayers. Thank God and the Blessed Mother. Ask them to help you stay out of trouble."

"Yes, Padre."

She was properly humble but he did not trust her humility. Spanish Americans, even the very good ones who went to church regularly, had an unorthodox concept of sin. It was understandable enough. Two or three families could crowd into a couple of rooms, and did. There was no privacy and children grew up with little sense of personal property, no sexual inhibitions, unable to associate any grave wrong with acts which were, to them, commonplace.

"God bless you," he said.

He went back to the streets and he thought about Raimundo Baca. The boy would be at work now but tonight was the long night at Guadalupe House, which would be operating until ten or later. He would have a chance to talk with Raimundo sometime in the course of the evening. He would give Raimundo all of the time he needed and he would go into the different aspects of his problem; the mother, the sisters, the job, his night study, the girl he wanted to marry, the specific problem of the automobile, how much money needed and when. He hadn't made a decent attempt to get close to the problem with him the other night. *Mea maxima culpa.*

The confessional at Saint Anselm's claimed his afternoon. The small children came into the box, and the old ladies, occasionally a retired man or the mother of one of the children. It was a slow, dull parade; little real sin, much observance of custom. Near the end of the afternoon, he had a homosexual. They came usually on Saturday night. There were an increasing number of them lately. What did one tell a homosexual? It depended, somewhat at least, on the individual case but one could not arbitrarily say: "You are living a sinful kind of life. Stop it!" Considering the nature of the homosexual that might be tantamount to telling him that he must live the life of a celibate. Celibacy was difficult enough when one was dedicated to the service of God.

There was no time in the confessional to go into the details that one would have to know in order to be truly helpful to people in real trouble. There was always another pentient waiting on the other side of the box, and a line waiting outside. Under the circumstances, one was too often perfunctory.

Father Lind had the rectory to himself again. The pastor and Father Guyton went out, each to separate destinations on Friday evening. They would be back for the evening confessions. Father Lind sat at the dining room table alone and Mrs. Wagner served him two fried eggs, with fried potatoes, and a salad. He had raisin bread for a change.

It was clear and chill, not quite as cold as it had been all week. Guadalupe House was having a big night. The parking lot was crammed with cars. Father Lind had to park nearly two blocks away. There was no one waiting in his office so he strolled down the corridor to the twin rooms of stenography and typing. He stood in the corridor outside the central door. Pamela Gibson was dictating to an earnest-looking group, male and female, who worked with heads down, fingers racing.

He had never seen her dictating before. She paced back and forth, gesturing as she read. She had eloquent hands. She enunciated clearly and she had a pleasant voice. When she glanced up and saw him, she did not lose a word. She curled the fingers of her left hand into a gesture which said clearly that she would see him when she finished what she was doing. She came to a paragraph's end, closed her book and came over to the door.

"Hello," she said.

"Hello, yourself. I didn't mean to interrupt, but I am looking for Raimundo."

63

"So am I. He hasn't come in. I've had no word from him."

"If he comes in, tell him I want to see him."

"Right."

She was already turning back into her classroom. Her manner had been entirely professional and he could not have meant less to her as a person, but her picture moved in his mind as he walked back to his office. He could see her sharply. She had worn her brown suit again tonight. It was far from new and, having seen her apartment, he was certain that she owned good-looking clothes. She just did not wear them to Guadalupe where girls had so little. He liked that in her. He wondered, as he had often wondered before, what she did in the daylight hours. She would do something; she would not loaf.

There were young people waiting in his office; two young men and a girl. There were a number of young women in classes but few of them came to him with complaints or seeking advice. This one was interestingly confused. Her name was Catalina Garcia. She was twenty years old and she had two children. She worked as a waitress in the daytime and she studied dressmaking at Guadalupe. She did not want to make a living by sewing but she would like to make her own clothes. Her mother took care of her children and she would like her mother to have them permanently. She wasn't certain that her mother wanted them. Her husband had left her and she did not know where he was. She wanted the Church to declare him dead. She would pay for a Requiem Mass for him if the Church would admit that he was dead. That was important to her. It was her big problem. There was a young man who wanted to marry her. She wanted to be married in the Church. The young man did not want her children. "He says that they belong to another man." She did not care about the children. "I work in the hamburger place. That is daytime. I come here to the school. That is night. My mother, she sees the children all the time. Me, I do not even know them."

Catalina was a strong-minded young woman. She knew what she wanted and she did not recognize any wants that conflicted with her own. She had a pattern of life in her mind, arranged as she wanted it arranged. She did not want the past to interfere with the present and she would not be interested in the future until it came. Father Lind talked long and earnestly to her but he succeeded only in arousing her hostility.

"I came to you because I thought you would be my friend," she said. "You are my enemy."

He was slightly depressed when she left. Any failure to reach a person who came to him was, he felt, a failure as a priest. He had missed with

64

Catalina and he did not have time to re-examine the problem in his mind; he had two other people waiting, young men. He had to give each of them his full attention. At nine-ten the phone rang.

"Father Lind? Sergeant Regan speaking. I have some bad news for you. Your boy, Raimundo Baca, was shot a few minutes ago."

Father Lind's hand tightened on the receiver. "Where? How?"

"Better see him, Father. Emergency Hospital."

"Right. Thanks."

It was, obviously, no time to discuss details. Father Lind was shrugging into his coat as he left his office. He made a sudden, fast detour on his way to the front door. Pamela Gibson was in the typing room.

"Raimundo has been shot," he said. "I don't know how bad it is. I'm going to the hospital."

"Oh! Let me know, please. Come out to my place. Can you?"

"Yes."

He was on his way again and he drove with his horn sounding. The Emergency Hospital was in the old town and only six blocks from Guadalupe House, a gloomy old structure with a half-moon area on the north side reserved for vehicles on trouble calls. The entrance to the accident rooms was at one tip of the half-moon. Raimundo was in the third room. There was a policeman and a priest, an intern in a white coat, a nurse. The priest was Father McMurray, the hospital chaplain.

"He hasn't spoken a word," he said.

"I'd like to speak to him." Father Lind moved to the side of the cot. He met the eyes of the surgeon who shook his head.

"Go ahead. There is nothing that we can do for him."

Raimundo's face was white, his eyes closed. He was lying on his back and there was a huge wad of bandage on his chest under his torn shirt. The priest bent over him.

"Raimundo," he said. "It's Father Lind. Your friend. Can you hear me?"

There was a slight twitch in the boy's left cheek. His eyes slowly opened, dark eyes with terror behind them.

"Sí," he said huskily.

"Save your breath, Raimundo. Tell me only one thing. Are you sorry for all of your sins because you have offended God who made you?"

The eyes widened. "Sí."

"Think then of your act of contrition if you can." He raised his hand and pronounced the absolution. "Deinde ego te absolvo a peccatis tuis, in nomine Patris, et Filii, et Spiritus Sancti, Amen."

The light left Raimundo's eyes on the "Patris." Father Lind prayed for him then and Father McMurray joined him. When they resigned the corpse to the hospital attendants, Father Lind turned to the policeman.

"What happened to him?" he said.

The policeman hesitated, then shrugged. "It was a holdup," he said. "This guy had a gun and he walked into the A-1 Loan Company just as they were closing. They stay open till nine on Friday. He got the money but someone stepped on the button and the patrol car rolled right over there. He tried to shoot it out."

"Did he hit anybody?"

"He tried. One slug in the patrol car door."

That was that. Gregory Lind walked out. He met Sergeant Regan at the door. The sergeant was built like a football player, in his early forties and fit.

"Gone?" he said.

"Yes. I just heard how he got it. I still don't understand."

"Neither do I. We never had him up on anything violent, never found a gun on him." A police car wheeled in to the half-moon area. Sergeant Regan glanced at it. "That will be his mother," he said. "I sent Jim Baker out after her."

"Good of you. I'll take care of her."

Gregory Lind braced himself for a bad half hour but Raimundo's mother did her weeping behind her mask. She had one of her daughters with her. They both sobbed when they knelt beside the body to pray but there was no hysteria, no big scene. Mrs. Baca turned to the priest when he helped her to her feet.

"He was a good boy," she said.

"Yes. Something went wrong for him."

"It was that girl, that Ysabel Jaramillo."

"I don't know. You don't. He was in love with her."

"I know."

Father Lind thought bleakly that he would know, too, if he had given time to Raimundo when Raimundo needed him. He drove Mrs. Baca home. She neither spoke nor cried. Her daughter cried softly. They both knelt for his blessing before he left them.

He did not see Ysabel Jaramillo. The news of Raimundo's death had reached her before he drove up to the house in which she lived. Her mother, a tired little woman, no more than five feet tall, had tears in her eyes and her voice broke badly when she tried to speak.

"Raimundo was good to my daughter. A gentle man," she said. "I do not understand this thing. My Ysabel, she is afraid that he did this for her. He had no money. His mother took all his money."

"She probably needed it. Say a prayer for her, and for him."

Mrs. Jaramillo's face was set in stern lines and he doubted that she would pray for Mrs. Baca. She knelt for his blessing, however, as did the neighbor women who were visiting her. The night seemed colder when he walked back to his car.

He drove to 751 Steuben Drive but not without misgivings. He had had to do many things and it was late. Pamela Gibson had to know, of course, about Raimundo. If he knew her phone number, he could call her; probably not. There was an honest something within him which would not tolerate self-deception. Even if he knew her phone number, he would do as he was doing now.

There was light in her apartment behind the curtained, draped windows. He climbed the stair and she opened the door to his ring. The inevitable question was in her eyes and he nodded his head to it.

"Dead," he said.

Her eyes closed momentarily. "I was afraid of that. Come in. You must tell me about it. I'll fix a drink. The fire is pretty good. You might add a log."

She was gone and he walked into the living room. It was a beautiful room, just as he remembered it, a room of serenity. A person could rest here or read or talk or listen to music, and nothing in the room itself would intrude; the room would share with one whatever one felt like doing. That, perhaps, was a fanciful thought but it had to come from somewhere; it did not belong in his everyday life.

He put one of the logs on the fire, easing it on gently, taking a sort of joy in the intense heat which, momentarily, singed his skin. It had been so unearthly cold out of doors. When he rose, Pamela Gibson was standing behind him. She had two glasses in her hands.

"That is nice," she said. "Here! You must need a drink."

"Probably not; but I'll enjoy one."

She sat on the small couch across from him, a duplicate of the one on which he sat. She was wearing an ankle-length green robe of some rich velvety material; a dark green. There was a thin edge of gold on the lapels and in a straight line across the top of the single pocket. She had her feet pulled up under her. She was wearing gold slippers without heels. Her hair was fuller tonight than normally, brushed out or fluffed out. Her eyes seemed larger, intent. Shadows moved across her from the fire, narrow ribbons of shadow that leaped and vanished and returned. "Tell me of Raimundo," she said.

He told her, beginning with the phone call. It was a relief to put it all into words. There was so much pent up inside of him. He did not tell her about Raimundo's distress over the bicycle order and it was difficult to explain Ysabel Jaramillo. He had to digress and link her to an earlier conversation with Raimundo. Pamela's voice moved into that chapter immediately.

"I made a mistake with that gift of a bicycle," she said. "How?"

The question was honest; an evasive answer would not be. "You did not know about the girl," he said. "Raimundo appreciated what you tried to do for him. Never doubt that. He appreciated it deeply but he did not want a bicycle; he wanted an automobile in which they could both ride."

"He told you that?"

"Yes. He was afraid that you would be hurt if he did not take the bicycle. I told him that you would not be, that you might even be willing to let him apply the bike money toward buying a car of some sort."

"Or buy him the car," she said. "If I'd only known the whole story! Let me fix your drink."

"I shouldn't. It's late."

"I know. But you probably won't sleep. I know that I won't. I need another drink."

She took his glass and her own. He stared at the fire. It seemed absurd that this girl should be upset over Raimundo, that he should be. In cold black newsprint, as he would appear tomorrow, Raimundo, the parolee gunman, would not be a candidate for anyone's sympathy.

Pamela Gibson returned and he took the fresh drink from her hand. "He never came to me," she said. "He stopped coming to classes. He did not buy a bike and he did not return the order. I did not know what to think. I should have listened to you. I upset him. Maybe I caused what happened to him."

"No. If anyone did, I did. I had a chance to talk with him, to sift out all the bugs, to seek answers with him. I didn't take it."

"I won't like it, I won't like it at all, I won't know how to live with it, if he bought that gun with the bike order."

"He didn't. I'm sure he didn't."

"But you don't *know*."

"No. I don't. It isn't something he'd do."

The denial seemed weak to Gregory Lind, even as he voiced it. Some of the girl's fear had communicated itself to him. He did not want that gun linked to the bike money, either.

"Look," he said. "You have no responsibility for Raimundo. His father walked out on the family. I don't know how many children Mrs. Baca had. She needed money from Raimundo. He loved a girl. He wanted a car to take her out, a lot of other things, too, maybe; sharp clothes, the price of shows, dinners maybe. I don't know. I'm guessing. There are a lot of people like Raimundo. That's why we have Guadalupe House. Raimundo was developing a skill, but he couldn't wait. It all built up too big on him. He tried to get money in a hurry."

"He was a sweet little guy," Pamela said. She dipped her glass. "You're pretty fine yourself."

The personal salute disconcerted him. He made an abrupt gesture, erasing it. "My job is people. When I miss, someone is hurt. I miss too often."

"That's something to remember, that your job is people. There's something wrong about that idea, very wrong, but I don't know what it is. Not now. I'll think about it."

He looked at his glass. His drink was nearly gone. The fire had lost its leaping exuberance. The hour was late and he no longer had answers for anything. The girl across the coffee table was lovely in the soft light and he liked listening to her. There was a pleasant tingle in his nerves, warmth in his blood. It was time to go.

He rose and Pamela rose with him. She walked slightly ahead of him to the small foyer and turned around. She was so close to him that he was aware of the faint fragrance that she wore. He was aware, suddenly, of all of her; of a straight, slender woman who had to tilt her head back to look into his face, of eyes that met his. His arms moved out, seemingly of their own volition, and she melted into them.

He held her gently and his lips met hers. There was a fierce drumming in his blood stream, a driving, rocketing force rising in him, blotting out all thought, and his hold on her tightened. She was warmth and she was woman and, above all that, she was someone who yielded to him, inviting him, wanting him. He felt that beyond any need of words, releasing her lips for a moment, looking into her wide eyes. She crossed one arm on his chest, pushing him away.

"No," she said. "No. *You* can't do this. It's my fault. You've got to go now."

He reached for her again and she twisted away. "You'd hate me," she said. "Just go! Please. Just go!"

He stood there, looking at her, and something inside of him was horrified but he did not hate her and he did not believe that he could ever hate her. She was right when she said that he had to go; very, very right.

"It's my fault," he said, "but I'm not sorry. Not sorry at all."

He left her and he did not notice the cold in the street. In his car, after he had turned on the lights, he wiped his lips carefully with a clean handkerchief and looked at it. It was streaked with crimson. Nothing like that had ever happened to him before. He was thirty-two

69

years old and, for the first time, his handkerchief was smeared with lipstick. He laughed and his laugh was shaky, without any mirth behind it.

– IX –

Father Lind led the rosary for Raimundo Baca at eight on Monday night. He led it in Spanish and the voices behind him were strong, singing voices. When he rose and made the sign of the Cross over the body in the casket, he turned toward Mrs. Baca in the first pew and his eyes swept briefly over the people. Pamela was among those who were leaving without coming down the aisle to visit the family. She had her back turned to him, moving toward the door. He had not known that she was there. He bent over the pew and spoke to Mrs. Baca.

Outside there were a few snowflakes drifting and it did not seem as cold as it had been. He did not see Pamela or her car, and he did not expect to see her. She had, obviously, taken time off tonight from Guadalupe House, as he had done. She had been in his mind, moving in his thought through a long weekend, through the doing of all the familiar things; the Saturday evening confessions, the Sunday with his mother, the early Masses.

He walked back to the rectory. He was, he knew, refusing to face a reality as far as Pamela was concerned; but the reality was not a solid, tangible thing that he could weigh or measure. Some mocking, derisive other self within him laughed at his stretching and expanding of molehills. He was a man and he had kissed a girl. This was a night in the nineteen sixties. Kissing a girl was a small matter in the long calendar of sins. Another inner voice reminded him that he who looked at a woman in lust hath already committed adultery. There was a question and a doubt. Had he actually looked at Pamela in lust? He had gone to her with grim news and they had shared much more than the Scotch, a harmless, companionable sharing. In the end, he had kissed her and, admittedly, he had wanted to kiss her again, and longer. If the kiss was impulse and not lust, where did the boundaries of impulse lie?

"I build things up. I rationalize them. When I cannot change something I should forget it," he said.

The embarrassing answer to that was the fact that he would not let a penitent get away with such an argument in the confessional. The pertinent inquiry did not concern the past at all; it was, simply, how do you feel about this girl now and what are your intentions? Well, he would have to see her, no avoiding that, and he wanted to see her. The apartment, if he granted seriousness to a kiss, was an occasion of sin and he should avoid it. It was a lovely, serene place and he had enjoyed it in all of his being; a warm fire dancing and music drifting softly in from two rooms away. He would not, lightly, now vow to avoid it.

Father Guyton's door was open when he climbed the rectory stairs. It was cool in the house and Tom Guyton was wearing an old gray sweater. "Heigh-ho," he said. "I was hoping you'd come in. Have you got a few minutes?"

"More than a few if you need them. I'm through for the night."

"Good man. Come on in. I haven't seen you over the weekend except in passing. I had a showdown with my confessional seductress on Saturday."

"What happened?"

"About what you'd expect. I followed your advice and added a slight twist of my own. I told her I'd discussed her with you and that we would both be waiting in the rectory at nine-fifteen to discuss her problem with her. I told her I was certain we could get her straightened out."

"That must have made a hit with her."

"She cussed me out. Real tall language. Then she banged out of the box without waiting for my blessing. I'm making a bet, too, that she won't be back. Not next week. Not ever. I think the whole deal calls for a drink. How about it?"

"I won't fight you."

Gregory Lind watched Tom Guyton mixing the drinks and the other priest seemed young to him, incredibly young. Guyton was a good priest and he handled the often-ugly problems well. He looked without blinking, as did his contemporaries, at the problems of marriage, the tragedies of unwanted children, the necessity of arranging care for the unmarried and pregnant. He went on sick calls and he helped the old and the young to die. He sat through the dreary boredom of the confessional week after week, prepared to meet those souls who needed new light on their problems, help in some spiritual crisis. He was a good priest, a dedicated, well-equipped priest, but he had a certain unhatched quality, a naïveté that was difficult to explain. There was no trouble in his face. His eyes were clear and he had fine skin. There was a wry twist to his mouth.

"No ice," Father Guyton said. "When it comes to raiding the kitchen, anything in the kitchen, my nerve fails me."

"We don't need ice. I wouldn't risk the wrath of Mrs. Wagner either."

"Terrible woman! Good at her job, heart of gold, but terrible, simply terrible. Skaol!"

They drank solemnly and it was a kind of bond between them, a bond that had no need of words. Greg Lind wondered what his companion would think of his other drinking companion. He would disapprove, certainly, because the potential of scandal was in that lovely room where two people sat, safely separated by a wide coffee table. He would think, too, as all priests do, in terms of the occasion of sin. As for the kiss, and Gregory's walking around with worry about it, he would probably laugh. That wasn't even a junior high problem any more; it was a problem of the grade schools. He heard it himself, dozens and scores of times; childish voices, male or female, confessing kisses or asking solemnly if kissing was a sin. He and Pamela Gibson were not, of course, children and that moved everything into a different perspective.

"I'd like to say action Masses," Father Guyton said. "I'd like to establish a floating parish and say Masses in living rooms, or kitchens, like some of those fellows in New Jersey and Washington and other places."

"Why, for God's sake?"

"It seems to me a good thing, a coming closer to the people; a doing what Christ did. I'd like to say Mass somewhere with just twelve good people present. That would have a lot of meaning for me."

"One of the original twelve sold out."

"Sure. And I know I'd have a difficult time getting even eleven. It is the kind of experiment that would attract crackpots and screwballs. But I'd like to try."

"The original twelve were all men. You'd have a tough time holding to that."

"No trouble. To me they'd be twelve souls; terms like man and woman would not enter into it."

Gregory Lind shook his head. He had an idea that the twelve, any twelve would get around eventually, if not immediately, to setting up rules and conditions, meeting dates and a rotation system which would include each dwelling of the twelve in the holding of the sacrifice. When that stage was reached, Father Guyton would discover that he was not merely dealing with souls, that he was dealing with men and women, mostly women.

"If you start playing around with sideshow liturgy like that, you may get your wish about leaving this parish," he said. "You'll be pitched out on your ear."

"I suppose so. The bishop is as bad as Schafer. Same breed of ecclesiastical cat. I wouldn't have a chance. Maybe someday! Anyway

I like to think about it. I'm not going to leave the Church, you know. A lot of things I don't like are changing, some new things I like are coming in. I'm a priest forever. I like it that way."

Tom Guyton took the glasses and fixed fresh drinks, drawing the water from the basin faucet in the bathroom. Two drinks seemed right, in Pamela's place or here, and lonely people talked more easily. It was strange that conversation took on flavor and interest with the two drinks. Conversation that was without any great significance, not at all memorable. The answer was, probably, that conversation was the real need and not liquor. If one went beyond the two, continued drinking into satiety, there would be no conversation, no relaxation, merely drunkenness. Gregory Lind had never been drunk, but he had taken care of people who were.

"The Holy Father is slow in making the contraception ruling," Tom Guyton said.

"Wouldn't you be?"

"Probably. The writing is upon the wall, though. One way or another, we are going to have an O.K. on contraception for married people. And no stupid rhythm business, either."

"That O.K. will have many, a great many, rules and regulations, footnotes and fine print. There will be no *Carte Blanche*. Don't expect it."

"Why not? There's *Carte Blanche* now, with nothing official about it. *You* don't pound the wall of the box and tell the poor wretches they have to keep having babies if they want to keep on having sex. You don't damn them to hell if they can't make rhythm work and if they try something else."

"No. I don't. You touched the heart of it there. I've always felt that the Church forever compromised itself when it O.K.'d rhythm. The intent governs in the value of an act, or in the blame for it. When we approve the intent not to have children, the method is none of our business."

Tom Guyton laughed. "I have never put it so compactly but that, I guess, is how I've felt. I hate facing the question with people because I know that I'm beyond my authority, but their problem is tougher than mine. I just can't back away from them."

"Neither can I."

There was a sudden silence between the two men, as though they had simultaneously run out of words. Gregory Lind had experienced this silence before. The subject of contraception and birth control was apt to bring it on among priests; after, of course, a few vehement opinions had been expressed. They were not all agreed on the subject.

There were still priests, usually old-timers, who generated a lot of steam behind the idea that the individual priest had no problem whatever with birth control decision because he had no right to attempt a decision. "Roma locuta est. Causa finita est." ("Rome has spoken, the matter is finished.") It wasn't all that simple. Gregory drained his glass and rose.

"Nice drink, Tom," he said. "I shall dream fondly of you."

He crossed the hall to his own room and the thoughts which he had escaped for a time were haunting his mind again. Raimundo Baca was a rather frightening reality. He could not turn his back on the sense of guilt or wave it away. He had been given an opportunity to help another human being who was on the verge of desperate action, and he had failed the opportunity, he had let a personal interest of his own intrude on the time which a young man had complimented him in seeking. The young man was gone and the opportunity was gone and he could call neither of them back. He prayed on his knees for Raimundo Baca before he went to bed and, on the following morning, he sang his Mass.

He did not bring Raimundo's body before the altar of Saint Anselm's without a struggle. When he first suggested it, the pastor had replied with a short, curt "No." He had not accepted that.

"Raimundo Baca lived in this parish," he said. "His mother attends Mass here. He is one of ours."

Father Schafer's eyes widened slightly. He was not accustomed to argument on his parish rulings. He sat back in his chair; a big man with a hard, deeply lined face. His eyes measured the priest before them and when nothing in Father Lind betrayed any tendency to yield, he sighed.

"Father Lind," he said. "You are looking at this matter narrowly. You have to think in terms of the parish. We are, in these days, a poor parish. We no longer support a school. If we did not draw on the downtown area, on transients in several large hotels, we could not meet our expenses. Those who come to our Masses find a quiet, dignified old church and sober, decent, devout people. We must keep it that way. If we encouraged these Mexicans to come, the whole personality of the church would change. Soon we would have nothing else; no one else would come."

"You wouldn't tell Spanish Americans to stay away?"

"No. They have a church of their own, priests who speak their own language. That is where they should go. That is where, I would suggest, this Mass be said."

"I have to disagree. Raimundo was a pupil in a school that means much to me. He was my friend. I want to sing his Mass—here."

74

The older man sat without moving. He was, if he cared to interpret it in that way, being defied; he had, if he cared to invoke it, the unchallengeable reply. He could repeat his "No" and state flatly that there was no more to be said. That would close the door of appeal to this young priest. He raised his hand and made a gesture of dismissal.

"I deplore your persistence," he said, "but I am not going to forbid your saying this Mass, nor am I going to close the door of the church to the body of a young man whom you identify as a parishioner. I will ask you, however, to discourage publicity of any kind. You cannot want, any more than I, a three-ring circus, or an emotional carnival in Saint Anselm's."

"No, I'll guard against anything like that. And thank you."

He had tried to guard against publicity and he had appreciated the fact that Father Schafer had not referred to Raimundo's criminal background. The church might occasionally bury a saint but it did not expect to do so; it served sinners. In the morning, the body of Raimundo Baca, enclosed in a cheap, dark gray casket, lay before Saint Anselm's high altar and the Church, in the person of Father Gregory Lind supplicated the Creator for him; it had no more to offer a Cardinal or a Bishop than he received.

There were many people in the church. They did not crowd it, but one was aware of them; poor people, many of them shabbily dressed, but strangely dignified in their shabbiness. The Mass was the calling down of God upon the altar and in accepting a miracle they made themselves a part of it. When Father Lind approached the casket for the absolution after the Mass, he was aware of the two young men in the side aisle, alien to the scene. One of them raised a camera and there was a brief flash of light. There was nothing that one could do about that. Father Schafer would see a photograph of Saint Anselm's interior in the paper tomorrow and whatever the caption on the photograph stated, the statement would flatter neither Raimundo nor the Church which paid him the last sad service.

In those few minutes of seeing a camera and of thinking momentarily of publicity, Father Lind saw Pamela. She was sitting alone in a center aisle seat, two thirds of the way back in the church.

"Pie Jesu Domine. Dona eis réquiem. Amen."

She was present again at the cemetery when he consigned the body of Raimundo to the earth. Only a half dozen people made the long trip. There was a light covering of snow on the ground and a savage wind blowing. She came up to him after he spoke to Raimundo's mother and sisters. She was very cold, as he was, and a flake of sleet lingered on the skin above her cheekbone when she raised her head.

"It was beautiful," she said, "truly beautiful. I had no idea. I had never attended a Mass before."

"I'm glad that you attended this one."

"So am I. I owed it to Raimundo. But you were in it, too. I am impressed. More than a little awed. There are so many questions I'd like to ask." She hesitated. "Could you come to my place again tonight after the classes? I'll understand if you can't. I have no right to put you on a spot."

"It isn't a spot." He smiled at her. She looked so damned defenseless. Warning bells were ringing inside of him and he ignored them. "You are patient to put up with me," he said. "I'll come and I'll try to answer the questions."

"Thank you."

She turned away abruptly and, in walking to her car, she strode. It was a matter of mood, probably, that walk of hers. He did not like to see her striding. She looked awkward in a long stride and he would not watch her when she was less than graceful. He went to his own car and his hand trembled with the cold when he put his key in the ignition.

He was back in the day again, a day in which news stories would flow across his desk, in which people would have problems, in which he would receive directions from the bishop and urgent memoranda from the absent Father Peter Coyle.

"And while I'm mentally complaining," he said, "it's damned cold and one of these times, this automobile isn't going to start when I kick the button."

The snow moved in with the evening, heavy clinging snow that veiled the houses and that blotted out the pavement. Gregory Lind went home and bathed and shaved. He had dinner with Tom Guyton who was in a talkative mood, quoting in detail from his *National Catholic Reporter* which was delivered on Monday. The *Reporter* was a Catholic paper, specializing in everything newswise that the *Star* skipped, ignored or suppressed. The day of the *Reporter* was always a day of bright gossip and Gregory Lind enjoyed the condensation of it; which, at the very least, took one's mind off Mrs. Wagner's cooking.

It was still snowing, harder and heavier, when Gregory drove to Guadalupe House. Monday was one of his busy nights there. He put in an intense three hours and he did not see Pamela until she opened the apartment door for him at nine-thirty.

She was wearing the long green garment that he had seen and admired before. He identified it in his mind as a robe, as a hostess gown, a formally informal kind of thing that was very becoming to her. It

76

was a rich dark green and it fitted Pamela like a sheath. She looked very slender, small, pictorial.

"You are precisely on time," she said. "I have just lighted the fire."

"Good for you. And I'm sorry that I am precisely anything. I try not to be."

"Do you? Charge me up with a figure of speech. You know where to put your coat."

She did not mention the snow although she must have just come in from it herself. She turned away as she closed the door and there was no striding in her tonight; she moved like a dancer. There was music coming from the mysterious inner realm of the apartment, *Kiss Me, Kate* music, old but still among the all time best of its kind. Greg Lind hummed along with it as he walked into the living room. There were flowers in vases and they added something, a special color. The room, as far as he was concerned, had never needed one extra touch beyond what it had; but he liked the flowers.

Pamela returned with two glasses on a tray. Scotch was taken for granted now when he came. It had not taken long to establish a custom. He accepted his drink and stood, looking down into Pamela's face. He felt tall. The fire tonight was singing and it was a sort of waltzing fire, its flame undulating to a rhythm of its own. None of their other fires had been like this one. Pamela's eyes seemed amused. Her hair was fluffed out and it was a decided chestnut shade. She had never, in the time he had known her, looked lovelier. She sat in her place on the low couch which faced his across the coffee table, smoothing the green fabric across her knees with both hands.

"It surprised me to hear you sing," she said. "Your voice is truly fine. I was wishing that you had something to sing besides church music."

He tasted his drink, inwardly amused. So many people were sold on the idea that all priests had dull, parched voices, with cracks in them, as a sort of occupational ailment.

"I've sung other things," he said. "How about you?"

"Yes. My piano is home. In my parents' home, that is. I considered bringing it here but at the last minute I changed my mind."

"Your parents, are they here? In Culverton, I mean?"

"Of course. Didn't you know?"

"I know about Gibsons. There are quite a few. I didn't know if you belonged to any of them or not. You remember, I tried to find you in the phone book."

"That's right. You did." There was a compelling intensity in her eyes. "It just didn't occur! Oh well! I warned you once that I don't listen often. I like to talk. Tonight is going to be one of my talking nights. If I bore you, it's your own fault. You triggered me."

"Fine. It's a good night for listening."

"I hope so." She looked away from him, staring into the fire. "To start where you stopped, my father is Ralph Gibson. If one has to say that someone is *the* Gibson, he would be it. The rest of them are his brothers, or nephews, a cousin or two."

Gregory Lind watched her, content to be watching her, not tempted to interrupt with comment which could be only absurd. He knew a little about Ralph Gibson. He had been hearing about him and reading about him for years; the senior partner of Gibson, Paskert and Rowe, Culverton's top brokerage firm. He was always leading drives or serving community causes; a tall, florid, impressive man whom one linked at sight with banks and country clubs and blue chip neighborhoods. One could not live in Culverton and not be aware of him. It was a bit of a shock to think of Pamela as his daughter.

"We are an impressive lot, we Gibsons," Pamela said. "My mother is sleek and slender, one of the most compellingly attractive women you will ever meet; gracious, magnetic, accomplished, instinctively right. I grew up with the conviction that I would always have to compete with her and I couldn't match her; not in any manner, shape or form. That is a hell of a situation for a girl."

"I can see that it would be," he said softly. "You dislike her, don't you?"

"No. I worship her. I think she's the everything. She's just what a woman should be, and never is, but I've never wanted to be like her." Pamela made a fluid dismissing motion with her right hand. Her hands were eloquent. "You won't understand that. It's a feminism."

"She would be a man's type of woman?"

"Decidedly. They forever flutter about her. All ages of them. She expects it, so she takes it for granted and she never inflates with it. My father is the only one who matters to her. He really matters."

"That's a fortunate situation. All marriages are not like that."

"They damn well aren't." She was frowning at the fire. Her face in profile had lean, sharp lines but the moving shadows softened them. "My father is big business. He breathes the stock market in and he breathes it out. He thinks in fractions, small, intense fractions. He plays a good game of golf and he enjoys a few drinks with friends and he contributes to both political parties without involving himself with either of them. He's a good mixer and he always knows a new joke and he walks wide of women."

Pamela turned and spread her hands wide. "I want you to know us as we are."

"You're doing fine. Now, how about you?"

"We need another drink."

She rose swiftly with a jackknife motion that, somehow, lacked the mechanical quality of jackknife motions. She took his glass and vanished with it into the other room. Gregory put another log on the fire. He liked the way in which the flames leaped and then settled, the small, crackling sound as the new log established itself. It was interesting about Pamela's parents. She exaggerated them, of course. She would not be able to see them straight. There would be a struggle for control between two such persons as she described; neither would permit the other to dominate. He did not believe, either, that Pamela actually liked her mother.

Pamela was in the other room for so long that he was beginning to wonder before she returned. She had sliced cheese and crackers on a plate. There were small sausages, freshly browned, on toothpicks.

"It isn't civilized to absorb liquor without food," she said. "Yet we always seem to do that."

He smiled at the "always." As she said it, one would have the impression that such sessions as this were a regular thing, a tradition blessed by years, or months, or many repetitions. She had the drinks, too, on the tray. It *was* pleasant to have food with liquor. He took one of the sausages.

"This is the first time we have ever dined," he said, "or eaten a meal of any kind together."

"It isn't a meal. But it will have to do." She lifted her glass. "To many of them."

"Right." He could hear the warning bells again as he raised his glass. He had no right to be drinking to future food and future drink with this woman, with any woman. The bells rang somewhere, in his soul perhaps, and he knew they were ringing but he ignored them. "You were going to tell me about you," he said.

"Was I?"

"You know you were."

"It's a long, involved story, and probably not worth telling."

"I'd like to hear it."

"You're nice."

She stared at the fire, sipping her drink. "All right," she said. "Me! I've told you about my mother. She was a separate star, you know. We whirled around in different orbits. My father was another matter. He expected that I would orbit around him. Never doubted it."

79

"And you didn't?"

"I tried, I guess. Not very hard, probably. Daughters are women. They try to please fathers, who are men. It is that simple, really. They are supposed to practice on their fathers; practice being women, I guess. I did a lot of that. I was pretty good at it. Daughters don't practice forever. They grow up and they don't need the practice any more, and fathers do not understand what is happening. At least my father didn't understand."

Gregory sat silent with her, watching the fire. She had to tell her story her own way. The wrong questions might throw her off the direct line. She sipped her drink slowly.

"Daughters don't understand, either," she said. "Although, being women, they are damned sure they do. Girls growing up are an insincere lot; hypocrites, actresses, being a lot of things they really aren't, pretending a lot of big emotions they haven't got, not giving an honest thought to what other people are feeling. Boys, most of them anyway, are different. They are curious about a thousand things, but girls are just curious about themselves."

"Rather hard on girls, aren't you?"

"Maybe. If you really believe I am, think about girls you've known. Really think about them; don't sentimentalize. Oh never mind! Maybe you can't. That's all right. Anyway, my father was crazy about me. I was his only chick. He wanted me to have everything—and I damn near did. I had all the toys there were, and horses to ride, and the best schools and the last word in clothes. I went East to the best schools and I came home to big holidays. I didn't worry about money. It was always there."

"Did your mother go along with all that?"

"Spoiling me, you mean? By herself, she wouldn't. Not for a minute. But she was not by herself, you see. My father was very real to her, and I wasn't real at all. Yes. She went along with it."

The room was quiet save for the soft flow of distant music, the crack and sputter of the fire. Pamela had drawn her legs up under her. She looked very small. She had not, the man thought, painted a flattering picture of herself but that made no difference. She rose above her own picture of herself, not seeming to exert any effort to rise.

"My father was a Yale man," she said. "He sent me to school in his old hunting territory and it did not seem to occur to him that the hunters are still hunting. He didn't like it when I met Yales and Princetons, even a few Cornells. At that period, I couldn't figure out what he wanted or expected. I didn't try. I was excited over being me and I wanted other people, men of course, excited, too."

"They were, naturally."

"A reasonable number of them. Reasonably excited." With a sudden gesture, Pamela lifted her glass and finished her drink in a swallow. "To hell with it," she said. "It's a boring story, so I'll get it over with. I married Rodney Keller when I was twenty. He was twenty-five. My father never liked him but, then, he never liked any man I had. I wasn't impressed. I wanted a big wedding, a great big wedding, and, by grace of a mother who wanted that, too, I had it."

Her face had tightened. She was staring at her empty glass. "Then what happened?" Gregory said.

Her eyes came up slowly. "Rodney was everything that a man shouldn't be," she said. "He was, and is, an affront to human dignity. I had pride and I didn't quit easily, and I didn't ask for help, but I finally rang down the curtain. I divorced him. Catholics don't believe in divorce. Well, all I can say to you or to anybody, is that a Catholic unlucky enough to be married to Rodney Keller would believe in divorce."

It was not the time or the place to enter into debate even if one felt like debating. Gregory waved his hand to the room and the fire and the music.

"You are all right," he said. "You didn't let anyone destroy you. You have the humanity to give yourself to others at Guadalupe House. You have the good fortune of being yourself and living in beauty."

The girl was staring at him. The shadows were heavy in the room and she was a softly done portrait, with her feet on the floor, her fingers locked across her knees, her body inclined forward.

"It is probably still snowing hard," she said, "and your car is probably buried in it. You will have a terrible time going home because you listened so long to me. Another drink would make it all more difficult, even dangerous." She paused and her voice sounded very young, like a child's voice. "Do you suppose we could have another drink?"

Gregory laughed. "I suppose we could. I'll still be able to dig out and there won't be any traffic and I've got snow tires."

"Good. Help me mix them."

She rose swiftly to her feet and as he followed her to the wide doorway at the end of the room, Gregory thought that, at last, he was going to see beyond the boundaries of this room. It was an idle thought, an empty thought, and the only thought he had.

The hallway in which the credenza stood was a surprise. It had two doorways opening off it, a bedroom and a bathroom, but it led directly to a small dining room. Beyond that was the kitchen. There was a bottle of very fine Scotch standing on a low shelf beside the refrigerator. There had been ice cubes in an ice bucket but they had melted. There were a few inconsequential pieces of cheese left on the plate where Pamela had obviously prepared her cheese and cracker spread. She stopped in mid-kitchen, looking around the room, helplessly, as though it had presented her with a problem which was beyond her. She turned slowly and raised her eyes.

Gregory Lind was only one step away from her and he took that step; he took it without thought or planning or foreknowledge, instinctively. She seemed to float into his arms and his lips came down on hers. He could feel the softness and the warmth of her through the thin robe and her lips responded to him. There was no time, no thought, no other person in the world. He released her mouth. Her eyes were closed but she opened them.

"You're wonderful," he said.

"No."

He kissed her again and the full tide of feeling broke inside of him. He could feel his blood rushing, a great roaring something, a madness, a blind insensate urge. His hand found the girl's bare flesh beneath the garment and then he swept her from her feet, holding her lightly in his arms. He could feel the nipple of her right breast with his lips as he held her close to him. He turned then and walked with her down the hall. Her arm curled up around his neck.

The wild unbelievable reality of it all was her response, her wanting him as he wanted her. There was no holding back, no protest, no denying. She was his and she rolled with him, accepting him, feeding her body back to him, her voice uttering strange, small sounds in her throat. He lay quiet at length with his arms holding her close to him and even the lying quiet was a soaring thing. Her hand stroked him.

"I wanted you," she said.

He had no words, none at all. His lips found the underside of her chin and he kissed her. He was becoming aware of himself again. It surprised him that he was naked. He did not remember removing his clothes. He must have flung them about the room in that frenzy which was a part of the experience, that frenzy which blocked out the awareness and the memory of itself. His hand moved up the girl's back. Her skin was so smooth and she, herself, was so small. There was no need for speech between them. There was a touching, an awareness of the touching, and then the storm broke again.

They lay together and there was a great drowsiness now, a deep peace, a relaxation of the senses, a sense of fulfillment. There was no need for any other thing. This was all of life, rich and warm, a spending of oneself and a drawing upon one's other self for renewal. One's other self? Certainly. That was it. One was a half-being until one discovered that. He turned, lifting her face, his hand beneath her chin.

"I couldn't get you out of my mind from the moment I first saw you," he said. "Now I know why."

"Do you?" Her lips were so very red and her face was pale. Her eyes seemed to mock him and then she laughed. "You don't know anything about me," she said. "You don't know how I make my living or anything. You don't know anything about me and yet you know everything about me. Everything. Does that sound crazy?"

"No. The things I don't know, I'll find out eventually." He drew a deep breath. "I didn't want to leave. I want to stay all night."

"Of course."

She accepted his decision as she accepted him. He drew her close, liking the feel of her body against his own, the sense of nearness. He was not aware of any weariness, of any need for sleep. Thought came to him, however, moving out of his own decision. He had not been thinking at all. Being had been sufficient without thought. Now, with relentless logic, his decision to stay all night challenged him with the awareness of morning beyond the dark. He closed his eyes, refusing to see the morning in detail.

"Have you an alarm clock?" he said.

"Hasn't everyone?"

"I don't know. Where is it?"

"On the dressing table. I'll get it. What time do you have to leave?"

"Five."

"Impossible."

"No. I must."

She slipped away from his arm and out of the bed. He saw her cross the room, a naked silhouette. She brought the tiny clock back to him and lighted a small lamp on the bedside stand. He set the alarm for five and turned out the light.

"I'm sorry that it will wake you, too," he said.

"If you keep me awake, it won't."

She was close to him and she was no longer a silhouette. There were many hours till five.

83

Steuben Drive was dark at five A.M. and no life moved on it. The snow was falling in a slow precise pattern and it had, obviously, been falling all night. Gregory Lind moved laboriously through an unbroken field of white, sinking to his knees in it. He reached his car, recognizing it solely by location. It was another of many white mounds along the curb. Opening the door was difficult and the engine awakened reluctantly. It seemed excessively noisy on the deserted street when it caught. He turned on his heater and defroster, left the engine running and waded into swabbing conflict with the snow which covered his car. He was aware of the time element and he worked fast. He was curiously detached, not thinking past the moment, heavy-eyed from lack of sleep but not notably tired. When he had the car clear, there was another thin veil taking form on it. He slid under the wheel and, even with snow tires, the car made hard work of pulling away from the curb. He held the speed to a walk but he slipped and slid and skidded in the four block descent of the hill. The windshield wipers struggled valiantly against the new snow and he had no rear vision at all.

Saint Anselm's was stunted by the storm, the upper part of its steeple invisible. When Gregory reached the sanctuary, Father Tom Guyton was already there, and vested. The younger priest looked at him with raised eyebrows.

"I knew you didn't come in last night," he said, "but I checked your room anyway this morning. You better let me say this Mass."

"No. It's mine. I'm all right. Sorry if I worried you. Does the pastor know that I didn't get in?"

"Not so far as I know. He wouldn't. Neither would the Wagner. You look like Saturday night in Sodom and Gomorrah. Are you certain that you want to say this Mass?"

"Positive."

Father Guyton offered no further objection. He helped his fellow priest to vest and one altar boy, looking half frozen, came in before Father Lind was ready. He blew on his hands and jigged for a few moments before he donned the cassock and surplice.

There were only a few people in the church, a scattered dozen. Gregory Lind, walking out to the altar behind the altar boy, was a priest of God, aware of himself as a priest of God and simultaneously aware of the incredible night. His mind separated two different, unrelated experiences, laying the one aside temporarily, concentrating upon the other. He made the sign of the Cross.

"I will go to the altar of God," he said.

He preferred the old way and always said, mentally: Introibo ad altare Dei. The Church, however, was changing. The altar boy, who knew the old response as well as he did, said: "To God who gives joy to my youth."

He was saying his Mass, moving solemnly, slowly, toward the climax. He experienced a great hesitation of soul, bowing his head to pray before the consecration. He was a man in mortal sin, unworthy to be where he was. The Church said that sacraments were valid, the Mass a source of grace, no matter if the celebrant was steeped in sin. He was a priest still, whatever he was as a man.

He held the white wafer, the round wafer of unleavened bread, and he had Latin on his lips now; "Hoc est enim Corpus Meum." ("This is my body.")

All of his faith was in this moment, the unquestioning belief of his childhood, the fully realized conviction of his seminary years. He held in his hands, at the instant of consecration, the body of Jesus Christ. This was the miracle of miracles, the enduring reality of twenty centuries. Princes and peasants, untold millions, had accepted small white wafers on their tongues, *knowing* that Christ entered into them in the receiving. Countless men had performed brutal penances for their sins in order to justify their approaching the great sacrament and innumerable priests had died, or suffered crippling injuries, in rescuing the Host during fire or flood.

He held the newly consecrated Host high and the altar boy's small silver bell sang. The bell tone echoed in the vast space of the church and there was no other sound. The people in the pews knelt with their heads bowed.

Father Lind's sense of unworthiness was suffocating him. He placed the Host upon the Corporal and uncovered the chalice. He made the sign of the Cross and intoned the Latin:

"Hic est enim Calix Sanguinis mei . . ." ("For this is the chalice of my Blood.")

He elevated the chalice and again the little bell sang. Jesus Christ, whole and entire, was now, in his unquestioning belief, personally present with him on the altar. He offered his prayers solemnly and hesitated before he took the Host into his mouth and drank the wine in the chalice.

"Domine non sum dignis," he said ("Lord, I am not worthy"), and the words never had held the meaning that they held on this morning. The faithful were coming to the Communion rail and, taking fresh Hosts, he went down to them.

At the end of the Mass, priest and altar boy left the altar and bowed to the Christ of the Crucifix in the sacristy.

"Thank you, Fred," Father Lind said. He reached into his pocket, found a dollar bill and passed it over. It was unusual but the morning was bad and the boy had been faithful to a duty. The thought, the decision to reward the boy, were on the surface of the man's mind; beneath that surface he was a different being, concerned with other thoughts. He removed his vestments slowly and placed them on their proper hangers. He did not hear the boy leave. His eyes lifted to the suffering figure on the cross and he sank slowly to his knees.

He did not pray. He looked upward into the face of the God-man who, in his final hour of agonizing death, had exerted himself to console a man who was dying with him. It was quiet in the sacristy and Gregory Lind searched his own mind. He was sorry that he had failed his priesthood, had violated his vow of celibacy, had appeared unworthily this morning before the altar of God, performing a rite that called for purity of mind and flesh. For all of that he was sorry, yet he could not in honesty, kneeling here alone before the image of his God, say that he was sorry for last night or that he regretted what had happened. He was poised and balanced on a contradiction.

He made the sign of the Cross, rose to his feet and walked out.

Father Guyton was waiting for him in the dining room. "I'll have a cup of coffee with you while you have your breakfast," he said.

"Thanks."

Mrs. Wagner served his breakfast and Gregory Lind ate what she served without looking at it, without any awareness of what he was eating. Tom Guyton talked brightly of weather, of items in the morning paper. Finally, Greg Lind pushed his plate away.

"So much for the shoes, sealing wax, cabbages, kings, Tom," he said. "Now what?"

The younger priest met his eyes. "That is up to you, Greg," he said. "If you are in trouble, can I help?"

"Good of you to try. I don't know."

Gregory Lind was thinking that he would have to go to confession. Father Guyton would be understanding, not likely to be easy on a man because he knew and liked him. He would be a good confessor but Father Lind did not believe that one should, if he could avoid it, find his confessor in the house in which he lived. This matter of Pamela was not something that he wanted to discuss with anyone outside of the Confessional either.

Tom Guyton finished his coffee. "I hope you won't need anybody's help," he said, "but if you do, sing out."

He smiled broadly, waved his hand and was gone. Greg Lind had no desire to leave the table, or the dining room. If no one disturbed him, he would be content to sit where he was through the day. It was strange, he thought, that he and Tom Guyton had never been close friends, living in the same house, sharing the same responsibilities. He was a good priest, a fine human being. If Greg had not returned in time, the six o'clock Mass would have been celebrated and no issue made of it.

Mrs. Wagner came in for the dishes, gracing them with an importance that did not belong to them. Father Lind rose. It was time to go.

Out of doors, the streets were narrow channels where the plows had gone through, and the channels were banked by huge mounds of snow. The snow was still falling but thinly. A man had to drive carefully. He drove slowly and thought moved in him.

Gregory Lind thought of Pamela Gibson here as he had not been able to think of her in the church or in the rectory. The night was incredible. He did not remember it, or run it through his mind as film through a camera; he lived it again, within it and yet holding it within him, part of himself forever. He could not regret it and that would be a difficulty. There was a sweetness in it, a gentleness, a great sharing. To call it a sex experience would be to lessen it. There were authorities in the field of sex and he had read some of the works they had written. According to theory he should be experiencing a revulsion this morning, feeling hostility, repelled by the woman with whom he had shared the night. That was not true; not in any small degree was it true.

He could remember now with tender amusement her awakening when he did to the call of the alarm clock.

"I'll fix your breakfast," she said. "Stay right where you are; I'll fix your breakfast."

She had gone back to sleep then, immediately, and she had been sound asleep when he left the apartment.

The parking lot of the *Catholic Star* was lost in snow. It was impossible to enter it. He drove two blocks to a garage and walked back to the paper. Father Peter Coyle, back from his trip and filled with significant ideas, came in at eleven. From that point on, the day was filled with discussions of great things to be done, most of them obvious things and, in one way or another, already in the process of being done. Five-thirty arrived slowly and brought with it another line to be toed.

There was a dinner scheduled, an ecumenical thing, with a rabbi, three Protestant ministers, several priests and laymen of various faiths. There would be hearty fellowship, speeches proclaiming the love of man for man, a straining toward graciousness, brotherhood, charity to all. It would be quite humanly constructive, a small step toward essential understanding, a soft blow at ancient prejudices, and it would be frightfully dull. Father Gregory Lind, representing the *Catholic Star* and perhaps the entire Catholic press, would be seated at the head table. One of his many roles was that of symbol; he stood for things unspoken and, if the truth were told, things undefined and totally unclear.

Pamela would not be at Guadalupe House tonight. She worked only three nights, as he did. He wanted to call her but he did not have her unlisted phone number. It seemed one of life's incongruities that he failed to have it now, but he had not given phone numbers a thought when he might have easily obtained it. He could not run out to her apartment. The time element would be too close for that even if the streets were free of ice. He accepted the impossibility but he was impatient with small details as he dressed.

"Slow down!" he told himself. "You have to break clear of all this anyway. You know that. There isn't anywhere you can go with it."

He drove to the dinner and he was seated beside Monsignor Raftor who was known as one of the real gung-ho pastors of Culverton, red hot for anything that called itself an implementation of Vatican II. The surface Father Gregory Lind talked glibly, effortlessly, meaninglessly to the monsignor, who talked himself but who never listened; while, deep inside, the hidden man, the inner Gregory Lind sat quietly and played with the chess pieces of his own life.

He was a man in mortal sin. There was no blinking at that. He had defined mortal sin too often for others; he could not escape the definition of it when it was applied to himself. He had to rid himself of that sin. He had to seek absolution, express his sorrow for having offended God, accept his penance and resolve not to repeat the offense. There was the compounded difficulty.

He was a priest of God. He did not want to offend God through any act of his own, and he would be sorry if he did so inadvertently; but he could not feel in his soul that he had been in conflict with God through his sweeping want of a woman. He had not planned to take her. The climax had come with sudden fury; an avalanche, a hard blown storm, a river at its flood.

He stopped there. There was no point in rationalizing. He had not walked blindly into that avalanche, flood, or whatever it was. There had been warning signals posted along all of the way he had come. He had known that the intimacy of two in an apartment, "and a nip of likker," was dangerous. He had identified it in his mind as an occasion of sin, then closed his eyes to all the warning signs. He was within himself both confessor and sinner. The confessor would not accept from the sinner an evasion of truth. He had seen where he was going and he had plunged ahead. Right? Probably. But he had not seen clearly. Grant him that.

The insoluble difficulty, at least right now, was the fact that he could not regret what he had done. He could not be "sorry" in the accepted sense of the word. Pamela had brought something precious into his life before he ever touched her. She had offered companionship, a glimpse of strange beauty, the stimulation of a keen mind that was at variance with his own. He could not wave her out of his life as without meaning, nor as a menace to virtue, an occasion of sin. To do so would be to reduce her from herself to a figure of phantasy. She was a human being, a fascinating human being, with whom his own life course had collided.

"Granting all that," the stern voice inside himself said, "you know that your life is dedicated to the special service of God in the priesthood. You have no right to seek 'strange beauty' or the 'stimulation' of a feminine mind. You have learned the controls so there is no excuse for your 'colliding' with other human beings. You are a man apart and some experiences are denied to you because you have been granted other, greater, experiences. You are not deprived: you are disciplined."

Gregory Lind closed his eyes. He was weary. He felt like some winged thing beating around within a cage that was too small, trying to escape.

He should, certainly, regret his failure to maintain the inviolability of his own priestly vows. He had chosen the way that he had walked the years, and his leaving the path was a personal failure. He looked at that failure and he still could not regret Pamela Gibson, nor could he wish last night undone. Last night had been the fulfillment of his physical self, a night of magic, a night of exultation and joy and the knowledge of a woman. God had given him the instinct that he had satisfied, the driving urge that sought the woman. Whatever he was that had made him a priest, he was also a man, a man whose whole nature launched him in the quest of woman. He had discovered facts about himself last night that he had not suspected, and he was not ashamed.

There was a burst of applause in which he joined mechanically, his inner self and surface self coming back together again in awareness that the meeting was breaking up. He rose from his place, shook hands with a dozen people, added his voice to the chorus of voices which approved the program of the night, and moved toward the door. He saw Leo Darrell, Father Coyle's favorite reporter, in the crowd. All was right with the world. Leo had been assigned to cover the meeting; no point in expecting notebook work from an assistant editor at the head table. He drove home and there was a light in the pastor's study, a band of light under Tom Guyton's door. He didn't give a damn. He was in bed within ten minutes and asleep within another five. He did not dream.

There was a sick call in the morning after the six o'clock Mass. The messenger came directly to the church. A man was hurt and dying, he said. Father Lind went down with him to the grim, gray old furniture factory on the levee. The man was lying on the rugless floor of a time-keeper's office. He had been almost broken in two by some piece of machinery that had swung out of its normal arc. Father Lind did not receive any detail on the accident and would not have understood it if he had. There was an ambulance attendant kneeling beside the man. He shook his head.

"He wouldn't let me do anything for him, Father, till you came. Says his head has to be clear."

The man was, perhaps, forty or forty-five. His face was pasty white and the black stubble on his skin was visibly composed of many individual hairs, each seeming to stand alone. There was agony in his eyes.

"Gus Orcutt, Father," he said huskily. "No church in ten years."

"Can you tell me why not?"

"Marriage. She had divorce. Our marriage no good. But it worked. As good as most. I didn't go to Mass, sacraments, nothing . . ."

Sweat was bubbling on the white face. This man had gambled through all the ten years and now, at the end, he was afraid to gamble. There was no strength in him for a general confession. If he could make it, it would be what any experienced Confessor would expect. There were no original sinners. Father Lind bent over him.

"God is good," he said. "Say your act of Contrition if you can. Be sorry for all your sins. Ask the mercy of God—and trust Him. He loves you."

The man made his act of contrition, or most of it, and he died on the timekeeper's floor. Father Gregory Lind absolved him before he died and prayed for him afterward. He left the factory depressed. The man, someone told him, had four children. Was it reasonable to expect a man to be sorry that he had shared ten years with a woman who gave him four children? Could he die regretting her, and the children, wishing them non-existent for the welfare of his own soul? God was a reasonable God and would not demand that. What, then, had a reasonable God actually asked of this man, Gus Orcutt, during the past ten years? What had God expected from him?

Gus Orcutt knew more about the mind of God now than did the priest who absolved him.

The *Catholic Star* picked up Gregory Lind's day and arranged it for him; or, at least, arranged assignments of work that were his to do. At three-thirty he was sufficiently caught up to leave his desk for a while. He drove out to Father Philip Dorker, a Franciscan, who had been his Confessor for several years. Going to Confession was going to be difficult, the decision to go was more difficult still. This was Wednesday and tonight he would see Pamela at Guadalupe House. He wanted to see her. It was not unreasonable to imagine that she would invite him to the apartment. He was going to Confession this afternoon because he would not be able to face the saying of his Mass tomorrow if he did not go; he could not fit Pamela into the time between Confession and his Mass, not in honesty, he couldn't. He had to face his Confessor with a sincere desire to escape from sin; otherwise, the whole procedure was a mockery.

Father Dorker was a young, lean, long-faced man with sad brown eyes and an abrupt manner of speech. He listened to Gregory Lind and he did not dwell on the issue of fornication. A man with nearly a decade of priesthood behind him would know all about that.

"You are in a situation which you could have avoided," he said. "Every situation confronts us with a choice. You are a priest. Your choice lies between God and this woman. What are you going to do about her?"

"I don't know. I can't help seeing her. I can avoid intimate contact."

"You must. Is it possible for you to leave town for a month or so?"

"Not at all."

"It is important that you break off all relations with this woman. If you cannot go away for a while physically, go spiritually. Lent starts next week. Consider it a desert and go to it. Live in it and mortify yourself. Live in Lent as you would in a desert, the essentials of living, nothing else. And leave that woman behind you."

It was tough and direct and Father Lind knew that, as counsel, the words made sense. He was one thing or another; a priest or a bachelor. He could not think of himself as a bachelor; if he was a priest he had to live like one.

There was work to be done yet at the paper, nearly two hours of work. He had a hurried supper and went to Guadalupe House. He had to brace himself before he entered. It would, he imagined, be difficult

91

meeting Pamela, a bit awkward. He did not meet her until nine o'clock
when the classes were disbanding for the night. They almost collided
in the corridor.

"Hello," she said. "I wondered where you were."

"Penned in the office. Tonight was full of trouble."

"Some nights are like that. The moon, maybe. It has phases."

"So I've heard."

The conversation did not make much sense but it was relaxed. Confronted with the reality of Pamela, Gregory wondered how he could
have anticipated anything else. She was wearing a brown suit tonight,
one that he had not seen before. It had a small jacket, not a regular
sized jacket. She had a pin on it, a small owl. An owl seemed a strange
choice for her; maybe not.

"I wanted to call you yesterday," he said. "I didn't have your
number."

"That's easy. Write it down. It's 222-6844."

"Thanks. I'll guard it as an unlisted secret."

"Do! In the meantime, there's some Scotch in the bottle if you'd
care to stop in tonight."

This was the moment that he had dreaded. He had hoped that she
would not invite him and was fairly certain that she would. After all, he
had no place to which he could invite her and they both knew that. He
wanted to say "yes" but he was only hours away from confession and
the stern words hung over him. He had a Mass to say in the morning.

"I'm sorry," he said. "I can't tonight."

Her eyes lifted to his face, then turned away. "Suit yourself," she said.
"It was just an idea."

"I'm sorry. You know that."

"Of course."

She smiled at him but there was a note in her voice that disturbed
him. She was reading regret for the other night into his refusal. She
seemed to be walking out of his life as she walked away. He had to
resist the impulse to pursue her.

"Damned fool!" he said. "It's what you want, isn't it? This is the way
it's got to be."

He did a half-dozen unnecessary things in his office before he turned
his back on it and closed the door. When he walked out to the parking
lot, she was gone.

The weather warmed. There was a lazy breeze from the south that did not chill in its crossing of the river. On all of the hillside streets of Culverton there were creeks and streams and small rivers, headwatered by melting snow. Driving was a messy business and walkers were splashed. Citizens on street corners and in lobbies talked of an early spring.

Thursday was a good day for Father Gregory Lind. He had an exceptionally large number of people at six o'clock Mass and he was at peace with himself in the saying of it. There was a letter for him from *The Catholic Digest.* They were going to reprint an article that he had written about Spanish American students who studied at night. There would be a check for that eventually. At three o'clock, one of the boys he had talked into staying in his classes at the school came down to see him at the paper. Pedro Gonzalez had passed the examination for the fire department. He would be the first Spanish American fireman in Culverton.

"Wonderful, Pedro," he said. "We'll give you a party at Guadalupe when you get your uniform."

"*Sí!* A party will be good." White teeth flashed in contrast to dark skin. "But at this party we must not burn down the house."

It had been a good day, certainly. Father Lind, rationalizing consciously, assured himself that there could be no harm in sharing good news with a friend, that it was, actually, the thing to do. He called Pamela Gibson's number and there was no answer. He called three times more in the course of the evening without a response. He lay, fully clothed, on his bed with his FM set playing and thought about that.

He did not, Pamela had told him, know a thing about her. She had added, of course, the paradoxical statement that he knew everything about her. The first statement was fact and the second hyperbole. He knew now who her parents were, and a little about the types of people they were. He knew that she had been married and that the man had been no good. She was presumably divorced. Beyond that, he drew blanks. He did not know why she lived alone when she had a family in town, nor who her friends were, nor even why she had ever become interested in Guadalupe House. Being the kind of person she was, she would work at something during the day, but he did not know what work she did. He had no idea how she spent those evenings which she did not spend at the school. Did she read, like motion pictures, watch TV, visit other people in their houses or apartments? He came eventually to the question which had formed dimly in his mind when first he failed to obtain an answer to his ring. Were there other men? Was she with one of them tonight?

There had to be other men. He faced that, staring at the ceiling, listening to his music. Anyone as attractive as Pamela would be a target wherever there were men. It was strange that she never had any of them call for her at Guadalupe. A girl like that could have a different escort every night in the week. He found the thought disturbing and that led him into another strange thought.

Like every other normal male, he had been aware of girls at the various stages of his life. He had had a few dates before he went into the seminary, not many. He had gone to a few parties during summer vacations from the seminary, parties which had included young people of both sexes; again not many. He had thought about girls whom he knew, girls he met, girls whom he saw here and there, even about girls in the occasional motion pictures and girls in many novels. He had definite ideas about the kind of girl he liked and he had some strong convictions.

He had taken it for granted that any girl who interested him would be a Catholic. No question about that. He had taken her virginity for granted, too. A woman who had belonged to another man, or who had had sex experience with someone else, would not attract him. He would, if he married, go to the woman as he expected her to come to him, without having shared the sex experience with anyone else. He liked dark-haired girls better than blondes, and he liked the small, shy, slightly helpless ones, the girls who needed protecting.

That is how he had been. Pamela was neither dark-haired nor blonde. She was not shy, nor helpless. She was not a Catholic. She was divorced. The fact that she had belonged to another man did not, amazingly, disturb him; there was no reality in it. He was disturbed by the thought that she might be out with a man tonight, but not by the fact that she had lived with another man.

He continued to think about her, staring at the ceiling. She was something that had happened to him, something that he had not willed to happen. He had even written an editorial in defense of celibacy; a good editorial, one that was written sincerely. He had been a good priest, within his limitations as a person, causing no trouble to his superiors, begrudging no service he could render to any layman who needed him. He faced his priesthood now and still found it good, but he did not believe that he could do as his confessor instructed. He could not walk into the desert of Lent and fast there, forgetting Pamela. He could fast. He had the strength for that. He could walk difficult ways and do difficult things, but he could not give up the woman who had come into his life. She belonged there. She completed him.

"There is no future with Pamela Gibson, no possible future," the relentless logical mind within him said. "Even if you were not a priest, this whole affair would be impossible. She belongs to wealth and social position, to a way of life that you do not even understand. She cannot be tied to you, will not be. She will find someone of her own kind eventually, if she has not already found him, and she will leave you then. Do you believe you will still be a priest? What will you be?"

He stared into space and he listened to all the arguments that his other, saner self, hurled at him. He had no sound argument to offer in return; he knew only that he would not turn his back on Pamela and walk away, not to the desert of Lent or to any other place, spiritual or material, where he could not see her, hear her voice, touch her.

It was a long night and he slept badly.

Some stubborn streak asserted itself in him on Thursday and he did not try to call her. On Friday, at Guadalupe House, he saw her. He walked down the corridor and stopped at the door of her classroom. She was walking back and forth, dictating from a thin book to a class, mostly girls, who were writing in notebooks. When she saw him, she gave the rest signal to the girls and walked to the door, her finger holding her place in the book.

"Hello," she said.

"Hello, yourself. I've been wondering if I'm invited to call this evening."

She shook her head slowly. Her eyes met his but he could not read anything in them. "I can't invite you tonight," she said. "Sorry. Monday maybe."

"Right," he said. "I'll check with you on Monday."

It was, he felt, a weakness in him that accepted Monday, a hypothetical Monday at that, instead of tonight; but it was her apartment, certainly, and she had the right to invite whomever she chose, with no obligation to explain her actions to anyone. He had no right to know her plans for tonight, no right at all.

He had a difficult time concentrating on the problems in his office and the weekend loomed as interminable. He went into the Confessional on Saturday evening for three hours. The lines were long because this was the last Saturday before Lent. There were a number of tough sinners, some people who had been away from the sacraments for a long time, a great many intricate spiritual questions to resolve in one way or another.

Father Gregory Lind had never been as relaxed in the Confessional, never as close to the people who hesitated and stumbled and expressed themselves badly. He felt with them and he gave them understanding, but he had always done that or tried to do it; the added element was the feeling of union with them. He was not aloof or detached. He knew why they rationalized their motives and their actions, he knew why it was difficult to regret some sins, he knew why some sinners despaired when facing the need to change their way of life. He, no less than they, was walking that difficult road. He did not compromise standards nor accept sin as anything other than sin, but he sympathized with the sinners. It was his most memorable evening in the confessional and he recognized that it was when he knelt before the high altar to offer his thanks.

He closed his mind to his personal problems and he slept soundly through the first half of the night. He awakened suddenly in the dark with the thought—"This is Saturday night. I only have to get through Sunday and Monday; just Sunday and Monday." The thought frightened him and he prayed his way back to sleep.

Monday night, when it came, was as balmy as a night in spring. He left his topcoat in the rectory when he went to Guadalupe House. He was early and he saw Pamela driving into the lot when he stepped out of his car. He waited for her and she smiled when she saw him. Her smile when the eyes of her class might be upon her was a brief, flickering affair, but, in the open with an audience of one, she smiled brightly. She had beautiful teeth. Her suit tonight was a plaid, a subdued maroon in color. She was wearing a small black hat which curved in the crown.

"This meeting saves me a walk down the corridor," she said. "I have cold chicken and rye bread at the apartment. Want some?"

"It sounds great."

"Good. The bar opens at nine-twenty."

She walked ahead of him into the school and he noted, as he had noted before, the deference she commanded. Young men, tough young men who were not in her classes, discovered some ancient layer of Spanish courtesy in their systems when she was around. Father Lind turned in to his own office and, now that he was committed to seeing her again tonight he remembered all the reasons why he should not. He had been off-balance when he met her and her opening statement had taken him by surprise. He did not try to convince himself that the

96

result would have been different under any circumstance; he made a brushing gesture with his hand and dismissed the matter. There was a young couple waiting for him and he concentrated his attention upon them.

At nine-twenty Steuben Drive was quiet, no cars rolling, no pedestrians strolling. There were lights behind windows but the windows were heavily curtained and draped. It was a discreet street, a pleasant, comfortable, financially stable street, a street such as Gregory Lind had never lived on. He had never seen any of Pamela's neighbors in 751 and he did not see any of them now. Pamela opened the door for him.

"I haven't a bit of chicken or rye bread," he said, "but I brought a bottle."

"You didn't have to do that. I had a bottle."

"It's about time I did."

She laughed. "You shared the fire, too. If you come up here some night carrying a log, I won't let you in."

The first few minutes were always like this, tentative and unsure, but tonight she did not go alone into the other room. She took it for granted that he would go with her. She unwrapped his bottle, told him to open it and turned her attention to the refrigerator. As he poured the drinks, Gregory Lind thought wryly of what a dent one bottle of Scotch could make in a priest's meagre funds; Pamela probably bought hers by the case.

They went into the living room and there was no need of a fire tonight. He missed it. A fire seemed part of the room itself, an aspect of its personality.

"Have you ever been in Jamaica?" Pamela said.

"Not I. Nowhere close. Why?"

"It's popular this winter. A lot of Culverites have been going."

"People you know?"

"Not particularly." Her eyebrows lifted. She held her glass suspended, halfway to her lips. "It didn't occur to me until now. You don't know what I do, where I work."

"No. You told me, remember, that I know nothing about you."

"I remember. Fondly and without shame."

She disconcerted him and that amused her. "I work for a travel agency," she said. "Chase and Melrose. I book people to places I'd like to visit myself, and I make their reservations and I see that they are treated like kings and queens."

"You have traveled, though?"

"Yes. A little."

The little, as he drew her out, seemed like a fair share of the globe.

97

She had flown and she had traveled shipboard and she knew both oceans. Gregory Lind had been to New York and Washington on press junkets. He had never seen the Rocky Mountains or the West Coast. He had spent all of his life, with the exception of two trips, within three states, most of it within one. He mentioned that, half apologetically, and Pamela looked at him doubtfully, her head cocked on one side.

"You're kidding."

"I'm not."

"I thought that all priests traveled, traveled a lot. I thought that Rome must be a must."

"You have lovely ideas."

"That's right. I do. I should be Pope." She leaned forward, her glass in her hand. "How does a man become a priest?"

That question seemed to obsess her. He remembered that she had raised the subject before. "He becomes a priest the hard way," he said lightly. "Tough study of tough subjects, the putting in of a long time in a seminary."

"Poof! That's the outside. That's studying engineering to be an engineer, or dentistry to be a dentist. I don't care about that. I mean, inside; deep inside. What makes him? Someone like you, I mean."

"It would sound trite to you. The love of God, mainly."

Pamela took a swallow of her drink. Her eyes were far away, looking over and beyond him. "The love of God," she repeated slowly. She shook her head. "No. I won't buy that. I don't believe it. You don't know him. You can't even prove that he exists."

"I can."

"I know. I've heard it. It's verbal hocus-pocus. Never mind. The thing is, you can't love him; couldn't do it. He's too big to love if he made the universe and everything in it; too overwhelmingly big."

"He knew that. He came down to man, and to man's level."

"Christ, you mean? It's difficult to talk to you. If I believed in a God that created everything, that would be going pretty far for me. The rest of it would be impossible. I just couldn't take seriously all the fairy stories of stars and wise men and a virgin birth and miracles, and God himself dying for our sins."

"Not that way, you couldn't! You're taking the easy way. It's easy to oversimplify anything and then ridicule your own oversimplification. That's what you're doing, you know."

"Possibly! You do the same thing in reverse. You find something in your own mind and you say you love it. Maybe you do. You don't have to shut yourself away from life for it."

"No, Pamela," he said. "That isn't the way it is."

Their eyes held across the coffee table. She smiled. "Maybe yes; maybe no. Do you realize that is the first time you've called me Pamela?"

"Is it? I've thought of you as Pamela."

"Nice. I'm glad that you did. You'll have to tell me what you thought. But first, let's fix these drinks."

She scooped up her glass. He took his own glass and followed her, startled that most of the chicken and rye bread had vanished in the course of a conversation. That, perhaps, was the true measure of the conversation. It was all a bit absurd, looking back at it. One did not approach faith in that way. He had encountered Pamela's catch phrases on university religion nights when he had had a half hour for a lecture and another half hour in which to answer questions; a full hour in all for the dispelling of total disbelief in bright young people who knew how to make shallow argument sound clever. He had never succeeded with them.

The light from the kitchen fell across Pamela like a leaning shaft as she came within range of the door. She was wearing the green floor-length hostess gown. He liked the long skirt after an overdose of miniskirts and comical legs. Pamela's legs were slim and straight and lovely. A long skirt did not betray the beauty of her body. She moved in a soft sheath.

"You've never called me anything," he said, "now that we're on the subject."

"We aren't on it. We left that subject in order to pour ourselves a drink."

She took his glass and held it up against the light, tilting it slightly as she poured the whiskey into it. Her eyes narrowed with concentration.

"It would be simpler to use a jigger glass," he said.

"I don't believe in the middleman." She poured water into the glass. "I never called you 'Father' if that's what's bugging you. I always considered the father business pretentious and phony, utterly without reality. You weren't my father. Nothing like it."

"O.K. You have never called me Gregory, either."

They walked back into the other room. "No, I didn't. It's a good name. I like it. I think that I like Greg better."

They sat in their places again, facing each other. It seemed such a simple point to reach now, such a simple beginning point, when they had come so far together. They had been picked up in a great tide and swept into intimacy without terms of endearment, without even names for each other. He felt, looking at her, that Pamela held the same thought that he did. He felt, too, the magnetic current that flowed between them when they looked at each other. He had tried to tell himself before this that he was being a high school romantic when he thought such nonsense, but the magnetic current was there whether one called it nonsense or called it something else. He set his glass down.

"I don't want a drink after all," he said.

She set her glass beside his, looked at the two glasses, then raised her eyes. "What do you want, Gregory?" she said.

"You."

He was on his feet and she rose into his arms. This was inevitable, he thought, but it hadn't been planned. Thought closed with that fragment. He held the warmth and the softness of her and her fragrance was in his nostrils. Her lips moved to meet his and he swept her up into his arms, carrying her as easily as if she had no weight. Her arm curled around his neck and she kissed him deeply before he laid her down upon the bed.

It was a long time later that she turned in his arms. "I am afraid that I am in love with you," she said.

"I *know* that I am in love with you."

His voice was husky. He had never expected to say that to a woman. This did not seem to be the proper time or place or circumstance but the words spoke themselves because he felt them. He held her naked body close to him glorying in the holding, knowing that he wanted this woman beyond all the reckoning, not merely now but again, and beyond the again. Her voice came up to him.

"Do you really love me, Greg?"

"You know I do."

"You might be just carried away. You could get over me."

"No."

"I'm being fair, I think. I'm telling you the truth. If I'm just a woman, the first woman you've known this way, you'll get over me."

"How about you? Will you get over me?"

"I couldn't. Not even if I should."

He tried to think about that, about the meaning in the words that people speak. His thoughts would not march. There was languor in him, lazy languor. It was enough to be alive and to be here; neither his mind nor his body demanded more. The woman in his arms laughed softly.

"Everything with us is out of sequence," she said. "Do you know what I've been thinking?"

"I couldn't guess."

"If you fly from Bergen or Copenhagen west in the daytime, over the North Pole to the United States, you see sunsets in reverse. The setting sun comes up instead of going down. Everything is out of joint. That's us. We're doing everything backward. I am not sure that we were ever introduced. Maybe, someday, we will be."

"I doubt that anyone will. We don't know the same people. Is that right about the sunsets unsetting?"

"Of course. Figure it out for yourself. Those jets fly fast."

She twisted out of his arms and went into the bathroom, trailing the green garment. Greg rose reluctantly. There was a small lavatory off the entry hall. He dressed there, marveling when he looked in the mirror that there was no change in his appearance. After he had doused his face with cold water, he did not even look sleepy. He went into the living room and he was only seconds ahead of Pamela. She was wearing a blue robe and he could not tell if she was wearing anything under it. Her slippers were cream colored, without heels.

They took their accustomed seats, facing each other. It seemed natural, easy. There was relaxation in the room atmosphere, in his nerves, in all of his body. Greg tasted the drink that he had deserted. The ice had melted in it but that made no difference. Pamela did not touch hers.

"Do you know what I'd love right now?" she said.

"What?"

"A cigarette."

"Oh. Did you?"

"Yes. For years and years. I quit them three years ago. Cancer had nothing to do with it. I wasn't afraid. I was just bored. It seemed that everybody smoked. I didn't want to be everybody. So, I quit. Sometimes I look back. Like now. If I had a cigarette, I'd smoke it."

"I can't help you."

"You don't either. Did you ever?"

"Yes. Not very seriously, I guess. I tried a pipe, cigarettes, in the seminary. Poverty helped me quit as much as anything. When I had any money, I needed it for other things. No merit for me in quitting."

"I guess not. You wouldn't look back, either."

"No. I've never done much looking back. That is, in the sense of wanting something that I used to have."

Pamela tapped her teeth with her middle finger, an odd gesture that, somehow, conveyed the idea of thought. "You'll look back and wish that you hadn't met me," she said.

"What made you say that?"

"Realizing it. I'm a problem to your priesthood. I don't understand very well what I've done to you because I don't understand priesthood.

I know I've hurt you. I wish that I could be sorry. I guess that I am, in a way."

"You don't have to be sorry on my account for anything connected with me. You are responsible only for yourself."

He frowned, realizing that he had expressed that thought badly. The word "sorry" had thrown him off balance because it was the key to his own dilemma. He took a swallow of his drink.

"I'm bad for *you*, Pamela," he said. "I did not mean to be. I can't earn a place in your life. I can't do anything for you. I can't offer you anything."

"You do all right."

He made a dismissing gesture with his right hand. "You know what I mean. I don't like saying that I can't do this and I can't do that. It sounds self-pitying. Hell! What I'm trying to say is that you'll have to break off from me eventually in self-defense. When you do, I'll understand."

"You think so?"

"Yes."

She rose and crossed the room. He followed her. It was, of course, the time to go. She helped him on with his coat and when he turned, she held him away with two fingers against his chest.

"There is one thing I want you to know," she said, "if you do any looking back, and whether we break up or don't, you must never blame yourself for me." She drew a deep breath and she seemed to grow tall with it. "I did exactly what I wanted to do and with whom I wanted to do it."

She kissed him then and that was good night.

– XII –

Lent came in solemnly on Ash Wednesday. In Saint Anselm's church, long lines of men, women and children queued slowly up the aisles to the altar rail where the priests moved back and forth, inscribing black crosses on their foreheads.

"Remember, Man, that thou art dust and unto dust thou shalt return."

Father Gregory Lind repeated the formula countless times, aware of faces, foreheads, eyes, but not aware of them as belonging to individuals. He placed the ashes on foreheads in the morning, knowing that many of those receiving them would wear them all day; a proclamation of faith, an act of humility, a symbol of penance. As far back as his memory went, black forehead smudges were linked to Ash Wednesday. He had a feeling of kinship, of affection, for those who came to the church and knelt to receive these ashes. There was no compulsion about it. The Church did not say that they must come; but morning, afternoon and evening the Church offered this reminder that forty days of penance lay ahead and that the truly repentant sinner would walk the way of the Cross.

"Remember, Man, thou art but dust."

Gregory Lind was tired when the last service of the day was over. Guadalupe House had had no claim on his time tonight and neither had Pamela. Tom Guyton's door was open when he climbed the stairs and he paused outside of it. Father Guyton was slumped in his easy chair; not reading, not listening to music, merely slumping. He waved his hand.

"Come in if you like," he said. "There's no whiskey. I've sworn off for the stretch."

"Good man. I won't stop in. I'm going to do what you're doing. We walked a few miles along that rail today."

Tom grinned. "And carrying the coal."

"Aye."

Gregory crossed the hall to his own room and despite his vow that he would slump immediately into a chair, he paced restlessly, picking up objects and laying them down. He was aware of the fact that he had developed the habit of avoiding Father Tom Guyton. He had read speculation in Tom's eyes, sensed that the other priest was concerned about him. He could not settle the speculation nor endure the concern. A younger priest like Tom, one of today's younger priests, would probably sympathize with him and with his problem more readily than an older priest, but if he had to talk to someone the older priest would be his choice. He was not going to talk to anyone.

He had decided that he would not spend a solitary forty days in the desert of Lent, that it was an impossibility for him. A man could walk away from liquor or tobacco, from any number of things he liked or loved, but a woman who entered his life, who was not a mere passing indulgence, was another matter. A man had to experience the relationship, with its overtones and undertones, to understand how it enmeshed a man. He did not believe that the priests whom he knew best understood how strongly spiritual forces asserted themselves in something that was ostensibly a physical relationship. If a man loved a woman, he could not merely love her physically.

There were times, as now, when a man moved like a beast in a cage but, unlike the beast, with a doubt in the reality of his bars. A man could be trapped in the meaning of his own mind, of course. The arguments which took form so swiftly and that seemed so firm could, if extended, be used to condone any sin or any indulgence of man. Still, if one acted sincerely and did not harm another human being in the acting, could his sin be truly grave? Even within the Roman Catholic Church since Vatican Two there had been a revolt against any stereotyped authoritarian definition of sin.

He stood beneath the crucifix on the wall of his room and there was agony in him. "Lord, I don't know," he prayed. "Even now I cannot be sorry that this experience has come to my life. I cannot return to confession. It would be a mockery under the circumstances. I cannot desert the work that I am needed to do. I cannot pretend that I have never met Pamela, or walk away from her. If we have sinned so that absolution is necessary, I cannot seek it for myself when she cannot have it. I need time, Lord, and grace and more wisdom than I have. Be patient, please, with what I try to do and help me."

All of the simplicity of his nature was in his prayer. He stood for a long minute staring at the figure on the Cross before he turned away and made ready for bed.

The question of Lent, the personal pattern of it, was settled in those few minutes. Right or wrong, he accepted certain things as the realities of his life, realities that made their demands and offered their compensations in the immediate now. He moved with those realities, feeling closer to God rather than alienated, and he did not look back.

He had to be a priest. Lent made enormous demands; stations of the Cross, extra sermons, longer hours of confession, a greater number of people in the church on weekdays, evening devotions in addition to the morning Masses. The *Catholic Star* became more demanding, too. It was heavily devotional but it stirred, too, to anger, lashing out against the evils of a revitalized modernism. Gregory Lind welcomed the anger as a change from complacency but he, of course, was called upon for the labor involved. Father Peter Coyle was a pronouncer of ideas, a spokesman for the bishop, a journalistic symbol, but never a toiler in the vineyard.

Guadalupe House suffered in Father Lind's schedule. He could find only occasional hours free during school periods. He had less time for Pamela Gibson, too, but he had time.

Pamela, he discovered, was a girl who respected a man's working time, and she did not have to understand the work that he did. They found late evening intervals, practically the only periods which they both had free, and they enjoyed their time together even when sex was not involved. There was music and there were books. Pamela was far ahead of him on novels and he had to allow her that lead. He thought that she read a lot of junk. There was no reading time in his life at the moment.

They achieved three hours on a Saturday afternoon and drove in her car southward to the small city of Jerome. There was spring in the warm sunshine and in all the fields. The redbud was in bloom on the low hillsides and the wild plum thickets were scattered like snow along the fence lines. There were daffodils and Johnny-jump-ups and field daisies turning green. Birds were flying from tree to tree, seemingly aimless but actually working hard. Gregory saw cardinals and woodpeckers and jays. He knew that there were dozens of varieties which he did not see. In one field that they passed there were early lambs.

It interested him that Pamela saw so little when there was so much to see. She looked at him suspiciously when he called birds or flowers by name.

"I thought that you grew up on pavement," she said.

"I did. I was also a Boy Scout. I did a lot of nature study when I was a kid; bird-watching and the whole ticket."

"I didn't. I watched boys. I guess I neglected the birds. I never knew what went on in the country."

"The boys were probably more appreciative than the birds would have been."

"I don't remember any boy being particularly appreciative. About the time a girl first becomes interested in them, boys are a dull lot. She makes do with them but it takes work." Pamela made a dismissing gesture. "What else did you do that was interesting?"

"Damn little. I went to the seminary early and the only interesting thing a seminarian does, if he does anything interesting at all, is on summer vacations."

"Such as?"

"I worked as timekeeper for a power company construction crew one summer. I drove an ambulance two summers."

She looked at him speculatively. "You would be good with accident victims."

"What makes you think so?"

"You are gentle."

They talked, in great part, along the surface of things, whether on a ride in the country or in a few snatched city minutes. They sought depths only in discussions of books or plays, or of people in the newspapers. They made no attempt to look ahead, to see any tomorrow of their own, and yet the sense of belonging together was strong in them.

Father Peter Coyle came into Gregory's office one afternoon after the pace of the day had quieted. "I hear you were riding a girl around town the other night," he said.

Gregory had known that this would happen sooner or later. Someone was bound to see him with Pamela and do some speculating or commenting. He shrugged.

"A girl from Guadalupe House," he said, "I took her home. Where do you hear such things?"

Father Coyle chuckled. "Here and there. I just wanted you to know that a Roman collar can't steal a dime. Little old ladies are watching."

"Dreadful thought!"

"Yes. Isn't it? Anyway load a couple of boys in the car whenever you let a girl get into it. Just for balance. You're carrying our press tags on that car, you know."

Father Coyle waved and went out. It had all been good-natured and cheerful. Gregory knew that Father Coyle did not take the matter of a girl in the car seriously; but there had been a phone call obviously and for one person who called there would be ten or twenty, at least, who would merely make mental notes. He had not taken Pamela in his car very often; obviously it would be discreet not to take her at all.

He did not mention Father Coyle's phone call to Pamela but he had a drink with her in her apartment on Friday night and she had her own bulletin.

"I'm never one for bringing skeletons to feasts," she said, "but we may have to halt these tête-à-tête things in the apartment."

"Why? What happened?"

She shrugged. "A couple of anonymous letters and a discreet warning from my landlady. That uniform of yours stands out, Greg. That's what raised the issue, I'm sure."

"It's too late to leave it off, even if I could. Sometimes I can get away with jacket and slacks at the paper." He hesitated. "Damn it! I'm sorry, Pam. I should have thought about you and the spot I could put you in."

"Why? I didn't. Don't be silly. It's bad for you, too. Your reputation is probably more sensitive than mine."

Gregory thought about that, holding his drink in his hand, looking into Pamela's grave eyes. It was incredible that he should be in such a situation. Discretion was second nature to a priest. A priest was aware of the possibilities for scandal in even the small, careless acts that a layman would not think about; but he, Gregory Lind, had been in the grip of a fantastic madness since he had known Pamela. He had been unaware of other people. He had invited trouble. He had not been sensitive to the need for preserving her reputation or his own.

"I'm sorry, Pam," he said. "I'll stop coming here, of course."

She spread her hands wide. They were lovely hands, expressive hands, and she used them very effectively. "We haven't any place else."

He faced that, sitting quietly in this room that he loved. The FM was playing in the near distance of the apartment and the music that flowed into the room was *Swan Lake*. They did not have any place else, not any place at all. People had drinks and dinner in lounges and clubs and restaurants, but he and Pamela could not do that. Too many people knew him, as a priest and as the associate editor of the *Star*. He had gone to so many civic affairs, had had close contact with so many Catholic laymen, Protestants and Jews. He had no doubt that a great many people knew Pamela Gibson. They would be a marked couple wherever they went. Culverton was a fairly big city but it had its small-town aspects.

"I haven't an immediate answer," he said, "but I'll have to stop coming here. This is your home. I can't embarrass you."

"You could come, as you have been coming, for a little while yet, I guess."

"No."

They sat quietly, sipping their drinks. There was no way of discounting the situation in which they found themselves, no way of shrugging it off. Gregory groped in his mind for some immediate alternative, even if it were only a stop-gap; an alternative to the acknowledgment of no-answer.

"I could break away reasonably early Tuesday night," he said, "if you could have dinner with me. There was a place just this side of Jerome, remember. A restaurant. Not a nightclub. It adjoined that big motel. I don't imagine that there would be any Culverton people there. I'll leave off the uniform. I'll wear a jacket and slacks."

She weighed what he said, frowning slightly. She seemed self-sufficient most of the time but when she was perturbed, she lost her assurance. There were sensitive lines in her face. Her mouth, without the pronounced lipstick might be very vulnerable. That, perhaps, was the reason for the lipstick. She could be hurt and probably had been. She nodded slowly.

"Yes," she said. "I would like that. It should be all right. We'll use my car. I'll pick you up someplace."

"Fine."

He left early and he had a sense which he was certain that she shared, the sense that the apartment no longer represented sanctuary;

a feeling that, somehow, privacy had vanished, that they were observed in even the slightest action, as in the simple act of saying good night.

The weekend rolled over him and there was little time for thought, grim or otherwise. He had a particularly difficult Sunday with his mother who was subjecting herself to fasts and abstentions which were not required of her and whose nerves, as a consequence, were quick and jumpy, seeking relief in words that were ill-balanced and unkind. His sister, Janet, had none of her usual sparkle; she was pale and tense.

"I can't take much more of it, Greg," she said. "And it isn't fair to Joe or the children. It just isn't. Their home is like something that's ready to explode any minute. She's got to realize that we are human beings, too, just as she is. If she won't, I won't try any more. We'll have to put her in a nursing home."

He did not mention the nursing home idea to his mother. It would sound like a threat if he did, and he did not believe in threats. He tried to calm her down, tried to reason with her, tried to change the subject, tried to take over the conversation and talk about the church, its priests and the *Catholic Star*. He left her ultimately with the familiar sense of failure and with the equally familiar and humiliating thought that he had not lifted one ounce of his mother's chronic unhappiness, that he had been of no assistance whatever to his sister who needed help. All that he ever did for his family on Sunday could be summed up in a sentence. He put in a little time, then walked away, leaving all the problems where they were, safely out of his life for another week. A man could not give himself much of a diploma for that.

Tuesday evening was slow in coming, but it came.

Pamela picked him up at the Harper Street corner of Fifth, the Guadalupe House corner. She slid her car into the curb and waved him over to the driver's side when he would have entered by the passenger door.

"You drive," she said. "You know the route better than I do."

He liked to drive. He picked up the Interstate Highway a dozen blocks from Harper and rode it south. There was a full moon, slightly tinged with yellow.

"Idiot's moon," Pamela said. "Lovely, isn't it?"

"It is."

In his growing up, a full moon had been called "Madman's Moon"; if Pam wanted idiot for madman, that was all right; on the same folklore wavelength. The night was a night for singing but all the songs that passed swiftly through his mind were corny, none of them equal to the occasion.

"I like your jacket," Pam said.

"Thanks. How about the necktie?"

"I'll tell you when I see it across a table."

"It's blue. The only place I can shed the uniform is down at the paper. I went in for loud-splash ties at first, fried eggs and Mexican dinners."

"Why did you tone down?"

"I don't know. The flamboyant stuff was an escape, I guess, but it didn't express me."

"Do I express you?"

"No. You express you and gorgeously. Why?"

"I wondered. I wouldn't want to be an escape. You would tire of me, like a fried egg necktie."

"You think?"

"Yes."

"I'll never tire of you."

The "never" hung on some star of no-time and Gregory Lind recognized that when he spoke the word. He and Pamela had no measurable interval together in which they could tire of each other, or tire not; they lived in a perpetual present which was not linked to plans, hopes, dreams, or a vision of tomorrow. There was yesterday of course, but it was segmented, divided, half to each of them; they had not known the yesterday of years together.

Pamela was riding quietly, slumped a little, watching the road. "I have always wondered how you discovered Guadalupe House," he said. "You are doing something pretty wonderful down there. It isn't easy. Why do you do it?"

Pamela raised her head. "You don't know, do you? You've never seen the office where I work. You've never played any of the games I play. You don't know any of the people I know."

She paused, then made a brushing gesture with her right hand. "We're still moving backward. Do you realize that this is our first date, the first time we've gone out together, the first time you've taken me any place?"

Gregory winced. The truth behind that multiple question was appalling. "I can't introduce you to my family," he said, "because there isn't supposed to be a you. You still haven't told me how you heard of Guadalupe House."

"Oh! Well, it isn't mysterious. I eat lunch often at the main restaurant of the Lantern chain. It is on Griffin Square. I met a girl named Sarah Mendez there. She is dietitian for all the Lantern restaurants. She plans the menus. She has a lot of responsibility. She is Spanish American and she is young and she is attractive. An airline copilot wanted to marry her. She decided not."

"Why not?"

"Lantern has a rule. If a girl marries, she has to resign. Old-fashioned and maybe unconstitutional. I don't know. Anyway, that's how it is. Sarah was in a spot where she could help young Spanish Americans find jobs. And she did. She decided that she would be closing a door to opportunity for a lot of her people if she married her copilot. She was completely sincere about that and she did not marry him."

Gregory Lind frowned at the road. This was another version of celibacy.

"I know Sarah Mendez," he said. "I did not know her story, not any of it."

"She wouldn't be likely to tell you."

"And she's the cause of your joining Guadalupe House?"

"Yes."

"I owe her much."

"Probably not."

There was a winking sign ahead of them on the left hand side of the road. This was the Triangle Motel. Beyond it and independent of it was Cynthia's Kitchen, a restaurant and lounge housed in a structure that was vaguely Swiss. The lounge was dimly lighted and the dining room nearly as dim. Gregory and Pamela were seated at a corner table and Gregory ordered Scotch. When it came, he lifted his glass and dipped it.

"To the first drink I've ever bought you," he said.

She acknowledged the salute with a slight dip of her own glass. "You forget," she said. "You bought me a bottle."

"A different matter entirely."

Gregory was relaxed, content, happy in being where he was. He had been uneasy when he contemplated this evening, a bit tense on the way down, but now he was able to put everything behind him and live in the immediate moment. Pamela looked lovely. He told her so.

"This semi-darkness is becoming to me," she said.

"You would thrive on any amount of light they gave you."

"Keep on believing that. I'll purr like a kitten."

They passed words back and forth across the table, words that were inconsequential in themselves but which served as messages between two people who liked each other. There were so few subjects open to them, so many subjects to be avoided, so much that suggested the brief halting of two people who were traveling in different directions. This half was theirs and belonged to both of them; their destinations had no common identity that they could name and discuss.

Pamela had fine line eyebrows softly penciled over. Pamela had eyelids that widened and narrowed, eyes that looked upward when she lowered her head, sidewise when she tilted it. Pamela had a short, straight nose and firmly defined cheekbones. Pamela's upper lip and lower lip were identical twins, two equal parts of a whole and boldly lipsticked. Pamela had a soft contralto voice and there was music in her laugh. Her hands had life of their own, reaching for meaning and expressing it when she could not find the words she wanted. Pamela, the man thought, was unlike any woman he had ever met or known.

The highway was quiet on their drive home with few cars rolling. Pamela sat close to him in the seat and Gregory drove below his normal speed. The night was magic in its way and for long stretches they found speech unnecessary. Steuben Drive was dark when they reached it, the spire of the Presbyterian Church on Pamela's corner a sharp silhouette against the sky. There was only the entrance light at 751 and a faint glow behind the curtain on the second floor, Pamela's apartment.

"I left it on," Pamela said. "People will think I'm home, reading. You'll come up for a nightcap, won't you?"

"I hadn't better."

"I think so. We'll be quiet. Very quiet."

There was no will in him to resist. He wanted to go up with her. They moved on the staircase like shadows and that, too, was adventure, like taking part in a burglary. She turned briefly and kissed him when she opened the door, then swiftly moved away from him. He was sharply aware of the scent of her in his nostrils.

They sat in the living room with their drinks and it was their first evening together without music.

It was three o'clock when Gregory Lind left, descending the stairs quietly, closing the door carefully, literally holding his breath. The air out-of-doors was chill, not cold. He drew it into his lungs and, momentarily, he regretted the car. He was not tired or sleepy. He was alive in all of his being. If he did not have the car he would enjoy walking back to the rectory.

– XIII –

The morning came too soon. Gregory Lind rolled over in bed and turned off the alarm when it rang. His alive quality had evaporated and rising was an effort. His shower did not pick him up. He went to the church in a deep gray darkness and he felt both chill and weariness when he vested for six o'clock Mass. He felt, too, as he had felt before something that was close to horror. He was a man in mortal sin who was about to go up to the altar of God and consecrate the bread and wine.

He walked out of the sacristy and the people in the pews rose to their feet. Some part of him always seemed to continue this walk, moving into the pews where the people were while he, as priest-celebrant, stopped at the altar. He had a feeling of oneness with these people who were the sharers of the sacrifice that he was about to offer, a feeling of identity. Most of them would receive Communion today and to receive the Host from his hands they were obliged to be in the state of grace. He was unworthy of them.

He bowed low and intoned the Confiteor, accusing himself of sin. He had accused himself thus in many Masses through the most innocent years of his priesthood. He was strongly aware now of the presence of God but, strangely, despite his own sense of unworthiness, he did not feel God's anger. A spirit moved in the Mass, a spirit of deep peace. He loved today's Mass, aware of the words he was saying as he was not always aware, aware of response from the altar boy, from the people in the church. When he raised his hand in blessing before he pronounced the *Ite Missa est*, he was neither justified in his acts nor absolved of sin but he was oddly at peace with himself.

He was weary again when he went back to the world. There was no opportunity to stretch, to compensate for even an hour of his lost sleep. He went to the *Catholic Star* and he did his job as a split personality; one person hammering at a typewriter mechanically or talking to people without thinking about them, the other person standing aloof and looking idly on, finding no reality in anything that was said or done. In the intervals when the two personalities merged, Gregory Lind longed for evening, for a quiet evening that would bring only duties that could be evaded.

At three-thirty his telephone rang. His brother Bart was on the line, gruff, abrupt, impatient with small talk, as he always was. There was an added note of belligerence in his voice which seemed to belong to this day.

"Gregory," he said. "I want to see you tonight. At my office. I have to go home first. Can you come out at eight?"

"I'd rather make it tomorrow, or another night."

"It wouldn't do. You can make the time later if you like."

Greg sighed. Later, or earlier, what difference did it make? "No," he said. "If you have to see me, eight will be all right."

"Good. I'll look for you."

Gregory stared at the phone after he had cradled the receiver. Bart was four years older than he was, and Bart had always had a tendency to dominate, but he could not recall when Bart had been as curt as he was today, or as downright uncompromising.

"Something is bugging him," he said.

There were always family problems, of course. Their mother did not often call Bart. She considered him unsympathetic. She would, however, be capable of calling him if she was bored or if she felt neglected or if she experienced a need for a fresh audience. She could quite possibly stir him up if she did call him. Bart, of course, had problems enough in his own family. Gregory had a twinge of conscience every time he thought of Bart's children. He never seemed to find time to do anything for any of them. He did not do anything for Bart, either, or for Barbara, Bart's wife. He had always liked Barbara, a frail and exceptionally pretty blonde girl who had given Bart four children. Janet, his sister, and Barbara were about the same age. They did not like each other. They did not get along at all. His mother, of course, followed along with Janet. The antagonisms created an awkward family situation even if one tried to stay clear of all conflicts.

Bart's headquarters were established in a suburb known as Stanhope. Bart had followed his father into the construction business and although John Lind had always worked for other people, Bart had his own company. Bart suffered, and always had, from a lack of capital but he had made a place for himself on the edges of the city. His construction work consisted mainly of suburban houses in rows and clusters. He was not very proud of them but the Lind houses were honestly built.

The headquarters building of the Lind Construction Company was off the road on the left as Greg drove into Stanhope. It was a two story brick building and there was a light behind one of the windows on the ground floor. Greg parked his car and walked in. Bart was sitting behind his desk. He was a big, broad-shouldered man with a heavy chin and a series of fine line scars on his left cheek. He raised his hand, almost mechanically, in greeting and waved to a chair. He lighted a cigarette slowly, deliberately, then extinguished the match in an ashtray, crushing it into the glass.

"Who was the woman last night, Greg?" he said.

"A friend of mine. A teacher at Guadalupe. Why?"

"She's more than a friend. She's more than a teacher at Guadalupe, too," Bart said. "I was at Cynthia's Kitchen last night. I saw how you looked at each other. Now, what in hell is it all about?"

"Frankly, I don't believe that it is any of your business."

"Think again! If you are blind enough to walk on the edge of scandal, that affects your whole family. You're a priest. You have no damned business batting around to night spots with a woman. You know that as well as I do. Now, what is she to you and what are you going to do about it?"

Gregory had asked that question of himself and had been unable to answer it. He had no answer now. "She is a lovely person, Bart," he said. "She is good company. A priest is not a statue in a corner of a church with votive lights burning in front of him; a priest is a human being."

"He is, is he?" Bart crushed out his cigarette and lighted another. "So, he's a human being? Well, he's not a woman-chasing human being. Not under any license in the book. Get that idea out of your head. Are you, for God's sake, going high school at your age? The one girl! The only girl! Hell. That nonsense belongs to the age when a man snaps at bait. A taste for honey takes him right into nature's backyard where he starts breeding babies for the good of the nation, and raising them and feeding them and educating them. That isn't for you."

"I didn't say it was."

"No. No man ever did. But men get themselves into it. Now you listen to me!" Bart leveled his lighted cigarette like a gun. "This girl may look like a fresh peach to you. Judging by the way you looked last night, you're panting after that body of hers right now. Her body isn't any more wonderful than yours or mine. She sweats and she gets pimples and she has a hell of a time once a month and she gets constipated and . . ."

"We got all of that stuff in the seminary."

Bart blinked, then banished the blink with a sweeping gesture of his heavy right hand. "Did you? O.K. I suppose you did. It's the truth. A man looks at a woman and all he thinks about is sex. The woman acts like that's all she's thinking about, too. Don't kid yourself! She knows exactly what she wants, and sex is the least of it. She'll take the sex part and maybe she will even enjoy it, but there's a lot else on her mind behind the baby blue eyes. One hell of a lot! A man, no matter how close he is to her, never knows what she's really thinking until she lets him know. Maybe she's laughing at him."

"I suppose that's true. Women are human beings. You act as though I've been living in a cave like a hermit. A priest knows a lot of people, and he knows a lot about people."

Bart sat deep in his chair, rocking it back. There was anger in his eyes. "I don't give a damn what a priest knows, or who he knows," he said. "I have to judge him by what he does. I watched you last night and I didn't like what I saw. You've been evading my question. What is that woman doing in your life?"

Gregory took a deep breath. "I don't know, Bart," he said. "Maybe I'm in love with her."

There was a silence in which that statement floated. Bart Lind was a study in arrested movement. His cigarette, halfway to his lips remained there motionless between his two fingers. His eyelids narrowed over his eyes and then his hand came up, completing the cycle of movement. He drew smoke into his lungs, letting it flow gently out between his lips.

"In love with her," he said slowly. "Lord God in Heaven! That's a choice you are offering yourself. A choice between God and her. Whoever, and whatever, she is, are you handing her your priesthood?"

"No. I told you that I don't know where I am with her. There is no reason why she would want anything I've got, no reason at all. I don't own anything. I don't have any money. There is no reason why a woman would be seriously interested in me. None. I told you that she is good company. She is. Maybe I need somebody who is good company. For a little while anyway."

Bart shoved his chair back violently. Standing, he was an impressive man; an inch over six feet, with no noticeable fat on him. He was wearing a blue suit with thin stripes in it. He walked the length of his office and walked back.

"You're kidding yourself," he said grimly, "or you are trying to do so. You know damned well what kind of good company a woman is for a man when they end up forty miles from home at night, with whiskey in their glasses. You're a priest. A celibate. You can't hold a woman's body in your hands at night and hold the body and blood of our Lord in those same hands the next morning." He punched his left palm with his broad right fist. "Companionship," he said softly. "Christ!"

Gregory wanted to get up and pace, too. He could feel the nervous tension tightening the muscles in his calves, in his back. It would be too ridiculous if they were both moving around in one small office. He envied Bart that big, powerful body that he had. It was an ancient envy. He had wanted to be as big as Bart when he was a small boy. He was nearly as tall but he had never been able to develop the muscles. He felt the old awe of Bart, the envy and the hero worship, whenever he was long around him. He was feeling it now, but he could not let himself be intimidated.

"It is just fine for you to talk about being a priest and a celibate," he said slowly. "I know that I had a vocation for the priesthood. I'm not certain that I had a vocation for celibacy. I'm not certain, either, that the two should be inseparable. Do you remember what celibacy is really like, or did you ever know?"

Bart stopped pacing. He stopped behind his desk and settled into his chair. His mouth was set in a hard, straight line. His eyes were fixed on his brother's face. Gregory leaned forward, his own right fist clenched.

"The simplest thing about celibacy is avoiding the women who like to tease the animals," he said. "Most of them good Catholic women! A man knows what that is and what he should do about it. He does it. He knows how to insulate himself, most of the time anyway, in the confessional. He works on staying in a group of women, not encouraging the loner who wants a confidential chat. His life is full of techniques. As I said, that is the easy part."

He thrust the words at Bart; intense, passionate, knowing this subject all too well. Bart listened to him, unblinking, moving only to light another of his interminable cigarettes.

"The hard part of celibacy is nights without sleep," Gregory said. "It is thoughts that come, perhaps at your own invitation, perhaps not; you can't always tell. Celibacy is nocturnal emissions, wet dreams; the awakening with a sense of shock, aware that your body, pent up too long, is automatically ridding itself of the seed that you never use. It is the momentary excitement of that shock and of the violent emission, followed by the doubt in your mind. Did I will that to happen? Did I think something, read something, open the door to evil? Is it evil? If it isn't, why not? It's the wasting of seed, isn't it? We thunder enough about that. The Church doesn't allow a husband to waste his seed if he can get babies with it."

Bart shook ash into the ashtray. There was no flicker of expression in his face. "Other priests go through the same thing, don't they?" he said.

"I suppose so."

"Other priests have been going through it for centuries?"

"Most of them, I guess."

"You don't guess. You *know*. There are priests who slip but they are exceptions. Nobody can tell me different. I've grown up in this church. I've known too many priests. I'm not a damned bit impressed with your speech on celibacy. You wouldn't have even thought like that before this woman entered your life."

Bart kicked the chair back again. He stood, leaning forward, his weight supported on his fist against the desk top.

"Now you listen to me," he said. "A married man has his wet dreams, too, for more reasons than I am going to go into. That's the least of it. You're willing to split things up now, aren't you? You'll take your vocation but not the celibacy. You'll be a priest and you'll have what the married man has, too. All right. Are you willing to take all that the married man has, the whole package?"

Anger was glowing in Bart's eyes. He did not wait for an answer to his question. He straightened his body, no longer leaning his weight on the desk.

"You don't take a woman, flop into bed with her when you want to romp," he said, "and put her away, out of sight, when you've got other things to do. You damn well don't. She's suddenly the big part of your life; all of her aches and pains and jealousies and her quaint ideas of how you should run your business. She's got needs and wants that you would never dream of. She's got an automobile and some other woman she knows has a better automobile; so she wants a better automobile. That goes for everything, stuff to wear, stuff in the home; everything. You're tired to the teeth and she wants to go to a party, or go dancing, or go to a show. She knows and likes the damnedest people, so you've got to know them and like them. Hell! She looks like an angel and you cannot, just cannot, imagine her doing a mean thing, a nasty thing, lying about anything . . ."

Bart stopped suddenly. He walked away from the desk and walked back. He snapped his fingers. "You could get the wrong idea out of that," he said. "Don't get the idea that I'm talking about my wife. I'm talking about women. I'm generalizing. Giving you the rough picture. I know how the family feels about Barbara. Hell, they all show it. That's Janet's fault. Barbara is worth any two women I've ever known. That includes my sisters."

Gregory nodded. The steam and the drive and the anger seemed to leave Bart in the moment when he turned defensive. Bart had, of course, been talking about Barbara. He was late in trying to cover up. He obviously knew that he had lost the point that he had been trying to make when he personalized his argument. He sat down heavily, took a cigarette, fumbled it in his big hand and failed to light it.

"I got carried away," he said. "I'm just sick at the idea that you might leave the priesthood, Greg. I couldn't sleep last night. I got up and walked around the goddamned bedroom like I've been prowling this office tonight. Barbara thought I was nuts. I had to tell her I had a toothache." He ran his hand, absently, through his hair. "In a way, it was the truth. I do have them."

Gregory met his eyes, sorry for him now. "I'm sorry," he said. "I've got a problem, too, Bart. No matter how you feel about it, I've got a problem. I'm trying to find my way through it. I haven't left anything. I am still a priest."

"Thank God for that." Bart's shoulders moved, seemed to contract.

He leaned forward. "Look, Fella, I'm on your side. I'm your brother. I talk rough. It's the way I live. I can't find smooth, polished things to say when I want them. I couldn't debate with you if that's what you wanted to do. I haven't the mind for it. I've had experience where you haven't had it. I tried to tell you what I knew. All wrong, maybe, but honest."

"I know that."

"Sure you do. Well, all it amounts to is that you've got the finest life a man can lead, the best job any man ever had. You're a Catholic priest. You should hear my kids, Greg. I guess Janet's kids are the same way. They tell other kids that their uncle is a priest. Proud! Hell, that gets to you. Then there's mother. She doesn't know I'm on earth. She doesn't give a damn really about Janet. She's the mother of a priest. That's her whole deal, all that her life comes down to; she's the mother of a priest."

"I know all that, Bart. It's part of my problem; a big part. People forget sometimes that maybe a man just can't do the job that they take such pride in, that he just can't do it."

Bart's face was suddenly without expression. He threw his unlighted cigarette away and took another from his pack. He lit this one.

"You did all right with the job until this woman came along," he said flatly. "Look! Suppose I admit that's none of my business. O.K. Then, I'll say this. I don't know the girl. She looked pretty from where I sat. O.K. Whoever she is, and whatever she is, she wants something. Women always want something, especially when they are around men. You don't rate yourself as having anything. Maybe this girl doesn't need the things you haven't got. Hell, I don't know; but she wants something. O.K. She's going to be sugar and cream in a time of roses until she gets what she wants. All you know about this girl right now is her sunny weather side. That's all she'll let you know."

Bart drew a deep breath. "So the bait is less than you think, Kid. The bait is less than you think. And being a priest is the greatest thing on God's wide earth. That's all of it from me. Let's go home."

– XIV –

A young white woman who lived in the northwest corner of Saint Anselm's parish was going to marry a Negro youth from Saint Francis de Sales parish. She wanted to be married in her own church and Father Schafer was upset about the situation. He took his concern to the breakfast table after the six o'clock Mass. Father Gregory Lind, accustomed to solitude at breakfast, was surprised to see him. The pastor had had a phone call from the girl's mother the night before.

"She approves of it," Father Schafer said. "She actually approves of her daughter marrying a Negro, or she says that she does. Same thing, I guess. A woman named Enswin, Mrs. Natalie Enswin. Widow probably. I never heard of her. We don't have her name on the parish records. The address she gave me is on Kilgallen Street, 818. You wouldn't know her, I suppose."

"No. That's a poor neighborhood. Some Spanish Americans live on Kilgallen. People down there are apt to stay off the parish records unless they get into trouble. They might be good Catholics at that."

"They might not be, too. I told that woman to have her daughter and the young man come to the rectory tonight at seven-thirty. I want you to be here. You talk to them. Negro-white marriages are wrong. Nothing but unhappiness in them. I don't want this marriage in my church."

"We can't tell them that."

The pastor frowned. He was obviously worried. His strong face was a mask of grim lines. "Try to influence them," he said. "The marriage is not in their own best interest. Try to make them see that, Father Lind. A journalist like yourself can find the suitable words if he has time to think about the problem. Seven-thirty tonight, remember."

The old man rose. He did not wait for acquiescence and he would not, of course, anticipate dissent. He was the pastor and an assistant did what he was told to do. Father Lind's breakfast had lost its flavor.

"What a nice little tea party that will be," he said.

The day brought its own problems, as all days did, and Father Lind forgot his "tea party" until the shadows moved in. He planned then to talk over the problem with Father Guyton before dinner. Father Guyton was elsewhere for the evening and that, Father Lind thought, left a journalist like himself very little time in which to find those suitable words which the pastor had suggested. He walked into the visitor's parlor at seven-thirty without anything in his mind that he could recognize as a suitable word.

The two young people were ten minutes late and delay gave the priest time in which to run through the facts on the two cards which the pastor had left for him. The girl was Mildred Enswin of Saint Anselm's parish, age nineteen. She had finished three years at Sacred Heart High School and was now employed as a beauty shop operator. The young man was Don Ballinger, twenty-two. He had graduated from Saint

Francis de Sales High School. A bell rang in Father Lind's brain. He had heard of Don Ballinger. He frowned, then he remembered. Don Ballinger had been a star football player, a standout in the Parochial League. The card said that he had taken courses at Zimmerman Business College and was now employed by Minelli Mercantile Company as an accountant.

The young people arrived at seven-forty without an apology for being late. Don Ballinger was a light-skinned Negro, only medium tall but broad in the shoulders, deep in the chest. He was neatly dressed in a gray suit. His necktie was gray with a broad green stripe. Mildred Enswin was light-haired but not exactly blonde. Her hair was long, falling to her shoulders and it was the first feature that one would notice. There was no life or sparkle to it. She was short, slightly overweight. Her eyes were blue and she had added eye shadow, quite a lot of eye shadow. Her face was round with no particular delineation of feature.

"Good evening," the priest said. "I am Father Gregory Lind."

Both of the young people were hostile, obviously carrying chips on their shoulders. Father Lind could understand that. People had probably given them a bad time. They were on the defensive. The young man introduced the girl and then himself.

"We're Catholics," he said, "both of us. We want to marry each other. We want the wedding here in Mildred's church. That is proper, isn't it?"

There was belligerence, challenge, to every line. Father Lind nodded. "It is indeed proper," he said. "The bride should be married in her own parish." He saw the scowl on the young man's face relax. "I remember you when you played football," he said. "I never met you but I saw you play many times. I always rooted against you, I'm sorry to say."

Don Ballinger's head came up. "Why?"

"You were a menace. I was a Cathedral rooter. I played for them once. Left Half. I was never All-Parochial back as you were. I wasn't that good."

"I was lucky," Don Ballinger said. He was an ex-football player talking to an older "ex" for a minute or two and he was relaxed; then he waved football away. "That's a long time ago," he said. "Now I'm going to be married."

"A lot of people are against us," the girl said. "Some people say we can't get married in the church, but we know they're wrong. Sister Marie Agatha says they're wrong. She's the one who introduced us."

Father Lind did not know Sister Marie Agatha but he thought about her. One of the worst after effects of the Vatican Council was the so-called freeing of the nuns. They were everywhere now, night and day, gaining community contact, communicating with citizens, broadening social horizons, meddling in everything. This nun evidently fulfilled her need for a social role in contemporary living by doing a little liberal, or ultraliberal, matchmaking. Father Lind felt suddenly that he was in agreement with the pastor on this whole affair.

"By saying that people are against you," he said gently, "I presume you mean that they do not approve of mixed marriages in color. The Roman Catholic Church has no rules against your marrying. It asks if you are Catholic, but makes no inquiry about your race or nationality."

"I knew it," the girl said. She had a sharp voice; whether from nervousness or keyed-up hostility, her voice was pitched too high.

"Those who do not approve the idea of your marrying each other are not necessarily against you," the priest said. "They may be trying to save you from unhappiness. You know, of course, that there are problems in any marriage. You would have many special problems added to the normal ones. You would have to accept the fact in advance that you are going to have hurts and humiliations, a great many limitations that will distress you."

"Why should we have?" the girl said. "We're human beings, citizens. We have the same rights that other people have."

"I wasn't speaking of what should be. I can speak only of what *is*. I would wish you ideal conditions of living but you have to face conditions as they are, attitudes as they exist."

Don Ballinger had been sitting quietly, his eyes fixed on the priest's face. "We know that, of course," he said. "We know that what you say is true. Mildred gets excited because she thinks that some things should not be." He drew a quick, short breath and his shoulders twitched. "We know we can't make quick changes in anything. We know we've got to take it if people don't understand us. We figure that we're pioneers. We're kind of proud of being pioneers."

Father Lind liked this young man. He did not like the girl. He wondered what the young man saw in her. That was futile wondering.

"Pioneers," he said thoughtfully. "Yes. I suppose you would be. You could think about that, perhaps, and be so carried away with the idea of being pioneers, of being different, that you would not give sufficient thought to more important things. It isn't really important whether you are pioneers or not; it *is* important that you lead honest, useful lives with a fair share of happiness. If you go into anything for the wrong reason, even if it is a great thing, you will end up disappointed."

"We haven't any wrong reasons," the girl said. "We love each other."

The young man leaned forward. "What are you trying to tell us, Father?"

"I have told you as a priest that there is no obstacle to your marriage in the Roman Catholic Church," he said. "I would like to tell you now, as a man and as someone who would like to be your friend, that I wish you would test your desire to marry, not plunge in. I wish that one of you could take a trip, that you could be apart for a while and look at the problems you would face in a marriage."

"We don't have to be apart. We have looked at the problems. Everyone tells us about the problems."

The girl's voice had edge. It was not a pleasant voice. Don Ballinger's eyes narrowed slightly. Father Lind nodded.

"You have looked at some of the problems, no doubt," he said, "but marriage is for life, till death parts you. You are attracted to each other now, strongly attracted. You are pulled by a sex magnet that won't pull so strongly a year from now. You will still have to depend on each other more than you realize now. There are a great many white people who will withhold friendship from you, who will disapprove of you; and a great many Negroes who will disapprove as strongly. You will have a difficult set of adjustments to make, and to keep on making. Maybe you will be strong enough to handle your problems and to be patient with each other."

"We will be," the girl said.

"I hope so. What about your children? They will have difficulty discovering where they belong. Will *they* be strong enough?"

"Father, are you telling us not to marry each other?" Don Ballinger said.

"No. I have no right to tell you that. I am merely asking you to wait for a while, and I hope that you will pray for guidance while you are waiting."

"No!" Mildred Enswin's fists were clenched. "We have waited long enough. We want to be married. We want to be married in this church, Saint Anselm's church. That's why we came here. We want to set a date."

The priest looked at the young man who hesitated a moment before he nodded. "That's right, Father," he said. "We want to set a date."

Father Lind took a pad of forms from his pocket. He was remembering his brother's voice from last night. A woman always wanted something, Bart said. It would be interesting to know what Mildred Enswin wanted, or thought she wanted. Whatever it was, she would serve that want with a degree or two of fanaticism. There would be little relaxation in her.

"We will have to set a date after Lent," Father Lind said. "Now, let us see what date would be best for all concerned."

Later, after the two people had gone, Father Lind went out and walked around the block. This nuptial Mass would be his to say. He would hear these people recite their vows and he would bless them. He was not happy about it. The matter of racial difference was a big stumbling block, a strain on any marriage, but he was not feeling either racial prejudice or racial loyalty. Of these two people, he liked the young Negro and had grave reservations about the girl who was white. He completed his walk and turned in at the church.

The sexton would lock the church at nine. At this moment it was empty. A few votive candles burned before the image of the Blessed Mother and the sanctuary lamp glowed red above the main altar. There was a deep hush, a sense of suspended presence. He walked down the side aisle on the gospel side, genuflected and entered a pew. He did not kneel. He sat in the pew as he would sit in a chair if he visited a friend's home. He was facing the Blessed Mother's altar. The white image stood in shadow.

"The shocking truth is that I was talking to myself tonight when I spoke to those two young people," he whispered. "The saving grace is that I did not know that I was talking to myself until afterward."

He looked at the dancing candle flames. He had told these young people to wait, to separate for a time and to seek perspective, to face the difficulties that were inevitable, not to skip lightly over those difficulties. He had told them that they were responding to a sex magnet which would not be as strong in a year. He had told them that neither whites nor Negroes would welcome them as a couple. This couple would not accept his advice. They were going ahead, two people against intolerable odds, into a marriage.

Where did they differ from Pamela and himself? He and Pam were, of course, both white; but he was a Catholic priest and she was an agnostic divorcee. He and Pam, it might be said, were not planning to marry. What were they planning? Where were they going? Why couldn't they do what he had advised two young people to do? Why couldn't they get away from each other and gain perspective? Simple, orderly, reasonable procedures were invincible when one put them into words and inoperable, seemingly, when launched in the churning seas of emotion. He was a disciplined man, a man capable of seeing clearly and of stating inevitables, a man who had developed strength in battles against innumerable temptations, a man of prayer. Why couldn't he resolutely put Pamela out of his life, or remove himself from hers?

He sat in the pew with questions in his mind and no voice spoke to him. There was no need for a voice. He could see clearly what he should do, what he must do—and he did not move. He could not do it.

The candle flames flared and diminished in turn as some draft from a hidden source moved in the church. Light touched the white image and receded. The glimpses of white in shadow were like brief views of a road. There was a road, of course. Father Gregory Lind could see it leading off into darkness, and himself walking it. He was walking away from his priesthood, from his faith, from his family, from his position in the community, from the respect of his fellow men. He knew where he was, and he could see what he was leaving, but he could not see where the road led.

"Madness," he said.

He rose and left the church. The rectory was quiet. He did not know if Fathers Schafer and Guyton were out or if they had already retired. He did not care. He sat at a desk downstairs and wrote a report on Don Ballinger and Mildred Enswin for the pastor. He went to bed, then, and refused resolutely to think of his problems. His mind, with nothing else to do, went to sleep.

The night was still black beyond his window when he awakened. There was no sound of traffic, of human motion. He lay on his back and blinked at the ceiling, or at where the ceiling should be. Everything was suddenly simple, obvious, inevitable.

"She is myself," he said. "She is the other half of myself, as I am half of her. We are indivisible. I cannot stay where she cannot be. We have to go, wherever we go, together. If I had never discovered her, if I did not know that she existed, I could have been half happy; entirely a priest, perhaps, but never more than half a person. Now that I know, I can't turn back. The reason that it is impossible is that no man can walk away, leaving half of himself in the road."

In the dark of the room, on the edge of sleep, it all seemed remarkably clear.

– XV –

Gregory Lind saw Pamela at Guadalupe House during the week. They spoke briefly in corridor encounters but there was no more than that.

He did not know what to say to her, and that seemed absurd. There was no place in a city the size of Culverton to which he could escort her. He could not wear the Roman collar and go anywhere with her, and he had no right to go anywhere in layman's garb. She could no longer invite him to her apartment, so she had to leave the initiative to him. He did not know what to do with that initiative. He had not told her that Bart had seen them on the evening they had shared in Jerome. Finally, the initiative slipped away from him and Pamela took it.

On Friday evening she stopped in his office after she closed her classes. "I would like you to see my family's home," she said, "and to meet my mother. Could you make it on Sunday afternoon?"

He hesitated. "I have a Sunday obligation as a rule," he said. "I usually visit my mother."

"Could you cut the visit short for once, or do you want to do so?"

"You know that I want to. Yes. I could cut it a bit. What time?"

"Drinks in the sun room. Five. Five-thirty. Old family custom. My father probably will not be there. He will probably be sitting around the club after eighteen holes. Just you and mother and me."

"Fine. I'll aim for five."

"That will be perfect." She turned toward the door, then turned back. "You won't wear the uniform, of course. Jacket and slacks will be fine. Mother will try to discover what you do and where you fit in. Don't tell her anything. Just politely confuse her."

They smiled at each other and the smile was the intimacy of the week. "I'll make myself hard to place," he said.

"Do."

She waved her hand at him, palm turned outward, fingers straight up, and went striding down the corridor. He gathered the memos of his evening counseling. He had follow-up work to do on most of the cases, people to see or phone calls to make. He fitted the sheets of paper and the small cards into the tough brown dime-store envelope which he used as a briefcase. He would think about those problems again ultimately and he would do whatever had to be done about them, but at the moment his mind was far away from them.

It would be interesting to see the home that was Pamela's background. He was not certain that he would be at ease with Pamela's mother, despite all the flattering things which Pamela said of her. The Gibsons lived in a world he seldom touched, a world of wealth and comfort and country clubs. He would not be ill at ease in that world but he would not have much in common with its people.

There was, of course, the exception and the contradiction; Pamela herself.

The Sunday omens were good. He had dinner at Janet's and there was less friction than usual. It was a sunny day and his mother was in better humor, with few complaints. She had such days and he was glad that this was one of them. There was no serious objection raised when he said that he would have to leave a bit early because of a meeting. No one asked what the meeting was, nor where. This was, he assured himself, a meeting; at least, in a sense, it was a meeting. He had not lied so much as he had evaded truth.

"Which is a hell of a nasty distinction," he thought.

He drove the River Parkway, south-southwest, following the river in its bending course. The Gibson home was built on a hill, four miles beyond the city limits. There were stone pillars topped with images of solemn griffins, a curving driveway and then the house.

The house was a vision of white columns rising from a bricked terrace floor to a second-story roof; of third-story dormer windows; of a classical doorway with fan steps. Pamela completed the vision by appearing in the doorway as Gregory stepped out of his car.

"Bravo," he said. "I expected a butler."

"Not on Sunday afternoon. There is a butler, however. Do you mind?"

"Not particularly."

Pamela was wearing a blue dress with fine line strips of red at the neckline, at the edge of the one pocket, and at the cuffs. It was the simplest dress that he had ever seen on her and he knew instinctively that it was the best.

"I was watching for you," she said. "One can see the road curve into the gate when one sits in the sun room. Mother is eager to meet you. Mainly because she is curious." She paused. "That jacket is new, isn't it?"

"Yes. So are the slacks."

"Nice."

He did not tell her that he had bought them only yesterday and that he had inspired cries of anguish at the store by insisting on having them last night. They had cost him a big hole in small savings. He could not mention that, either.

He had a swift, confused impression of the house; high ceilings, white pillars and columns, stately hall doors, a room with walls of Pompeian red, a drawing room with an immense Chinese rug. The sun room was like an oval bubble at the rear of the house. It commanded a view of the river through the trees and, as Pamela said, one arc of the road that seemed quite distant. Winter still lingered over the landscape and there was an evening haze which blurred detail.

"Carina," Pamela said, "this is Greg Lind."

The woman in the big chair seemed too young to be Pamela's mother. She looked up at Greg and extended her hand, a slender right hand with rings on two of the fingers. She lifted her head when she looked upward. She had a long slender neck. Her hair was dark, almost black, and she had sharply penciled eyebrows. Her mouth was as vivid as Pamela's with, seemingly, less lipstick. Her eyes were a deep, vivid blue.

"It is good of you to join us, Mr. Lind," she said. "Pamela and I were growing tired of each other. You drink, I hope."

"If you waited for me, I am glad that I do."

"We waited for you," Pamela said.

She moved to a portable bar and when Gregory would have joined her, she waved him back. "I can do simple bartending," she said. "Entertain my mother. Try her name for an opener. She thinks she is the only woman in the world who is named after a constellation."

"I do not. I merely hope that I am."

"Carina?" Greg said.

"Yes. How did you know?"

"I heard Pamela call you that a minute ago."

"That's right. She always does. Did you ever know anyone named Carina?"

"Never. It sounded like a pet name, or a family code."

He did not mention the bell which rang in his brain when he heard that name. He did not know anything about the constellation but there was a Saint Carina who was the mother of Saint Antoninus. This was obviously not the time or the place to mention that.

Pamela brought the drinks and winked at him when she served his. No one clung to the discussion of names. Names had served simply as an opening conversational gimmick and they had served admirably. Greg was relaxed. He had been tense in facing the meeting with Pam's mother. Pam had made her sound formidable; obviously without intending to do so.

Actually, Carina Gibson was as casual as Pam. She had the same soft carrying voice that Pam had. It would be difficult, he thought, to tell them apart on the telephone. There was the same clarity, too, the same sparkling diction. He was aware of her eyes. She watched him while not appearing to do so.

Carina spoke easily of many things, one subject flowing into another. She timed her pauses after the name of a person or a place, giving him an opportunity to come in. He enjoyed the game, dropping his comments where she did not expect them, where they told her nothing. She obviously knew nothing about him or about his background, and she wanted to know. She would not ask questions. When she mentioned the Oberwitte family she penetrated his guard. She read immediately the signal, whatever it was, that revealed his familiarity with the name.

"You know them?" she said. "The Oberwittes?"

"Yes. Of course. Not well. Carl's death was a shocking tragedy."

"Indeed it was. I hadn't seen Carl since he was a little boy." She paused and when Gregory did not say how well he had known him, her voice moved on. "My husband and I are not Catholics," she said, "but we attended the Mass. We felt that we should."

"So did I."

Gregory had been aware of Pamela's tensing from the moment that the Oberwittes were mentioned. He looked calmly at the woman who had attended the Mass and wondered what she would say if he told her that he had been one of the three priests at the altar. She had not noticed, or remembered, which made her performance average.

"You remind me of someone," Carina Gibson said. "It's like a name on the tip of my tongue."

There was a thoughtful expression in her eyes and she held her head tilted slightly to one side. She tapped a cigarette against the back of her hand and Greg rose to light it for her. He might have been premature, he thought, in writing off her powers of observation. He did not look at Pam.

"I'm pretty average," he said. "I can walk into a clothing store and take a perfect fit off the rack."

"Youth," Carina said. "You won't be able to do it in ten years. But that's not what is moving around in my memory. Not costume. Not size." She turned to Pamela. "What is it, Pam? Where did I see Mr. Lind before?"

"You didn't. Not as far as I know. He's from out of town. Chillicothe."

That, Gregory thought, was a quick diversion. He remembered telling Pam where he had been born. Carina raised her eyebrows.

"Chillicothe," she said.

A door closed noisily somewhere and there was a sound of heavy footsteps. A big, bronzed man came into the sun room. The spirit of the out-of-doors seemed to enter with him. Greg rose. The other man, he guessed, was at least three inches taller than he was. Pam introduced them and they shook hands with perfunctory friendliness. This was *the* Gibson, Ralph Gibson. The big man sat in the chair beside Carina, which seemed to be waiting for him. He looked around.

128

"Everyone seems to need a drink, Pam," he said, "and God knows I do."

Pam moved to the bar. "Coming right up."

Carina lighted a fresh cigarette, not waiting for masculine aid. "You must have taken the boys for money on those eighteen holes," she said.

"What makes you think so?"

"You're in such good humor."

"Completely irrelevant. I am always in good humor. As a matter of fact, I did win a few dollars. No sense in playing golf for mere exercise."

Greg studied Pamela's father with genuine interest. Here was a personality which took over a room as she claimed that her mother did. Ralph Gibson was easy, relaxed, impressive. With Culverton just beginning to emerge from winter, it was difficult to explain his rich skin tone unless he used a sun machine. He probably did. His scalp was bronzed, too. The only hair he had was over his ears, two white strips. It was difficult to imagine him with hair. He had a cheerful grin, excellent teeth, and features that seemed roughly assembled. If one subtracted the affability, the air of genial ease, this would be a definitely homely man. He took a deep swallow from the glass which Pamela gave him, turned the glass in his hand, looking at it, then lifted his eyes to Gregory.

"Lind!" he said. "It's a name that one doesn't see very often. Are you, by any chance, related to Bart Lind?"

"He's my brother. Do you know him?"

Greg felt that this was dangerous territory, but how could one avoid it? He had seen Pamela's eyes widen. She hadn't ever heard of Bart. The subject had never come up. There were so many things!

"Yes. I know him," Ralph Gibson said slowly. "Not well. My brother, Ted, would know him much better. I am interested in these young men who are building, and rebuilding our city."

Ralph Gibson took another swallow of his drink. "Your brother interests me particularly because he is a man of integrity and of poor return on his investment. I have a meddlesome urge to straighten him out."

"How?"

"It doesn't matter really. There is no reason why he should pay any attention to me. He's doing what he wants to do. Still!"

Ralph Gibson leaned toward Greg. "There are really only two ways to build houses, Mr. Lind, and to make money building them. The best way is to build fine houses for people who can afford the finest. When you do that, you build churches and a lot of other interesting things, too. It takes capital, a lot of capital."

The women did not try to speak when this man was holding the floor and it did not seem to occur to him that he might be interrupted. Obviously, one did not interrupt him.

"The other way," he said, "is to build cheap houses, a lot of cheap houses, and to build them cheaply. Your brother is building houses for the cheap-house market but he isn't building them cheaply; not cheaply enough. The extras he adds are, mostly, out of what should be his profit. He can't add them to his list because he's selling to cheap-house buyers. You can't compromise in building. You are one thing or another; not somewhere in the middle."

"I guess you are right."

"I know I am right." Ralph Gibson emptied his glass. "I should have asked first, of course, before I sounded off. Are you in your brother's firm?"

"No. I'm not."

"I don't place you. What are you then?"

The question, from some men, would have seemed impertinent or prying, but not from Ralph Gibson. He was expressing an older man's interest in a younger man who happened to be his guest. Greg Lind was sorry that the question had been asked. This was not fencing with a lady, this was direct inquiry. Whether he ever saw Ralph Gibson again, or not, he could not have a lie standing between them.

"I am a Roman Catholic priest, Mr. Gibson," he said.

"A priest!" Ralph Gibson chuckled at a bad joke; then the chuckle died as he realized that this was not a joke, bad or otherwise. He straightened in his chair, then lunged to his feet. "A Catholic priest!" he said. "In those clothes? Out with my daughter! Drinking in my house! You get the hell out of here—and as fast as you can make it!"

Pamela was on her feet, too. "He doesn't have to get out," she said. "He is my guest, not yours."

"If he doesn't get out quick, I'll throw him out," Ralph Gibson said.

Greg looked at Pam. Her eyes were opened wide, the corners of her mouth drawn down. "I'm sorry, Pam," he said.

Carina was staring at him. Her expression could only be described as horrified fascination. She was probably remembering now where she had seen him. He bowed to her, repeated his "Sorry" and strode away through the rooms and the great hallways to the door. He was about to enter his car when Pamela ran out. He stood and waited for her.

"Why? Why did you do that?" she said. "Why did you tell him? Why did you stand in the middle of that room, bellowing that you were a priest?"

There was anger in her eyes, in her voice, in the poise of her body, the clenching of her fists. He had never seen this side of Pamela; the tightening of her eyebrows, the forward thrust of her chin.

"Your father asked a question," he said. "I gave him the only answer I had."

"It wasn't necessary. You didn't have to tell him anything. He was only making conversation. You put me in an awful spot. I trusted you. I asked you out here because I trusted you. You let me down."

She was still tense with anger and she was, he thought with a sense of shock, childish. Her features seemed sharper and the music was gone from her voice.

"I didn't mean to let you down," he said.

"You did. You made everything impossible." Her face seemed to break up and there were sudden tears in her eyes. "Impossible," she repeated.

She turned away and half ran up the path to the house. Greg Lind watched her go. She was, he thought, running out of his life and there was nothing that he could do to stop her. This was how a story ended. One time or another, it had to end in some such way as this.

He drove back to the city and he felt alone as he had not been alone in many weeks. He lay on his narrow bed, staring at the ceiling and he saw again the anger in Pam's face. There had been shock in seeing it, in recognizing childishness and unreasonableness in her attitude. There was shock still, in reliving the scene. Then, the tears! He had seen many women cry. A priest dealt often with the material out of which tears are made. He had never associated tears with Pamela before this; not in his thought of her, the pictures in his mind, or the living reality. He had the urge to reach out to her but she was not there, not any place in his life.

"How could she be?" he thought. "It is absurd that she ever was. You saw that place out there. Acres of it! That is her life. That is her background. That is where she belongs."

He tried to leave her there and he could not. The heaviest work load of the year was moving in on him but he did not release Pamela from his mind in the doing of it. He did not make any serious effort to banish her and he had periods of impatience with himself, with his lack of resolution, with his inability to accept what was obviously best for both of them.

There were only two weeks left in Lent. Next Sunday would be Palm Sunday. There would be few open spots now on the schedule of a parish priest, even if he was only partially a parish priest. The *Catholic Star* Easter edition was the largest edition of the year and most of the deadly routine of it was Gregory Lind's. He had to miss Guadalupe House on Monday night. He wondered if Pam would expect him, look for him, credit his absence to herself. He had the impulse to call her on Monday and again on Tuesday but he resisted it. He did not want merely to talk to her; he wanted to see her.

He cleared his desk and went to Guadalupe House on Wednesday night. There was one young man awaiting him, a young man with the familiar problem of discouragement. The young man was tired and it was too much to work in the day and to study at night. Father Lind gave him time and let him talk himself out of the feeling of defeat. When the young man left, Gregory Lind sat alone for a few minutes. He played with a pencil, spinning it in his fingers, then tossed it down on the desk top and walked the corridor to the typing room.

A short, heavy girl was dictating to the class, a cheerful girl who wore glasses. "I am Emily Nugent, Father," she said. "I am filling in for Miss Gibson. Is there anything I can do for you?"

"No, thank you. I was just looking around. Where is Miss Gibson?"

"I don't know. I used to work with her. She called me and asked me to sub for her this week. She didn't say where she was going."

Gregory Lind returned to his office. There was no one waiting for him and he welcomed the solitude. He looked at the telephone. His instinct had been sound on Sunday when she turned and ran away from him. He had seen her then as running out of his life and he had been unable to stop her. He reached for the telephone, hesitated, then gripped the receiver firmly. He dialed Pam's number and listened to the ring signal, imagining the bell ringing in the apartment that he knew so well. There was no answer. He called again from a pay station on the way home with the same result. He kept trying, at odd hours, during the next few days and finally he conceded. Pamela had gone away, out of town, back to her father's home, somewhere, and if she had wanted to hear from him she would have told him, in some way, how to reach her.

Palm Sunday opened Holy Week, a week of great solemnity, a week of extra services. Christianity's greatest story was re-enacted in the single week; the agony of Christ in the Garden, his trial, crucifixion and resurrection from the dead. Men and women who had not come to confession all year were in the long lines before the confessionals and most of them were from other parishes. They came to Saint Anselm's because it was a quiet, pleasant church and close to downtown, a church where they were not known. It was easier to make one's confession in a strange church, rather than in one's own, when one had been long away. Bedridden parishioners of Saint Anselm's phoned the rectory and priests went out to hear their confessions. Priests brought them communion, too. It was something that priests did all year, of course, but as Easter approached, there were more people asking for the sacraments, a quickening of the spiritual forces. On Good Friday, for the three-hour services in the afternoon, the church was crowded, lines of people standing in the vestibule.

During the long week, Father Gregory Lind lived through a unique spiritual experience of his own. He heard confessions but he did not go to confession. He was, by all the rules he had been taught, the rules which he applied to penitents in his box, a sinner, a grievous sinner, an enemy of God. It was a fact of his faith. If he could accept the fact, he would be unable to say a Mass, consecrate the bread and wine, counsel sinners in the confessional. He would stand in terror before the throne of God—and he did not.

He could not, in honesty, return to his Franciscan confessor. He lacked the essential ingredient of a good confession. A man should hate his sin as an offense against God and resolve never to repeat it. He could not do that. He could not regret knowing Pam nor hate any minute he had spent with her. He could not piously resolve to avoid her, to stay away from her, to wrench her out of his life. She *was* out of it but if she came back, he would not regard her as a source of sin. She was the other half of himself. He had accepted that strange idea as truth one night and it was still truth to him. There were fires within them, or magnets, which drew them together and welded them. He had periods during which Reason, or what he called Reason, took over. He could see clearly then the wide gap which existed between two people who had chosen to be close. He could see clearly the economic and social and religious absurdity of two such people as Pam and himself ever hoping to be and to share, to live and to die together. It was all impossible. They had no place to which they could go for even an hour. There were too many people, too many rules, too many circumstances against them. And yet?

He faced the problem whole, and in part through Holy Week. He was gentle, but firm, with the sinners in his confessional, sharing their confusion and their humility, offering his firmness as a reinforcement to their wills. He prayed alone in the church and he prayed at night in his room. He brought love to his Masses, love of the Mass and of all that it represented, and he preached simply, feelingly, sincerely. He was a man about to embark upon a journey and these were the beloved associations of his home.

On Easter Sunday, Father Gregory Lind said three Masses. He went to his sister Janet's home for dinner and he was a cheerful guest. The dinner party needed cheer. His mother was in one of her sad-sweet moods; speaking, without detail, in a soft voice about "remembering happier Easters." He helped Janet and Joe and the children to enjoy their day, he joked with his mother and teased her and paid her extravagant compliments. When evening came, he went to his brother Bart's house.

Bart was bluff and cheerful; Barbara was startlingly pretty. Looking at Barbara, and talking to her, Greg could not help wondering what was wrong, or missing, in her marriage and Bart's. She was a lovely girl, a very feminine girl who even played up to a priest brother-in-law; Bart was bitter about women and Janet actively disliked Barbara. It was strange. A man had no answers for riddles of that kind; at least, a man who was a priest had no answers. When it was time to leave, Barbara kissed him, as she always did, a sisterly kiss; Janet, who was his sister, obviously did not feel right about kissing a priest, and never did. Bart walked out to his car with him.

"Is everything O.K. with you?" he said.

"Yes. Just fine."

"Good. I'm glad to hear it."

That was all. Two men might remember a stormy session and leave it in the past where it belonged, leaving with it the issue which had sparked the stormy session. Women, perhaps, could not do that.

Before he went to bed, Gregory wrote to his two married sisters out of town: Agnes in Palo Alto and Anne in Scranton. They seldom heard from him but, then, they seldom wrote to him. He walked around the room when he finished the letters, picking things up and laying them down, rearranging the books in his bookcase. When the hour was late, Easter night was as quiet as any other night. He stretched and turned in.

The *Catholic Star* was experiencing a holiday hangover on Monday, with nothing going right and nobody caring. Guadalupe House on Monday night was lively. It had been closed during Holy Week and the students were cheerful after the one-week break, seemingly glad to be back. Gregory walked down the corridor to the typing room. Pamela was on duty again. He stood in the doorway and she came to him. She took her time but she came. There was inquiry in her eyes but she waited for him to speak.

"I would like to see you tonight after classes," he said.

"Do you think that wise?"

"I don't care, really, if it is or it isn't."

Pam seemed listless. Her shoulders moved slightly, a half shrug. "All right. You could come to the apartment, I guess."

134

"No. Not the apartment. If you drive your car home, I'll drive after you and pick you up."

She hesitated, looking away from him. "I'll leave here at nine-ten," she said.

It was a mild, clear evening. Pamela parked her car around the corner from 751 Steuben Drive at nine-thirty and stepped into Greg Lind's car. He drove over the hill, then southward to Downing Park. There was a paved overhang which commanded a view of the roofs of town with the river in the distance. There were only two other cars parked there and Greg stayed clear of them. There was a waning moon, a cloud cover that obscured all but a few stars, an arc of city lights below the wall of the lookout point. There was a magic of location but Pam sat well over on her own side of the car.

She was not making it easy for him. He fixed his attention on a distant light. "I may have let you down, Pam," he said slowly, "but I love you. I want you to know that. I have never said that to another woman."

He heard her stir in the seat beside him but she did not speak. He felt detached, distant from her, distant from himself, a voice speaking in a darkness that was surrounded by light. He turned slowly toward her.

"There is something else that I want you to know," he said. "I have not told anyone else yet. I am leaving the priesthood."

"No!"

Pam straightened and her head came up. "You can't," she said. "It's your life. It's more than that. It's you. It's the way you express yourself. It's the way you relate to other people. If I hadn't come along, you were all right in it. I upset things. I didn't give you enough to balance what I upset. I couldn't. I can't. You must not leave it. You'd be lost."

"I've thought about all of that, Pam. I've looked at myself. I could face a sin in my life, a wrong to others, and be sorry for it and renounce it. I could put it out of my life and be a priest still. I cannot be sorry for what you have meant to me, or renounce as sin the loveliest experience in my life. I cannot love you and love that experience and be a priest. Priesthood demands from me something that I no longer have to give it."

"I am still your problem, your only problem," Pam said. "I've looked at myself, too. I went away. I went up to Chicago. I saw a few shows, I shopped in stores, I sat in a hotel room and wrote words on sheets of paper, and tore them up. I do not belong in your life. I could see that clearly. I am bad for you, Greg. I'm staying out of your life from now on. I'm staying away from you. I'm quitting Guadalupe House. I may leave town."

Either one of them could have reached with a hand and touched the other, but neither of them moved. Greg found his distant light again and fixed his eyes on it.

"I'm the one who will be leaving town, Pam," he said. "I'll have to see what kind of a living I can earn in the world. I don't know. I've never tried, naturally. I have no money. I have nothing at all.to offer you. In a year, perhaps, if it works out O.K., I'll come back looking for you."

"Would you?"

"Certainly. You know I would."

Pamela threw her arms around him, her head against his chest. She held him tightly and Greg could feel the tremor that swept through her. She was crying and he patted her shoulder. He had no words for tears. Pamela let go of him and lifted her head. She brushed one hand across her eyes.

"Do you think I'd let you leave your priesthood and go off alone for a year, with no money and no job?" she said.

"You will have to let me."

"I won't. You listen to me!" She gripped his right hand with both of hers. "I'll go anywhere you go—and I'll start anytime you start." She straightened her body. "And I love you. I will always love you."

He held her in his arms and he could feel the warmth in her body, the beating of her heart. "You don't know," he said. "You don't know what it's like to have no money."

"I could learn. I don't really have any money of my own now. I'll tell you about that sometime. No capital. No income. I work. That's unimportant. I think you should remain a priest. If you don't, if you leave and you go somewhere, I want to be with you. I belong with you. If we've got something to prove, we'll prove it together."

"I'd like that. But I'd be afraid for you."

"Why?"

He did not try to answer her. He held her and the lights hazed in his eyes. He had not expected this, any of this. Tonight was to be good-bye. His leaving the priesthood had not hinged on Pam. He had reached his final decision when there was nothing between them. He would never have asked her to leave with him, gamble with him. He had not held even a faint possibility of that in his mind. If life never held another thing, he told himself, tonight was enough. He kissed her fingers, one at a time.

"When do we go?" she asked.

"You shouldn't. I can't linger long. I'll tell everyone tomorrow. After that, the sooner I leave, the better. Is the end of the week too soon?"

"It is soon; probably not 'too.' But yes. I can make it. Where are we going?"

"I don't know."

"Good. We'll figure it out."

"And another thing." He turned her body, gripping her shoulders. Her eyes raised to his. Her eyes seemed very dark when normally they were gray or green. "We'll have to get a license and arrange for someone to marry us. I can't make it big or gay or festive for you. It can't even be in a church unfortunately."

"Are you proposing?"

The question disconcerted him. He loosened his grip on the girl, then tightened it again. "Yes," he said. "Yes. I am. We always do things backward, don't we? That should have come first. I'm sorry. Pam, will you marry me?"

Her voice, slightly shaky, came up to him. "I'll marry you, Greg," she said, "or live with you. I'll go anywhere in the world with you, and do anything you want me to do . . . just so long as you keep on loving me."

– XVI –

There was tomorrow.

Father Gregory Lind said the six o'clock Mass, knowing that his right to say it was debatable and sharply aware of the fact that this would be his last Mass. He sat in the pastor's study, facing Father S. K. Schafer, within a half hour after he left the sanctuary. The pastor's heavy face seemed to grow heavier, grimmer, sterner as he listened to his assistant's declaration of intention. A priest charged to his direction and to his care was calmly telling him that he was about to leave the priesthood, in effect that he was leaving the Church, that he was about to attempt marriage with a woman.

"I do not intend to see Bishop McKone," Father Lind said. "I have met him many times but he does not know me. There would be no point in seeing him. I cannot ask him for anything that is in his power to give."

"This woman," Father Schafer said, "is she pregnant?"

"No, Father."

137

"Thank God for that. I tell you what I'll do. I'll get in touch immediately with an abbot who is a friend of mine. You'll go to his monastery and you'll stay at his discretion. You'll do penance, as you should, and none of it will be easy, but it will be the saving of your priesthood and of your immortal soul."

"No, Father."

"Think on it. You're in the grip of a madness, a madness of the senses. That madness passes, either with the woman or without her. Think of your years as a priest, the powers and the privileges. You're a good priest, Father Lind. Think on that. You can't choose a woman over the life that is yours in the Church, walking daily with Christ Himself and doing the work He has called you to do. You can't do it."

"It isn't a choosing. A great many people are going to see it as that. It isn't that simple. I did not—ever—weigh one life against another or consider for a moment that I could choose anyone in preference to God Himself. It's a change in me. I've discovered that I can no longer serve as a priest. I lack something that I once had; I have something else that I never had. I may be responsible for the change in myself but I didn't make a choice."

"God help you," Father Schafer said. "Will you give the monastery one week?"

"It would be no use. I've already given the monastery several weeks, right here in this rectory. I've been all over it and through it, in prayer and out of prayer, and I have to do as I told you. I have to leave."

Father Schafer sat with his head bowed. "You leave me no alternative. I will have to report your decision to Bishop McKone. Until I do, I will accept your decision in his name. Once I have accepted it, you are in suspension as a priest. You may not perform any priestly function. You understand that?"

"Yes, Father."

"Do you want me to accept your decision?"

"I do."

"Accepted."

Father Schafer rose. His face did not soften. "I do not suppose you have any money," he said.

"Very little."

"Well, I can do little about that. You may, however, stay here until you have completed such plans as you have in mind. I shall make no announcement on your change of status until I hear from the bishop."

Gregory Lind, too, was standing. The grim face before him was still grim but he wondered what had prevented him from knowing, and

138

valuing his pastor. Something in the pastor, he supposed, and something in himself.

"I am grateful for that," he said. "You have been very good to me, very understanding."

"I don't understand you at all," Father Schafer said gruffly. "You are a great disappointment to me, but you have been a good priest. Be off with you now. My prayers will follow you."

Gregory Lind was crossing the hall to the stairs when Father Guyton returned to the rectory after saying the seven o'clock Mass. "Hel-lo," Father Guyton said. "Come in and have some breakfast with me. I haven't seen much of you lately."

"I'll have coffee. I want to talk to you, but I'll save it till after breakfast."

"Nonsense. I absorb bad news beautifully with bacon and eggs. I never miss a bite."

"Good for you. How do you know I have bad news?"

"Easy guess. You look it, and you have been acting it for a long time."

Mrs. Wagner served them coffee. She brought bacon and eggs to Father Guyton while Gregory was telling him of his decision. Tom Guyton spread butter on a corner of toast.

"I knew you were in for it and that there was a woman somewhere in the picture," he said. "I was hoping that you would work it out and stay in the trenches."

"There was only one way to work it out—for me, that is."

"I doubt that. I'm utterly unsympathetic to your point of view. I will always have a quarrel with celibacy and I may even write articles attacking it, but I shall remain a celibate. I cannot put myself in the place of a man who is willing to leave the priesthood."

"You are, perhaps, fortunate."

"I know that I am. Damned fortunate." Father Guyton had lived up to his own claim. He was eating his breakfast with evident enjoyment. "My lack of sympathy with your reasoning and motivation does not lessen my sympathy for you," he said. "Is there anything that I can do for you?"

"Nothing, thanks. The pastor has invited me to stay here until I'm oriented."

"Unfrocked?"

"In a sense. I have no priestly duties."

"Somebody will draw your six o'clock Mass. I hope that he gets some missionary to do it. I like seven." Father Guyton buttered the last of his toast. "Who is the girl, by the way?"

Gregory hesitated, then decided that it could make no difference. It was not a secret that could be kept. "Pamela Gibson. She's the daughter of Ralph Gibson."

"Yes. I remember." Father Guyton's eyebrows lifted. "She was married to Rodney Keller. Messy divorce."

"I don't want to hear about that."

"That's all right. It wasn't her fault as I remember. Still? A divorce is a divorce is a divorce. You know where you will put yourself with the Church if you marry her?"

"I know."

"It will hit you eventually. Hard! Even a lot of money won't balance it."

"There isn't any money. That is, Pamela doesn't have any."

Father Guyton looked off into space. He shrugged and took a final swallow of coffee. "Greg," he said, "I'll see you again before you shove off. I hate to see you go and I wish you would change direction at this last moment, but keep me posted with addresses and I'll write. I'll send you such news as we have."

"Thanks, Tom. I'd like that."

Everything was awkward. Gregory sat in the office of Father Peter Coyle of the *Star* who listened to his story quietly and who shook his head when it was finished.

"The bishop will hate you," he said.

"Why?"

"He will have a nasty parish problem back again, with Schafer demanding a full-time priest; and he'll have me on his doorstep, demanding two men to take your place."

"Hardly."

"You think I'm kidding. You've been better than you know."

Father Coyle lit a cigarette and leaned back in his swivel chair. "You didn't surprise me with this, though. I felt it coming. There have been rumors about you for some time."

"Why didn't you tell me?"

"Would it have done any good?"

"Probably not."

"I floated one trial balloon at you. You ducked. You're a big boy now. It was up to you to make your own mistakes, or not make them. I was hoping you would come back in line."

Gregory Lind had no ready answers. He and Pamela had been reckless. He had known that at the time but he had glossed over the risks they were taking, assuring himself that they were discreet, that no one would notice or draw conclusions. Father Coyle was smiling at him. It wasn't a particularly pleasant smile. He had a wide mouth and he smiled at a slant, his lips climbing up the left side of his face.

"It's the Gibson girl, isn't it?" Peter Coyle said.

"Yes. Pamela Gibson."

"A non-practicing Protestant! A divorcee! You certainly went all the way, didn't you?"

"That's all outside the discussion, Pete."

"But not irrelevant. Well, leave it that way. You better clean out your desk if you have anything personal in it."

"I will. But I have a few days. I can help to get the next issue out while you're finding a man."

The eyes of Father Peter Coyle were cold. "You were all through five minutes ago," he said. "I'd like you out of here in the next hour. I'd like the keys to the car, too."

Gregory Lind rose. He had not given a thought to the car. No one else had ever driven it, so it had seemed like his. He laid the keys on Peter Coyle's desk top and that was his farewell to the *Star*.

He had his mother and Janet to see; after that, Bart. He stopped first to see Father Diego Montoya, S.J., who had been eager for some time to take over Father Lind's office at Guadalupe House. When Gregory Lind left him Father Montoya had his wish. Guadalupe House was his.

Loyola, the Jesuit church, was Midwestern Gothic, an imposing church. Gregory Lind entered it and knelt in a pew that was halfway down the middle aisle. It was nearly noon and there were only three other people in the church, an elderly man and two women. Gregory Lind prayed first, as he always did, for those who shared the church with him, then for those he must hurt and finally for Pamela and himself that they would prove worthy of grace. He felt at peace in the hushed and dimly lighted church before the great altar. He left reluctantly.

A hamburger drive-in provided lunch. There were too many miles in the triangle of rectory, Janet's house and Bart's. He rented a car for the day, frowning over the expenditure. They would have to use Pamela's car, he and Pam, when they left town. He would feel better if he could, at least, provide a car. He had less than three hundred dollars in his savings and checking accounts combined. He would have to buy some clothes out of that. There was little leeway in time. He would have to have a job in a hurry. He did not know where they would be so he could not imagine the job that he would have. He pushed the problem aside, consigning it to the future. This day already had problems enough. He drove south.

Janet's children were in school, even the five-year-old, who was a pre-schooler. Joe was, of course, at work. Janet looked startled when she saw Gregory. His mother, sitting in her big chair was obviously delighted.

"Gregory, my son, this is a nice surprise. What brings you out on a weekday?"

He sat down beside her and, gently, he told her. There was a moment of stark surprise that distorted her face; then she screamed. She screamed and kept screaming, uttering unintelligible sounds. With Janet's help he quieted her and as she brought her voice down to a comprehensible level, she upbraided him.

"You cannot do this to me," she said. "Your own mother! I'll never be able to hold my head up again. Some woman did this. Some foul, unspeakable woman! You must have nothing to do with her. You must be a priest. My priest!"

She screamed again. Janet gripped her under the armpits and, with surprising strength, lifted her. "You'll be damned, damned," Gregory's mother shouted. "You'll be damned for all eternity. You'll burn in hell."

Janet half-carried her into the bedroom and the screams became loud, sobbing cries. Janet came back. Her face was pale and her eyes seemed larger. She had been a very pretty girl and she was pretty now, with the appealing little-girl quality that she had always had.

"I'm sorry, Janet," he said. "I didn't know any other way to do it."

"She'll be all right. She's done this with less provocation. She'll come out of it." Janet lifted her head, looking up into his face. "Your trouble is a woman, isn't it?"

"It isn't trouble. I'm in love with her."

"It's trouble. You're a fool if you leave the priesthood for a woman. We're not worth it, Greggie. Not any of us."

Janet did not cry but her eyes misted. Gregory put his arms around her and held her close to him. He was three years older than Janet and he had had closer ties with her in his growing up than with any of the other children in the family. She was the only one who had ever called him "Greggie" and, until today, she had not called him that since his ordination. She pushed him away.

"You had better go now," she said. "I'll have to go back to her. We won't be seeing you again, will we?"

"Not for a little while."

"Not ever. There's nothing we can do for you, but write to us, please."

"You are doing a big thing for me. Mother is the big concern. I couldn't handle her."

"No. And if I was a better wife and mother myself, I'd put her in a home. Never mind. You better go. Sinner that I am, I'll pray for you."

"Do."

He went out into an afternoon that was clouded over, turning chill. He thought, as he had thought about so many people, that he did not know Janet, did not know her at all, the strengths and the weaknesses which combined and which added up to what she was as a person. He had glimpses into her, into her life and motivation; no more than that.

The traffic was fairly heavy on the route into downtown; fast cars, slow cars, weavers and lane changers. Gregory watched the other cars, accommodating his pace to the situation he found, but driving did not employ more than a small surface section of his mind. He drove automatically. He thought about his mother. He did not know her, either.

Through most of his growing up, most of his life, his mother had stood above all other human beings. She had firmly believed that she knew what was best for anyone in her household, in any situation or in a life plan. She was sweet and sunny, always interested in what one was doing, devoted to the church, proud of her home which she was always trying to make more attractive. She had attacks of nerves sometimes, or she was upset, or she had to lie down with a "sick headache," but these situations won sympathy for her. To children growing up, she was the person to be thought about, and saluted with cards or presents, on a long calendar of holidays and anniversaries.

It was rather remarkable through the years that Greg's father had been so taken for granted by Greg and his sisters and his brother. There were no halos for his father, no glorification of any kind although he was dependable in any emergency, able to build toys or gadgets when he could not afford to buy them. His children often resented him when they held him responsible for one of mother's headaches or attacks of nerves. John Lind's death in 1961 had opened the door of understanding to his children, had thrown people and events into a different perspective.

Mother's virtues had been, in the main, the easy, pleasant virtues of a person who is getting her own way. She could not stand being denied, being crossed, being considered wrong about anything, not getting something she wanted. Her immediate answer to any denial, any thwarting, any frustration, was an attack of nerves or a headache. She never changed, never adopted new tactics because the old tactics had always worked and, almost hysterically, she insisted that they must work again. John Lind, however, was gone and his children had not inherited his patience. Cecilia Lind had destroyed her own legend, and her own image, but she never understood that.

Gregory was aware of his mother as a tragic figure and he was sorry that he had had to hurt her. He felt, looking back, that he might have handled the situation more adroitly, but it probably would have made no difference. He had never satisfied his mother as a priest because he had failed her in not being a pastor.

He drove to the rectory. It was still his home, no matter how tentatively, and he had to guard his few dollars. To his surprise, the pastor had his dinner in the dining room. Father Guyton was absent. Even at table, Father Schafer was a grim man in appearance, a man of rigid facial lines, but he made no allusion to the interview of the morning; his conversation, what there was of it, was confined to the news of the day as it appeared in the evening headlines. At the end of the meal, he offered thanks and then, for a moment, looked at Gregory Lind.

"And may Almighty God in His mercy grant you every grace you need," he said.

He stalked off then to his own quarters; stiff-shouldered, stiff-necked, heavy-footed, expecting no acknowledgment and waiting for none. Gregory, watching him go, knew that he would remember him in tonight's framework and he was glad of that. It was the picture to remember.

Bart's house was the last of his major calls. There were a few priests who were fairly close friends and he would see them in the next day or so, but he had to see Bart today. Moreover, he had to see Bart at home and not in his office.

It was a fairly long drive to Bart's house, a big modern house in the suburbs. Bart's eldest girl, Cecily, answered the door and there was brief visiting time with the four children before Greg was alone with Bart in his study; a large, untidy room with a long table that was piled with papers, rolled blueprints, maps, letters. There were four chairs, big comfortable chairs designed for masculine sprawling.

"I have to tell you that you were right, Bart," he said. "I'm leaving the priesthood."

"I'd rather be wrong."

"I know it. That's how it is. And the answer isn't as simple as it looks. It isn't merely the three letter word, s-e-x."

"No? What is it?"

"It is the discovery of another self in me, a self that cannot remain a priest. I've been useful as a priest. I'm not deserting jobs that need me, or people that need me. There is something else that I am meant to do. I feel it. I cannot continue on the jobs I'm doing but I am not merely chasing a personal want, Bart. I've been able to deny myself personal wants and desires. I'm not self-indulgent. There is something. I've been given a mind and a body, an assortment of skills, abilities, ideas. I am meant to use what I have, all of it. A woman is right for me. She completes me as a person. I have found the right woman."

Bart smoked a cigarette, his eyes fixed on his brother's face. "You're kidding yourself," he said.

Barbara appeared in the doorway. She was wearing a simple blue housedress. Despite four children she was still flatteringly slender. Her hair was golden blonde and she had lovely skin. Her eyes were a warm blue.

"I could fix drinks for you boys," she said. "What will you have, Father?"

"Scotch and water."

She did not ask Bart. That was one of the small aspects of marriage, one that had definite value. A person knew what the other person wanted without asking. Bart crossed the room to a small desk in the corner. He sat there writing and Greg could see his back and his shoulders. He was a big man, Bart, and he seemed to exert muscular effort even in the simple task of writing. Barbara came back with the drinks.

"Aren't you having one with us?" Gregory asked.

"Not tonight. I'm rain-checking."

He was relieved and he had an idea that Barbara sensed that. She wasn't crashing the conference of two males. It was one of the many grand traits she had, her capacity for judging a situation and of staying out without making a point of it. He liked Barbara and had always liked her. He knew that, somehow, her marriage and Bart's was less than a shining thing, but he could not understand why. It was impossible to look at Barbara, or talk to her, and imagine her as possessed of any grave faults, of any downright unpleasant qualities.

Bart came back from the desk and picked up his drink. "Cheers," he said.

"*Salud.*"

They drank solemnly. "There is something else you should know, Bart," he said. "This girl is Pamela Gibson."

Bart lowered his glass. His eyes widened slightly. "Christ!" he said. "You don't know her."

"I know the family. In a slight, threshold kind of way. I remember her divorce." Bart took a quick swallow from his glass. "Hell, Kid, you're too far off base. You can't handle a woman like that. You don't belong with those stuffed shirts. Nobody, the woman included, speaks your language."

"She does. I couldn't make you understand."

"No. You damn well couldn't."

"I'll try. Ultimately. Not now. We're not staying here. We're going to another town."

"On her money?"

"She hasn't got any. The family has. She hasn't. She differed on a lot of things with her father. She isn't taking any money from him. She didn't take alimony, either."

Bart lighted a fresh cigarette and looked at it as though he had never seen a cigarette before. He was quiet for a full two minutes, then he rose shaking his shoulders.

"O.K., Greg," he said. "You've got your ticket. It's a little late to change anything. I hope it works out for you. If she isn't picking up the tab, and I hope to hell she doesn't, you'll need money. I wrote this before I knew who she was. I wish it was bigger."

He held out a folded check. Greg backed away from it. "No," he said.

"Don't be a damned fool! You'll need it. I'm not giving you anything I haven't got."

"I'm not your responsibility."

"No, thank God!" Bart's smile was an effort. No more than that. "But if you get in a jam, write me or wire me or call me on the phone. I've always got a few bucks lying around."

"Thanks."

Greg pocketed the check. There did not seem to be a decent alternative. The two men stood facing each other, then Bart slapped his brother's shoulder. "O.K., kid," he said. "I appreciate your telling me about it."

They parted on that. Half a mile from the house, Gregory stopped under a street light and looked at the check. It was for two hundred and fifty dollars.

He lay that night in his narrow rectory bed and listened to the ticking of his clock. It would tick all night but it would not awaken him in the morning if he happened to be asleep. Someone else would be saying the six o'clock Mass. He thought about that, counting the ticks, and he realized, fully for the first time, that he was no longer a priest. That was all behind him.

BOOK TWO

Portrait of a Woman

-I-

Pamela Gibson was born on March 20, 1942, in Culverton. She was christened "Pamela" because her mother liked the name, which meant "beloved elf." There was a war and her father left for service with the infantry when she was two months old. She lacked masculine influence in her life during her first three years but, according to her own testimony, she "made up for that later." This was a little less than accurate, a feminine exaggeration. She was not actually popular with her contemporaries, male or female, during her school years. She was the spoiled single-child of a wealthy family and she was arrogant without the awareness of arrogance, given to snap judgments, defiant when lacking an answer or when she was in the wrong. She freckled easily when she was a child and considered freckles a curse. They made her self-conscious and, although few people recognized the fact, shy. She hid the shyness behind an aggressive attitude and she was forever nervous inside when faced with the necessity of meeting strangers. She knew that she was considered homely by other girls when she was twelve and she distrusted mirrors. It took her a long time to see even potential beauty in her red hair, freckles, high cheekbones and odd angularity of build. She exaggerated her worst features for years in defiance of her distressed mother and in defiance of everyone else. Her father considered her ugly-duckling attitude "cute" and supported her even in ideas and conduct which he did not approve. He bought her anything and everything she wanted, good, bad, or ridiculous.

During the unhappy years of being homely and unaccepted, Pamela discovered within herself a wide assortment of skills and talents. She had an instinctive understanding of music and played the piano from her pre-school years, with none of the normal rebellion against practice. She had an ear for speech, too, and an early love of languages. She was a mimic, limiting herself at first to mocking imitations of people whom she disliked. All of which, over a period of time, served as compensation for many defeats.

In the summer which followed her freshman year in college, Pamela emerged suddenly from all the gray make-believe in which she had been trying to hide herself. She swam and she danced. She developed soft curves and her hair darkened to chestnut. She discovered how to limit, if not eliminate, the hated freckles. By concentrating her make-up on her mouth, she developed a somewhat alarming, but fascinating appearance. She had absorbed unconsciously the Gibson sophistication and the Gibson belief in money. She was a snob in a circle where snobbery was a virtue. Men discovered her and for a year and a half, she had a heavy play. In her junior year, she married Rodney Keller, five years older than she was and from the same general background.

Ralph Gibson, for probably the first time, opposed something that his daughter wanted. He did not like Rodney Keller and he did not want him in the family. Neither did Carina Gibson. Pamela was accustomed to having her own way. She not only married Rodney Keller, she had the most impressive wedding of the year. The marriage lasted less than two years.

Ralph Gibson opposed the divorce more violently than he had opposed the wedding and this was one of the few issues on which Carina Gibson could not, at least, modify his attitude. He told his daughter that she could not expect one dime from him, for support or for anything else if she became a divorcee; and to his intense surprise, she told him to keep his dime.

The Pamela Gibson who came out of the Keller marriage had many of the characteristics of an earlier Pamela. She had lost confidence in herself and she did not want to go back to the life she had known, or to the people she had known. She traveled for a few months and she thought things out and she returned to Culverton. She found a job in a travel agency and she rented an apartment. She donated her services three nights a week to Guadalupe House. She had, she felt, restored herself to dignity and she was, she knew, a source of knowledge and of strength to other people; but she lacked direction as a person. She was not moving to any recognizable goal and she could not convince herself that she was needed in the life that she had found for

148

herself. Anything that she did could be done by others if she was not available for the doing.

Gregory Lind came into her life and, once again, she ignored the danger signals or failed to see them. He was unlike any man whom she had ever met. She brought to him what Rodney Keller had never commanded, the volcanic passion of her young maturity. She fell madly in love with him and all things were secondary to that. She had still, of course, the faults and the weaknesses which she had taken out of her childhood but she had learned and she had grown and she had suffered and the elements of her character were assembled in different proportions. She could not see herself clearly but she could see what she hoped to be.

– II –

The Gibson women sat in the sun room of the big house in midafternoon. They drank coffee and Carina smoked innumerable cigarettes. The discussion had not been easy or comfortable.

"I cannot repeat too often," Carina said. "You will be making a bigger mistake than you made the first time if you marry this man. He's impossible. Absolutely impossible."

"No, he isn't. You are wrong there."

"Impossible for you, I mean. I do not doubt his virtues or his charm or his sterling character, or any of the rest of it. They are all fine for someone else; not for you."

"He is very right for me." Pamela's voice was low. There was intensity in it. "I did not believe that anyone like Greg existed. Thirty-two years old and there was never a woman in his life! A tall, strong, virile masculine man. Think about that!"

Carina's slender fingers held a cigarette suspended, halfway to her lips. Her eyes widened slightly, then narrowed. "One scarcely believes!" she said. "A woman would think about him. Yes. It's rather staggering." She gestured with the hand that held the cigarette, scattering ashes with the gesture. "You're living with him, of course. I can understand that. Your father wouldn't. Never mind. The point is that you won't lose much, living with him, if you're careful. It would be madness to marry him. Sheer madness."

"I am going to marry him. He asked me."

"Asked you! What difference does that make? A dozen men or more, drunk or sober, asked me to marry them once upon a time. I had sense enough to wait for your father."

"And luck enough. Never mind. A dozen men, at least, drunk or sober, asked me, too. This one never asked anyone else."

"A priest! He couldn't. You are allowing yourself to be seduced by the maddening idea of masculine virginity. I understand that. It gets to me, too, when I think of it. But it is irrelevant, absolutely irrelevant."

"If there was any seducing," Pamela said slowly, "I did it. I was aware of him, very much aware of him, before he knew that I was on earth. I made him notice me and I knew where he was going before he did."

Carina drew hard on her cigarette. She lifted her head, throwing it slightly back. "All right. I don't know if I believe all that. Suppose you did. So, you taught him about women. You awakened him. Now that you've got him out of his silly collar, out of his cage, do you think he's going to stop with one woman?"

"Yes. I do."

"You are being childish. You wouldn't be the first woman who has educated a man for somebody else." Carina waved with her left hand. "Deliver me from amateurs in anything. They never know how to begin or when to stop."

"He doesn't know he is an amateur. I didn't believe that there was a man on earth, a mature man's-man type of man, who had only an academic knowledge of sex. That's what he had. And he'd heard the Confessions of a lot of women!"

"That must have confused him—utterly."

"I don't know." Pamela sat with her legs stretched straight. She looked at the toes of her slippers. "I am not happy that I know more than he does about sex. I wish that I didn't. I wish that we could start even."

"Birds and bees! I never heard such nonsense. Unless it is your idea of a man with a mere academic knowledge of sex. Academic!" Carina blew a puff of urgent smoke through a lazy smoke cloud that floated just above her. "Do you remember that botanist-psychologist, or whatever he was, who came here to lecture? Floyd something-or-other? He said that sexual intercourse is a form of communication. I never liked him either."

Pamela made an impatient gesture. "Nobody was talking about sexual intercourse. I wish you would stick to the point."

"I was. That, precisely, is what we were talking about, and there is no need to get prissy about it. We were talking about this priest of yours learning from you and practicing with someone else."

"We weren't. Never mind. I'm not worried about women with Greg. No woman is going to take him from me. The only thing that worries me is the Church. The Church had him for a long time. It taught him to think in a certain way and act in a certain way, and there is a lot of mystery in it that a man loves. If I missed with him, he might go back to it. Even if I didn't miss, he might still want to go back."

"He couldn't, could he?"

"I don't know. Probably not. That makes no difference. If he wanted to go back, really wanted, even if he couldn't, I'd be through. That would kill something in me."

"You're talking like a Victorian novel."

"I know. I feel like a Victorian novel. This is all damned important to me." Pamela raised her eyes. "It's so important to me that I'm going to give him a baby."

Carina dropped her cigarette. She scrambled ungracefully to pick it up before it burned the rug. When she straightened, her face was red. "Are you pregnant?" she said.

"No. I will be, if I can be, and I believe I can."

"This is too much," Carina said. "Now you listen to me. The only way this young man knows how to make a living is by being a priest. Well, that is a job he can't have if he marries you. What is he going to do?"

"There are a number of things he can do. He is a journalist for one thing."

"You can't do without money. You've been spoiled. Rotten spoiled. Have you got any money?"

"Damned little. If I had a lot, I'd hide it. He has a right to his pride."

"Pride! Somebody named Lind! Well, the Gibsons have pride, too, and they have something to be proud about. Your father cut off your allowance when you defied him and insisted on marrying Rodney. He was right."

"O.K. He was right."

"He was. And not in that tone of voice! Your divorce hurt him. He wouldn't unbend. He couldn't. You paid no attention to him."

"You mean I should have stayed married to a heel like Rodney Keller so that my father wouldn't feel hurt?"

There was electricity in the air. Pamela had her feet on the floor now, her fists clenched in her lap. Carina sat stiffly.

"No," she said. "You know that I do not mean that. You know, too, that you could have mended the bridges to your father any time that you wanted to mend them. It would have only taken a little kindness, a little love, a little melting."

"Oh, certainly. And he was just waiting, all full of his own kindness and love and melting—just waiting for me to come on my hands and knees to him."

"Sarcasm does not become you, Pamela. It wasn't like that and it isn't. You have always exaggerated things, always exaggerated yourself, ever since you were a little girl. If you marry this priest you won't have to exaggerate anything as far as your father is concerned. Not for a minute. You'll never get a dollar from him. Never! He'll write you out of his will, too. If you don't know your father by this time, believe when I say that I do."

Pamela left her chair. She walked the length of the room and back, a slender, long-legged girl who was, at the moment, angry.

"I don't see anything fair about that," she said. "He may have a legal right to disinherit me; he doesn't have a moral right."

She came to a full stop, facing her mother. "He may outlive me. You both may. Fine! I'd rather live on what Greg and I earned than embarrass Greg with Gibson money. But I am a member of this family, damn it, and I don't like being read out of it because I do not conform."

Carina lighted a cigarette. She was always lighting them and the process was usually mechanical, a swift flash of match and an inhale. This time she was deliberate; even her shaking out of the match flame was deliberate.

"What you like, or dislike, makes very little difference, my dear," she said. "Your father is not going to accept a priest son-in-law. And while you are saving your Greg the embarrassment of Gibson money, and having a baby for him, I hope that someone will be earning something."

Pamela picked up her black and white check coat from the back of a chair. "Sarcasm does not become you, either," she said.

She turned away and her heels clicked sharply as she marched across the great hall. She was at the door before her mother caught up with her.

"Pamela," Carina said. "I'm sorry we lost our tempers."

"I didn't lose mine."

The eyes of the two women locked; then Carina laughed. "I pity that young man, even if he is a priest," she said. "You'll lead him a hell of a life."

"I won't. He'll do all right."

"I hope he does because I hope that you do. I wish that I could help. I really do, even though I disapprove of what you're doing. I'm almost sick thinking about it." Carina's right hand opened and closed. "I can't even help you financially because I can't work against your father behind his back. I never will."

"Nobody asked. Nobody will."

Pamela was turning away when Carina's fingers tightened on her arm. "Another thing. Please. If you marry him, and I hope you don't, please don't marry him in or near Culverton."

There was desperation in Carina's face and it was a face that she normally controlled. It would, of course, be a bad experience for the Ralph Gibsons if there was sensational publicity about Pamela and a man leaving the priesthood. Some of the other Gibsons would be hard to take under the circumstances and some of the family friends would be impossible. Pamela's hostility melted. She threw her arm around her mother's shoulders.

"Don't worry, darling," she said. "We'll get far out of town."

She kissed her mother then and hurried to her car. There were so many things which she had wanted to discuss but the conversation had taken its own shape instead of hers. It had been an unhappy afternoon.

"Dammit, I love them too," she said. "I just never get that across."

She drove faster than she normally did, taking a certain pointless satisfaction out of passing cars, almost hoping that she would be flagged down by a policeman. There was fear in her, a genuine fear. She could hear her mother's voice through some microphone in her mind:

"You can't do without money. You've been spoiled. Rotten spoiled."

"Pride! Somebody named Lind!"

"You have always exaggerated things, always exaggerated yourself."

"I pity the young man, even if he is a priest. You'll lead him a hell of a life."

It was all so possibly true. She did love comfort and luxury and she loved money for the things it would buy. She was a snob. She probably did exaggerate herself and the things that concerned her. All that had made her what she was, all that still made her what she was, might be beyond Gregory when he knew her better, might be very difficult for him.

"I love him," she said.

There was reassurance in saying that, reassurance to a degree, but the fear remained. She parked down the block from 751 Steuben Drive. There was no one around when she climbed to her apartment. The apartment looked stripped, no longer her home. She had had two men in to help her pack and the movers were coming tomorrow morning. She was sending her possessions, practically all of her possessions, to her father's house. Her father would not know that they were there because her mother would store them in an attic. The apartment as it looked now was the last chapter of a novel. The thought added to her feeling of fright.

She looked at the telephone. It should be connected still. She crossed the room and tested it. The receiver was alive. There was no number at which she could call Gregory except the rectory. She did not know the number. It would be in the phone book. If he was not at the rectory, and the chances were that he wouldn't be, she could leave her number for him to call. Leaving a message for him would help to drive the woofits away even if she didn't speak to him. She picked up the telephone book and laid it down again without opening it. Somebody at the rectory would answer the phone and she would have to ask for "Father Lind." She had never called him Father anything and she was not going to begin now.

She walked through the apartment. Her bed was made and her dresser was intact. Some of her clothes were in the closet, and her shoes. She had three suitcases and a wardrobe case to pack. The bed and the dresser would go with the other things tomorrow. Everything was winding up.

The phone rang.

Greg's voice came over the line and everything in her world seemed intact again. "This is telepathy," she said. "I was trying to conjure you up."

"It's the third time I've called. Who was conjuring me the other times?"

"I was. I just wasn't near a phone. Could you come up to the apartment for a little while or are you too busy?"

"I'm not too busy if you want me."

"I do."

"Fine. I'll be along."

She went out to the kitchen. There were things there which she had not sufficiently valued to pack, including glasses, quite ordinary glasses. She had a Scotch bottle that was half full. She had thought that she would give the bottle to the moving men. She took it from the shelf and placed it beside two glasses.

"Poor moving men," she said.

She and Greg had not had a drink together in a long time, she thought, and they certainly would not be able to afford Scotch when they went off together. For a while, at least, they would be separating themselves from income. It seemed right and proper that this afternoon they should have a drink here to all of the things in the apartment that were over, and perhaps another drink to things beyond the horizon that were in the beginning.

"Why am I making excuses to myself?" she said. "The sun is over the yardarm, or whatever that silly expression is. It is growing dark and that is the right time for a drink."

She was emptying ice in a tray when the bell rang. Gregory was dressed in his basic black, with the Roman collar, and that, momentarily, disconcerted her. She had been thinking of him as through with all of that. He kissed her and walked into the apartment with his arm around her.

"Lord!" he said. "You've been bombed out."

"Just about. There's still something to sit on and we have a few conveniences left. Sit you down."

"How about helping with the conveniences?"

"I'd rather do them myself."

"O.K."

She did not know why she wanted to serve him this drink; she just did. It might have had something to do with the fact that this was how they had started. She never pursued an idea too long through her mind in a quest for origins; there were too many twists and turns.

They took their usual places, facing each other beside the fireplace. Greg, she thought, looked very well in the clerical black. His hair and his eyebrows were dark. The lines of his face were strong. He had a firm chin. There was a cleft, or hollow, definitely not a dimple, on the right corner of his mouth. The word, perhaps, for how he looked, she concluded reluctantly, was spiritual. Sometimes he was careless and unpressed. The spiritual impression, then, was not so pronounced. Today he was pressed and shining.

Gregory seemed to read her mind, as he did often. He dipped his glass to her. "Does the uniform disconcert you at this late date?"

"No. I remembered that you were still living at the rectory. You would wear it, of course. It astonishes me that they let you live there."

"Only a few days. But I am astonished myself. The pastor, however, has never quite given up hope on me. He has had a couple of talks with me. He is a grand old man. I never realized how fine he is."

She watched his face. "Gregory, are you sure that you want to give all of that up?"

There were many possible answers to that question and she knew in advance that he would not reply as she wanted him to reply. He was singularly blind to a woman's need for reassurance and he, seemingly, did not hear the plea for that reassurance which a woman wrapped into a simple sentence. His eyebrows lifted slightly.

155

"That matter is no longer open. I am not giving up; I am extending."

She sighed. It was the wrong reply, of course. "Cute," she said. "I'll think of you as extending yourself instead of giving up."

Gregory sipped his drink. "How did you make out with your family?" he said. "Rough?"

"So-so rough with Mother. I didn't see my father."

"Perhaps you should."

"No. There would be nothing to say; no meeting ground. How about your family?"

"I did it all with one swoop. No replays."

"That sounds callous."

"If it does, that is because of the way I expressed myself. Actually, that is all that I could do. I do not feel callous."

"Your family and me," she said slowly. "That will always be impossible, won't it? Always."

Gregory looked down at some vague point of reference just above the floor, frowning. He lifted his glass and took a swallow of his drink. "I'm afraid so, Pam. There are so many things! I won't make it with your family, either."

"Not now. But you never know. With time?"

"Don't hope on it. I think you should see your father. He won't accept me but it will hurt him if he loses you—and it will probably hurt you."

Pamela did not answer. She drank quietly. She had never welcomed advice from anyone. People offering advice always sounded stuffy; even Gregory did. She liked to turn a question over in her mind, preferably in a fast rotation, and then make her own decision. Her decisions were, as a rule, snap decisions, not always right or even sensible; but even when she knew that she was wrong she defended any decision of hers stanchly. It was instinctive with her.

"Mother hopes that we won't stir up publicity in Culverton," she said. "She hopes that if we get married, it will be over the hill and far away."

"That's reasonable enough. Fortunately, the *Catholic Star* never mentions a priest who checks out. We'll take off quietly and we are already married to each other by mutual consent. We'll just make it legal along the way. In another state, perhaps."

"Yes."

They looked at each other. Today was a mistake, Pamela thought. They weren't saying what they should be saying. Everything came out stiff and unreal. The apartment had lost its charm and they could not find charm in themselves amid the chaos of packed and half-packed possessions. Gregory was evidently feeling it, too. He set down his glass and rose.

"If there isn't anything useful I can do for you, Pam," he said, "I'll settle for one drink and check along. I have details to round out."

"I know. So have I. I'm lazy. I've been trying to outwait chores in the hope they will go away."

"They never do."

They walked to the door together and suddenly Pam's control broke. This was the man, the one man, whom she had never expected to find in her life. She threw her arms around him and held him tightly, her head against his chest.

"I've been dull and horrid and contentious," she said. "I'm sorry, Greg. I never mean to be like that. I did want you. I am glad you came. I'm scared to death of you now that we are getting away together. I'm afraid that I will miss some way, that I will fail in something important that you want of me."

He lifted her chin gently with one curved forefinger under it. "I'm the one who is afraid," he said. "You are doing a perfectly wonderful thing in going with me, risking with me."

"I can't help myself."

"I'll try, Pam, to justify what you're giving me. I can't say that as I'd like to say it."

"Why not?"

"I haven't the vocabulary. I just do not know how to talk about my own emotions, about the way I feel."

He kissed her and in that his lips were eloquent. He broke off abruptly, squeezed her fingers and opened the door.

"Good night, Pam," he said.

She understood the abrupt leave-taking. She understood, too, her own surrender to emotion, even as she deplored it. She walked to the window but she did not look down into the street. She listened for the sound of a starter, the brief thunder roll of a starting engine. There was no sound at all and she frowned, puzzled; then she remembered. He did not have a car. He probably could not afford to rent one every day. It was a long walk to, and from, Steuben Drive out of downtown; but he had not mentioned the walking. She thought about that.

Life with Gregory Lind would be unlike any living she had ever known.

Gregory Lind and Pamela Gibson were married in Limefield, Illinois, on April 27. Illinois was a good state in which to be married because the law required only an overnight stay after a blood test. Most states required a three-day wait. They selected Limefield when they drove into it because it was a charming town, with tree-bordered streets and a red brick courthouse. There was a well-weathered bronze statue of a Union soldier on guard before the courthouse entrance and he seemed a fitting symbol of all things solid and secure. He had stood there for a long time.

The name of the judge who married them was Hugh Wheeler. He had a broad forehead, friendly eyes, and a firm mouth that could curl into a genuine smile. He wore a blue necktie with immense white polka dots.

"I like to marry people," he said, "and I always hope for them that their marriage will be as happy as mine."

Two of his staff served as witnesses. It was a wedding short on ritual and rhetoric, brief in time. It was ten-ten by the courthouse clock when they passed the Union soldier again on their way back to the car. Pamela did not feel like speaking, was convinced that she could not. There were tears filming her eyes, stinging them, and she did not brush them away because their removal would call attention to them. She did not want that for Gregory. He stopped suddenly, just short of the sidewalk, turned her around and kissed her.

"I am sorry, Pam," he said.

He did not elaborate and she could not speak. His face, she noted with surprise, was pale. There was a tight, drawn expression across his eyes. He would, of course, be upset, she thought. He had never expected to be married to anyone and he had taken vows against it. Today had had no God in it, no religion, no beauty of ceremony or ritual or costume. He had probably performed the wedding ceremony many times as a priest and he would, inevitably, compare his own wedding with those he had known.

He helped her into the car and walked around to the driver's seat. "What are you sorry about?" she said.

"Sorry that you didn't have what you should have had; music, flowers, a bit of glory and a blessing."

"I had all that was necessary. As you said, we were already married. This was to make it legal."

"Good of you to put it that way."

"You put it that way yourself. How far will we go today?"

"Topeka, Kansas."

"We should have two drinks and a big dinner. This is a very special day."

"You're right. We'll settle for Kansas City."

She was feeling better and she believed that he was. He no longer looked pale and, with highway under him, he drove fast. She let him do most of the driving because he so obviously liked to drive. She enjoyed driving herself and she liked her own driving better than his; not that there was anything wrong with his driving, it was merely different from the way she did the same thing.

She had discovered with delight on this journey that Greg shared her own gift for writing light verse and that he enjoyed doing it. It was a frivolous side to him and he was a man, she thought, who must often have needed a little frivolity of one kind or another to balance the solemnity that surrounded him. She played to that frivolous side now.

"In Kansas we will chow and drink," she recited, singsong.

"The time is later than you think," he said.

"The clock is fast and tells bad time."

"It won't, at least, write awful rhyme."

"With a hey nonny nonny and a hot cha-cha," Pam said solemnly.

The knack to these things was a poker face and a funereal delivery. Either one of them could feed back a rhyming line instantly to any kind of nonsense. It was a means of breaking monotonous stretches, of picking up when they grew tired; of, perhaps, asserting their oneness. They created these transient lines together, letting them blow away in the landscapes of strange states.

They made fast time across Missouri on the main highway which flowed through Columbia. They reached the outskirts of Kansas City in the deep dusk. They were fresh enough to carry on but they had set a goal and had reached it.

"Enough," Greg said.

They rolled into a motel driveway. It was a more pretentious motel than they would seek on ordinary nights but this was special. Greg signed for a single bed unit but did not quite achieve nonchalance in doing it. Last night an unanticipated question had taken him off guard. Asked whether he wanted a single or twin beds, he had chosen twins.

When they were alone in their unit, Pam had pointed her finger at each of the beds in turn.

"Why?" she asked.

It delighted her that he had flushed. It still delighted her, remembering. Tonight they had a deep room with the bathroom at the far end where the open-face clothes closet stood. There was a dresser and a desk, the single bed with a beige spread, two stands for luggage, a coffee maker on the wall with two cups, a radio on the small table to the left of the bed, a television set.

"No place to keep a horse," Pam said.

Greg opened his bag and took two Scotch miniatures out of some depth. They were small bottles holding two ounces each, or maybe an ounce and a half; she never could remember.

"These will get the road out of our systems," he said.

She could feel the road in her system, the subtle vibrations which came up out of the tires and traveled through the framework of the car. There was a faint dancing haze in her eyes, too, and an untranslatable sound in her ears. Her nerves seemed to jiggle a little when she sat in a chair under the floor lamp.

Greg brought her drink, the Scotch in a tumbler with water poured over it. There was no ice in the room and it seemed too much trouble to go after it. Greg lifted his glass and dipped it to her.

"To us, Pam. For always."

His voice was husky. She did not believe that her voice would be husky but she did not risk it. She merely dipped in return. She liked the way Greg looked. He was a bit mussed up, as she was, after a day's driving and his beard was a shadow on his face but he was ruggedly, masculinely handsome. He was wearing a dark brown jacket with Oxford gray slacks, a yellow shirt and a maroon necktie. She had groaned at first over the color combination but she had to admit now that the colors blended. His hair needed combing and his eyes were bloodshot. He sat in the chair on the other side of the lamp. It wasn't necessary to say anything, nor necessary to hear his voice; it was enough to know that he was there. They had finished a fairly long day's journey today and they had embarked on a longer one with their simple responses in the courthouse of Limefield, Illinois.

"If we start early and beat at it all day, we can make Denver tomorrow night," he said.

"How many miles?"

"Let's see—663 miles on my map."

"Too much. Let's go some place else."

"Limon, Colorado, ninety miles from Denver, or Burlington, Colorado, just over the Kansas border, about 500 miles."

"Let's take Burlington," she said lazily.

"O.K." He looked around the lamp at her. "I was about to give you another drink, but I won't."

"I know. I'm getting languorous."

"Let's eat." He rose, then hesitated. "Do you want the bathroom?"

"Help yourself. I'll take it later."

She watched him walk the length of the room. He was having difficulty in growing accustomed to small quarters with her, to intimacy. He had had no practice in sharing a room with a woman. There had been her apartment in Culverton, of course, but he had come and gone there; in a motel, there was a limit to one's privacy. He did not strain the limit. There was a lot of tiger in him when he was aroused, a lot of don't-care and abandon, but he had no need of furtive things and there was nothing of the exhibitionist about him.

She sat sipping her drink, thinking about him, content. He came back the length of the room and he had combed his hair. He had shaved, too. He must have worked fast.

"I have to take a bath," she said.

"Baths later. We have to eat."

"I don't care about eating."

"I do."

That settled that. She resigned the bath temporarily. There was a full length mirror in the bathroom and she confronted herself. Her lipstick had faded and there was dust coating her skin. She had effected repairs several times during the day but she could not seem to travel and stay orderly. Her scarf was awry and her hair windblown. She liked the scarf, a solid dark green. Her suit was a plaid, predominantly green. She liked that, too; it traveled better than she did. She removed her lipstick with the idea of startling Greg, then stepped back away from the mirror, her head on one side, frowning.

Her arrogance went off with the lipstick, her assurance, her look of being able to cope. She looked vulnerable and she hated that. She restored the lipstick, laying it on heavily, vividly. She wanted a bath and reluctantly conceded that she would have to wait. A man waiting to be fed was a woman's first responsibility; if he wasn't, he should be.

They ate in the motel dining room, surprisingly attractive and surprisingly expensive. They were relaxed, with no more work to be done this day, and they talked easily of inconsequential things. They talked, too, about the trip ahead. They were going to Albuquerque, New

Mexico. The state was new to both of them and the city was their second choice.

Denver had appeal. It was big, many times the size of Culverton, and there would be jobs there. It would take far less driving to end the journey in Denver. The city had a large Spanish American minority, which interested both of them. It was an attractive place to live. On the debit side there were two big negatives. Carina's brother, Pamela's uncle, was the president of a large Denver bank. The *Register* chain of Catholic newspapers, largest in its field, headquartered in Denver and Gregory knew several of the priests on the staff. So, they were going to Albuquerque.

They walked back to their unit from the dining room, making an elaborate production out of keeping in step. Gregory drew on a deep bass voice to state:

"Kansas City is called K.C."

"Capital letters, as you can see," she said.

"If I loved you and you loved me."

"We'd marry each other in old K.C.—Boop-boop-a-doop."

They reached the unit and Gregory lifted her easily in his arms. "I forgot about the threshold," he said. "You are entitled."

"I am indeed. You also forgot to unlock the door first."

He could not unlock the door until he put her down. She was carried across the threshold on the second attempt. "And on the second trip in," she said.

It had turned chill out of doors and it was good to be in, to feel the warmth, to have Gregory hold her in his arms and kiss her. It was good to look at the motel-supplied newspaper, not caring what was in it, while Gregory showered. It was good to soak in a warm bath and to come out in a terrycloth robe, to sit around for another drink with Greg and to feel his eyes possessing her. It was good to lie in his arms in the dark and to know that they belonged to each other.

"You are the loveliest creature ever made," he said, "and the sweetest."

"I'm glad that you think so," she said sleepily. "I work on myself. I buy miracle lotions. I try to stay neat."

She did not know if he answered. Sleep did not float in on her or wait for her to float gently out to it: Sleep snatched her and rubbed out her consciousness in one swift swoop. She came back into a room that was still black dark and she had a moment of terror, convinced that she was back with Rodney and in bed with him. The moment passed on the rhythm of Greg's breathing. Rodney had snored, gustily and explosively; Greg slept like a child.

"It's a physical thing with us," she thought, "a simply terrific physical thing. It's more than that, too, of course. It has to be. It's many things."

Sleep came for her again and she drifted off with it, more gently this time but out into the darkness beyond darkness where there was no thinking, no wondering and, only occasionally, dreams.

They took the long day's driving across Kansas on a divided driving basis which called upon them to change seats every hundred miles. Kansas was incredibly flat and the roads astonishingly straight. One could see for great distances and one was encouraged by conditions to drive fast. The towns were far apart and much alike. The day that they drew was clear and cool. Pamela discovered, to her own amazement, that Greg did not like the way she drove. He shifted restlessly, or fidgeted while she was behind the wheel.

"You spurt," he said finally. "You will drive any driver behind you crazy."

"If he's behind me and he's crazy, he can pass," she said. "What do you mean, spurt?"

"You go fast for a while, maybe over the speed limit, then you get talking, or thinking about something, and you slow down, sometimes away down. When you realize that you've slowed, you speed up. You are not consistent."

"I'm as consistent as you are."

Once she was made aware of that driving habit, she discovered that he was correct. She liked to talk and when she talked she cut speed. It was true, but she did not admit it. When he was under the wheel, she watched every move and called him for any fault, no matter how small. She saw his jaw harden. He retreated from her into silence.

"Petty," she thought. "I'm being petty. He has a right to be annoyed. I've got to stop it."

She tried, but she did not stop it. Once embarked on a campaign of criticizing his driving, she seemed committed to it. It was like her driving, she thought miserably, a spurting; periods of steady, happy driving and then more needless comment that created tension between them. After that one comment on her driving he had not mentioned it again.

It was a relief to drive up to the borderline sign which welcomed them to Colorado. Kansas was behind them and the town of Burlington straight ahead. They went to the hotel instead of a motel because a filling station operator told them that it was a good place to have dinner. Pamela wanted Scotch and she thought that they would be justified in celebrating their crossover into Colorado. Greg shook his head.

"We can't afford it," he said.

She deferred to him but she had reservations. The money thing was going to be difficult and she did not know how it would ultimately be settled. She could not affront his pride and she knew that he had little money, pitifully little money. It had meant much to him that she was on her own, a bit outcast, without access to her family's money. She told him that she had a little saved, not much, and she had not been specific. She had left most of what she had in Culverton and yet, with what she brought along in traveler's checks, she had much more, very much more, than he had. He would not, of course, understand the way her people, and their contemporaries, referred to money.

The Gibsons, or their friends, might say that someone they knew had no money. If the someone was in their set, or had been, he probably had more money than the Linds, or their associates, would ever dream of having. A person with a little money was someone who had much more money than someone with "no money." It was all a manner of speech and a matter of relativity.

Pamela had lived on her own, and through her own efforts, since her divorce without asking money from anyone, but she had had money in the bank when she declared her independence and she still had money in the bank. She had earned a good salary from Chase and Melrose, the Culverton travel agency, and they had written ahead of her to Albuquerque, introducing her to travel agencies there. It was going to be difficult for her, with her habit of doing precisely what she wanted, to hold herself within Greg's limits.

"If only he gets a job, a good job, right away," she thought. "That will make a difference."

Greg was taciturn tonight and she did not feel like talking, either. They checked into the hotel instead of a motel and their room was quiet. He did not make love to her and that was a shock. She lay awake for a long time after he went to sleep.

"He is tired," she thought, "and I am tired. It was a long day. I guess I did nag him. I'll have to watch that. It is awfully soon to be getting sore at each other. Maybe I should just stop analyzing everything that happens. Most things that are said and most things that are done have no meaning at all. No use in looking for meaning. No use."

She went to sleep on that thought and she awakened to a bright morning. Gregory was up before she was and he was cheerful. She half-resented the cheerfulness and was about to ask what was the matter with him last night, but changed her mind. She matched cheerfulness with cheerfulness and it was an easy day's driving. They first saw the Rocky Mountains at a small place called Genoa and they were in Denver for lunch.

This was the west and they were happy with it and with each other. If there had been a cloud, even a small one, it had blown away. They made verses and they did tourist things and they headed southward in the morning, every mile talking them closer to the land of the Spaniards where once the Conquistadores rode. The mountains were on their right and then, after they had crossed a pass, the mountains were on their left. There were mountains and semi-desert, few automobiles and few people, sunbaked adobe houses off the road, flat topped buttes which were mountains that had volcanoes in their past, streams of black lava frozen by time and visible from the road, incredible color in sky and rock and soil. They ran into Santa Fe in the early evening, a city that looked and felt and sounded foreign.

"I love it," Pamela said. "All of it."

"So do I."

They were in a city that had been a seat of government for a decade before the Pilgrims landed on Plymouth Rock. Gregory wanted to see the cathedral because it had been built by Bishop Lamy, the hero of Willa Cather's novel, *Death Comes for the Archbishop*. He entered it and stood appalled. Pamela, to whom it meant nothing, shared his sense of shock. The cathedral had been gutted by a post-Conciliar Archbishop. The high altar and the small statuary were gone and there was only a small altar, dwarfed and out of proportion to the huge, empty space around it.

"I'm sorry I saw it," Gregory said.

His face was hard set and she knew that for the little time they had been in the cathedral, he had been a priest again, that perhaps he remained always a priest, looking at all things with a priest's eyes. The thought frightened her but he was ardent that night and she matched his ardor, clinging to him and afraid to let go.

They drove to Albuquerque and here was a modern city with a population of more than 300,000 people, with a skyline of rectangular buildings. They drove Central Avenue from the Country Club motels to the University of New Mexico where they stood on the campus and looked at the famed statue of Lobo.

"This is the most honest university in the United States," Greg said. "The statue of a wolf on its campus."

"Highly symbolical," Pamela said. "Do you suppose it is a strain living up to it?"

He grinned. "Not with Spanish blood."

They went to Mass in the morning, Sunday morning, in the church of San Felipe de Neri. Greg seemed to take it for granted that she would accompany him and she was happy about that. She had been wondering how they would handle the problem if, and when, it came up. There was no problem. He merely went to Mass and so did she. It was the way they did everything else.

This was a very old church, built in 1706 and little changed, medieval in appearance and mood, crowded with Spanish-speaking people. The Mass was solemn, reverent. Pamela did not understand it but she watched Gregory, kneeling when he did, standing when he did. She watched his face without being obvious about it. He was praying, she knew, and praying rather desperately. He wanted to make good here, to establish himself, to take care of her. She was lifted out of herself in thinking of that, kneeling so close to him that she could almost feel his prayer. He did not know how difficult it would be. He did not know the world that he was going into. He had been aloof from it in a very special niche. He did not realize his own limitations when it came to coping with a commercial, moneymaking society. She raised her eyes to the altar.

"I wish that I could pray, too," she thought. "I wish that I could and that I could believe in it."

When the Mass was over they walked out into the sunlight. Gregory turned and stood for a minute looking at the simple, sturdy adobe structure. "Mass has been said in that church every morning, without one miss, since 1706," he said. "We will do all right in Albuquerque, Pam. We will do all right. I am glad we came."

– IV –

Bernard Maxing was the travel agent whom Chase and Melrose preferred in Albuquerque. Pamela called on him first. He was a thin, medium-tall man who looked Spanish. He had dark hair and dark eyes and a precise black mustache. He symbolized the far places, and exquisite manners and the right wines by merely occupying a room and permitting people to look at him. It was, Pamela thought, a bit overdone but she could see where Mr. Maxing would make an impression. He told her that he was pleased by the letter from Chase and Melrose and that, fortunately, he had an opening. She could, he was certain, be of great assistance to him. He called her "Miss Gibson" ignoring the

166

fact that she had given him her name as Mrs. Lind. When she called his attention to his oversight he raised his eyebrows.

"My dear Miss Gibson," he said, "it must be obvious to you that I cannot use another married woman in the key position which your experience and command of languages entitles you to hold. My wife is, inevitably, Mrs. Maxing. There is a definite value. There are people who prefer to deal with a married woman. Most people do not. Two married women in an office such as this would be too many."

Mr. Maxing had introduced his wife early in the interview; a slick, sleek, continental-looking woman who was heavy on eye shadow and who appeared vaguely French. Mrs. Maxing had not missed any detail of Pamela Gibson and Pamela had come to Albuquerque prepared for people who would look her over. Greg would not know that she was wearing a designer dress and he would have no idea of its cost; but Mrs. Maxing knew. Pamela thought about the Maxing position on her name.

It seemed rather foolish to argue the point. In an agency like this, names meant no more than they did on the stage. The salary arrangement was better than she had anticipated and, judging by its appearance, the Maxing Agency had an interesting clientele.

"I prefer to use my own name, my married name," she said, "but I suppose that I can be Miss Gibson if you insist."

"I do insist. Regretfully, I would be unable to use you if you could not yield that point."

She would not, Pamela felt, ever be fond of Bernard Maxing, but that was, obviously, not a condition of employment; not with Mrs. Maxing so much a part of the firm. Once the name question was settled, everyone was friendly. It was like being admitted to a sorority or, perhaps, becoming a member of a Lodge; one experienced a change in status. Mrs. Maxing introduced her to an attractive Spanish girl at one of the inner desks. This was Miss Mora who worked mainly on the outside, concentrating on the groups who wanted, or who could be made to want, trips at special rates. Mr. Armstrong, who also worked for the agency, was out and Pamela had the impression that he would be consistently out, that he, too, worked away from the office, calling on people. It was quite an agency, more strongly staffed than Chase and Melrose in Culverton.

"Many people in Albuquerque are traveling now," Mr. Maxing said, "and there will be more. There are many people here with money."

The Maxings were interested in her living problem. It was important, they said, to know the neighborhoods and to live in a good address. Mrs. Maxing, whose first name was Lucille, drove her out to look at apartments after first talking to a real estate man who was a friend of hers. The first apartment that she saw was charming and exactly what she would have wanted, and rented, on her own, but the rent was too high for Gregory. She could not take command of things in that department; it wouldn't be fair to him. The second apartment was a sharp drop down in price, not even comparable to the first but charming in its own way. She sensed the fact that another drop down the price scale would be too great a compromise.

"I want my husband to see it," she said.

"You'll risk losing it and this apartment is a bargain," Lucille Maxing said. "Pay a deposit now and show it to him tonight."

"He might not like it."

Lucille laughed. "You can take care of that."

It was true, of course. She knew that she could make Greg like, or at least admit as likable, anything that she liked; but it did not seem quite fair or honest to do that about an apartment, a place where they would both live.

She paid a deposit. If he doesn't like it, she thought, I do not have to tell him that I paid anything; I can just let it go.

She walked home to their motel on Central Avenue. Traffic was heavy and there were a great many people walking. Albuquerque had a bustling big city air but it also had touches of a small town. The people dressed more colorfully than they did in the Midwest; not sloppy or hippie but casually Western, a quality difficult to describe. There were Spanish faces and Indian faces but she did not see Indians in tribal costumes on the streets as she had in Santa Fe which was just seventy miles away.

Their motel was bright, fairly new, but the unit was lonely when Greg was not in it with her. She did not feel like doing anything. She was hoping that he had walked into a job but very doubtful about the probability of her hope. He had planned to start searching at the top, with the big companies, and he had been vague about the type of job that he wanted, the special skill that he had to sell. One could not be indefinite about the fundamental realities of job hunting, but he was, and it was impossible to tell him because he did not understand. That sounded like an indictment of his intelligence and it was not. The simple truth was that he had been educated, and granted experience, in a narrow field that touched, but did not penetrate, the materialistic realities by which he would now have to live.

It worried her that her own job had come so easily and so fast. She had walked in with an introduction because she had asked Chase and Melrose, once she knew where she was going, to write letters ahead of her. Why hadn't she taken the same chance that Greg had to take, coming into a town cold? She would still have had a great advantage over him without the letters.

"It wouldn't be sensible, or do him any good," she said defensively, "to throw away an asset that is legitimately mine."

She had not, of course, thought of Gregory or of his problem when she asked for the letters. She waved the recollection away now because it rebuked her.

An automobile drew into the space in front of the unit, the engine sighed off, and then Gregory was in the room. He came in breezily, cheerfully, but she knew that he had not connected with a job. There was effort in his cheerfulness. He threw his arm around her and kissed her and there was no effort about that. She looked up into his face.

"I missed you," she said. "It's good to have you home. How did you do?"

"No good," he said. "I really didn't expect to hit those big fellows. I'll tell you about it later. How about you?"

She hated her good news in contrast to his, but she told him about her job and about the Maxings. They sat facing each other, which was in their habit, and she could watch Greg's face. He wasn't jealous; he was honestly pleased for her.

"That's swell," he said. "I would worry about you if you had to wander around a strange town looking for work."

"I know. I worry about you."

"It's different for a man. Entirely different."

"Tell me about it."

"Not too much to tell. This town got its boom from the atomic bomb, of course. Most of its industry is connected with it in one way or another, so the people I called on today were people with government contracts. They have personnel departments and forms to fill out. I'm afraid they found me difficult to classify."

"How?"

"Well, judging by the questions, I should have had a college, at least one degree; experience with other firms; certain easily described skills; earnings in one bracket or another last year." Greg grinned. "I have an idea that they punch the cards after they are filled out and run them through a computer. I wasn't giving them anything that a computer could work on."

"No. You wouldn't fit in a computer at all. Did you have to tell them you used to be a priest?"

His face sobered. "Yes. Of course. No avoiding that. They have to be able to trace a man back. That is the only backtrail I have."

"Do you think they were prejudiced?"

He frowned and his right hand clenched momentarily. "It is difficult to tell. Where I had a chance to talk to anyone, it seemed all right. You know. Polite. The best I got, however, was the promise that they would call me if something opened up. I didn't have a number or an address, of course."

Greg shrugged, jackknifed to his feet. "Time to feed you," he said. "I'll buy you a drink to salute your job."

Pamela wanted the drink. She shook her head. "We'll hold the drink idea," she said. "Let's celebrate your job and mine together."

She was glad that she had thought of that when she saw his face light up. "O.K.," he said. "That's a deal."

They dined in a small place which specialized in Mexican cooking. Neither of them understood the food but they were surprised to discover that they liked it. Pamela did not mention the apartment until after dinner since they had committed themselves to one more motel night anyway by staying past the checkout time. The apartment looked well at night. It was small but there was room to move around; a tiny entrance foyer, a living room, a bedroom, a small room with a desk in it that Pamela said would be Greg's study, a fairly large kitchen.

"I'm not much of a cook," Pamela said. "I could do a chop or something for myself when I had the apartment but I never cooked for two."

"I don't know much about cooking, either."

They stood in the kitchen and it was one of the realities that they had never faced. The question had never been raised. They had not had the problem of meals together until they were on the road; then they had eaten in restaurants and in small cafes. They would probably have to do a lot of that in Albuquerque. It would be expensive but, if they both worked, inescapable.

"How much would this layout cost?" Gregory said.

Pamela told him and he whistled softly. "I know," she said. "It's a fairly stiff town on prices. The budget people say that one's rent should not be more than one week's salary. This is more than one week of mine, but there are two of us. We can handle it."

"I haven't a salary yet."

"You will have."

They walked through the apartment again. Pamela knew that he was comparing it with her apartment on Steuben Drive. It did not compare well. It was cheerful, however, and it looked comfortable and the Southwestern touches were discreet; they belonged and there were not too many of them.

"I like it," Pamela said.

"Do you, really?"

"Yes. I do. It's a bright beginning."

"O.K.," he said. "We'll take it."

They returned to the motel. The wind was rising and it was good to be in, to shut the world out and to be together. Pamela sat beside Greg and watched three television programs. It was the first time they had ever done that. She held his hand.

"We have a lot of firsts ahead of us," she said. "We haven't seen a movie yet."

"Nor a ball game."

"Do you like ball games?"

"Baseball, yes."

He had, he admitted, very few athletic skills but he would have worked hard at baseball if he had ever been anyplace where he could seriously play. He had been pretty good in grade school and high school.

"In the seminary we had some softball. Very, very amateur," he said.

It was fascinating to Pamela, glimpses into the kind of person Greg had been, the kind of person he has aspired to be. There were so many things she did not know. They did not matter now, perhaps, but nothing about Greg was dull as far as she was concerned. It was odd that he lacked athletic skills. He was straight and strong and he had a superb body.

She remembered one of their stops on the drive across country. He always rose at an ungodly hour in the morning and stepped quietly out for a walk. He came back that one morning while she was doing her exercises. There was a routine of twisting and leg lifting and rising from the ground without reaching out for help. Greg had been surprised and then impressed.

"You ought to do these with me," she said. "I'll show you how."

"No, thanks. I used to work out with barbells at the rectory. It entertained and amused Tom Guyton."

"Why didn't you bring the barbells with you?"

"Too heavy. Too clumsy."

"When we settle in, can you send for them?"

"I could. Tom Guyton would send them but they would be a curse to pack and ship."

She had known then that he would never send for the barbells but she believed in exercise. She would not, she thought, ever permit him to grow lazy and fat; not any more than she would permit herself to let down. They would exercise together, one way or another.

They moved in the morning, a simple process which consisted of tossing bags in a car and driving to a new address. The motel had seen many people come and go, obliterating all trace of them within an hour of their leaving. She and Greg were now among the many. Greg drove her to Maxing's and she stood on the sidewalk watching the car grow smaller in the unknown and menacing distance. There was work out there for him to do, or there wasn't. It would be a lonely job for him, the finding out. She could not help him. There was something bleak about that.

Her first day at the Maxing Agency consisted of familiarization. She was in a different time zone, dealing in a different set of distances, working with different transportation systems, particularly in the airlines. She had to study a changed schedule of rates from the one that she carried in her head at Chase and Melrose and there was a new orientation on hotels and cooperating travel agents. She sat down with a brand new notebook and memorized what she had to know by writing neatly on the pages.

Greg was home before she was, pacing around restlessly. He shook his head to her glance of inquiry and took a pint bottle of Scotch from his pocket.

"No good," he said. "This is a consolation prize. Maybe it will help you to think up an answer for me." He frowned at the bottle. "Lord, but whiskey is expensive in this town!"

"What is the question?"

"Wait till I fix us a drink. Nice to have a kitchen again, isn't it?"

He walked out to the kitchen and she could hear him running water and clicking ice out of a tray. She went to the bathroom and looked at herself in the mirror. She looked all right for someone who had finished the day. When she returned to the living room, her drink was on the coffee table. Greg was seated, facing her drink, but he rose when she came into the room. It was one of many nice qualities about him, his instinct for correct things.

"There are couples who sit, all cuddled up, side by side," she said, "and couples who like to face each other. I'm glad we are facers and I'll bet we love each other as much as the cuddlers."

"More. Much more." Greg lifted his glass. "Here's to our home. First night in! A housewarming."

"Cheers!" she said. "I do not imagine that the apartment expected a fuss to be made. What was that question?"

"It's a bit complicated." Greg tasted his drink. He sat straight and his forehead wrinkled slightly. He had gone to one of the Albuquerque newspapers, seeking a job, and he had seen the city editor who, at the moment, was short of staff. The police had just captured, in the home of his latest victim, the phantom rapist who had eluded them for months. The brutal attacker of women was a freshman at the university, nineteen, a young man from a good family who had never been in trouble before.

"The editor told me that he would give me a shot at a job," Greg said. "He told me to shoot out to the university, find out from this lad's professors, and any classmates I could find in a hurry, how he was regarded, how he stood in his work and in his social contacts; all that sort of thing."

Greg took a swallow from his glass. "This was all very different, of course, from anything I'd ever done for the *Catholic Star* but I went out on it. I did pretty well, I believe, in finding profs and students, jotting down verdicts and getting back fast to the paper. Would you like another drink?"

"I want to hear the question but I'll have a reinforcement in this drink. That was a very tough assignment you drew."

"Yes. It was."

Greg took the glasses to the kitchen. Pamela waited, aware of the silence in the apartment, experiencing the sense of being in a strange place. The end of Greg's story was no secret, of course. He did not get the job, obviously. Why not?

He returned with the glasses which tinkled cheerfully as the ice cubes floated against the sides of their container. He seated himself again and he did not look at her. He seemed detached, a man telling a story of something that had happened to someone else.

"I wrote the story, a bit long perhaps, and turned it in," Greg said. "The editor read it and he told me that they would pay me for getting the facts which he would turn over to a rewrite man, but that he could not offer me a job."

Greg's eyes were still far away. He lifted his glass, drank, and set it down. "He told me that I could not write a newspaper story, that I had good material and did not know what to do with it. He said that I should try something else, that I wouldn't learn because I'd already learned, and learned wrong."

Greg drew a deep breath. "I asked him if he could tell me what, specifically, was wrong and he said that it was my style."

Greg came to a full stop and picked up his drink. "He said that my style is mealy-mouthed."

His eyes met Pamela's now and she could read the humiliation in them, the embarrassment. "He's crazy," she said. "There isn't one mealy-

mouthed thing about you; so how could something come out in your
writing that isn't in you, that hasn't ever been in you?"

"It came out to him."

"He used the term carelessly."

"Mealy-mouthed." Greg repeated the term as though it fascinated
him. "It could be, you know. The *Star* was a lousy newspaper. I
learned to write their way. Come to think of it, it is probably a mealy-
mouthed newspaper. What cuts me down is that I didn't know I was
writing that way. It seemed all right to me. So, he's right about something else. I can't learn now. No taste."

Greg rose abruptly and strode out to the kitchen. He did not ask
Pamela to have another drink but he, obviously, was going to have
one, his third. Pamela frowned at the two ice cubes in her glass. She
did not want to cross Greg when he was hurt. If he wanted to drink
too much, that was his privilege. She would fight it if he showed a
tendency to drink too much steadily or consistently but she did not
believe that he ever would. He came back and he was steady on his
feet, walking a little more slowly as he was talking a little more slowly,
but under control.

"There are other jobs besides writing jobs," he said, "other places
besides newspapers."

"Of course. But if I were you, I'd forget this stupid editor and try
other editors."

"He wasn't stupid."

Greg waved his hand, dismissing the subject. He asked her about
her day and drank slowly, listening, while she told him. It seemed
absurd to think of going out for dinner, but they had no supplies in
the apartment except the few things she had bought for breakfast.

"Would ham and eggs do for supper?" she said.

"Perfect."

She went out to the kitchen and Greg fortified his drink again while
she cooked the ham and eggs. They ate at their own table in Albuquerque, which they had not planned to do, and Greg helped her
with the dishes. He did not mention the newspaper again but he made
gentle love to her that night and she could feel the hurt in him when
she held him.

Pamela had her own desk at Maxing's and there was an identifying triangle on it that she hated, an elongated pyramid with a brass plate and the legend: Miss Gibson. There she was, in a cage and identified, a specimen in the Maxing zoo. There were customers assigned to her, too, regular customers, in addition to the drop-ins, the trip-yearners who wandered in off the street, or the trip planners who read the Maxing ad in the telephone book Yellow Pages. Meeting the regular customers, she understood why she must be Miss Gibson and not Mrs. Lind. They were young men, in the main; wise-cracking, conceited, superficial, operators in the entertainment arm of big business which had developed into an arm of consequence. It was their mission to plan trips for customers, or employees, to arrange for banquets and luncheons, to import speakers and to send them away again. Detail work was trying on geniuses so they were willing to pay money to Maxing in order to avoid detail. After all, it was legitimate business expense, wasn't it?

The young men liked to appear daring and a girl who did business with them had invitations to lunch, to dinner, to cocktails, particularly to cocktails. She had to use finesse in avoiding entanglement while never flatly refusing. She had to not-hear a number of things that were said and she had to—blankly, without expression—fail to catch the point of an occasional joke. Seeing the points of jokes only encouraged the tellers.

Bernard Maxing would, Pamela felt, prefer it if she accepted invitations from good customers but he did not interfere with her. From her first five minutes behind her desk, she had commanded it; and he knew that she did. She had maps in her brain, an instinct for distance and direction and mileage. She had patience with dull detail and a quick comprehension of foreign currencies. She belonged in a travel agency by virtue of many skills and abilities and she should not have had to flatter brash young men, nor endure them, but they were inseparable from the work that she did.

She liked Albuquerque. It was exciting, as she had not expected it to be exciting. It was old, with a long and colorful history, and yet it was new, painfully new, and riding a boom. She and Greg explored Indian villages and drove west on Route 66 to the big, rambling lush motels on their Sundays. They liked the Sandia Mountains which dominated the skyline and they loved the color in sky and in sun-touched rock. If only Greg could find a job! It was three weeks now and he had not missed a day in his searching. Even on the Sundays, when there was no object in pounding pavement, he read want ads and made notes. He was game and he did not complain and he did not take it out on her, but she knew that he was growing desperate. In comparison her own job was a joy, and often amusing.

There was a Thursday, a rather lunatic Thursday, which marked the takeoff of Mrs. Corbett McDonald for Japan, Hong Kong and the places far away. Mrs. McDonald inundated the agency offices with flowers, a ridiculous gesture which beautified the premises and which made the efficiently small space assume the impressiveness of a capsule world fair. At four P.M. Tony Hibbard came into the office.

Tony was one of the bright young men, public relations officer for one of the large firms with government contracts. He wanted to arrange a ten-day tour to Mexico for fifteen members of an employees' travel club and he wanted to make a highly personal thing out of the transaction. He was fairly good looking, highly conceited, well tailored and a crashing bore. Pamela played him off the top of her mind, paying little attention to what he said or she said. The Tony Hibbards of the world had never given her any trouble, and she had known many of them in one place or another. When she had this one's order all written up she would ease him out so swiftly and so smoothly that he would not know what had happened.

She did not know when Gregory came in, nor how long he stood around while she dealt with Tony Hibbard. When she became aware of him, standing just inside the door, she experienced a sense of shock. She had a swift mental picture of how she must have looked, in scene, with the ubiquitous Tony draped across her desk, smirking at her like a combination of Don Juan and Peter Pan. Greg had never visited the office before. And the office! Lord, the flowers! It must look, to him, like a bordello.

There was nothing that she could do about the bright young man. She had to go right along with him until his Mexico trip was all written up. She would never be able to explain him, either, or how she had to work, even if she was good at explaining things. She just did not explain or apologize or beat her breast about anything. There was nothing that she could say about the flower-draped office, either.

She got rid of Tony Hibbard eventually, slipped a half-dozen form sheets into a file folder while he was going out the door, then crossed the room to Greg. He was wearing his second-best sports jacket and slacks. They needed, at the very least, pressing. His wardrobe was pitifully meager; two sports outfits and a suit. She would have to do something about him, some way.

"Hello, darling," she said. "This is a surprise. I'm sorry I kept you waiting."

"That's all right," he said. "I should not come in when you're working. When will you be free?"

"Five minutes. Maybe six. I'll hurry."

She went back to her own desk and placed the Mexico trip folder in the right hand drawer. She would work out the detail of that, reservations et cetera, the first thing in the morning. She told Lucille Maxing that she was leaving, walked straight back to the powder room and returned. She had a hunch about Greg when she saw him again, standing patiently inside the door.

"He has a job," she thought.

She could not hurry that hunch. He would have to tell her in his own way, in his own time. She looped her arm through his and they walked out into the street. He was a tall, grave individual today. She flashed her eyes upward at his face. It was a strong face, a very masculine face, nothing pretty-boy about it. He walked for a half block without speaking.

"I did not know that you were Miss Gibson in there," he said.

"Oh. Didn't I tell you? It's a silly idea of theirs. And my references, of course, read Pamela Gibson."

He walked another half block in silence, not holding himself as straight as he normally did, his head inclined forward. His voice, when he spoke, was flat, without emphasis.

"I got a job today," he said.

"Greg, no!" She stopped in mid-stride, half turned toward him. "Where? What?"

"It isn't much," he said. "It's in a grocery store. A big supermarket. I'll tell you when we get home."

"It's fine. Whatever it is, it's fine. You'll take off from there. Let's stop and buy that celebration bottle of Scotch."

"It isn't a Scotch celebration job. Not that good."

"It is to me. And we said we'd celebrate. We'll buy something to fix at home, too."

"I'd like that."

They bought the Scotch and they bought TV dinners, with some extra side dishes, at a market. Pamela was not pretending, to herself or to anyone else, that she was a cook who could work with raw materials and whip up meals from scratch. They sat in their own living room, with the rest of the world outside. Pamela said: "Now."

"There isn't much to tell," Greg looked almost apologetic. "They needed a man at this big market and they didn't seem to be a bit interested in my background. It's mostly a strong back and muscle job, I believe, and the pay isn't wonderful, but it's better than walking around on pavement with no payday at all."

"Of course it is. But how did you find it? How did you know that they needed a man?"

"I didn't know. It was the simple process of ringing doorbells. I tried every place I saw."

She stared at him, trying to comprehend that. She had known, of course, that he had run out of newspapers and big companies long ago. He could not teach because he had no teaching credits in his education. He had ruled out selling jobs, even when they were not straight commission because he was certain that selling was beyond him, something that he could not do. He had religiously studied the want ads but he did not have the training or experience demanded in most of the ads. He wasn't an accountant, barber, draftsman, meat cutter, upholsterer, fence installer or baker. It had discouraged him, she knew, to see the jobs for which men were wanted, the jobs that he could not handle, but he never voiced discouragement. He found humor in his predicament, even when there was little that was humorous. She remembered one ad that he had read to her from the *Albuquerque Journal:*

"Permanent position for dishwasher in exclusive establishment. Do not apply unless you have at least one year experience and references."

They had both laughed at that ad but it was sad rather than funny. There wasn't any activity of man in which Greg could claim a year's experience except the Catholic priesthood.

"What's the matter? Why are you staring at me?"

Greg's voice snapped her out of her reverie. She shook her head. "Was I staring? Sorry. I was thinking."

He reached into his pocket. "Do thoughts still sell for a penny?"

"Mine never did. I was wondering about your hours. What days do you work and how long?"

"Monday is the day off. And Sunday, of course. I go to work at seven most mornings. There may be some night work. I'm new. I can be moved around."

She nodded. Their time together was important to her. That time was going to be menaced by this job. Greg walked to the bedroom and brought back a package. He had come home evidently before he called for her at the office.

"I had to buy some working clothes," he said. "Good clothes couldn't stand up to this job, and shouldn't. Luckily I had enough money. Just enough. I'll have to borrow from you now till payday."

He was spreading out the contents of his package as he spoke. He had a rough looking pair of gray work pants, four colored shirts and a cheap jacket. She felt something close to horror, just looking at them. She wanted to cry but that wouldn't be fair.

"I always lend and always demand interest," she said solemnly. "I come from a banking family."

"With a hey nonny nonny and a hot cha-cha," Greg intoned.

They looked at each other and laughed. It had been a bad moment but their world was back together again.

He left the clothing on the floor where he had spread it for display. Pamela stared at it. She had never known anyone who wore clothing like that. There were people, of course, who had a functional relationship to her life and nothing else; she never noticed what they wore, nor cared. She would never have known Greg if he had worn such a uniform rather than his clerical black. It would have been impossible for her to know him.

She was aware that many people would brand her as a snob for thinking such thoughts but she did not believe that she was a snob; she was a realist facing the truth of her own life. What in her training, education, daily experience or aspirations could she share with a man in working clothes? People living in totally different worlds could only touch casually and in passing. They had nothing to offer each other that was not casual and transitory. What, now, of Greg? He had stepped into the world of this deplorable uniform because he, seemingly, had no choice. She was part of him. He could not take that step alone. She stared at the heap of clothes.

Greg, working in a supermarket at manual labor would not comfortably associate with the Maxings, phonily pretentious though the Maxings were. She, Pamela, could not imagine sharing an evening with the people whom Greg would know on this job. They could not, simply could not, she and Greg, walk separate paths—and yet?

He relaxed now and he talked. He talked brightly, cheerfully, of news in the papers and street scenes around town, of events and of people and of herself. He did not mention the "Miss Gibson" identification on her desk and he made no reference to Tony Hibbard or to the way in which she conformed to the demands of her work. He ignored her office and his visit to it as he ignored his supermarket.

In the middle of the night, he rolled over and put his arms around her, holding her tightly against him; as though he sensed a danger that she would slip away from him.

– VI –

Two weeks and three days after Gregory started to work at the supermarket, Pamela awakened with a sense that the apartment was being gently rocked. She attempted to rise and the rocking became violent. The room in which she slept seemed to tilt sidewise, then stood on end. Her stomach seemed to fall away, then rise almost to her throat. She slid out of bed and raced to the bathroom, violently, nauseatingly ill. She rocked there, on her knees, and when the spasm had passed, rose shakily to her feet.

"If this is what I think it is," she said, "the sickness bit is starting too soon."

Greg had left early, as he always did, and she was alone. She looked at herself in the mirror apprehensively and the image stared back, apprehensively. As far as appearance went, there did not seem to be anything wrong, anything apparent, except fright. There was no deception about that, she thought; she *was* frightened.

She went through her regular morning routine, including her exercises, and went to work. The day was like every other day as far as the office was concerned but she found it difficult to concentrate on the work before her. She wondered if she should see a doctor, then decided not to do so. She thought seriously about telling Gregory when he came home, then shook her head. "Not yet," she said.

She had several bad mornings and one, inexplicably, that was fine, without a sign of distress. On Saturday she only worked half a day and that was Greg's long day. She felt lost in the afternoon, restless, with nothing to do that she felt like doing. There were letters piled up, unanswered. Her mother had written two brief letters and she had heard from several of her friends as soon as she established an address. It was an odd quality in Greg that he had never exhibited any curiosity about her friends. He seemed to assume that she did not have any, that her life, until he entered it, was practically a blank page. He had never once shown concern that leaving friends was a part of her uprooting in the leaving of Culverton. Nor had he ever shown interest in what she did on the nights when he had not seen her. She looked at the small pile of envelopes.

"He may have been right," she said.

She had had few friends after her divorce compared with the great many of the period before Rodney Keller. She had kept up with the friends she retained in a desultory fashion; shows, small dinners, concerts. There was no one to whom she felt like writing today. She decided to write to her mother and she stared for a long time at the sheet of stationery before she touched it with her pen. Once she made the first stroke, she wrote steadily:

"Carina, dear:

"You have been neglected. It is difficult to defend the non-answering of letters and pretty old hat to mention that there have been adjustments to make down here. I've just been lazy. I did tell you about my position at the Maxing Agency. The Maxings are doing very well indeed and making a surprising amount of money, but I do not like them too well as people and neither would you.

"Greg has a position with a mercantile establishment, not as good as he deserves but a start. I do not worry about him. He has such a very good mind. Our apartment is crude in some ways and it is impossible to think of it as anything but a *pied-à-terre*. We are comfortable in it. Gregory and I, contrary to your pessimistic anticipation, are very happy. We go well together and there is no friction. To show you that I am not merely pink-spectacled, I'll list his faults as well as his virtues. I know him very well by now, of course.

"His worst fault grows out of the fact that he lived a completely womanless life for so long. He forgets sometimes, I am certain, that there is a woman in his life now. He is not thoughtful in the little ways. He does not anticipate things I want or would like and he seems astonished when he discovers that I want, or need, anything. There are occasions when he notices what I am wearing but he does not really know what I own. My clothes and shoes and gee-gaws have no reality for him. On the other hand, *I* do have reality. He is very much aware of me apart from anything I wear, and he is never stingy with compliments.

"You thought that other women would get him and I worried about the Church. He does not know that other women are on earth, but religion has a strong reality for him. It still frightens me, that quality in him. He does not know that I know it, but he goes to six o'clock Mass nearly every morning, even when the weather is mean. He did it when he was facing long, solid days of discouraging job hunting and he still does it. He has an odd feeling, an involvement, or something, as far as six o'clock Mass is concerned. That is the Mass he used to say when he was in the Church. I go to Mass with him on Sunday and he genuinely feels something that is not there for me. He prays, and I can't. Maybe that is the answer. I don't know. I don't know if he still considers himself a Catholic. He probably does, but I'm fairly certain that he was excommunicated when he married me. He never discusses any of that when we talk together. We have the present and the future, not the past. Two thirds of the package is a good score.

"I am pregnant. I am glad that I have finally written that down. I have been talking all around the barn, haven't I? Well, I have just discovered that alarming little fact and I am not used to it yet. It is what I wanted. I told you that. Still, wanting or not wanting, now that I'm caught, I am just plain scared. I haven't told Greg yet. I will tell him tonight. There is something repulsive about the idea, in spite of all the sweetness and light and gay balloons that are written about it. I have never felt so much like an animal as I feel this moment and I am just starting on this with all of the most unpleasant features ahead of me.

"I suppose, as one bit of unpleasantness, I shall lose my job. I do not recall if I told you that the Maxings insisted on my retaining my virginal Chase and Melrose identification. They would not hire me unless I met their public as Miss Pamela Gibson. I cannot imagine a place on their staff for the heartily pregnant Miss Gibson when I reach that stage. My condition and my public identity just will not decently gibe.

"Now that I have broken my news, let's change the subject. I wish that I could tell you more about Albuquerque. There is much to tell but none of it seems real to me. It is a strange city in a strange setting. I never have any conviction that it actually exists. It seems like a stage set, or a wide-screen movie in mad color. Greg, I am certain, knows far more about it than I. He fits in here and belongs somehow. I cannot even believe in the people. I was truly interested in people with Spanish blood at home but here they are different. It is hard to explain. Maybe the simple explanation is that they were a minority in Culverton and that here they are a majority, or seem to be. It is warm here now and the summer, I am sure, will be damned hot. According to the figures in our book down at Maxing's, the temperature in Albuquerque is just about the same as in Culverton on an average, but the sun is blazing bright here, very little cloud, and I hate that. You know how my skin reacts to sun. I am going to look like a leper.

"I hope that I have a son. I do not know at this second whether I want him to be born in New Mexico. Maybe when it is time for him to be born, I will love the place. It is difficult to project ahead. I cannot even see a cloudy vision of the future. Maybe I lack imagination. I always considered myself imaginative. I don't know.

"Anyway, I've told you what I started out to tell you. Don't tell Dad yet, but give him my love whether he wants it or not.

All my love to you,

Pam"

Pamela felt tired. She walked around the apartment and then returned to her desk. She read her letter with distaste, tore it into pieces and dropped it in the wastebasket. She had written many letters in her lifetime that the recipients-of-intent never received. The writing of the letter had released something that was pent up inside of her, but the thought of anyone reading it, even her mother, was embarrassing.

Greg came home a little after eight o'clock. He was weary, and dirty. It was difficult for her to accept the fact that he came home dirty. That was one of the inescapable facts of his existence but something in her that was perhaps caste or station rebelled against it. She had never seen herself in even the wildest of mental fantasies, sitting in a humble, mediocre apartment, waiting for a man to come home with the grime of toil on him. It wasn't the way Gibsons lived. Once, no doubt, there had been Gibsons who ended a day with the dirt of it in their skins, but that was long ago. She had not known any of them.

"I'll take a shower before supper," Greg said. "Are we eating in?"

"We could. But I'd like a Mexican dinner."

"Good. So would I."

They had developed a taste for Mexican food and they had a favorite place that was priced to the pockets of people who spoke Spanish. Arturo Aliso's place had shaded low-powered lamps on little tables and all of the employees were Aliso relatives. There was no planned entertainment but sometimes someone would sing and often there would be someone with a guitar. Gregory looked dark and romantic across a table. It was eight blocks from the apartment and they walked there and back in preference to driving. They had a route which took them along a narrow street which looked like a picture from Old Spain.

"I like to walk along here with you," Greg said. "I pretend that the wealthy Lind is honeymooning in Valencia with his lady."

"Why Valencia?"

"It sounds right. Perfect name for a honeymoon spot. The place looks right, too."

"It does. We do." She had her arm linked to his. She looked up into

183

his face. "The only wrong note, Caro mia, is that the lady on that honeymoon is slightly pregnant."

Greg took four steps before her statement registered, then he stopped abruptly. "You can't," he said. "Are you sure?"

"There are signs and portents. And you must admit that there is every reason why I should be."

They stood facing each other on an empty block. Pamela had an adobe wall at her back. She looked at him and pitied him for his bewilderment. Incredibly, he seemed overwhelmed by surprise, as though it had never occurred to him that this might happen. His Church in his time had been in a turmoil about births and pills and all manner of post-coital controversy, but he had lived cheerfully, and more than a bit paganly, with her; assuming, apparently, that they were immune to hazard.

"What are you going to do?" he said.

"Have a baby. What else?"

"Of course. I meant, there are things to do like finding a good doctor and stopping work."

"Not yet. There are months ahead of us."

She started walking again and his touch on her arm was tentative, as though he feared to touch her at all. He would have to get over that. "I'll have to buy you a book on how to be a father," she said.

"Is there such a book?"

"I don't know. There should be."

When they entered their apartment, she turned and kissed him. He held her softly, seemingly afraid to press hard on her body. His cheek was against her head, his voice muffled.

"I'm glad I've got a job," he said. "I'll take care of you. I know how to make more money than I'm making."

"How?"

"Never mind. I will. You can quit work any time. I wish you would."

She felt safe with his arms around her even when something in her mind told her that that was nonsense. She was no safer than when his arms were not around her. Long after he was asleep, she lay awake. Her thoughts formed into confused patterns and she made no attempt to sort them out. Ultimately, she cried into her pillow and she did not know why she was crying.

It was nearly two months before she told the Maxings that she was pregnant and she had a nasty scene with Bernard Maxing. He was neither understanding nor sympathetic, neither polite nor courteous. She was Miss Gibson to him, and had always been Miss Gibson to him. She had no damned business getting pregnant. He took her pregnancy as a personal affront, a betrayal of the confidence that he had placed in her. Lucille Maxing, for her part, was frigidly withdrawn. It was a distressing termination of a relationship.

Pamela Lind did not know how to spend days with nothing to do, without people or conversation or a sense of function. She had not missed friends when she had associates in the office, trip-planners coming in through the day, Greg at night. She had learned before she knew Greg, how to live alone and how to fill lonely hours with music or books, an occasional phone conversation, but she had learned in Culverton where she had an apartment that was a projection of herself, where she had friends and work and a dedicated mission to the less fortunate on three nights of the week. The equivalent did not exist for her in Albuquerque. She had no women friends; the apartment rubbed her nerves raw when she had to spend long hours in it; no one called her on the phone and she called no one; she had no sense of useful function. The fact that she was developing another human being within her body seemed more of an abstraction than a concrete idea.

"And it's an abstraction to Greg, too," she said. "He has no feeling about it at all. No sense of fatherhood."

She often talked to herself and when she was aware of doing so she dismissed the talking as the mere growling of an animal in a cage. She made Greg the object of much of that "growling," vowing to herself later that it was unmeant, that he was the available target and hence the only innocent bystander within range.

On the matter of the baby, she made no mental apologies to Greg. He had never, from the beginning, discussed her condition in any way apart from herself. He was concerned for her, worried about her, uncomplaining about anything that he was called upon to do; but he never, at least in conversation, seemed to link her pregnancy to the idea of a baby. He never projected ahead, never speculated on boy or girl, never assumed for a second the role of parent-to-be. Until he did, she could not speak either in such terms. It was not only baffling, it was frustrating.

The money was running out. She had spent nearly all of the money that she had taken from her account to go away with Greg. She still had money in a Culverton bank but Greg did not know that and this was a bad time to mention it. He was taking the full load of their expenses on his own shoulders and he was meeting the essentials. He had never known about the little things that Pamela called "civilized." He had no idea how much it cost in a beauty shop to keep her hair looking well and he did not know the prices of purely feminine things in the stores. He knew that a woman came in to clean the apartment twice a week and he approved the idea without ever asking how much Pamela paid her. He was always generous about anything that he thought she wanted, but careful about spending even dimes or nickels on himself. He had no sense or understanding of money beyond the immediate, visible need.

The need which followed upon her loss of a paycheck was all too apparent. Her check had been appreciatively larger than his and Greg had approximately the same overhead to meet with the diminished income. He met the situation through the only means available to him and without consulting her. He became a moonlighter; working eight hours a day at the supermarket and four at a filling station, five days a week at the market and one at the gasoline shop.

"You can't do it," she told him. "You'll kill yourself."

"No. A lot of men do it. I pace myself. It looks worse than it is."

However he felt, Greg managed to act quite casual about the idea of two jobs and of a week with little but work in it. He was lean and hard, every soft ounce on his body melted away, and there were shadowy arcs beneath his eyes. His hands were toughened and they felt rough, with black worked into the pores. He left the apartment early in the morning and he came home late at night, but he was never too tired to sit and talk with her. She needed him and she needed conversation and he seemed to know it. He did something that living in Albuquerque had not done for her; he made the place real, a city populated with human beings.

"We couldn't work in a Guadalupe House down here, you and I," he said. "No one could start one. It is different. There are no Spanish Americans and if a man is from Mexico, they call him a Mexican. He is proud of that. If you called anyone in Culverton a Mexican, he was insulted. These people, most of them, are Americans with Spanish names. This state, and all the best part of its history, belongs to them. They have a fine university here. People with all kinds of names go to it, a lot of them Spanish."

She liked to listen to him when he got wound up on any subject. On the Spanish, he would pick up the phone book and read names.

"Look at the doctors," he said. "They are in the minority but they are there; Castillo, Garcia, Martinez. Or lawyers; Apodaca, Baca, Civeralo, Diaz, Duran, Lopez. Walk down the street and see the Spanish names on signs. I think it is great."

He knew so much about this land in which he found himself, the names of desert flowers and of cacti, the times when they blossomed.

He was concerned about Indians because they were the people on the bottom, the pawns, seemingly, of capricious government agencies.

"I frankly don't know why you give a damn," Pamela said.

"I can't change anything if that is what you mean," he said, "and I will probably never try to change anything."

"That," Pamela said, "is not what I meant."

She doubted the depth of his interest in people, never doubting his sincerity. There was a priest pattern that seemed quite apparent. He was accustomed to dealing with people, with becoming involved in their births, deaths, sins, and problems; but his involvement was brief as a priest's, a temporary thing. He did all that he could to help a person over a bad spot and then he moved on, to another person, another problem, another duty. He was still like that. He touched the lives of people, gently and compassionately, but he did not admit those people to his own life. He could not, of course, but it was rather frightening to contemplate.

Pamela wrote letters. It was difficult to start but, once started, she wrote a great many of them; to her mother and to the girls she knew best in her later Culverton period. She never mentioned any of her worries or her problems but the writing of letters which did not mention trouble was an aid toward the banishing of trouble. She plagiarized Greg's discourse on birds and flowers and cacti without crediting him and she mentioned the names of doctors, lawyers and accountants in the phone book as though she, herself, had discovered them.

She had a great many days when she did not feel well, when everything that she attempted was an effort. On a rainy Saturday she visited her doctor and he was cheerfully reassuring without spending too much time on her. He gave her a prescription for pills. She did not like pills of any kind or color so she did not bother to have the prescription filled.

It was still raining on Sunday but she did not want to miss going to Mass with Greg. The Mass meant something to him and she shared the attending if not the meaning. She did not want him to go alone, or to feel that he had to go alone; as long as it was a part of his life, it would be a part of hers. Her reasoning on the subject did not go very deep and she had never held any self debate on it.

Greg brought the car around and she got in. The rain was falling steadily and she put her umbrella down beside her. She felt something under her on the seat as Greg drove away from the curb. She reached down and brought up a woman's scarf.

It was a cheap blue scarf with two thin lines of red at the borders.

She held it in her hand staring at it and her voice did not sound like hers when she spoke.

"Whose scarf is this, Greg?" she said.

"What scarf?"

He was watching traffic. He did not look around but there was surprise in his voice, perhaps shock.

"What scarf?" she repeated, mimicking him. "Never mind the scarf if you are so innocent about it. Who is the woman? And don't say, 'What woman?'"

Her voice was sharp, almost shrill, to her own ears. Greg pulled the car over to the curb in a space reserved for bus loading. He turned in the seat.

"She is a girl named Mary Montoya," he said. "She works at the market where I do. It was raining yesterday and she was waiting for a bus. I ran her home."

Pamela was watching his face. "It isn't the first time you've taken her home," she said.

"It's the third time. When you see someone you know waiting for a bus, it's only natural, Pam."

"It's too damned natural. I won't have it. I won't sit in that apartment, all bulged up with your baby while you run around being natural with any little tart who is waiting for a bus."

"She isn't a tart. She's a decent working girl. And I didn't run around with her. I merely took her home."

"I don't know what you did. And I wouldn't have known anything about your decent working girl if she hadn't left her damned scarf in my car."

She said the "my car" without forming the intent to say it. Having said it, she could not check the repeating of it. Her fists clenched and her voice rose beyond her control.

"I won't have you going around picking up floozies in my car," she said.

Greg's face set, without expression, and he drove away from the curb. "All right, Miss Gibson," he said. "Let's go to Mass."

Her breath caught at the "Miss Gibson." Her career at Maxing's was over and this was the first time Greg had mentioned the triangle sign on her desk there, the first time since he discovered it. He had to be thinking about that, of course. She hadn't known that he was carrying that memory. He had probably been silently resenting the sign through the months. It was a side to him that he had kept hidden from her, she thought, and not a pleasant side. He drove now to the entrance to the church and stopped.

"I'll park and join you," he said.

She had a half-formed resolve to stay in the car, not to enter his church. The rain, however, was falling steadily and it did not seem worth the effort to raise an issue. She went into the church. The Mass had already started which, for some strange reason, embarrassed her. She waited in the vestibule for Greg and went down to a pew with him. He was reverently attentive, as always, his eyes on the altar. She had no interest in the altar today, nor in him. Her thoughts turned inward on herself.

Why, in the name of everything ridiculous, was she in this strange city, with no friends and no money, sitting in a Catholic church and growing heavy with a baby? Why in hell was she? A man had all the freedom. He wasn't pinned down. He could wander wide and free. How could she know how many women had been in that car? Only one of them had left a scarf. Her mother had warned her. Carina said that when this man learned about women he would be curious about a lot of women. He had been detached from them, insulated against them, until he met her. What made her think she could hold him?

"I can hold him," she said.

Gregory half turned toward her but her words were blotted up in the public recital of the Apostles' Creed. She stared straight ahead, letting the Mass and all the public praying pass her by. She filed out beside Gregory when it was all over and she waited in the vestibule until he brought the car. The rain was a thin, ugly drizzle now.

It was a normal procedure for them to stop for midday dinner on the way home from Mass. Greg did not deviate from it. He stopped at Arturo Aliso's. She wanted to say that she did not feel like eating and she had a silent reservation that she did not plan to express, a reservation about Mexican food. It did not seem like a good idea. Once she had had a quaint thought that she did not express to Greg because Greg did not regard the baby as a human being. She thought that their child would probably live in New Mexico all of his life because he would be addicted to Mexican cooking before he was born.

They went into Arturo's place and Arturo greeted them. Pamela did not say that she did not feel like eating; she was, in fact, suddenly hungry. Greg had retreated into an unaccustomed silence, far away from her, and she did not pursue him. They ate their dinner with the exchange of only a few words, then drove back to the apartment. The apartment was, at best, a dull place with no imagination in its furnishings and today it seemed particularly unfriendly. It was, Pamela thought, definitely hostile toward her. Greg walked around the living room then came to a stop with his hands rammed into his pockets.

"Look, Pam," he said. "I'm sorry that all this happened. I haven't let you down in any way. I haven't done anything I'm ashamed of. Since it disturbs you so much, I'm sorry I ever picked up anybody in your car, but—"

"I don't give a damn about the car." She could feel her body thrusting forward in the chair, hear her voice pitched much too high. She saw Gregory through a haze. "I do care about this woman. I don't want you to take her home ever again. I don't want you playing the gallant gentleman and the friendly helpmate to any women anywhere." She drew a deep breath. "If you want to cut loose from me and go your way, with a woman or without one, just tell me! That is all you have to do. But I won't share you, not for five minutes, with any woman on earth."

Gregory stood straight, listening to her. He was pale under his tan. "I understand, Pam," he said quietly. "You won't have anything to worry about. You haven't had any cause for worry about other women, whether you want to believe that or not."

Pamela did not answer him. It was impossible to make anything important clear to another human being. She had said much to Greg that she felt deeply, that she meant with all of her soul, and she had said some things she would like to recall. They all ran together and she could not sort them out.

Greg turned on the radio and they listened for a little while but neither of them was interested. They turned it off early and went to bed.

The dark pressed down on Pamela and there was an element of terror in it. She did not feel right, not humanly whole and integrated. She had told the doctor that and he had not taken her seriously. He had been masculinely superior and reassuring. She had not wanted to eat Mexican food today. She should not have eaten any. She had something the matter with her. She could not define it but she always knew when she was in or out of tune. She closed her eyes, trying desperately to sleep. Her eyes opened wide and she screamed when the pain came.

It was a sharp, merciless, penetrating pain deep inside of her, a plunging pain that did not seem to find bottom. Greg wakened instantly and she felt his arm under her shoulders.

"What is it, Pam?" he said.

"Pain. Oh, Greg. Please. Do something."

He was on the phone then and his voice seemed to come from a hazy distance. He was talking to the doctor and then he was throwing on his clothes. The ambulance came for her and she remembered the crazy angles on everything she saw when they carried her down the stairs, the pell-mell, unreal series of images that flowed past the ambulance. It was the next day before she was able to talk to Greg.

He sat beside her hospital bed, holding her hand. It was impossible to believe that she had ever been angry with him.

"I lost our baby, Greg," she said. "I tried. I went through a lot. I really did. I must have done something stupid. I lost him."

"I know. It wasn't your fault. Those things happen, Pam."

"I wanted the baby, Greg. You didn't, did you?"

"Yes. I did."

"Tell me the truth."

"I did."

She sighed and closed her eyes, then opened them. "Greg!"

"Yes, Pam."

"I can't stay in Albuquerque, Greg. It has never been right for me. Never. I want to leave it. You'll take me, won't you?"

"Where?"

"I don't know. Texas, maybe. A woman who came to Maxings owns a travel agency in Hollister, Texas. It is near the Gulf. I'd like that, Greg. Big water. I liked the woman. I'll remember her name in a minute."

"Are you sure, Pam?" Greg's voice seemed far away from her. "You are upset now. Albuquerque is a lovely town. We haven't done much about it, really. We can do a lot more."

"I don't want to do anything about it."

Greg was silent for a long minute. He stroked her hand. "Don't leave just because some things went wrong here," he said. "Running away won't make them better. It won't solve anything."

"I don't want to solve anything."

He held her hand firmly. "All right," he said. "Don't worry about it. If you want to go to a place named Hollister, we'll go."

– VII –

There were a dozen cities in Texas, with populations exceeding one hundred thousand, and Hollister was not the least of them. Hollister claimed a population of 159,817. It was larger than Amarillo, Lubbock or Beaumont; smaller than Austin or Corpus Christi. Hollister was built on a series of low hills which looked down upon the normally narrow Rio de Los Tontitos. The river flowed to the Gulf and there was a four lane divided highway which connected Hollister with Harrow Harbor, twenty-seven miles away, the Gulf outlet.

Greg and Pamela Lind came to the city from the northwest through a forest of pine trees which opened up abruptly to reveal the town. It was late afternoon and the sunlight was pink on the roofs, a series of flashing reflections in the windows facing west. The hills stood unevenly above the river and the town clung to the hills. The highway that they followed was a series of curves ahead of them and below them. Greg was driving. Pam's fingers tightened on his forearm as she leaned forward.

"Greg, I love it," she said.

"I believe you. It looks pretty good to me, too."

He liked the freshness, the enthusiasm, the excitement in her voice. She had been listless after she came home from the hospital and far from her old self when they drove out of Albuquerque. He had hated leaving the city of the Dukes and she had wanted to leave it, but she had left most of the work and the worry to him. She had not even been cheerful.

He wasn't certain that she had ever forgiven him for taking that girl home from the supermarket, which was a great absurdity. For his own part, he had disliked the automobile since she raised the issue of "my car." That, too, of course, was an absurdity. In the marriages that had lasted many years, he imagined, there were many incidents like the girl and the "my car"; a series of dull, thudding rocks that took the sparkle and the gleam and the resilience out of marriage. It was so easy to see the folly of such things and so difficult to do anything reasonable about the situations they created.

The curving road straightened and became a wide boulevard which led to the heart of town. Hollister was an old city, as Texas cities went, but it looked as though it had all been built yesterday or perhaps this morning. There were motels and drive-in diners and stores selling TV, loan shops and used car lots, the usual depressing sequence which was average Americana to the traveler. The standard array was, somehow, rather bright and cheerful here; probably because the town looked clean and the junky places of business looked temporary.

There was a small motel within a half mile of the main shopping area and they checked in. They had stopped at bigger, more exciting ones on their first trip together but this had all that they needed temporarily. Pamela was humming as she unpacked her bag. She stopped abruptly and turned.

"I have a feeling, Greg," she said, "a very strong feeling, about Hollister. We are going to be lucky here, both of us."

"I hope so."

"We will be."

She resumed her humming and her unpacking. He liked seeing her in this mood. She had a special magic. Her hair had a slightly wind-blown look but deep copper glowed in it. They had had some sun on the way down and she had lost her pallor. Her lips were as defiantly red as they always were. She was a lovely girl, slim and graceful. Hollister was something she had wanted, and she had it.

"I am going to run down to the post office while you are getting settled," he said.

Her head came up. "Why?"

"We're practically broke. I knew that we would be. I wrote to Bart and asked him to send me a hundred and fifty, general delivery, here."

"You shouldn't," she said. "I've never met Bart." She lifted a small cosmetic case out of the bag and looked at it thoughtfully. "One hundred and fifty dollars!" she said.

Gregory drove down into the town. The post office was on a side street off the main drag. His letter was waiting there for him, a few lines on the back of an estimate form.

Dear Greg:

The requested is enclosed. Let me know if you need more. Barbara will write when you have a regular address. Everything rocks along normally here. Nothing startling. Take care of yourself.

Bart.

There was a check for one hundred and fifty dollars enclosed. Looking at it, the check told its own story. Bart, being Bart, would have sent more than he was asked to send if he had been riding a winning streak. Quite obviously, Bart Lind was not prosperous at the moment.

"I am going to hate cashing this," Greg thought.

Hate it or not, he would, of course, cash it. Even if both he and Pamela got jobs immediately, they would have to live until their pay-days came around. They could not afford to go on living in a motel and without Bart's check they would not have the cash to rent an apartment. Standing in the post office, Greg remembered Pamela's saying "one hundred and fifty dollars." Despite all that they had experienced in a short time, she obviously found it difficult to take that amount of money seriously. It was, and would be, forever small to her.

"It's the way one has lived, of course," he thought. "Pamela and I did not learn out of the same book."

He had a fair idea now what Pamela's apartment on Steuben Drive must have cost; he had had no slightest idea when he was visiting her there. Priests, on the whole, even when confronted every day with people who had financial problems, tended to magnify the resources of any individual layman; they had good, sound clues to the incomes of parishioners and they always minimized living expenses on the layman's level. That, at least, was the conclusion he had reached from his experience of living as a layman. It was difficult for him to imagine earning, at any time present or future, the income that would be necessary to support Pamela as she had lived before she met him.

He drove back to the motel through the evening rush hour traffic. Culverton was a larger city than Hollister and Albuquerque was larger than either of them but the Texas city, in the rush hour, seemed like a very big place. Pamela, when he reached the motel, was wearing a light gray suit that he had always liked. She was looking at the telephone book. She raised her eyes when he came in and tossed off, in half chant, a challenge to verse.

"I am a denizen of Texas."

Greg shrugged. "You chose that tricky word to vex us."

"Lousy rhyme," she said. "I've been looking at the travel agencies. The Leland Barker one is the one I know. It isn't the largest."

"It doesn't have to be, does it?"

"No. Of course not. All it has to be is the place where I work."

"We'll hold that thought."

He did not look at the telephone book Yellow Pages himself but, after they had dinner, he turned to the want ads in the evening paper. The ads were almost interchangeable with Albuquerque. He could not answer any ad that called for a skilled barber, a plumber's assistant, a bookkeeper, fry cook, painter, auto body worker. There was one ad that interested him but he did not mention it to Pamela. She wouldn't like the job and he might not get it. He had very thin maneuvering time. He had to find a place on a payroll, and quickly.

Pamela picked up the paper when he discarded it. She read the ads under HELP WANTED MALE. He watched her reading them and their eyes met when she lifted her head.

"There are a lot of ads for salesmen, Greg," she said. "Why won't you try?"

"I'm not a salesman."

"You don't know. You have a fine personality. You talk well. People like you. You could sell mutual investment plans, insurance, any number of things that have dignity."

"No. My mind doesn't work that way. There's nothing in my background, my thinking, that would help me sell stocks, bonds or insurance."

"Other things then?"

He shook his head. "It's this way, Pam," he said. "If I was trying to sell a man something that he'd be foolish to buy, or that he couldn't afford, I couldn't go through with it. I'd tell him to skip it."

"You're odd," she said. "It isn't your responsibility if some stranger is foolish or is willing to buy something he can't afford. That stranger has a right to make mistakes if he wants to make them."

"I won't help him to make mistakes, or talk him into them. I couldn't do it, Pam."

He lay awake in the night remembering that conversation. He knew that Pam was not unreasonable in hoping that he would work where he could dress well and have, as she put it, "dignity." He had dressed well and he had had dignity when she met him. She had not been able to take any pride in the work that he found in Albuquerque and she had been embarrassed by his appearance. There had been a rift of sorts between them on that account, a loss of enchantment. He hadn't found an alternative and Hollister did not promise to offer more than Albuquerque had.

Half asleep, he thought as he had thought many times, that there was one position of dignity that he was capable of holding and he wondered why the idea had never occurred to Pamela. He had a fair command of two foreign languages, a good background in history and geography, and a better than average supply of patience. He would probably work well in a travel agency. He could not, of course, work in the same office with Pam, nor work in another agency competing with her, so that was not to be considered; but he wondered why the idea had never occurred to Pam.

He was out in the morning while Pam was still asleep and he left the car for her to use, walking fourteen blocks to the old section of downtown where Hollister General Hospital stood. The hospital was a series of red brick buildings spread over two square blocks. The emergency rooms were in a low building on the north side with two slots for ambulances and parking space for six cars. The six spaces were occupied, the slots empty. Greg walked up a ramp. There was a broad aisle on his left, right-angled to the ramp, in which a great many people sat. He did not know whether the people were waiting for medical attention or waiting for patients, but they were certainly waiting.

The corridor on his right was a series of small offices where doctors, presumably, examined patients. The emergency facilities occupied a wing that angled off from the end of the corridor. The ambulance slots fed into this wing which contained operating rooms and rest areas. There was a glass enclosed office with a black-lettered legend on the door which read: TRACY WELTON. Mr. Welton was the man who had advertised in last night's paper for an ambulance driver.

There was a man at the Welton desk who was being interviewed. Greg could see only his back, but there were chairs along the partition inside the door and when Greg seated himself he could study Tracy Welton without being obvious about it.

Tracy Welton was perhaps forty and could have been forty-five. He was slender, sallow-skinned, narrow eyed. He had thinning, blond hair and sharply defined eyebrows. He was wearing a brown jacket and a dark green ascot. He was smoking a cigarette. Behind him on the wall was a large calendar from which a worried-looking tiger looked into the room. Beneath the tiger there were two printed lines:

"If the meek shall inherit the earth,

What in hell will happen to all us tigers?"

The man being interviewed rose and left. The man behind the desk nodded to Greg Lind. There was no expression of interest in his face.

"You're an ambulance driver?" he said.

"I am. I worked two summers at it."

"How long ago?"

"About ten years."

"You don't look like a drunk."

"I'm not."

"O.K. Let's see how you look on the sheet." Tracy Welton took a printed form from the middle drawer of his desk. "You can fill it out right here."

Greg sat in the chair vacated by the applicant who had left. The form was very similar to a great many others. He could answer the questions in his sleep and even if he were tempted to lie or evade, he would not know how to do it. He was required to state his education, the what and the where, and then account for his employed time previous to this application. He filled in all the spaces, signed his name on the bottom, then raised his head. The man on the other side of the desk had been studying him. He passed the sheet across the desk and waited.

Tracy Welton read the answers in a glance. He flipped the form into the wastebasket with a languid sweep of his hand. A sneering smile moved over his lips but his eyes were cold.

"I would not give a Catholic priest the sweat from my huevos," he said.

Greg Lind pushed his chair back and rose slowly. He had had an uneasy feeling about Tracy Welton and he was certain now of what he had considered a mere possibility a few minutes ago.

"That is all right, Father Welton," he said, "if that is how you want it."

He had his hand on the knob of the door when the other man, circling the desk rapidly, gripped his shoulder. There were two curved white lines, like brackets, around the corners of Tracy Welton's mouth.

"Just what do you mean by that crack?" he said. "What do you mean?"

"Take your hand off my shoulder!"

The hand dropped. Tracy Welton was an inch shorter than Gregory Lind but he held himself erect and there was a hard quality in him.

"Where do you get that 'Father Welton' stuff?" he said.

"Why not? You're a one-time priest, as I am."

The eyes of the two men met and held, then Tracy Welton turned away.

"O.K.," he said. "You are the first one to spot it. What did I do to tip you off?"

"I don't know." Greg shrugged. "Your hands mostly. You do a bit of ritual with them. There's something in your voice, too."

"Marked and branded, aren't we? But it takes another priest to read the brand. That's why I never wanted one around." Tracy Welton seated himself in the swivel chair and reached into the wastebasket for the discarded application form. He spread the form flat on the desk top and his phone rang. He answered it, talking to someone named "Dr. Clyde."

"I'm sorry," he said. "I didn't think she'd make it. She was a nice little thing. I appreciate your calling me, Doctor."

He hung up slowly. "One of our customers just died," he said. "A girl of twenty-one. Two kids and a husband. Some punk on a stolen motorcycle ran over her."

He lighted a fresh cigarette, taking his time. "About this job," he said. "It's driving a hurry wagon, seven to three. I would rather have you on the first-aid side, with your experience but driver is the job that's open. Want it?"

"I applied for it."

"It's yours." Tracy Welton let smoke drift lazily from his nostrils. He was leaning slightly back, his eyes narrowed. "I won't ever like you, of course, but you're the kind of man I need around here."

"That's all that is necessary. We don't have to like each other."

"All right. That's settled. I don't suppose that you know the city."

"I don't. I can read a map, and study one."

"The man riding with you will keep you on the target. You'll need a driver's license. They cooperate with us at the traffic bureau. You can go down and get it this morning. You'll be starting on the wagon with a wise old-timer named Jack Serkle. Let's go down and meet him."

Tracy Welton was back in his role again, boss of an ambulance crew, a hirer of men with nothing of the ex-priest in his attitude. He walked with a trace of swagger, a roll of shoulders. The office next to his was a bullpen of sorts where the ambulance crews waited between calls. Greg Lind was introduced to Jack Serkle and his morning began.

It was a crowded morning. Jack Serkle was gruff, not overly friendly, but he guided Greg through the ambulance procedures, procured a manual for him and accompanied him when he went down to take his driver's test. It was almost impossible to guess Serkle's age. He was short, powerfully built, and his face was a series of lines, ridges and bumps, as though he had been beaten early and often. He looked patient, enduring, and he talked little; even when the two men shared lunch, he had no conversation in him. At the end of the day, fifteen minutes remaining before three o'clock, he sat with Greg in the bullpen and lighted a pipe.

"Quiet one, aren't you?" he said.

"I was with a quiet one."

"Aye. It's better. There's men that talk holes in your ears. I like that name of yours. Lind! I don't remember seeing it anywhere. Probably Lindberg or Lindquist or one of those Swede names if you spelled it all out."

"No. It's just Lind."

"Sure. That's better. Stick with it. My own name now. I like it. This job's the first place I've had it."

"Serkle?"

"John F. Serkle. Know what the 'F' stands for?"

"I haven't an idea."

"Full. John Full Serkle. That's me. Good, isn't it? Tells a story."

"I suppose that it does. I'd like to hear the story."

"You won't."

"I didn't believe I would. How did you answer all those questions in that damned application form if Serkle isn't your real name?"

"No sweat. I just put down anything. You don't suppose a stuck-up bastard like Welton is going to write to your references, do you? He figures he can tell about men. Just one sharp look from his bloodshot eye!"

"How about the social security card?"

"Anybody can get one of them. I've got three."

The man who had not talked all day was talkative enough at the end. He sat, smoking his pipe, obviously pleased that he had an audience. Greg didn't push him or try to invade areas which he did not open up himself. Jack Serkle drew appreciatively on the pipe.

"What's your trouble? The bottle?" he said.

"No. Why should I have trouble?"

"Everybody does. Nobody takes a job down here unless he has big trouble. Mine's the bottle."

Greg made no comment and the other man looked at him, one eyebrow raised. "Your problem is maybe women," he said, "or not-women. Maybe you're an ex-con. We get them, too. Me, I can go a year without a drink sometimes. Never touch the stuff. Then something lets go and maybe I drink steadily for a year; real, hard, stinko, rolling-in-the-gutter drinking. Makes a man a real slob, that kind. I've been church-going respectable this time for seven months."

John F. Serkle rose, knocked the ash out of his pipe and waved his hand. "Time to go home. See you in the morning."

Gregory Lind watched him walk away. It was surprising when a stranger opened up like that, but a great many people did; loneliness, maybe. Serkle was not as overboard-revealing as he seemed, at that; even if one believed all that he said, one would know very little about the man.

Gregory walked back to the motel. He wondered how Pam had made out. He hadn't called her. The day had been a busy one and he hadn't thought about calling her. He had not told her, either, about the job he was seeking. She would not have liked it in advance and she would not, he feared, like it now when it was a fact accomplished.

He measured off the blocks, walking them, liking the exercise. It would be impossible to explain to Pamela now how he felt about seeking work, even if he were good at explaining. He had not shared that seeking with her in the past. He could still see the masks which settled on the faces of potential employers, or personnel managers, when he told them that he had been a priest. He could see again, too, the faces which reflected dislike of him, or contempt, and there were many of those. A man walked pavement all day and he sought work and he looked at those faces. When he came home, he wanted to be cheerful, and tried to be; he did not want to relive his day.

It had been impossible to face it all again in a new town, to slip gradually down the scale of jobs and end up at manual labor. He had been an ambulance man once, and rather proudly. The people who had needed him were people whose need was great. Again, one did not explain such ideas well; one lived in the knowledge that his work was

199

worth the doing. One could call that knowledge "humble pride" perhaps. Was there such a thing? Humble pride? He believed that there was.

The blocks had clicked off under his heels and he turned in at their motel. Pamela was home ahead of him. She had a fresh hairdo and that was the first thing that he noticed. Her hair looked marvelous, soft, billowing out around her head, darkly copper in shade.

"Nice," he said. "I like your hair."

"Do you?" She touched it instinctively. "I didn't know how they'd do in Hollister. New places are so often distressing." She broke off abruptly. "How did you make out?"

There was little lightness in her. The angles in her face were marked, the inverted triangle of her features quite apparent. He knew that something had depressed her. It would have to be the job. She didn't get it. That seemed fantastic. He had not even considered that as a possibility. The thought made it doubly difficult to talk about his own good fortune. He threw himself down in a chair, facing her.

"I connected," he said.

Her eyes lighted. "No, Greg. You didn't?"

"I did. I'll be driving an ambulance, seven till three. Nice hours."

He was stopped by the shock in her face. Her voice, flowing in to fill the silence he had left for it, carried a note of dismay.

"Oh, no," she said. "You didn't try for anything else? You started at the bottom."

"It isn't the bottom. It's serving people, Pam; people who are hurt, dying, in danger. It's something worth doing and the pay is better than I earned in Albuquerque; much better."

"Damn the pay! Greg, you know you can do better than that. You have a mind. You should be someplace where you can move ahead, not someplace static, doing something that is always the same."

"Most jobs are what you call static."

"I don't care. You don't belong in them if they are like that."

He sat and looked at her helplessly. It was flattering to have her see him as the ideal junior executive, making important decisions, dictating to secretaries, giving orders to people under him. It was, however, a daydream. He wasn't trained for anything like that, did not know or understand the things he would have to know and understand in even the simplest business set-up. He was a bit old for the positions that he might be able to hold, and he was an ex-priest. He could not argue or explain, but he had absorbed knowledge of himself and of the world in which he lived while he was walking the streets of Albuquerque.

Pamela seemed to read the turmoil inside of him, looking into his face. She rose, crossed the room and kissed him.

"I'm sorry if I sounded harsh," she said. "It's just that I believe in you more than you do."

He pulled her down onto his lap. She curled lazily, softly, across his legs, her head against his shoulder. He was aware of the faint, elusive scent that had always been hers. She was a lovely person, lovely to hold.

"How about your day?" he said.

"I missed."

"How?"

"The agency I knew was Leland Barker. I wrote when I knew we were coming here. I wrote to Mrs. Barker. Her name is Roberta but people call her Bobbie. She's a nice person but she says they have a full staff."

"How about the other travel agencies?"

"I tried them all. Same story. They didn't need anyone."

"Damn! I never anticipated that."

"Neither did I."

He knew that she needed sympathy and he felt it for her. Walking into place after place, bracing one's self, being turned down, trying another place. He had been all through that. He rubbed her back. She always liked that. It relaxed her. He had had an impulse to buy Scotch on the way home. This was Texas. You had to buy it in a package shop and carry it home. Nobody served it to you. He and Pam had stopped drinking anything months ago. They got along fine without it, which was fortunate; they couldn't afford it. Still, tonight, if he'd brought it in, it might have been good for Pam.

"Let's look for an apartment," he said.

There was still daylight, not much but a little. He told Pamela to drive and she did exactly what he expected her to do. She drove up a curving street to a hill that overlooked the town. The streets on the hilltop were parallel, one street higher than the next. It was similar to the neighborhood of Steuben Drive but the apartment buildings were newer, larger, composed of many apartments rather than of few. Some of the apartment houses bore vacancy signs. The rents, in proportion to the Lind income and funds, were enormous. Pamela conceded that sad fact slowly, reluctantly.

"I guess we can't live up here," she said.

Greg had a sense of personal defeat. He had never known how much rent Pamela paid for her apartment on Steuben Drive. None of these apartments compared with it. Those that were furnished, the only ones they could consider, had no comparable furniture to Pamela's. They drove down the hill again and they had dinner in a small restaurant. At seven-thirty they rented an apartment in the low level of town.

The apartment was a slightly enlarged motel unit in design and in furnishing. It was on Del Rio Street, a fairly quiet residential block. The total effect, neighborhood and dwelling place, was mediocre. There was no lift or excitement in the renting. As they walked back to their car, Pamela said:

"Greg, I need a drink, a big drink. Do you suppose we could buy a bottle of Scotch?"

He looked at her face. She looked depressed, defeated. She had failed to find a place to work and the place in which she would have to live was without any touch of glory. She did not like the work that her husband would do. Liquor would not help her.

"No, Pam," he said gently. "No drink. Not tonight. The mood is all wrong."

– VIII –

Pamela Lind visited offices and met personnel managers and filled out application-for-employment forms. She found people who were interested in her command of languages but who did not have a need for that command at the moment. She discovered a fact which should have been obvious in advance; that a Texas city so close to the Gulf would attract a great many people with the approach of winter, and that a good percentage of the people attracted would seek work. Hollister gave her the first experience she had had with a tight labor market. She had held few positions and she had walked into the few without encountering difficulty. She began to understand Greg's problem but she was still at odds with his solution.

In November, she started a journal. The setting down of thoughts and ideas released tensions within herself and a journal seemed to make more sense than torn-up letters in a wastebasket. She did not write every day and she did not date her entries. She made no effort to achieve continuity but her entries constituted a form of narrative.

"Wednesday: We arrived in Hollister one month ago today. I am not certain what we were seeking, but I know that we haven't found it. The climate in this place is wonderful. It is November now and we have not had a cold day yet. There is moisture in the air and it does wonders for my skin and hair. Greg's hair, too, is curling. He is more handsome than ever. He has gained weight, muscle-weight and not fat. He has a rugged quality now and a strong sense of physical competence. I do not like his job and he does. He likes it too well and that liking underlines a great weakness in him. He is not ambitious. He has no drive toward success in anything. He does not aspire. This is probably the result of his training to be a priest. I imagine most of them are like Greg. I do not know what to do about it. He is living better now than he did as a priest, he likes the rough men with whom he is associated, and our way of life satisfies him, just as it is; the eating in shabby restaurants, the living in a hideous apartment, our lack of friends or any social life. I'd walk out on all of this in five minutes flat but I can't walk out on Greg. I'd follow him to worse, I am afraid, and it is not all physical, not nearly all. I don't know what to do.

"Thursday: I have a job, for two days. My friends at the Leland Barker agency phoned me today. One of their regular girls is ill. I shall fill in tomorrow and Saturday. Even two days will make a difference. Not so much financially, of course. It is a desperate situation, living entirely on Greg's earnings. He is wonderful about it and I have an idea that he likes it that way, but it means watching nickels and dimes. Preposterous, living as we do! I am frightened sometimes. Greg's top earning capacity is the top of our living and he is not doing anything at which a man can advance. When I tell him that he is fastened to a pattern of repetition, spinning around like a wheel on a wall, getting nowhere, he says that most jobs are like that. I would tell him that we are not 'most people' but I am afraid that he would say that we are. I do not want to hear him say it. He tells me about his adventures in the ambulance. I can see where they would appeal to a man. He has had some messy automobile accidents and he has had several suicides or would-be suicides. One, a girl, jumped out of a five story window. He says that she was conscious all the way to the hospital where she died, and she said to him, 'I didn't mean to do it. I want to change my mind.' I'm glad I didn't see her. I wouldn't be able to sleep. Greg worries, too, about the ones who die. He worries about their souls, I think, but he doesn't say anything to me about that. We do not discuss souls. I can't explain to him how I believe, so I don't try. I am Me. I believe that I will go on being Me after I die. I don't believe I will be rewarded or punished. I will merely have work to do and I'll probably only be trusted to the extent that I have been of value in this world: I'll have a good job or a bad one, in other words. As to what the purpose of it all is, I can't guess—and I do not believe anyone else can. The theories and the philosophies and the doctrines are all mere guesswork, and masculine guesswork at that. I cannot talk like this to Greg. He would laugh at me.

"Monday: I am out of work again. No luck today. Two days in a travel agency again just made my mouth water. If I could do what Greg did, step down, I could get a job. I could find work, I am certain, in stores as a clerk, and maybe I am cowardly. We need the money so what right have I to scorn anything? Well, I am not scorning. I am afraid that if I take a job that offers nothing to me but dollars, I will never have any position again that calls something out of me. It is different with Greg. I do not want to think about that difference now. We had a bad time at the Mass yesterday. I always go with him. He has been disturbed about the Mass since they started saying it all in English. He liked it best when it was all in Latin, then they reserved the part that means most to him and said that in Latin. Now, no Latin at all. Yesterday we went to a church named Immaculate Mother. Greg has been unhappy with all the Catholic churches down here. He says they are all 'gung ho' priests in Hollister, prideful progressives, the kind that would say a Mass in a kitchen. He says that he is more sharply aware of what is happening to the Church since he is out of it than he would be if he stayed in and got carried along. Anyway, yesterday was the climax. There was a fat, ham-actor type of priest and he was all over the altar space, tossing out asides to the congregation during the performance of what should be solemn ritual. Even someone like myself knows that it should be solemn. At one point, Father Fatso stopped the Mass to say: 'Come again with that Ay-men. I want to hear it loud, good and loud. You don't want to go back to mumbling Latin, do you?' I thought that Greg was going to get up and walk out. He had the blues last night. I worry about Greg and the Church. It isn't as bad as another woman, but it does disturb me. He has a loyalty there that is older than any loyalty he owes me and it tugs at him.

"Friday: I have my fingers crossed. The best advertising agency in Hollister called me in today for another interview. They need someone to handle their correspondence in Spanish. I read a lot of letters for them and I wrote some. I will know on Monday what they decide. My Spanish is damned good but I have a weakness in it; I studied the pure Castilian. Good old high-hat, snobbish me! I had most of a year in Spain but none in the dialect countries. I should try to speak to Mexico and Colombia, and Venezuela and the Banana Republics in the lisping accent of Castile! Oddly enough, ironically enough, Guadalupe House may get me through this. I learned a lot of dialects there, and a lot of gutter Spanish. I certainly did.

"Sunday: I am taking the pill, of course. I have been taking it ever since I lost my baby in Albuquerque. I did not feel up to going through that again and I have been timid about our entire situation. If people called children down at their own wills, and they don't, of course, this would be a most uncertain home to offer a child. We have just barely enough money on which to survive. We have no replacement money at all. My car is showing wear. It is squeaky and jumpy and the tires are thin. We do not have a hope of replacing the car, or even the tires. Greg needs clothes and so do I. We have no furniture of our own. My father and mother are fairly young people and should live the good long time that I wish them. My father has not softened or relented where I am concerned. He has not even sent me a line of good wishes in my mother's letters and she is too honest to fake anything like that. If he does not send his love, she does not try to enclose it. My marrying a priest was entirely too much for my father and I can understand that. My mother, as she told me, will never act behind my father's back. If he does not want to send me any money, she will not do so. I applaud that. I do not want money from them. It would embarrass me. I do not know, however, how we will turn out on our own. I was certain once that I knew. Now I don't. I have an idea about Greg that is rather alarming. I want to think a little before I try to write it down. This is a dull, lonely Sunday. Greg has to drive that ambulance every other Sunday. This is a work day. We went to six o'clock Mass today. It was quiet. Greg liked that. He hates all the singing, responding, jumping up and down. I have to say that I agree with him. If there is a God and one wants to pray, which is really talking to the unknown and the invisible, then one needs silence. There is meditation in it if it is any good at all, prayer, and nobody can meditate while he is jumping up and down, shouting responses. Well, anyway, I don't know anything about that, but I've been thinking about the pill and that is what I started to write about today. I haven't made up my mind but it seems to me that I should stop taking it. Greg and I are healthy, ardent animals and we should be able to produce healthy offspring. It seems to me that we should but I am not idealistic enough to submit myself as an instrument to a good cause or anything like that. I am selfish. I felt from the start, and I told Carina that I wanted to give a child to Greg; partly for the feminine reason that I love the man and want to complete myself as a woman, but mainly, perhaps, because I am married to a priest. I do not know how strong the hold of the Church is, and I do not know how long I will have magic for Greg. I may need help. I am frightened sometimes when I look around this ugly flat. I dominated situations pretty well when I had my own setting, that apartment of mine and my music and my privacy to which one had to be admitted. Now I have nothing to rely upon but myself, and I am not at my best. This setting is Greg's in obvious ways and subtle ways. He is paying for it and he is at home in it, oblivious to its shrieking ugliness. I would not like to call a child down if he would hate the life to which I called him. It would not be fair to ask for him and not give him what he needed. Greg and I are outcasts, if that does not sound too melodramatic. We cannot return to Culverton which represents security to me; not together we can't. Greg, I am certain, feels that he can never go back there and he is probably right. I'll never leave him while he needs me or wants me, but he has no ambition. I don't know. I am still taking the pill, but I don't know. There are so many things I have to work out.

"Tuesday: I am working again. There should be dancing in the streets. I had no idea, until I was out of work, how much it means to feel needed and wanted and useful. I am on the staff of Peckham and Potter, a fine advertising agency. The office here is only a branch, with the main office in Dallas, but this looks more like a main office than most main offices. We occupy half of the tenth floor in Hollister's newest office building, a tall rectangle which looks as though it were made of glass. I have my own private office. It is small but it is all mine and I can look down upon the silly river that flows through town. My aristocratic Spanish, with its touch of Guadalupe House, is highly esteemed and respected by the partners. I will handle anything that has even a trace of Spanish accent. There is a girl in the next office named Carol Dane. Carol is very dark, about my age and married to a man who knows how to feed facts to a computer and get answers. He is a graduate of MIT and works for a shipbuilding firm in Harrow Harbor which is twenty-seven miles from here. He commutes every day. She says that they are poor and struggling but they each have a car and they live in one of those apartments that Greg and I looked at on our first day here, half-way up that hill. Carol and I had lunch together. She talks a lot but I like her. Greg was delighted about my position. There is no envy in him, nothing small. I will be earning more than he is and he seems genuinely happy for me. I know that he enjoyed the idea that he was supporting me but he knew that I would not be happy unless I pulled an oar, too. He bought some Scotch to celebrate with me and I'll admit that I liked that. It was a little like old times, facing each other in our living room, feeling the liquor bite a bit and talking to each other about a multitude of things. If only the apartment was not so depressingly dull! It is almost vulgar. No matter how I rearrange things and add touches, I cannot get that low commonplace look out of the place in which we live, and I know that we did not bring that look with us. I am going to need some new clothes. I wrote to my bank in Culverton this afternoon. I am drawing five hundred dollars. I cannot tell Greg because it is money he does not know I have. I would have spent it happily when we both needed things and when Greg even worried about food, but I would have robbed him of something if I had come up with a bankroll. He had to get it, and he did. I had to endure whatever happened to us, and endure it patiently; and I did. Now, I need clothes. Greg has no idea what my things cost. He won't even be curious.

"Friday: I do not keep this book very well. I do not know why I keep it at all. It satisfies something in me to see my thoughts and ideas in words. I try to be honest. I believe that I am. I would not like Gregory to see this but if he did, and if he read it, it would not be a catastrophe; but he wouldn't read anything personal of mine. He just wouldn't. Honor, to him, is not something that he brags about; it is something that he lives with and never mentions. I receive quite a lot of mail from Culverton, a letter from Carina every week, letters from a half dozen girls I know, form letters from all the good causes that need money and ads from stores I used to patronize. Greg never shows any interest in them; they are mine. He receives letters himself. His mother lives with his sister Janet and Janet writes to him. I have never read any of the letters but from what he tells me, I am certain I would not like Janet. He has had a few letters from a sister-in-law named Barbara and he does not talk about her but he likes her. I would love to read her letters and he asks for it, leaving letters around carelessly, as he does. I never even glance at any letter of his. He hears from a priest he knows named Guyton and very occasionally from his brother Bart. That is about it. He receives far less mail than I do. He does not write many letters, either. Mail is an unsatisfactory substitute for people. Few people are real in the letters they write.

"Saturday: I went shopping today. Carol went with me. We had the afternoon off. Gregory was working. I don't know about Carol's husband. I am embarrassed there. We should have a party or get-together or something but I certainly cannot invite them to that place of ours and I do not know how Greg would work out with them. It is strange. Greg and I have no friends that were ours, not since we were married; no one to sit around and talk with us, or argue, to share a few drinks and a dinner, or a show. I wonder if there was ever a marriage like ours. The fact that Greg was a priest and that we literally married on the run turned everything upside down for us. I'm sure that I feel the lack of a social life far more than Greg does. As I must have noted before, he touched people rather obliquely as a priest, a few steps detached from them; yet he is wonderful company with me. I just do not know how he would be with anyone else, and we have to know. We cannot just go on being a twosome. I haven't told Carol what Greg does. There is certainly no reason to be ashamed of his work but something in me backs away from it. Until I married Greg there was no remote possibility that I would ever know personally a man who drove an ambulance. I am not yet, I guess, accepting my realities. Carol's husband's name is Richard and she calls him Richard, not Dick. I can see why. Dick Dane would be a rather comic name but Richard Dane has terrific dignity. I like the name Gregory Lind. That is very good. It is odd about names. Mine is all right, too, although Pamela Gibson sounds better than Pamela Lind. But I started out to discuss my shopping tour. I enjoyed it tremendously. Carol has good clothes and she knows the shops of Hollister. It is a long, long time since I had a friend who enjoys shopping. Carol had as much fun as I did. My check from the Culverton bank came in yesterday, so I splurged. I bought a cocktail dress that I love and a suit that I needed. I bought quite a few things. I think Carol was impressed. At any rate, she does not have me tagged as broke. I am not going to make any point of these things with Greg. I will just work them in without laying any emphasis on them.

"Wednesday: It is December. You would never know it from the temperature or the look of Hollister. It is like early fall with an occasional cool day and no cold weather. The trees are green. Greg and I have driven down to Harrow Harbor a couple of times. There is quite a bit of industry there, and a moderate amount of shipping. There is also a beach. We loved to watch the whitecaps breaking on all that off-white sand. The water is a bit cold for swimming now but it looks wonderful. I dread the coming of Christmas. It may be upsetting for Greg in many ways. He does look back, although he denies that he does. Even the simple matter of Christmas cards is a problem for us. I asked Greg what we should do, if I should order some, and he said that he had no one to whom he would send a Christmas card, that he will write a few notes. I believe that I understand. Christmas is a religious idea. He could not send anyone a card that was not religious in theme, and yet he probably feels that he cannot link himself to a religious idea in communicating with people. I will have problems myself. My father was always wonderful at Christmas before he and I reached the point of no understanding. I still do not believe that the rift was my fault. Anyway, it was all pretty wonderful once. Dad was generous, fabulously generous, and he actually had more fun in being that way than those who benefited from his generosity. He is such a big man and he has such a deep voice. I cannot help remembering but I do not know of anything I can do to help him have a good Christmas. I cannot bridge the gap between us. Anything I did would look like the seeking of an advantage. He told me I would never receive a cent of his money. I cannot do anything that he would interpret as an effort to change that decision of his. I cannot, will not, ingratiate myself with him. Carina is no help. She says, and she is probably right, that she will not work against my father or undo anything he does. I cannot let her think that I want one single thing from her. It is all going to be difficult but if it does not prove too much for Greg in one way or another, I'll be happy. He is wonderful with me and to me and I honestly do not believe that he regrets leaving the Church to marry me. The strange thing about that, now that I have written the sentence, is that he has never left the Church at all. I started to write about that once and then I did not face it. Greg loves, actually loves, the work that he is doing, his banging around town with an ambulance. All men, I guess, like loud, noisy, dangerous toys but it is more than that with Greg. The ambulance is his means of reaching people in pain or trouble. He talks of people who have been hurt and people who needed a fast ambulance to give them a chance to go on living. His skills go beyond first aid and he has some opportunities to use those skills even if he is a driver. Sometimes there are many people hurt in a single accident and sometimes the man who rides with Greg stands aside so that he can have a chance to handle a difficult case. I do not understand what Greg does, although he tells me many details. He accepts the salary that comes to him but if I were not around I do not believe he would care, one way or another, whether he got paid or not. Even with me around, he does not look one inch beyond the ambulance. He does not think in terms of promotion, of growing into a bigger job, of earning more money; all that matters is the chance he has to serve people, to alleviate suffering. He was trained for that by people who did not know that they were training him for an ambulance. He is a priest. He is not serving in a church but he is a priest, a priest forever; neither my love for him nor his for me can change that. It is a terrifying thought with which to live."

– IX –

On December 18, Jack Serkle failed, for the first time, to report for work. Greg Lind took one call alone, then reported to Tracy Welton.

Tracy Welton looked out of his window. He lighted a cigarette, taking his time.

"I'm damned sorry about that," he said. "I knew it was coming. I could see it building up in him. He won't be back."

"He could be hurt, or arrested for something."

Tracy shook his head. He was a thin-lipped man and his eyes were narrow, a cold, hard man. His face had not softened when he turned from the window and faced Greg across the desk.

"No good," he said. "I'm going to miss that guy. He's probably in Dallas or Houston or someplace, drunk as a Swede."

"Why Dallas or Houston?"

"A wild guess. It could be any one of a dozen places. Anywhere but Hollister. A top flight transient like Jack never falls off in a town where he's been walking proud. Never. He feels the strong urge coming, or he begins to see bottles going by, and he gets out. He takes off. Didn't you know that?"

"No. It seems that something under control to that point could be controlled all the way."

"It may seem so but it damn well isn't." Tracy leaned back in his chair. "O.K. Serkle is gone. You're promoted. You're the Doc. Somebody else can do the driving. You move up in money, too."

"Thanks."

"Skip it. I'm not giving you anything. I need you. About the driver, I want to say something."

"I'm listening."

"O.K. Listen sharp. There's a young orderly named Jerry Kagat. He wants a chance at driving an ambulance. I want to give it to him. You have to know about him if he drives with you. He's twenty-one. His family split up and he drifted. He stole a car and the cops down at Harrow Harbor picked him up. That's a tougher town than it looks, Harrow Harbor."

Tracy Welton seemed to be looking at something far away. "They threw that kid in a big cage in their lousy jail," he said, "and six tough punks raped him. That's an experience some young fellows never get over. Jerry Kagat is getting over it physically but that's the easy part, comparatively. He hasn't turned swish or given up, but he isn't friendly. He keeps to himself. He seems hostile."

"That follows."

"Well, I've got a hunch he'll be a good driver. He may be a good man some day. The point is, don't try to be friendly with him, don't be unfriendly; if there's any conversation, let him start it. Right?"

"Right."

"O.K. I'll get him for you."

Greg Lind left the office and went back to his ambulance. The other ambulance took a trouble call and he was in the alert slot for the next call. He thought briefly about the young man who would be his driver, and he thought longer, in greater depth, about Tracy Welton.

Tracy was tough; a belligerent, foul-mouthed straw boss who was not impressive physically but who was unafraid of any man who worked under him. Greg had heard him bawl men out and he had seen him handling tense situations when the victims of bad accidents were brought in. Tracy Welton might be impossible to like but it would be very difficult to find a better man for the responsibility that was his to handle. The Jerry Kagat affair presented another side of his character.

Tracy was not sentimental about the violence done to a young man. He did not raise his voice or express a sense of outrage. There was a situation, a lamentable situation, and he wanted to give a young man a chance to work out of it. He did not want any clumsy incident to complicate matters for Jerry Kagat, but he was not going to do anything for him beyond giving him a chance.

"Tracy Welton must have been a hell of a good priest once," he thought. "I wonder what happened to him."

He had a call before the other ambulance returned. It was a broken leg case, a boy of twelve who had fallen from a wall. He got the boy to the hospital and returned to the bullpen. Tracy Welton was waiting for him with Jerry Kagat. The young man was light-haired, slender, five feet seven or eight. He had pale blue eyes and there was no friendliness in him. Tracy Welton, once he had performed introductions, left the two men together.

"Have you got a driver's license?" Greg asked.

"Yes."

"Have you driven an ambulance?"

"I can."

"All right. Better climb in and get acquainted with it. If you need help, let me know."

Jerry Kagat did not need help. There was a series of calls, most of them routine, and then a bad one. A young woman in a sports car had run through a red light and hit another car broadside. There were injured people all over the intersection and one police patrol car was already on the job. Greg had his hands full but he could see Jerry in action. The driver was a good first-aid man, a gentle man with people who were hurt. The second ambulance joined them and they got the injured to the hospital. Jerry made no comment when the accident victims went to the emergency tables. He helped Greg silently in cleaning up the inside of the vehicle and then he lighted a cigarette. His hands were trembling.

At the end of the day, Greg walked home. The awkward point about his hours was his early quitting, at three P.M. when Pamela worked to five or five-thirty. He had time on his hands normally with no consistent plan for using it. He read newspapers or magazines, or he wrote letters. Today there was a letter awaiting him at home, a letter from Father Tom Guyton, with a *Catholic Digest* envelope enclosed.

Dear Greg: (the letter read)

The enclosed is months old. You will notice that the *Catholic Digest* people mailed it to you at the *Catholic Star.* Your old boss, Pete Coyle, let it lie around for a while and then wrote to the *Digest* people, telling them that you had left the priesthood and that your whereabouts were unknown. I guess the thing was cubbyholed at the *Digest* for some time with nobody taking action, then someone wrote to Father Schafer and enclosed the letter. Your pastor did not know where you were either but he figured that I did know and he was right.

How is Texas treating you? I would like to have a parish down there. I am not doing anything brilliant here, same old six and seven that we had when you were around and that I have reported in my dull letters. I saw three motion pictures last month, not one of them worth mentioning by name. This month I have read two dull books. My life is undistinguished.

If I don't write again before Christmas, I'll be praying for you.

Devotedly,

Tom.

Greg opened the enclosed envelope gently. There was a check and he removed it, turning it in his hands, looking at it, whistling softly. It was for one hundred dollars. He had forgotten that article that he wrote about the learning problems of Spanish Americans. He had packed humor into it but the humor had only been flavoring; the article had covered a subject that interested him. He stood, looking at the check and the check did not register on him as money; not immediately. This was a creative triumph. Someone had liked something that he had written, had liked it well enough to send him a check for it. One hundred dollars!

It became money suddenly and his mind reached out, finding a use for it. He did not have a Christmas present for Pamela and Christmas was only a week away. He had worried about that, wanting a present for her and not knowing how he could obtain one. His salary was pledged and committed, housing them and maintaining them, with no freeway, no nickel left over. He could not ask Bart again for money. There was no place else. Now, this.

The phone rang. It was loud and echoing, a bit plaintive, as though certain that no one would be in the apartment to hear it ring at such an hour. Greg crossed the room to answer it and Pam's voice came to him. She sounded breathless, a bit hurried, as she always did when something excited her.

"Greg? I'm glad you're home. Do you think you could make out if I had dinner downtown tonight?"

"Of course. What's up?"

"Oh, Carol and I thought we'd have supper downtown and do a little shopping. The stores are open. We might, just might, go to a show when the stores close. Are you sure you don't mind?"

"I'm delighted if you are. I can make out fine."

"I hope you can. Get something good for dinner. I must dash. All my love, darling. Thanks."

She was gone and he shook his head, seeing her on a screen in his mind. She always sounded different on a phone, not at all as she sounded across a table or in a room or in an automobile, or anyplace else. A telephone seemed to release something in her or release her from something. She had sounded happy tonight. She needed friends. It was good for her to have someone besides himself, someone who could share feminine enthusiasms with her. Loneliness was a bad human experience. He did not want it for her.

The stores were open. That was one point in the conversation which had significance. He had a hundred dollars in his pocket. He had nothing else to do except eat his supper and shop. The supper was the simplest part. He had no appreciation of fine cooking or of fine food. He ate at a noisy downtown restaurant where he sat at a counter. The spirit of Christmas was all around him in sound and symbol, the commercial spirit. He walked down a street thronged with people, under brightly colored lights, with off-scene radios or record players grinding out carols. Santa Claus figures on corners shook bells at him.

It was all vaguely exciting. He had rarely participated in this side of Christmas. The Advent season was always a busy one in the parish and the *Star* had always put out a big special edition. He had not had the time to wander around in the downtown section, nor any reason to do so.

Shopping, he discovered, was not simple, particularly at this season. He knew nothing about buying purely feminine things. He looked in windows with a feeling of helplessness and his mind kept returning to

213

the idea that he had held as a daydream before he had a hundred dollars. Pamela had not had an engagement ring from him. He had no doubt that she owned rings, but she never wore one; possibly because she had received none from him save the simple wedding band. He stood on a street corner, indecisive, jostled by passers-by.

"A ring is one thing that will make my hundred inadequate," he thought, "but it is right."

There were a number of jewelry stores, credit houses, but he had an instinct that walked him wide of big claims, sensational advertising and extravagant credit offers. He found a small, dignified jewelry store which displayed merchandise in its window without signs, posters or price tags. The man who waited on him was pale, quiet, dark-eyed. There were some charming little rings which mounted diamond chips, he said, but had the gentleman considered a ruby rather than a diamond. A ruby was a lovely and a valued gem. He had some oriental rubies. Greg looked at them.

Red was a color that Pamela never wore but a ruby was not red, it was ruby. He looked at one ring and he could see it on her hand. It was alive. He held it between his fingers and against the light, then low, in shadow.

"Do you know her size?" the quiet voice said.

Greg knew her size. He had needed that knowledge when he bought the little wedding ring. He had written the size on a piece of paper in his wallet. The man behind the counter nodded. Only then did he mention price. A hundred dollars would not buy a ruby either, not this ruby. Greg studied it, then raised his eyes.

"I'll take it," he said, "but I will need credit."

The man behind the counter did not answer him. His eyes were patient. A stranger did not ask for credit without justifying it. Greg understood that. He was thinking that he had a brand new raise that came with his change of jobs on the ambulance. He could forget that raise and continue to live on his old salary until he had paid for this ring. That was very simple. He laid his hundred-dollar check on the counter and his eyes read it as the jeweler did. He had forgotten something.

The check was made out to Reverend Gregory Lind and it was dated several months ago.

The jeweler raised his eyes and there was a question in them. That question could not be evaded, could not ever be evaded. It was the recurring question and this was one of the unexpected moments.

"I was a Roman Catholic priest when that check was issued," Greg said, "but it is still my check."

"I see. And you are now?"

"An ambulance attendant at Hollister General Hospital."

The man behind the counter studied him. There was neither dislike nor contempt in his eyes, no antagonism, no hostility; merely interest.

"If you will fill out our form, I'll see what I can do," he said.

"I'll appreciate it."

There were always forms to be filled out. When Gregory left the store, he did not have the ring but he had the assurance that every effort would be made to release it before Christmas. He had given Father Tom Guyton as a reference and the manager of the supermarket in Albuquerque and Tracy Welton. He had considered including Bart in his references and had decided against it on a delicate point. This was a present for Pam and none of the Linds would ever know Pam, none of the Linds would let themselves know Pam. He mingled with the crowd again and he no longer felt aloof from the other human beings on the street, no longer apart. He was one of them. He, too, had bought a present.

The press of people carried him along. He thought of his mother. He should buy her a present, too. He had only a dollar in his wallet and some change in his pocket. If he had not spent all of his money, and gone in debt, to buy Pamela a gift he could have remembered his family. The thought followed him home.

He was home before Pam was, and he had known that he would be. The Christmas gift problem haunted him. He had never had the problem when he was a priest. He had remembered each member of the family, and his friends, in his three Christmas Masses and he had sent out cards to tell them so. They had all known that he had no money and they had valued remembrance in the Masses above any material gift. He no longer had spiritual gifts to offer and he was still without money.

"I wouldn't know what to buy for them if I had money," he said.

He went mentally over his family. There were his mother and Janet and Janet's husband, Joe, and their three children. There were his sisters Agnes and Anne in Palo Alto and Scranton, with their husbands and children. There were Bart and Barbara and their four children. A hundred dollars did not have nearly all of the stretch in it that a man would need once he tried to reach around his own family. If he wanted to keep on stretching, there were good friends like Tom Guyton who should not be forgotten.

He walked restlessly around the apartment. There had been many people who made small cash presents to the priests of the parish at Christmas, and some people gave presents to mailmen, milkmen, laundry men, paper boys, a wide variety of people. Joe and Janet probably did all of that, and Bart and Barbara. How did they do it? He had taken the doing for granted when he was a priest, giving it no particular thought; but the layman he had become was aware of money and the lack of money, particularly the lack. There had been a great many people downtown tonight. They had been buying gifts. Somehow, they managed. Gregory Lind felt humble in the thought of them.

Pamela came in at eleven-fifteen. Her eyes were bright and there was color in her cheeks where the rising wind had roughed her. She was wearing a black hat and her light colored coat with the big black buttons. There was joy and sparkle in her. She had had a good time.

Greg kissed her and his life was right again. He had bought her a present and he was glad that he had. She was his wife. He did not have to buy presents for anyone else; not for anyone else in the world.

"Forsaking all others," he said.

Pamela blinked. "What?"

"Nothing." Greg waved his hand. "Nothing at all. It was just an idea."

She stepped in close to him. "I don't smell a thing," she said. "You must have been drinking vodka."

–X–

Greg Lind, with Jerry Kagat driving, answered nineteen calls the day before Christmas between seven A.M. and three P.M. Most of them were automobile accidents but there was one stabbing in a family altercation, one attempted suicide, two injured children and a filling station attendant shot in a holdup. The filling station man was twenty-seven and he had four children. He was the only one who died.

To Greg's surprise, presents came into the hospital for the ambulance men. He had two gifts personally from people he had attended; a bottle of Scotch and a five-dollar gift certificate on a department store. Tracy Welton divided the gifts that came to the ambulance section without individual names on them. Greg drew a fifth of bourbon, five cartons of cigarettes, a fruit cake and a ballpoint pen. He gave two cartons of cigarettes to Jerry Kagat.

"Merry Christmas, Jerry," he said.

His driver looked startled. He accepted the cigarettes awkwardly as though uncertain about keeping them. "Same to you," he said.

Greg walked uptown. He obtained a shopping bag at the department store and that made his package-carrying easier. There was electricity running through today's downtown crowd. Shopping time was running out. Greg felt the contagion, the urge to hurry, but he had only one thing to do. The ruby ring was ready for him, attractively wrapped. He walked home by a different route than the one he normally took and he passed a Catholic church that he had not previously seen. A wooden sign, anchored on the lawn, identified it as Saint Margaret's. He slowed his pace momentarily but he did not go in.

There was mail at the apartment. The past few days had brought brief notes on cards from his sisters, Agnes and Anne, a letter from Barbara which carried Bart's greeting with her own, and a card from Tom Guyton. Today's mail was all Pam's except one letter from Janet.

Dear Gregsie, Janet wrote. *I hope that you will find happiness in Christmas. It seems so strange, so different from other years. I do not know what to wish you, but you know my love goes with this. I have tried to get mother to write you a letter or a note, but she just won't. I am sorry. You know how she is. Her health is fine. No worry there. Joe is his same old steady, patient self. I cannot imagine my life without him and I do not deserve him at all. The kids are excited about Christmas as kids always are. Everything will be great here. No worry. Take care of yourself.*

> Love,
> Janet.

Janet always said a lot, even when she did not seem to be saying anything. It was good to know that his mother was well and he was not surprised that she remained behind a closed door as far as he was concerned. Greg paced the floor, thinking of his family situation. There was a thin line of communication left, and nothing else. He was glad that he had bought his mother a scarf. It was not expensive and it was rather corny but his mother had always liked maps. He had bought her a scarf with the map of Texas on it. It had taken his lunch money for one week to pay for it, inexpensive though it was.

He placed his gifts on the table so Pam would see them when she came in. The Scotch was a good brand and the bourbon was in a gift decanter. The fruit cake looked cheerful and he made a low pyramid out of the cartons of cigarettes. There was little that he could do toward displaying the ballpoint pen or the gift certificate but he was, for some inexplicable reason, particularly pleased with them. He had not anticipated personal gifts this Christmas.

"We need a Christmas tree, a small Christmas tree," he said.

The thought took form, translated into words and perished. He had no money.

He heard Pamela whistling as she came up the stairs. She was the only girl he had ever known who whistled. She did not whistle often but when she did it was a sign that she was happy. She whistled happy music. Her key clicked in the lock and then she was in her room.

She was wearing her light coat with the big buttons. The coat made her appear small, much smaller than she actually was. He still believed the effects she created although he had often watched, fascinated, while she was creating them. He had seen her tie a scarf before a mirror a dozen times, over and over until she had it the way she wanted it. The result would be a careless, offhand, casual look, as though she had flipped the scarf on without paying any attention to it. It was the same way with everything. She knew her colors and how to blend them so that they did not look blended. When she wore a hat, she adjusted it as carefully as she adjusted a scarf, but it created the impression that she had merely put it on, without craft or design, and that she looked wonderful in it because she *was* wonderful. He wondered sometimes if she really knew how calculating she was in her effects or if she was purely instinctive about it all. Most of the time he accepted the picture she created without thinking about it, accepting the picture she wanted him to have.

Today she was exuberant. "Merry Christmas, darling," she said.

She was in his arms as he rose from his chair. A spectator would believe that she kissed him but the spectator would be wrong. She made herself available to his kiss, and he kissed her. It was something that she did beautifully and he found it exciting. She had always been a woman who yielded to him, who responded; who, seemingly if not quite, left the initiative and the thrust to him.

She turned in his arms. "I've got presents."

He released her and she showed him her gifts, a bottle of body lotion and a jar of cream from a cosmetic client of Peckham and Potter. She was as delighted as if they had been jewels, and that was another quality of hers that seemed as natural as breath, or voice, or the touch of her hand; she loved all things that came to her, that revolved around her or that symbolized regard for her.

"You're ignoring *my* presents," he said.

"I'm not. I saw them the moment I came in. I saved them for climax."

He did not know whether she had seen them or not. It made no difference. She exclaimed over each of them and she knew, as if telepathic, that he particularly valued the ballpoint pen and the gift

218

certificate which were personal gifts. She bestowed the most comment upon them.

"What do we do with the cigarettes?" she said.

"Presents, for somebody. Whom do we know?"

"Not many people. There will be somebody. The bourbon?" Her forehead wrinkled. "We might give that to Carol if you don't mind. She's been very good to me."

"I don't mind. Of course not. Does she drink bourbon?"

"I haven't the slightest idea. Makes no difference. Whoever gave that bottle to you did not ask if you drank bourbon, did they?"

"No. The probable theory is that ambulance men are tough critters who drink anything."

A shadow crossed her face and he knew that his remark had been badly timed. She did not like to be reminded that he worked on an ambulance. She picked up the Scotch bottle.

"Nice," she said. "We'll save half of it for New Year's Eve."

She never knew, he was certain, that she took over the planning in their life together, that the decisions on what they would do, and when, were invariably her decisions. She seemed to consult him, and she was probably convinced that she did, but there was seldom anything that he could do except affirm what she proposed. In asking his opinion she rarely offered him alternatives.

"We really need a Christmas tree," he said, "but we can't afford it."

"I have money. I was paid yesterday."

"I'll be paid next week. Even if I had it now, it would be a silly expense."

"I don't know." Pamela picked up her body lotion bottle and looked at the label, humming softly. "If you think that a Christmas tree is a good idea, and if I think so, who is going to outvote us?"

"If I voted against you, we'd deadlock. Nobody to break a tie."

"You wouldn't dare."

Pamela took a twenty dollar bill from her bag and laid it on the table. "Christmas tree plus dinner," she said. "We celebrate."

"I hate to take your money for it."

"Our money. If you were paid yesterday and my payday was next week, that would be your twenty-dollar bill. So, it's ours, yours, what difference?"

Pamela and money could be another baffling chapter in his life if someone tried to write his biography. She had grown up with it and, until she married him, she had probably taken the possession of it for granted. She had worked for money in Culverton but she had had background money. She had taken money with her on their trip, more money than he had. Recently, in Hollister, she had bought a lot of clothes and had obviously drawn money from somewhere to pay for them; probably not from her mother, more likely from some secret account she had left in Culverton. She seemed to have taken it for granted that he would not notice her new clothes, as if he did not notice everything about her. She was generous, fabulously generous, with anything she had but still, the evidence indicated, a secretive person about money. It was difficult to reconcile the contradictions in her.

Greg wore his blue suit and Pam wore a simple little black dress. They went to the Hollister House, the city's leading hotel, and dined in the main dining room. It was a large room with few people in it. A tall silver Christmas tree stood midway on the window side and there was music from some hidden source.

"Two rooms away," Greg said solemnly.

"As it should be."

They toasted each other across the table and it seemed to him that Pam had never looked lovelier. There was a glow in her, a warmth, a semi-submerged excitement. She had undoubtedly dined in many large hotels against his very few but tonight satisfied something in her. She looked around and she possessed all that she saw.

"You belong here," he said, "in places like this."

"I'm not sure. I do like it. Perhaps no one belongs in places like this. Maybe it would be less exciting if one had it always. I don't know, Greg. But I am happy here. Are you happy?"

"I'm happy anywhere with you."

They walked out into a night that was windy, a bit chill, not cold. There was no chance of snow. Hollister did not produce white Christmases. The Christmas lights on strings, from pole to pole across the downtown streets, swung and danced in the wind. Traffic was thinning out. They drove to their apartment and it was shockingly shabby after the magic of Hollister House. Greg, who normally took it for granted, saw it suddenly with Pamela's eyes. He did not say anything about it because there was nothing helpful to say. He picked her up, carried her over to the most comfortable chair and sat down with her.

"We forgot to buy the tree," Pam said.

It was an incredible remark under the circumstance and he laughed at her. It did not seem possible that they could have forgotten the tree, but they had. It did not seem to make any difference.

"We'll create one," Greg said. "We will select a place to put it and we will imagine it into existence and every time we pass the place we'll see it."

"Yes. And we'll put those cute little blinking lights on it and ornaments, only a few ornaments but very good ones." Pamela paused. "I like you when you are this way," she said. "I like you every old way, of course, but I love creating a tree with you."

"I'll try to remember."

"Do." She placed her forefinger across his lips and pressed hard. "Stay right here. I have a present for you."

"I have one for you."

"Have you?" She stood still, looking at him. "What?"

"I'll get it for you."

"No. I spoke first. I'll get yours."

She turned swiftly and went into the other room. She returned with a large package which she laid on his lap. She crouched then, sitting on her heels, watching him open it.

She had bought him a plain navy blazer and gray slacks, the handsomest piece of attire he had ever owned. She was watching his face; anxiously, he thought, as though unsure how he would like her selection of clothing. Her eyes were intent and her face was small with none of the angles showing. She looked vulnerable and she was, of course. He dropped down on the floor beside her and kissed her gently.

"It's too much, darling," he said, "and too elegant. I never saw anything handsomer. You must have robbed a bank."

"No. It was my own money. I had some hidden for emergencies. I am like a squirrel, hiding nuts."

He kissed her again and held her close to him, and her voice came up to him. "Please. May I have my present now?"

"Immediately."

He brought in the small box and laid it on her palm. She looked at it, then removed the wrapping slowly, teasing herself he supposed. When she saw the ruby, she uttered one soft, low sound that was almost a moan. She lifted it out of its box and held it up to the light. She turned swiftly then and held it out to him.

"Put it on," she said.

She extended her left hand and he slipped the ring on the third finger, above the plain band. She held her hand away, staring at it.

"It's beautiful, Greg," she said. "Beautiful. I've never owned a ruby. I didn't expect a present. I knew you didn't have any money." She turned, her eyes widening. "Did *you* rob a bank? Did you?"

"No. I'll tell you."

She sat on his lap again and he told her about the article that he had written and about his raise at the hospital. Pamela held her hand away again, looking at the ring.

"I love it more because you wrote it," she said. "I knew you could write. I told you."

He did not answer that but he made ardent love to her and she responded, as she always did, to his ardor; intense, passionate, withholding none of herself. She went to sleep eventually in his arms. He lay then with the scent of her in his nostrils and the feel of her on his skin; and the thought that he had been evading moved in on him.

This was Christmas Eve, flowing into Christmas Day. He could not see the clock, nor move to see it without waking Pamela. There had been another man and woman, long ago, in a strange town, away from their own homes. There had been no room for them anywhere and they had taken refuge in a stable. That man and that woman had been a great reality to him. He had heard the confessions, and had done the many tasks of Christmas week, remembering them. He had celebrated, with genuine joy, and with three Masses, the birth of the child, Jesus, on Christmas Day.

It was all behind him. This Christmas Eve had belonged, selfishly perhaps, to Pamela and to himself. They had needed each other. He told himself that the need they had felt was the carrier of its own justification. His own memories, however, rebuked him. He had not said a prayer all day.

–XI–

Christmas Day was a long and lonely day. It was a working day for ambulance crews and Pamela Lind felt forsaken and functionless. She ate a braunschweiger sandwich for lunch and the day ahead of her was still possessed of too many hours. She took out her journal and wrote in it.

"Christmas. Greg is working and I am sitting in this drab apartment with no one I can talk to except this damn book. I have neglected it for a long time so I will not blame it if it is not companionable. If someone, even a year ago, had read the tea leaves or had shaken up the crystal ball to produce this picture of me I'd have laughed scornfully. It does not seem possible even when I am sitting in the middle of it. In the first place I went to Mass this morning at six. I have never had the spiritual feeling about Christmas that Greg has, and I find it difficult to understand, but his feeling is real, a part of himself, and even a moron would realize that and respect his feeling without the need for understanding it. It was a very bad Mass this morning, not that I am an expert on Masses. The priest was young and fat and sleepy. He was facing the people from behind the altar, and I expected that any minute he would yawn. He was an untidy priest with uncombed hair and vestments slightly askew. I did not say anything but I know that Greg was distressed. He did not like the church, either. It is a most unusual Catholic church. I did not see a single statue, not even a crucifix. The space behind the altar is plain, paneled wood.

"Greg is still a priest. I face that fact in so many ways. He never gets too far away from the Church and he stays *en rapport* with its problems. He has an odd conscience which draws strict, stark lines on many issues, but he is not intolerant or stiff or holier-than-thou. I would not be here, suffering out this day, if he were stiff-necked or professionally moral or, as he puts it, 'full of cant, pietism and good honest hypocrisy.'

"I do not know why I am here anyway. I can see no shred of a future in what we are doing. There is no line of promotion in what Greg is doing, no place for him to go, no way of earning more money. In the course of time, I could move upward a little, earn a bit more money, but that is no answer. Unless Greg moves, we stay where we are, limited in all of our living by the size of his check and his place in the community. He is just a little better than a common laborer and the fact does not seem to disturb him. He actually likes what he is doing. I do not believe that he minded leaving me and going to that damned ambulance today.

"What a hell of a way to write on Christmas Day. Maybe I am feeling sorry for myself. I'll have to watch that."

"Day after Christmas: It is a dull day at the office. I'm doing this on my work typewriter. There are a couple of things I want to reason out for myself and I do it better this way than if I sit static and try to think. We had a turkey dinner last night at a rather mediocre restaurant. Our Christmas dinner. I thought that it was depressing and an outrageous meal but I did not say so. Greg, I am certain, saw nothing the matter with it. He will eat anything, anywhere. I mentioned that fact once and he said: 'Darling, the food at the seminary was so very damned bad that it prepared us for anything the world could throw at us.' I cannot imagine Greg at the seminary. I cannot see him in my imagination, although I have tried. Everything in his past is inconceivable to me. It is alien territory, just as is his work on the ambulance. I never talked to a priest until I met him and I never thought of talking to anyone who drove an ambulance, but here we are, and I cannot imagine life without him.

"One would not think that cold turkey could possibly be a big thought. It is to me today. When we were walking home last night, after that deplorable dinner, Greg talked about his boyhood. He never reminisces about anything but cheerful things. Cold turkey was a cheerful thing. He remembered that his family had a huge turkey for Christmas and that the cold cuts and bones-to-pick lasted for nearly a week and tasted much better than the original dinner. I cannot give him that in his own home. I cannot even imagine cooking a turkey. I have no skills and I would not know where to begin. We eat most of our meals out. I just can't cook. In my growing up, the cooking was something done in the kitchen by people who were paid to do it. It is more expensive, eating as we do, and not as satisfying for a man, I am certain. I could only bring to a man such skills and gifts and talents as I have. Perhaps I should not have entered the life of a man who needs cooking done, and who needs other household tasks performed. That is the big thought of the day, and it haunts me, walking around with me. There are people, I know, who will say that I should learn how to do all the household things, that other girls have learned. Gently and respectfully, without one note of profanity, I reply that other girls aren't me. I leave it at that."

"Friday: Carol came in today. She and Dick flew to Chicago for Christmas. That is where his family lives. Her family lives in St. Paul, Minnesota. They went there last year. She has said several times that they do not have any money and I do not imagine that they have much, but they live nicely and they have little things that are important. I skipped over an account of our Christmas, Greg's and mine, and Carol must consider that strange. I have never told her that Greg drives an ambulance. I am not ashamed of his work, or of anything that he does, but I could never make anyone understand about us, and I shall never try. There are so many things that I do not understand myself.

"Greg told me about something that happened on Christmas Day and it is one of the things I cannot understand. He and his ambulance went out to a horrible old shack near the city dump. There were three old men who had been drinking wine for possibly a couple of days. They had some kind of a heater, oil I think, and it exploded. Greg and the young man on his ambulance, somebody named Jerry, went out there. They had to work with wounds and burns and drunkenness, and they had to contend with vomit and filth in that awful place. They did all their first aid and putting salve on burns and tying of bandages, and they took those sodden, repulsive old human wrecks to a hospital where doctors and nurses had to work on them. Now, my question is— Why?

"Why did a fine, decent person like Greg have to contend with a nauseous experience like that for three filthy creatures who were entirely responsible for their own condition? What good did he serve? Sodden creatures like that, insensitive to their own filth, won't change, won't improve, will not give back to decent humanity anything at all in return for what they demand. Greg says that it is the first time that Jerry, his driver, who is a young man, has even spoken more than a monosyllable to him and Jerry's approval seems to mean much to him. Why should it?"

"Another year: Greg and I saw a new year in, our first. It was oddly dull and yet there was that terrific physical thing between Greg and me that forever confuses my judgment about everything. Carol invited us to her apartment. 'Very simple,' she said, 'and only a few people.' I was dying to see her apartment and particularly eager to meet her husband, Dick, but I turned it down. I have no fear for Greg in any company. He mixes well and he has a unique view of people and events that makes his conversation interesting, actually arresting. You stop to listen when he expresses an opinion because it challenges you, or brings you up short. He is handsome and courteous and considerate. I am proud of him but, damn it, I cannot be proud of his job. I just could not face his moving in among those electronics people and admitting, as he would, that he drove an ambulance. That is not foolish of me, or snobbish. I am thinking of him more than of myself. He is better than anyone in Carol's crowd, in terms of education, fine instincts, any measurement at all, but he would seem less and they would consider him less and he would feel it. We went to a movie together, Greg and I, and we were home before midnight. When the new year came in, we toasted it in the Scotch we saved for just this occasion, but it seemed flat, without reality. The fault is probably mine. I've been accustomed to excitement and noise and people, especially people, on New Year's Eve.

"Greg and I are going to have people in our lives."

"Thursday: I have a raise. Five dollars a week. It is such a small sum of money that it is astonishing that it should make a difference to me. It does. We need so many things now but this won't buy them. No matter. It eases a little of the tension and it buys little things and it is good to feel that I am satisfactory in my work. Greg was pleased about my raise, and not for the money involved. He likes to have people like me. I could probably make him jealous if I tried and I am often tempted to try, but it really wouldn't be fair. He had one comment about the money, however, that sticks in my mind; probably because no one I have known in the past could ever have made such a comment.

"'My father used to say,' Greg told me, 'that every man who works has just ten dollars less than he needs every pay day. Ten dollars. It does him no good if he gets a raise. He still needs just ten dollars more when pay day comes around. Ten dollars. That is the margin that keeps a man poor.'

"I wish I could forget that. I don't know if it is true."

"Friday: Writing in this silly ledger yesterday I was obsessed with the ten-dollar quotation. I am still bemused by it as I am bemused by the idea of my receiving five dollars and discovering that I need it. All of which reminds me of Greg's minor mystery. His friend, Father Guyton, sent along a Christmas card which was mailed to Greg at the rectory. There was no return address on it. It was a very ordinary Christmas card with a Madonna and angels. It had, written in it, 'Wishing you a happy and blessed Christmas—Gustave Kaufman and family.' Tucked into the card was a ten dollar bill. Greg says that although that parish was full of Germans, he cannot remember any Kaufmans. He is curious and will probably write to his friend, Tom Guyton, about it. He says that he would like to know if the family had sent the remembrance in the belief that he is still in the Church or if, knowing that he has left, they were sharing with him in charity. He thinks of the damnedest things."

"Tuesday: I have stopped taking the pill. It is rather a big decision but I have been thinking about it for some time now. The uncertainties in the future for Greg and me are simply murderous and if I can have a baby, I hate exposing him to them. On the other hand, I want a baby, for many subtle, intricate and complicated reasons plus a few reasons that are not, perhaps, honest and pearly white. Never mind. Some of my reasons are decent and unselfish and may even be idealistic. I happen to love Greg greatly. When two people are drawn to each other as strongly as we are and as often and, I might add, at the drop of a hat, there are reasons that are not entirely physical. I am not religious, and will never be, but I do believe that 'to everything there is a season, and a time to every purpose under heaven.' Greg and I have no right to waste the fire and the spirit and the magnetism and the seed, and all else that is us. There is a purpose. I look at that and I cannot blink at it. Sex is not just amusement, entertainment, or—I hate that word—'fulfillment.' Sex should not be something you switch on like a TV for diversion's sake. There is more to it than that.

"I am the wife of a man. He may not always be easy to hold. Other women are going to feel that terrific magnet that he has inside of him.

Other women will be drawn to him. He does not hold the thought or go out looking for them, and I doubt that he ever will, but I do not know how he would cope with women who come looking for him. That is my job. I will not tolerate any woman who makes a pass at him.

"We are miles apart, Greg and I, in so many things. He does not understand the kind of living to which I was raised. He may even believe that he dislikes it, but he is wrong. He liked the glimpse, and the taste, of it that he had in my apartment on Steuben Drive. He could learn to like so many things but I do not have the key any more and I cannot open the way to much. I know one thing—we are going to have more than we have, and we are going to have friends. I am not going to bring my child into a world that has only two people in it.

"There is ambition. Greg does not have any, not a speck. I will have to do something about that. I do not know what. I heard someone say, years ago, that 'priests are the educated sons of peasants.' That may be fairly accurate as far as Greg is concerned, superficially nasty though it may sound. I do not know if his lack of ambition comes from his peasant ancestry or from his habits as a priest, but something will move him. I'm certain of it.

"At any rate, I want to bear a son of Greg's. I want a son of my own. I want to know everything that being a woman means. I believe that, somehow, the future is going to be all right."

-XII-

The hippies, flower children, draft card burners and drug addicts were a problem in Hollister as they were in other cities. The climate and the resort aspect of the city made it an attractive objective for drifters but a tough police force, and the reputation it had gained kept the numbers down. The marijuana, or "pot" smokers were on the increase and might be encountered anywhere. They were a particular source of irritation to Dr. Symons who was the chief of the hospital emergency division.

"We cannot prove that marijuana is injurious physically," he said, "or that people become physically addicted; but we do know that it destroys drive and initiative and will to achieve. A marijuana smoker just does not want to do anything and ultimately he is no good sexually, either."

LSD was a more grave problem but the ambulance crews had their experience with it mainly in the persons of young college students, not with hippies. The hippies, even in cases of bad trips, seemed to take care of their own.

The hippie neighborhood was not far from the hospital and was not, strictly speaking, a hippie neighborhood. Hippies lived in old rooming houses on Lafitte, Melton and Nolan Streets, one-time fine homes, later boardinghouses and now bleak unfurnished structures with pads spread on the floors. Not all of the citizens on the three streets, between Fourth and Sixth, were hippies but all of them were poor.

The ambulance call came from 411 Nolan Street at twelve-twenty on January 11. Greg Lind and Jerry Kagat made the run. The house was a three-story brick with dormer windows and Victorian trim. There were six or seven long-haired young men and untidy young women on the steps which led to the front door. The group parted to permit the ambulance men a passage through. It was a silent group except for one girl who called after them as they entered the dark hall.

"Look out for her! She's maybe dangerous."

The two men climbed stairs. There was a strong smell of urine in the house and some deeper, heavier odors. There were three more people at the head of the stairs, two young men and a young woman. One of the men pointed to a door but no one spoke. Greg hesitated, uncertain of his authority, and then opened the door.

The room was bare except for scattered mats. There was no article of furniture. A young woman sat on the floor in the middle of the room. She had a broken bottle in her right hand. A man lay face down beside her and there was an arc of blood to the left of, and under, his body. The girl's eyes were dull, fixed, uncomprehending, and she sat stiffly, unnaturally. Her grip on the bottle neck, however, was firm and she held it like a dagger. There was blood on it.

Greg remembered the warning call of the girl downstairs. It was indeed quite possible that the woman was dangerous. He did not know how fast she might be capable of moving if she snapped out of the spell that held her. Still, the man on the floor had bled a lot and might still be bleeding. If he was alive, it was imperative that they get him to the hospital.

He moved into the room, aware of Jerry behind him and aware, too, by some sense of presence rather than by sound or vision that the three people from the hall had crowded into the doorway. He could feel the cold current of fear moving down his spine.

The woman with the bottle was young, maybe nineteen or twenty, possibly younger than that. She was heavy, dressed in a man's shirt and a plaid skirt. Her legs were bare and the skirt was hiked halfway up her thighs. Her legs were very dirty, seemingly incrusted with dirt. Her face, too, was dirty, a round face with a broad nose and lips that were thin and flat. Her hair looked greasy and hung straight, to below her shoulders. There was no life in her eyes but, as he stepped closer, Greg could hear her breathing, a faint rasp in her nostrils.

"Drop the bottle!" he said.

There was a delay of three or four seconds, then the bottle dropped. It hit softly on a pad and lay there. Greg could hear a gasp from the group at the door. He watched the girl. No expression had lighted in her face when she dropped her weapon and there was no life in her eyes.

"Watch her closely, Jerry," he said over his shoulder.

He was uncomfortably aware that the girl, if she were quick in springing back to consciousness, could grab the bottle again and slash him with it as, presumably, she had slashed the man on the floor. He dropped to one knee and lifted the man's body by the shoulder, tipping it backward. Dead eyes stared at him. There was a solid, soaked mat of blood over the man's chest. He had been stabbed many times, a furious succession of blows. He was dead but Greg sought for a pulse. There was always a faint chance against the evidence of one's eyes.

Feet stamped on the stairs. Two policemen entered the room as Greg straightened and rose. They were husky, grim-faced men. The man in the lead looked with disapproval at Greg.

"Have you been touching stuff? Moving stuff around?" he said.

"No. I lifted the man and looked at him. He's dead and back where I found him. The girl had the bottle in her hand when we came in. I told her to drop it and she dropped it."

"Is that your job, telling people to drop bottles?"

"It was part of it this time."

The policeman grunted. He had only part of his mind, a small part, on Greg. He was watching the girl. He stepped forward and slapped her in the face. She cried out and her eyes blinked.

"What's your name?" he said.

"Sylvia."

She was looking up at the policeman and there was a dull sort of consciousness in her face, not intelligence but awareness of a sort. Greg turned away. There was no work for Jerry and himself in the room. The wagon would come from the morgue and someone would come from the coroner's office, and there would be more police. The patrolman at the door took his name and Jerry's; then they were on the stairs going down. There were a number of people on the sidewalk now, normal citizens and hippies. Several people in the crowd tried to ask questions but the men from the ambulance shrugged them off. Jerry's face was white when he slid under the wheel.

"That dirty cop!" he said. "Damned gestapo slugger, hitting that poor sick girl!"

"It was the thing to do," Greg said. "He didn't hurt her. He shocked her. He brought her out of that cave she was in."

Jerry swore under his breath. He put the ambulance in gear. Just before he reached the hospital, he turned his head momentarily.

"That took guts, what you did," he said.

"I'm afraid not. I was scared to death of her. That's why I asked you to watch her."

Jerry didn't answer. He turned the ambulance into the emergency space of the hospital and slid it softly into the slot. Greg went in to the long table of the bullpen and wrote his report. Within an hour a newspaper man and a photographer descended on the hospital and Tracy Welton brought them to Gregory Lind. They already had a story from the police record and the accounts of three young people who had watched from a doorway. An ambulance man was an acceptable hero, unique, someone who rarely wandered, name and photograph, into the columns of a newspaper. Greg would have balked at questions and pictures but Tracy Welton insisted that he cooperate.

"We're so modest, we turn our own stomachs," Tracy told the reporter, "but a good story might get us all a raise."

"I doubt it," the reporter said, "considering how the mayor is bellyaching about the budget. You guys get paid too much anyway. Lazy as firemen."

Greg gave no prominence to his own role when he told Pamela about the girl in a hippie pad who had killed a man with a bottle. He did not believe that he would actually rate much space in the newspaper account and he was astonished when he saw the paper in the morning. He did not see it until he reached the bullpen. The story was on page one and his picture was on page three. The girl, according to the paper, was the daughter of a public utility executive in the East and the man she killed had been married three times. It was a sensational story in all of its details and Gregory Lind was presented as the man who courageously disarmed the girl after the murder.

"Why didn't you tell me?" Pam said that night. "I didn't know. Carol saw it in the paper. She was popeyed. She wasn't certain that you were my husband. She came running into my office with the paper."

"The paper exaggerated the whole thing," he said. "I didn't disarm her. I merely told her to drop the bottle."

Pam was looking at him in the steady, disconcerting way she had.

"Now, let's start all over," she said, "and you tell me just what happened."

The story followed him. In his own rational appraisal of events surrounding the murder, Gregory Lind's role had been small, infinitesimally small, but he was astonished at how many people were suddenly aware of him, of how many people recognized him, days after the event, remembering him as a photograph in a newspaper. Doctors and nurses and miscellaneous people around the hospital greeted him, where once they had ignored him. He was, in a sense, a celebrity.

On Monday afternoon, as he was preparing to go home, Tracy Welton strolled into the bullpen. Tracy, too, was leaving and he did not go out to the world in working clothes. Tracy wore a light gray hat with a perfect curling dip in the brim. His suit was blue, pin-striped and his necktie was finely polka-dotted. He had in him the remnants of what must have been an impressive appearance at one time. He carried himself well.

"I'd like to buy you a drink, Lind, if you've got the time," he said.

Greg was startled. He did a quick mental caculation. He and Pamela did their shopping together on Monday night because the stores were open. Pamela would not be home for a couple of hours yet. It would be damned interesting to have a drink with Tracy Welton.

"You're dressed to the eyebrows," he said. "I'll look like a poor relative."

"So what? Poor relatives have to drink, too, just like everybody else."

They went out together, walking toward the bend of the narrow river that had been Hollister's initial connection with the Gulf. The remnants of the original small town still lingered here, a dull and dingy neighborhood that was concealed from tourists by bright and flashy traffic arteries flowing inward from the highway. It was the neighborhood of the railroad station, the old courthouse, the morning newspaper, shabby hotels and Army surplus stores. There were liquor stores and places which called themselves cafes but which were actually bars to which one carried his own liquor, buying setups. Tracy led the way to one called The High Handle. It was a dimly lighted place, even dimmer in the booths. Tracy took a booth.

It was obvious that this was one of Tracy Welton's regular stops. A waiter brought a bottle of bourbon and stood it on the table. He brought ice and water and soda and glasses, pretzels and a pot of cheese on a plate, surrounded by crackers.

"My personal bottle. I leave it here and they guard it zealously," Tracy said.

"I'll bet they do."

Tracy poured two stiff drinks. He added only one ice cube and a little water to his own. He dipped his glass.

"To fame," he said. "I don't often have a drink with a celebrity."

"Don't rub it in. I didn't seek all of that damned notoriety."

"If you did, you wouldn't be a celebrity. And I wouldn't think of buying you a drink."

Tracy's drink vanished in two swallows. He held the bottle out to Gregory who shook his head. "You're too fast. I nurse mine."

"Why?"

"I enjoy it more. Besides that, I am going shopping with my wife tonight."

"Ah, your wife! She'd be the reason why you walked away from the black suit and the black hat and the distinctive collar?"

Greg sipped his drink without answering. This was his own territory, not Tracy's. He wasn't going to introduce Tracy to Pamela, in person or in conversation. The other man smiled and the light from the low-powered, yellow-shaded lamp threw shadows in the hollows under his cheekbones, creating the impression that he had an abnormally long head and a narrow mouth.

"I don't give a damn about your marriage," Tracy said. "Don't tell me about it. Myself, I didn't leave the holy, holy priesthood for a woman. Believe that, or don't."

"Why did you then?"

"Many reasons. New reasons and old. Let's say my mind rebelled. So did my soul."

Tracy looked into empty space beyond the booth and Greg was fascinated to see anger build in him, anger that sharpened his features and lighted in his eyes.

"I can give faith to the positive and the undeviating," Tracy said, "even if error adheres to it or if it bends to bigotry." He grimaced. "I cannot give faith, or love and loyalty, to compromise and to apology."

"I did not mean to stir you up," Greg said. "I take it that you are not entranced with those open windows that let fresh air into the Church."

Tracy's eyes came back from their contemplation of outer space. He thrust his chin forward.

"Don't be too amused," he said. "It isn't funny. Those ventilating windows let all the magic out of the Church, all the nice misty fuzziness that we called mysticism. A bunch of exhibitionistic pragmatists sat around in Rome, living like Kings and sounding forth with a lot of bombast that knocked down every damned thing that the simple and devout believer held to be true."

Greg listened, fascinated. Tracy Welton, who looked tough and who was tough, had a voice of depth and power and resonance. He had all of the tricks and mannerisms of an actor. He gestured with a spread hand or with a leveled finger. He was a priest who had left the Church. His leaving was probably not as simple and direct in line as he pretended, but Greg did not care about that. It would be interesting to keep Tracy Welton talking.

"You know whether I'm right or not," Tracy said. "We still have the great true Church, and an infallible Pope, and nobody knows what to believe any more."

Tracy took a deep swallow, poured himself a third drink and looked at Greg's glass. "I talk only to fellow drinkers," he said.

"Fair enough. I'll take another."

Greg flinched when he saw the depth of the drink which the other man poured. Tracy lighted a cigarette. "We could always find answers under the old system," he said. "It made no difference what anybody brought up. We had basic principles, some of them patently absurd, and as long as we based all discussion on those principles, we were invincible. We were the custodians of holy truth and we could prove it. Outside of our ivy-covered walls were Protestants, Jews, heretics, schismatics, agnostics, atheists. We had them all named and classified and we had authority. If they wanted anything we had, anything at all, we wrote the rules."

"You think that was good?"

"You're damned right I do. If you are going to have a Church, that is the way to have it. Now we've got a damned Dutch catechism, and half-baked experts telling us why the Church is outmoded, and the dear old dedicated Catholic intelligentsia coming up with new translations and multi-explanations of everything, and nuns who look like characters in a fifth-rate British comedy, and no more Latin, no more Friday, no more transubstantiation, no more mortal sin, no hell."

"It's not quite that far."

"No? You haven't been reading the Catholic press. Let's have one more drink and then we'll take the air."

"I hadn't better. That last one nearly knocked me."

"One more will straighten you right up. And I tell you what I'll do, I'll prophesy. I'll tell you what is going to happen. You can write it down."

"I'd like to know what is going to happen."

Greg watched as Tracy Welton poured two more drinks. He was feeling the liquor in his fingers, in his legs. He was not certain that he could stand. He should, obviously, refuse another drink. He should walk out. He should go home. He was, however, enjoying Tracy Welton. This, oddly, was the only ex-priest whom he knew personally. It was a long time since he had had a session like this; "shop talk," if one wanted to call it that.

Tracy leaned back against the padded wall of the booth. His eyes were closed to narrow slits and the skin of his face was drawn tight. He held a cigarette a long time between puffs. "You remember the predictions of Saint Malachy?" he said. He spoke slowly but his voice was clear, controlled.

"Yes. Faintly. He predicted Popes."

"And very well. You could recognize any of them from his description, even Paul Six. And he wrote in the twelfth century. He had to take a long look ahead. Well, you know what? There will be only two more Popes. There are only two more on his list."

"You believe that?"

"Of course I do. He hasn't missed yet. The next one after Paul will be a foreigner, he says. Not an Italian. A foreigner. Want me to tell you who he'll be?"

"Yes."

"Remember, this is Tracy Welton making this prophecy. It isn't old Saint Malachy. But it's just as good. It's the way it's going to be."

"O.K. Shoot."

Tracy Welton smiled. He looked mocking when he smiled, completely lacking in sincerity. "Write it down," he said. "The next Pope will be Suenens, Cardinal, that is; Leo Joseph Cardinal Suenens of Belgium. Next Pope. Write it down."

"It's possible, I guess."

"It's inevitable. Inevitable. I've got another prophecy. Another Tracy Welton prophecy. The Church is all through. You know that. All through after two thousand years! A lot of literal-minded, unimaginative bastards broke it into little unbelievable pieces. So what happens? The Protestants are all mixed up, too. All these years they've been following Rome and didn't know it. Now they've got nobody to follow, nobody to protest against. Sad."

"O.K. What's the prophecy?"

"Very simple. Exceedingly simple. Pretty soon. Not long now. A fellow is going to show up. Glib fellow. Great orator. Rabble rouser. Maybe sincere. Maybe not. I don't know. Anyway, he is going to start the quickest religious stampede in history. Incredible. Sweep like a forest fire."

"How?"

"He'll preach simple. He'll tell people that Judeo-Christian is all one thing. Greatest religion in the world! Sad mistake broke it in two. Mistake in translation or something. Shouldn't be broken. Should be all one line. God revealing to man on Judeo-Christian line. Jesus Christ, the last and greatest Jewish prophet! Please everybody. Who wants to be a Judeo-Christian? Get in line!"

Tracy emptied his glass. "Damn near everybody will get in that line," he said. "It's the most ecumenical thing. People will swoon with it. Simplifies everything. Even the Jews will get aboard. All except the Orthodox. Not many of those left. No matter about them. They are like the old-fashioned Catholics. Conservatives! Just wait. New thing coming. Judeo-Christian, greatest religion in the world!"

"I think you're crazy."

"Wait and see. Let's get the hell out of here."

Tracy rose. He had a moment of difficulty in getting out of the booth but he drew himself straight once he was clear, took a deep breath and walked, without a trace of lurch or stagger, to the door. Greg had a difficult time following him and he had an idea that if he could see himself he was probably walking like a man with two feet asleep. He had not seen Tracy pay anybody and that seemed curious unless The High Handle operated like a club, which seemed unlikely.

The clear air of out-of-doors felt wonderful in his lungs, on the surface of his skin. He stood swaying a moment and the lights seemed to be out of focus, bigger than they should be, then smaller; far away, then close.

"Let's go," Tracy said.

"Wait a minute. Everything's disconnected. I can't drink the way you can."

"Nobody can. Don't let that worry you."

He felt Tracy's hand on his elbow and the other man was steering him. "You need food," Tracy said. "So do I. There's a place. It's got a show but we can eat there. There's something I want you to see."

"I couldn't see a show."

"You don't have to see a show. You'll see one thing. Never forget it. I go when I'm drunk. It sobers me right up. Every time."

"Just looking at something?"

"That's right."

"Are you drunk?"

"Certainly."

"So am I."

"Of course."

The place was in the basement of one of the old hotels. There was a sign that identified it as RICARDO's PINK SLIPPER. Ricardo sounded definitely masculine and the idea of his having a pink slipper was very funny. Greg tried to laugh and achieved only a hiccough. He went to

235

the men's room and saw himself in the mirror. His eyes were sunken and his skin had a mottled look.

"Look like a camel," he said.

He did not know what time it was, but he knew that he was late and that he should call Pam. He was in a strange place and he did not know where they kept their telephones and Tracy was waiting for him. He was fairly certain that Pam would be able to tell from his voice that he had been drinking. He didn't want her to know. He would, he assured himself, be sober again once he had something to eat.

Tracy was known at the Pink Slipper as he was at The High Handle. It was a low-ceilinged, smoky room with tables set around a cleared circular space. There was a man in the spotlight who was saying something but Greg did not know what he was saying, or care.

"Look," Tracy told a waiter. "I want you to bring out my bottle. And we're going to want some shrimp and soup and some soft stuff, scrambled eggs and English muffins and maybe some spinach. Dream it up nice for us."

The waiter disappeared and the man in the spotlight stopped talking. Gregory Lind was trying to cling to one thread of reality. He knew that he was in the Pink Slipper with Tracy Welton but he had no thoughts, no words that he could command. There was music and a girl dancing to it, or moving languorously to it. He was aware of her as a wraithlike figure in a mist. Tracy's voice came to him as though over great distance.

"I didn't like celibacy any better than anyone else," Tracy said. "I used to think about women, and want women, like everybody else. I never did anything about it. After I walked out, I did something about it, but doing something had nothing to do with my getting out. Do you know, women were a disappointment to me."

"What was the matter with them?"

Greg's own voice sounded thick and coarse, picking up its words one at a time. He knew where Tracy was, across the table, but he could not see his face.

"Don't get me wrong," Tracy said, "I never had any yen for men. Never will have. It just seems to me that sex is overrated. There's a drive there and a zing but I hate the hell out of women; whining and complaining and doing just what they want and blaming a man for everything that goes wrong. Dammit, the average woman isn't even as tidy as a man. She is satisfied if she just *appears* tidy."

"Maybe you know the wrong women."

"Maybe. Maybe. I sure as hell wouldn't marry any that I've known."

Pam moved fleetingly in Greg's mind. He should call her. She wasn't one of the wrong women. She would never be content to appear tidy.

236

Pam was dainty, fastidious, a person of glow and gleam and delicate scent.

"Eat your shrimp!" Tracy said.

He had not noticed the serving of the shrimp. He ate shrimp and crackers, then pea soup and scrambled eggs, paying no attention to the dancer. He did not know whether she was the first one who came on, or a later one, but the crowd was excited about her. She worked in a blue spot and there was a sickly blue color to everything on the table, including the eggs. Greg was drinking his coffee when the dancer exited to tumultuous applause. The lights came on, dim over the house, bright over the cleared circle.

"Now," Tracy Welton said, "this is what I want you to see. Better take a drink first. You will need it."

"Not me. I have had drinks."

Greg looked with surprise at the drink before him. There were many gaps in the action as he remembered it. He did not remember Tracy pouring a drink, yet Tracy must have done so. There was a bottle standing on the table. He had no desire for a drink. He could see it clearly and he could see Tracy clearly. His vision had returned to him and his mind felt reasonably clear. There was an offstage bang on a drum, a voice on a microphone saying:

"And now—Johnny."

There was a concert grand piano and a microphone in the center of the clear space. They had been placed obviously before the light came on. A short, stout, boyish-looking man came out, walking in a dance step. He had a round face and was almost totally bald. He was wearing eye shadow. He wore a white suit and there was a large red rose, which was probably artificial, in his lapel. He waved to the crowd which greeted him with applause.

"Thank you . . . Thank you . . . Thank you . . ." he said. "Did you notice my flower?" The crowd applauded again. "I thought you would. It's a big rose. I bought it from an old woman as I was walking down here. It was so big that it reminded the old woman of the story of the three dwarfs in a supermarket. Did you ever hear that one?"

No one, evidently, had heard it, so the man called "Johnny" told it. It was a very dirty story, an exceptionally foul story, and he told it deadpan in a high, clear, slightly lisping voice that was almost childish. His audience laughed loudly and again he said: "Thank you . . . Thank you . . . Thank you . . ."

He seated himself at the piano and his fingers moved deftly over the keys as though seeking a melody. He played the music of "Some

237

Enchanted Evening" with a nice feeling for the romantic values, and he sang parody lyrics to it that were as dirty as his joke.

Greg looked at Tracy Welton and Tracy nodded his head. "This is what I wanted you to see," he said. His face was grim, the lines drawn taut. "He is one of us."

"You mean?"

"Yes."

Johnny was giving his treatment now to "On the Street Where You Live." He was light and airy, almost innocent in expression, in his soft handling of the music, but he sent the most unpleasant words in the English language flying around the room. Greg stared at him, repelled. It was impossible to believe that this creature had been a priest. Tracy rose.

"Let's go," he said. Outside on the shadowy street, he stood for a moment to light a cigarette. "I'm dead cold sober now," he said. "It always works. That rodent chills me. He makes me want to fight. Maybe I should be sympathetic and kind and tell myself he's sick. I won't be. I can't be. He's lower than a cockroach."

Greg took a deep breath. He felt fairly well under control again. He, too, had experienced the shock that Tracy mentioned, the sobering effect of outrage.

"Did you actually mean by 'one of us' that that fellow is a former priest?"

"I damn well did. I could tell you his name and where he came from, and his parish, but I won't." Tracy turned his head. His mouth smiled but there was no smile in his eyes. "You see, he comes from the same city that I do."

He tossed his cigarette down and stepped on it. "Would you believe that I was once a Dominican?" he said.

"Yes. I'd believe that. I enjoyed the drinks with you tonight, and the dinner, and the talk. I'd like to pay my share of it."

"There isn't any share. Did you see me deal out any money?"

"No. You must have charge accounts."

"Guess again. An ambulance guy can do favors for joints like those, and he does. Never mind the details." Tracy Welton smiled again. "Now go home to your wife."

He turned and walked away, striding down the street without looking back. Greg, startled, watched him until he turned a corner, then he looked at his watch. It was eleven-ten.

"My God," he said. "What will Pam think?"

A cab rolled up in answer to his signal. Once inside it, with no conversation to key him up, he slumped. His brain felt foggy and the motion of the cab made him aware of his stomach. He had an idea that he had downed that last drink while the creature named Johnny was singing. He could not be certain. He had no clear memory. He did not want to think about it.

He stood for a minute outside the apartment house that was his home. He was feeling shaky, in no condition to handle a delicate situation. He dreaded going up. There was, however, no alternative. He mounted the stairs slowly.

Pam heard him coming and she flung the door open as he reached the landing. She was wearing a transparent robe over her nightgown, a pale blue robe with large dots of darker blue. It tied with ruffles around her throat that made her look like a little girl. She looked frightened and angry and she was very lovely.

"Where have you been?" she said. Her voice was a full octave higher than normal.

"It's a long story," Greg said.

She retreated into the apartment, walking slowly backward, permitting him room to enter. "You're drunk," she said bitterly. "Drunk. Having so much fun that you couldn't call me! You couldn't spare two minutes out of your evening for me."

"No. That wasn't it."

"What was it? Why didn't you call me?"

He sat in the overstuffed chair. It seemed to him that there had been a reason why he had not called Pam, a good reason. He couldn't remember. He had been able to talk all right and think all right when he and Tracy stood outside the Pink Slipper. Pamela disconcerted him and he couldn't think.

"I didn't know where you were," she said. "I couldn't imagine. I called the hospital and I called the police and nobody knew anything about you. I didn't know what to do."

Pam was crying. The tears were rolling down her cheeks. He wanted to do something about that but he was feeling dizzy and he couldn't call up the words he wanted. She would understand how it was if he could tell her about Tracy. Tracy was an ex-priest. Tracy used to be a Dominican. Top order, the Dominicans. It had meant a lot, talking to another ex-priest. He hadn't had a night out with another man since he met Pamela. That was O.K. Pamela was enough for anybody, but if he could call up the words, she'd understand what tonight meant to him and how he got all mixed up with the liquor and everything. He could make her understand if he could only put the words together. She was standing there looking at him and she was crying.

"Where were you?" she said. Her voice climbed. "Were you out with a woman? Were you?"

"No. No. Absolutely not." He felt shock at the mere thought. "Just Tracy and me. He's an ex-priest, too, Pam."

"Who is?"

"Tracy. Tracy Welton. My boss. He used to be a priest." He drew a deep breath. He wanted to push that thought now that he had started on it. It was important to him. "I was only going to take one drink."

He stopped. That seemed so long ago. It was afternoon, just after three o'clock. He had had that one drink. Now it was nearly midnight. He did not know where all that time had gone. He did not know why he did not call Pam. He couldn't explain anything.

The telephone rang suddenly, shrilly, clamorously. Pam turned jerkily and her shoulders shook. "You answer it," she said contemptuously. "One of your drunken companions no doubt. Maybe the woman you weren't with."

He rose shakily. He could not imagine. Tracy would not call him, or would he? He had to cross the room to the phone. He did not dare sit down. He stood and he felt better standing. He lifted the receiver.

There was an empty, hollow sound for a second or two and then a voice that he recognized immediately.

"Greg? This is Carina. I'm so glad you answered the phone." She was crying and the tears came through the receiver with the words. "Prepare Pamela a little, Greg, and take care of her. It is going to be so hard on her, so very, very cruel. Greg, my husband, her father, died a little while ago."

"No!" He had anticipated the news by seconds but shock hit him. An icy sponge seemed to move across his brain and he was suddenly sober. "I'm so very sorry," he said.

"I'll have to talk to Pamela. I want you both here. I'm wiring you the money to fly. Come as soon as you can, and take care of Pamela. Now, put her on, please."

"I will and I'll take care of everything."

He knew that nothing he had said to Carina Gibson made much sense, but it didn't matter. He turned and Pamela was standing straight, staring at him. She knew that the voice on the line was a woman's and there was hatred in her eyes. He had to walk through that hatred. He laid the receiver down and took three steps.

"Pam, darling," he said. "You've got to brace yourself. It's bad news."

"Don't touch me!" she said. She read his face then and her hand came up to her mouth. "What is it?"

"That's your mother on the line, Pam. Your father—"

He got no further than that. She pushed him aside in reaching for the phone and her voice climbed. "Carina!"

He stood, listening helplessly, while she wept and ejaculated and spoke in fragmented sentences. She hung up and dropped her head on her arms which she had folded across her knees. She cried then in sobs that shook her body. He dropped to his knees beside her but he could not reach her with love or concern or sympathy. She raised her head and brushed his arm aside.

"Wash the stink of whiskey off you," she said. "I can't stand it."

She walked away from him, into the bedroom and he stood for a moment staring after her, then he went to the bathroom. He showered in lukewarm water which he changed slowly, gradually, to cold. He stood under the icy shower and his teeth chattered. His stomach felt a little sick when he stepped out from under the water but his head was clear. He brushed his teeth and used a mouthwash of Pam's and sprayed himself with deodorant. He stood for a minute then, wondering if there was anything else that he could do. He decided that he had done everything necessary.

The trouble with him, as far as Pam was concerned, was not physical. He had given her a very bad evening through sheer clumsy neglect. She had been frightened and worried. She had probably had nothing to eat. It was a brutally unfair preparation for the bad news she had just received. Never since she married him had she been so badly prepared for trouble.

He did not have his pajamas in the bathroom so he put his street clothes on again. He paused as he was tightening his belt. He had not convinced Pamela that he had not been out with a woman. He might never convince her. She had convinced herself that the phone call was from some woman with whom he had spent the evening. Pamela had a strange mind in many respects. Those few minutes during which she stood in the room while he talked on the telephone might remain a reality for her. She knew now that the woman on the phone had been her mother, but she might still have him charged with all the sins she had imagined, charged in the end with talking to some lady love.

He shook his head. There was no point in going off on tangents. She needed him. He walked to the bedroom door. She was lying face down, sobbing. He wanted to go to her but he remembered the ancient wisdom which said that no one should be denied the right to shed honest tears. He went instead to the kitchen and made coffee. He sat there watching it while it perked and he thought of Ralph Gibson.

Pamela's father had offered him friendly hospitality on the one occasion when he had had social contact with him. He had sought for common ground and had spoken in friendly fashion about Bart. He had not accepted a Catholic priest in a sports jacket drinking Scotch with his daughter, and he had been right.

The coffee had perked sufficiently. Pam drank it black, as he did. He poured a cup for her and carried it to the bedroom. Pam refused to raise her head when he spoke to her. He set the coffee down on the small bedside table and laid his hand on her shoulder.

"Please, Pam," he said. "One cup of coffee. I won't bother you for anything else."

She sat up slowly and turned. She stretched out her right hand, groping in seeming aimlessness at empty air. "A handkerchief. Get me a handkerchief, please."

He took a handkerchief from the drawer and brought it to her. She wadded it in her hand and did not use it. Her eyes were red-rimmed but very bright. There were tear lines on her cheek. She kept drawing her lips in under her teeth and releasing them. He offered her the coffee and she accepted it, sipping it slowly.

"He was so very good," she said. "He was the strongest man I've ever known. He did what he thought was right and nothing could swerve him. Nothing. He was right about me and I was wrong." She swallowed hard and the tears flowed again. "I wish that I could tell him so."

The man who wasn't the strongest man she had ever known knelt beside the bed. He held her left hand and his fingers pressed it gently but there was no response. She did not look at him. He would, he thought, have to get out early in the morning and pick up the money that Carina Gibson was wiring. It was thoughtful of her in her grief, and wise, and knowing. He could not buy airplane tickets without her money. It would mean much to him if he could. He would have to buy the tickets in the morning and he would have to phone the hospital because he would not be going to work.

"Let's go to bed, darling," he said gently. "You will need all of your strength tomorrow."

-XIII-

They were flying over a snow-covered landscape during the last half hour of the flight to Culverton. Pamela had the window seat but she did not look out. Greg had encouraged her to talk about her father and she had wanted to do that. She had talked about him on the flight to St.

Louis where they changed planes, during the hour and a half wait for the plane to Culverton, and through most of the last lap of the journey; childhood memories, family legends, impressions and events of her more mature years. She was tired ultimately, or nerving herself to the ordeal ahead of her. She rested with her head on Greg's shoulder and his arm enclosed her.

He was, he thought, at least useful to her in his limited way, although God knew there was little that he could do. He could not have even brought her home without her mother's help.

They were losing altitude for the approach to Culverton airport. He could see the city when the plane swung out over the river and the port wing dropped. Culverton was shaped like a fan, with the old section and the downtown section as the handgrip and the streets radiating out. It was not flat, however, so the fan image did not persist when one was sufficiently low to be aware of the uphill slope of the streets running west. The river was south of the town and east of it, due to the bulging of the land and the curving sweep of river. Either south or east, one could look across the wide river into another state.

The plane settled and Pamela sat up straight. "Help me," she said. "Don't let me cry."

It was an odd request. He accepted it as that, patting her shoulder. They had not needed heavy clothing in Hollister but Culverton demanded it. They were too lightly dressed for the day. The snow on the ground was frozen there and there was a nasty wind that came in spurts. Carina did not meet the plane. Horace, the Gibson chauffeur, was waiting for them and he was a solemn man. They rolled in the big car over the River Highway south and memories moved with them. Greg looked at the highway exit that led to Janet's house, and his mother. It did not seem real; at best, an image out of some remote association.

"It is impossible, of course, to believe that I am here," he thought. "The idea is preposterous."

Twenty-four hours ago he had been riding an ambulance to an accident in Hollister, Texas, and last night he had been very drunk in that same city. The car turned in between the stone pillars with their griffons. The tires crunched a little and then they stopped.

Carina waited for them in the sun room. If Greg had ever doubted her dignity, he granted it now. She wore a black dress with a triangle of white below the throat line and she rose slowly from the chair in which she had been sitting. Pamela covered the last ten or twelve feet at a half run and the two women locked in an embrace.

Pamela hadn't wanted to cry, and she didn't. Neither did Carina.

Their need for each other and their shared grief did not demand tears. There was a poignancy beyond tears in every movement they made.

"I want to know all about it," Pamela said. Her voice was steady but it did not sound like her voice. "I did not even know that he was ill."

"Your father hadn't been ill. He was never ill, as you know," Carina said to Pam. "He was playing golf yesterday afternoon." She paused, with an odd break in her voice. "Good God! Was it only yesterday afternoon? Twenty-four hours ago!" There were tears in her eyes. "This time yesterday. He was on the golf course. The sixth hole. He did not say a word. He just toppled over."

Greg was thinking that this time, yesterday, he had been walking into The High Handle in Hollister, Texas, with Tracy Welton. He looked at a space in the rug where the sun touched. Ralph Gibson had stood there, on approximately that spot, the last time he had seen him. He could see him now as he had been then; tall and bronzed, genial, commanding. He had just won some money playing golf and he was delighted. The money could not have meant anything to him; he had been happy about winning.

"They took him to the hospital and they called me," Carina said. "He never regained consciousness. I called you shortly after—after . . ."

She did not complete the sentence. Pamela was crying again, silently, her eyes fixed on her mother's face. There was no glare in the sun room and the sun was not in anyone's eyes, but light flowed cheerfully through the room, touching everyone impersonally. Greg remembered Pam talking on the plane, telling him how homely she had been as a girl and how her father always insisted that she was beautiful.

"I knew that he was wrong," she said, "but it helped. It helped so very much."

It was difficult to imagine now that anyone, anywhere, at any time, could have considered Pam homely. She had had a bad day and night yesterday, a harrowing journey today, and there were tears in her eyes. The marks of fatigue and grief were in her face but he knew that he would never forget the picture that she projected at that moment. She was the loveliest woman he had ever seen.

"I will not go to the—mortuary—until evening," Carina said. She laid the words down one by one. "I will go with Ted and Elinor. Why don't you and Gregory go this afternoon, Pamela? I know you would want to—"

"Oh, yes. May I?"

"I'll have Horace drive you in."

"Please don't. I would like to drive if you will lend me a car."

"Take mine. The keys are somewhere. Horace will know. Ring for him."

Greg felt like a spectator; a favored spectator, of course, permitted to stand in the wings during the playing of scenes but still not an actual participant in anything that was said or done. It would have to be that way, inevitably, he supposed, but it was a strange sensation. It seemingly did not occur to Pam that he might like to drive, that driving might offer him an outlet for some of his own repressed emotion. She did not think of him at all. They stood together, waiting, until Horace brought her mother's hardtop convertible around. There did not seem to be anything to say until she said, "Thank you, Horace."

The River Highway flowed past familiar streets, church steeples against the skyline to which he could put names. At the warning sign of ROHLMAN STREET NEXT EXIT, Pamela pulled into the right hand lane. They came off the freeway then. Rohlman was the main street of newer downtown. The banks were there, the investment houses, the large insurance companies. A right turn took them into Chasen Street. They passed Saint Mark's, the Episcopal Cathedral, and the Rinehart Mortuary was in the next block. Pamela pulled in to the curb before the mortuary and that seemed to be the peak of her effort. She turned her head.

"I'm frightened, Greg," she said. "I don't believe I can go in."

"You can. There is nothing to frighten you. It will be difficult but just remember—your father isn't in there, Pam."

Her eyes widened. "You're talking about immortality, aren't you? He didn't believe in it."

One could not tell her that any individual's belief, or non-belief, in immortality was irrelevant and unimportant. He reached for her hand and enclosed it in his arm.

"We will go in," he said.

They climbed stone steps and they spoke to a precisely mannered, deferent man, and they walked a short corridor to a room in which two tall torches burned, a room in which flowers were arranged; not too many flowers.

Ralph Gibson's body lay in a handsome bronze casket. His thin hair had been carefully arranged and the skin of his face had a deep tan. He had not been handsome in life and he was not handsome in death, but he had been strong and masculine, a powerful man, and that was how he appeared now; a strong man asleep.

Pamela sobbed only once and then stood looking at him.

Gregory Lind stood beside the coffin and remembered that this man had been friendly to him, had served him a drink and had spoken about

245

his brother's business. This was a man who had offered a little girl disbelief in her homeliness, who had loved that girl greatly but who had refused to compromise, even for her, with what he could not respect.

Gregory Lind had sung Masses for the dead. He had blessed coffins and prayed above bodies and offered priestly supplication to God for souls. He was close to Ralph Gibson, family-close, and he was helpless, an unfrocked priest without an altar. There would be no religious service of any kind, Carina had said, and there was outrage to Gregory Lind, a touch of horror, in this burying of a body without a blessing or a prayer, this resigning of a soul to eternity without addressing oneself to God.

He was as helpless as Pamela, standing in the presence of death. "I wish I could say a Mass for him," he said.

Pamela did not answer and he did not look at her. He was remembering the many who had died and for whom he had offered Masses. He had led rosaries, too. The rosary was a simple offering for the dead, one in which Protestants, Jews and atheists participated, at least in offering their presence, when Catholic friends died. One did not need a priest for that. For fifteen minutes, a few people or many could pray in unison, identifying themselves with the soul who had passed to judgment, asking mercy for that soul and for themselves.

Gregory Lind stood straight, looking at the strong, calm face of Ralph Gibson. He turned his head and Pam was looking up at him.

"Will you say the rosary with me, Pam?" he said.

Their eyes met and she read, perhaps, the great need in him. She hesitated only a few seconds.

"Yes, Greg," she said. "Thank you."

He sank to his knees and he felt her presence when she knelt beside him. He made the sign of the Cross and raised his voice in the "Our Father." Pamela said the response and his voice swept on to the "Hail, Mary." Pamela faltered and he helped her until she could carry that response alone. He did not look at her. He had his eyes fixed upon a point above the coffin. They said a decade and then the break prayer.

"May he rest in peace, O Lord, and may perpetual light shine upon him."

His voice led and Pamela's followed. They were very close again. Their voices rose and fell and the echoing walls in the small room gave the voices back, rising, falling, rising . . .

BOOK THREE

Tomorrow and Tomorrow

–I–

There was no religious service for Ralph Gibson but there were a great many people at the mortuary and at the cemetery. Gregory Lind escorted Pamela, walking behind Carina and Ralph's brother, Ted. Ted's wife, Elinor, walked with her son, Arthur. To Gregory it was an ordeal, walking in the clothing of a layman, consenting by his presence in this burying of a man without a prayer. He did not glance at the bystanders. Some of them would be people he knew, people who knew him. He did not want to see the expressions on their faces.

Ralph Gibson had been a prominent citizen, a leader in community activity. The newspapers had been generous in space and tribute. The accounts had dealt with the man and with his family, with his widow and with his daughter, Pamela, who was Mrs. Gregory Lind.

Greg had been able to read that "Mrs. Gregory Lind" with eyes other than his own. He could read it as priests would read it, as his own family would read it, and the neighbors, the family friends, his former parishioners. To the many that line in the paper would be a revelation; anyone who had not known of his marriage to Pamela Gibson would know of it now. He was startled at his own shrinking from public opinion. He was not apologetic for his marriage to Pam; he was proud of it. He would do the same thing again if time rolled back. He just could not be comfortable in Culverton in his identity as a husband, an identity which so many people would forever refuse to accept.

He had called Bart and Bart had been gruffly pleased at the call.

"I thought you'd be back," he said. "I was sorry about Gibson's death. It gives you some problems, doesn't it?"

"A few."

"What do you do now?"

"All of our personal possessions, or most of them, are in Hollister. I don't know how long we'll have to stay around here."

Bart was silent for the space of a long breath. "How about seeing you?" he said. "Could you make it for dinner this evening?"

"Not for dinner. I could come about five. Or I could come to the office."

"No. Come to the house. Five is fine. I'll scram the kids. I haven't prepared them yet for you in civilian clothes."

"Sorry."

"No. My fault. Should have done it. I'll see you."

It was difficult, thinking of Bart's children and the necessity for preparing them for their uncle in layman's clothes. They must know by this time, of course, that he had left the priesthood and they would be adjusted to the knowledge. Actually seeing, and meeting again, an uncle who had been a priest was a different matter; a matter of attitude rather than of mere knowledge. It would be the same problem at Janet's home, with her children. A man could collide with many lives when he left an accustomed track.

He had called Janet, too. "We knew you would be in town," she said. "I was wondering if you'd call."

"You knew I would."

"I didn't. I'd have known about you once."

"All right. Have it your way. Will mother come to the phone?"

"She will not."

"How do you know?"

"I hate to tell you this, Gregsie, but she said that if you called I should hang up."

"I thought she would soften with time."

"She hasn't. She made an awful scene about the things in the paper that mentioned Mrs. Gregory Lind. You can see why she would."

"I guess so."

"Why don't you come out, Gregsie? It might make a difference if she saw you."

"Thanks, Janet. I'll try."

He remembered the phone conversations as he rode to the cemetery. There was no possible chance, even in the wildest daydream, that his family would ever accept Pamela. Her family had accepted him, with obvious reservations, and it was possible that he could establish

248

a relationship of a sort with most of the Gibsons, that he could be on friendly, even warm, terms with Carina. A man did not, comfortably or happily, exchange his own family for the family of someone else, even if he loved the someone else. A man did not govern all of the things that happened in his life, either.

It was cold at the cemetery and cold coming home. The house of the Gibsons seemed too big, too imposing, too impersonal, but there was warmth within it and beauty; beauty that was a bit withdrawn from a stranger, unwilling to share with him, and consequently, a bit formal and stiff to his eye. Carina went to her room immediately for a rest and Greg accompanied Pamela to the room that had once been hers and which was now theirs.

It was a youthful room, done in blue, with too many soft surfaces, pillows and cushions, a large room with three windows and two exposures. Greg felt uneasy in it as he felt uneasy in all of the house. There was, he supposed, an art to relaxing when surrounded by luxury. He knew nothing of that art. One who was at home here would own the lamp of Aladdin. A finger on a button was all that one needed to command almost anything conceivable.

He wondered momentarily if Rodney Keller had ever occupied this bright blue room with Pamela. He probably had and so the subject was better skipped.

Pamela was pale. Black was not becoming to her when it was unrelieved and she had worn unrelieved black to the cemetery. The skin of her face was drawn tight and the cheekbones were prominent, angular. She had softened her characteristic lip coloring to a weak pink and her mouth appeared oddly small.

"I need a nap," she said, "maybe a sleep. Is there anything you could do if I just let go?"

"Of course. If I can borrow a car, I would like to poke around town a bit."

"The car is easy. Take mother's. It's all tanked and in good shape. Tell Horace to bring it around."

"Thanks."

"Don't say that!"

"Say what?"

"Thanks. As if I was giving you something, or anybody is giving you something." Pam gestured sweepingly. "Anything around here that I have or that I command is yours, too."

"It's a bit difficult for me to feel that or to accept it. You belong here, always have belonged here. I'm a stranger to all of it."

Pam nodded slowly. "Yes. I guess I can see that. It seems absurd but

I can see it. We'll have to do something about it." She closed her eyes and opened them again. "Greg, I don't want you to have a bad time but I'm just too tired to even think about it."

"I know. Don't think about it." He dropped to one knee beside her and held her against him. "I'll visit Bart tonight," he said, "but I won't stay out late."

"Good. I'm glad you've got some place to go. I'm sorry that I'm such a mess." Her voice caught. "I'll make up for it. Kiss me now and take off!"

He kissed her, stirred as he always was by the softness of her, aware of the faint, characteristic scent. "I love you very much, Pam," he said. "Please do."

He left her and he felt like an intruder, an alien, walking through the silent halls. Pamela had spoken of "Command" and he was certain that he would never achieve command over anything in this house of the Gibsons and that those who belonged in it were very well aware of his incapacity to command anything. It made no difference, of course. It just didn't matter.

Once in the car and headed for downtown Culverton, he was confronted by choice. More than anything else, he wanted to see Saint Anselm's church. It would not be changed in any slight degree, of course, but he would like to see it. He would be uncomfortable if he encountered former parishioners, as he would, of course. He was not ready for Tom Guyton yet, either.

There was not much traffic, so he drove slowly. He could call on his mother and Janet but he did not feel up to that either. He needed a quiet afternoon, a peaceful afternoon, but there was little peace and quiet in aimlessness; he had to have some objective. He was approaching the Rohlman exit when he remembered the Christmas greeting which he carried in his wallet. He had wondered about the identity of Gustave Kaufman who had sent him ten dollars for Christmas. Now was a good time to find out who and what he was.

He drove off the freeway. He and Pamela had gone to the mortuary on his last visit to Rohlman Street. He stopped at a drugstore and consulted a phone book. Gustave Kaufman lived at 27 Downing Court, which was in a new subdivision east of town, a long way from Saint Anselm's. Gregory Lind frowned at that discovery but he had to accept it because there was only one Gustave Kaufman in the book.

Downing Court when he reached it was one street in a subdivision like the ones Bart built; acres of houses which resembled one another in all but the superficial details. Number twenty-seven was a bungalow. It had blue trim on shutters and door canopies. The bungalow on its right had red trim and the bungalow on the left had yellow trim. The man who answered Greg's ring was in his sixties; a short, gray-haired man, settling into a little weight but not fat. He had blue eyes, alert blue eyes.

"You're Mr. Gustave Kaufman?" Greg said.

"I am. Come in, won't you."

"Thank you. I am Gregory Lind."

"I know you are. I've still got good eyes in my head."

The living room was simply furnished but it did have comfortable chairs. Gustave Kaufman shrugged into the jacket of his suit. He wore a white shirt and a necktie that was reddish brown.

"I knew you when you were a small boy," he said.

"I'm sorry. I didn't know. I never wrote to thank you for your Christmas gift. It puzzled me."

"I guess it did. That didn't occur to me. I thought you'd remember. No thanks necessary. Your dad was my best friend. We worked together a great many years."

Greg looked at the other man and he had no memory of him. Gustave Kaufman sensed that. He chuckled and reached for his pipe.

"You have no recollection of me," he said. "Well, I'm little surprised. You had small knowledge of your father or his work, or those he knew. Your mother held you pretty close."

"I appreciated your gift," Greg said. "I wondered if you thought I was still a priest when you sent it, or if you knew I had left."

"Oh, I knew you'd left. Those things get talked about. My wife heard about it from someone. I'm sorry she isn't here. She's visiting our daughter and the grandchildren this afternoon."

"How many grandchildren have you?"

"I have nine. Not all in the same place."

The conversation was difficult, without a foundation and seemingly going no place. Gustave Kaufman lighted his pipe. "I didn't know you'd married the Gibson girl until her father died. My ten dollars must have looked mighty small to you."

"On the contrary, it looked mighty big. I needed it. Pamela and I were on our own. We had nothing except what we earned."

"Strange, that. Well, you can't tell about people. If a man's been a priest, I don't imagine jobs come easy. I figured you might be having trouble and I remembered your dad with affection."

The statement was flatly made but there was emotion in it for Greg. Stated in Gustave Kaufman's terms that ten dollars was like a present from his own father. He had never really known his father in life.

"A better-looking man than you are, your father," Gustave Kaufman said. "A strong man with a fine face. He was not as tall as you. He had a mustache, English kind of mustache. Made him look more important than he was."

"Wasn't he important?"

"No. None of us were. We were employees. We wanted to branch out and start a little company of our own, him and me. We talked of it often and your father wanted it pretty badly; more than I did, I guess. Anyway, we never found any capital."

Greg looked at Gustave Kaufman, trying to imagine how he had been as a young man, a friend of his father's. It was sad, hearing now of a great unfilled want that his father had cherished for years. It was sad, too, that his father had looked more important than he was.

"I remember when they ordained you a priest," the man said. "Your father was proud as a man always is about the things that come to a son. I think he'd rather you'd gone in the contracting business. I can't say for sure because I'm a Lutheran and I was more apt to argue with him than anything else when it came to religion. He was a good Catholic, a fine, upright man, but I'll never believe he wanted you to be a priest. You were more your mother's son than you were his. Bart was the one that followed him."

"You know Bart?"

"I know him."

There was a coldness, a note of hostility, in the man's voice. Greg rose. "I am glad that we had this time together," he said. "I wanted to thank you for your thoughtful gift. I didn't expect to hear about my father."

"I could tell you more. Another time maybe. I'm sorry I can't offer you a drink of something. I quit it a long time ago, drinking. Your father did that for me, made me quit; saved my job and my life, too, no doubt."

"I didn't know. He drank a little himself."

"Aye. He did. Sometimes more than a little. He was a man that could. I am a man that couldn't. There was that difference between us, among other things."

"I am glad that I know. I would like to come back another time."

"Do that. A man that's retired has nothing but time. It's not always a blessing, having it."

"I don't imagine that it is."

He went out to a street that was quiet save for a single boy on a bicycle. He wondered how it would feel to be old and to be living here. He shook his head. He wouldn't like it. His father wouldn't have liked it, either. His fragmentary memories of his father were of a restless, active man. He looked at his watch. He was half the town away from Bart and he didn't have much time.

Bart's home, when he reached it, was as he remembered it, with nothing changed. His time away seemed so much longer than it actually was and he was surprised that all the familiar places were untouched.

Barbara opened the door for him and if she had changed, he thought, it was to grow prettier. As she stood in the doorway for one hesitant moment, she was a study in blonde beauty, her hair bright about her head, her eyes warm, her lips slightly parted. She moved forward then and kissed him, the fingers of her right hand pressing hard upon his forearm.

"I was almost afraid to kiss you," she said.

"Why?"

She laughed. "You were a strange man."

It was one way of getting over the hurdle of a missing Roman collar. He went down to the game room with Barbara and Bart was waiting for him, big and hard-handed and obviously happy to see him.

"You're looking fit," Bart said. "You didn't get like that pushing a pencil."

"I haven't seen many pencils."

"We'll hear about what you did see. I'll fix a drink. You like Scotch, don't you?"

"Yes, if you've got it."

"I've got it. I seemed to remember. It's a parlor-snake whiskey, but every man to his taste."

They sat in an intimate circle, the three of them, with their drinks. "Now, tell us," Bart said.

"Tell you what?"

"What you've been doing. The work, the recreation, the living. Anything."

"And Texas," Barbara said. "I've always wanted to visit Texas."

"It's a big order. I'll try."

Something stiff and tense and wound-up inside of Greg let go. He was suddenly relaxed as he could not remember being relaxed in a long time. This was home and these were his people, and they were concerned about him. They really wanted to know about the life that he had been leading and they would not consider it dull.

"I've been working on an ambulance," he said.

He put the ambulance first because it was the most interesting, the latest, the work that he had found most rewarding. He had always talked well when he liked his subject and his audience. He knew how to break narrative with humor and he presented people well. He pictured Tracy Welton as he had known him and he mentioned that he was the only former priest he'd known, an ex-Dominican.

"Did he quit or did the Dominicans throw him out?" Bart said.

"Why did you ask that?"

Bart shrugged. "He sounds like somebody who might have been thrown out."

It was an interesting thought but there was no time to pursue it. Barbara had her question. She was leaning forward.

"What I want to know is, how your—well, your Pamela—liked the idea of your working on an ambulance?"

"I don't believe she liked it too well, but we had to live and she is a good sport about anything and everything. She adapts."

There was a moment's silence. He could feel Bart's eyes on him. Barbara laughed softly. "That's nice," she said. "Does she still work in the travel places, ships and planes and glamour?"

"No. She has a post in an advertising agency, reading and writing Spanish."

"It sounds grand," Barbara said, "but it is kind of difficult to mix the advertising crowd with the ambulance boys, isn't it?"

"We don't mix them."

"You don't? Well, what happens to your social life?"

Greg hesitated. It was a difficult question because he had never given any serious thought to a social life. It was important to Barbara or she would not have brought it up. It was probably important to Pamela, too. He spread his hands.

"We don't have a social life," he said.

"How odd. I'd expect that your Pamela would insist on one. On a whole lot of social life, in fact."

"She doesn't. She doesn't insist on anything. You should see the place we live in. After all she's had, it must be terrible for her but it's what we can afford." The tension was building in him again. "I wish you knew Pamela. I wish I could tell you how she is."

"I'm sure she's lovely," Barbara said. "Now you and Bart have another drink and I'll fix some sandwiches. I'd like to do much better than that but I didn't have much warning."

"Sandwiches will be fine," Greg said.

Bart rose and walked to the bar. He fixed two drinks and came back. "Don't ever try to sell a woman to another woman, Kid," he said. "They never buy. How are you doing on religion?"

"I'm not doing. I go to Mass every Sunday. Pam goes with me."

"The hell she does."

"Yes. I told you that she'd surprise you, that she isn't the way you imagine."

Bart took a swallow of his drink. "Maybe not. Anyway, you've been making out all right."

"Yes. Thanks in large part to you. I owe you a lot of money."

"Not a lot. You'd owe me more if I'd had a big surplus. You can tie a heap of money up in building."

"I'll get it back to you. I may need time."

"Forget it."

They sat for a minute, looking at each other and emotion flowed between them. There was very little that they could say, very little of what counted.

"I saw Gustave Kaufman today," Greg said.

"That crusty old bastard! I didn't know you knew him."

"I didn't. He sent me a Christmas card with ten dollars in it. I looked him up because I was curious as well as grateful."

Bart drank slowly, his eyes fixed on something out of sight and far away. He shifted his weight in the chair, nodding his head.

"Yes," he said. "He'd do that. Dad was about the only friend he had. Old Gustave was a hell of a good man around a contracting shop. He knew where you could buy or rent anything from a screwdriver to a crane, and he could probably get it cheap. He could do all the jobs that nobody else wanted to do and he never forgot anything, but I could never see how Dad put up with him."

"What was the matter with him?"

"He was a drunk. A noisy, offensive, loud-mouthed drunk. Dad straightened him up and got him off the bottle but he was still a suspicious, cranky, cantankerous old bastard. Nobody could get along with him."

Greg grinned. "He doesn't seem to like you, either."

"I guess not. When he had to retire, age-limit, he hit me for a job. I'd have jumped at the chance to have him around the shop; not for what he was, God knows, but for what he could do. I couldn't take him on. I couldn't afford another man on the payroll."

"Couldn't he understand that?"

"Hell, I never told him. You don't tell people that you can't afford something. Not in business, you don't. He probably thought I was slamming the door just because he is a disagreeable, evil-tempered old hell-raiser. How is he?"

"He looked fine to me. He looks too healthy to be idle. I imagine he is bored to death."

Bart shook his head. "I still can't afford him."

Barbara returned, full of bright apologies for having taken so long. She had a big plate of sandwiches and she went back for a bowl of salad. The conversation switched emphasis immediately. Barbara had been a good listener to tales of the ambulance and tales of Texas, but now she had tales of her own to tell, mostly about her children. She had four. Cecily, age eleven; Bill, ten; Stephen, eight; and Mary, six.

"You have no idea how it is, raising children today. They are so sharp. An idea that gets in at the top filters down, in one shape or another, to all of them. There is this nun. Cecily has her. She used to be Sister Mary Gabrielle. Now they have all gone back to their family names, you know, and she is Sister Marian Bortsch, which is no improvement. Anyway, she tells these kids that they have to learn to express themselves and their personalities in order to be complete human beings and that they are not to suppress impulses. And the kids thought that she means, and she probably does, that anything they want to do is all right because they are expressing themselves."

"Will you tell me what else she can mean?" Bart said. "Or what she is trying to say."

"I'm sure I don't know."

"Well, they don't express themselves too much around here," Barbara said, "and there are some impulses that they jolly well suppress, but it doesn't make things easier for parents to have nuns putting nonsense into their heads. There is enough nonsense there already."

Gregory was awkwardly placed. He could not discuss the Church, or its schools, freely any more. He was standing on the outside now. Barbara was still talking about nuns. Monsignor Joseph Annixter, pastor of the church that she and Bart attended, Saint Bernard's, had a choir nun in the school who brought a guitar to Mass. She played the guitar and the children sang what she called "a modern Mass." The Monsignor said she couldn't play the guitar at a Mass and the nun's Mother Superior said that she could. The Mother Superior threatened to take the nuns out of the school and the Monsignor backed down. There were now two guitars playing at Masses, the nun and one of her pupils twanging them.

"It has made an old man of him," Barbara said.

Gregory had been watching Barbara as she talked. She was older than Pamela by about eight or nine years. There were fine lines in her skin and she was not quite as slender as when he had first known her, although that was not apparent in casual contact. She was still startlingly pretty, as she had always been, either in a first impression or under observation at a table; but she did not have Pamela's striking beauty or Pamela's grace or Pamela's eloquence of voice and gesture.

He felt guilty, inwardly embarrassed, sitting at Barbara's table and making mental comparisons which did not favor her; but the comparisons came to his mind unbidden.

It had been a pleasant evening. When he rose to go, Bart walked to the car with him. "Nice little wagon you have," he said.

"It isn't mine. It's Pamela's mother's car."

Bart nodded. He was standing straight and tall. "You don't think you'll be staying in Culverton?" he said.

"I can't. You know how it would be."

Bart looked away, then looked back. "Well, if you go," he said, "let's have another session."

"We will. Of course. I enjoyed tonight."

"So did I."

Greg drove away and he could see Bart in his rear vision mirror, standing on the curb looking after him.

–II–

Greg and Pamela had breakfast in their room, served by a maid who had a serving table on wheels. Pamela was clear-eyed, rested, wearing white negligee which was not absorbed by the blue of the room.

"I'll never get used to service like this," he said, "particularly not with breakfast."

"One can get used to anything. You're not complaining are you?"

"In a way. It's great, of course. No effort. I guess I'm an effort guy. Maybe I don't fix a breakfast but I have an idea that I ought to be out hunting for it."

"Remind me to give you a club before lunch. You can go out and kill your own rabbit."

Pamela rose and stretched and walked across the room. She was lithe, graceful, long legged. He liked the way she swooped down twice, once with her right hand and then her left, picking up imaginary objects from the floor. The swooping did not slow her progress to the bathroom; she made it part of the process of walking across a room. She could find exercise in anything that she did and she never made a show of it. She was not an exhibitionist.

The attorneys were coming at eleven. Greg went to another of the many bathrooms and when he came back Pamela was gone. She would, of course, want to see her mother. He walked around the room and he

257

stood at the window, looking out. The roads had been cleared but the fields were white. There were heavy banks of cloud on the horizon. The flat layers of snow seemed strange after balmy Hollister. It was, of course, still January, with a good part of Culverton's winter still to be delivered. He wondered how long he and Pamela would have to stay, how soon they could decently plan to get away.

Pamela came back to the room quietly. She seemed grave, preoccupied, and she made one circle of the room as he had done. She was wearing a navy suit that he had not seen before, probably one that she had left here in the house. This huge house probably contained a great many things of hers that he had never seen. The suit had golden buttons shaped like half walnuts.

"Let's go for a walk, Greg," she said. "I want to talk to you. I can't talk in here."

"Neither can I. Walking is fine."

He had a sweater that was beginning to show its age. He wore it under his brown jacket. Pamela wore a fur coat. He hadn't ever seen that before, either. She had a shapeless felt hat and a white scarf around her throat. They walked on the motor driveway down toward the road. It was a cold morning with heavy gray clouds dropping low.

"Greg," she said, "I want you with me, close to me, when those attorneys read the will."

"Of course. But what do you think will happen?"

She had been walking with her head down. She lifted it suddenly, looking up into his face. "Carina says she is certain, or fairly certain, that my father never changed his will. He said that he was going to toss me out of it, and he said that he *had* tossed me out, but—"

Her voice trailed off and she dropped her head again. He was walking in step with her. His own voice sounded strange when he spoke. "Suppose that is true," he said. "What would it do to you?"

"I don't know. I never like to think ahead. Never. I don't believe that Carina knows. She's guessing. I won't go farther than that. But stay close to me."

"What could I do, close or far?"

"Nothing. You don't have to do anything. Having you there, near me, is enough."

They walked back to the house and there did not seem to be anything to say. The subject that they couldn't discuss hung over them and casual topics lacked vitality. They returned to their room and once inside the door, Pamela turned and kissed him. She kissed him softly, gently, without passion.

"Thanks, Greg," she said, "for being you."

It had been a strange half morning. Greg saw himself in one of several full length mirrors and decided to change into the blue blazer that had been his Christmas present. At ten minutes to eleven he walked down the stairs with Pamela. They entered the library and they were the first to arrive. It was a large, dark-paneled rectangular room with tall windows. The books were leather bound and of amazing uniformity. There were long rows of books, shelf after shelf, to the ceiling level, and a ladder, an elegant ladder in appearance, on which one could climb for the books that were out of reach. Greg selected one of the books at random. It was *The Byzantine Empire* by C. W. C. Oman, M.A., F.S.A., published by T. Fisher Unwin of Paternoster Square, London, in 1892.

"Did your father actually read these books?" he said.

Pamela hesitated, then shook her head. "He wanted a fine library. He thought that he should have one. He admired people who wrote and he talked about reading but he never got around to it." She looked embarrassed. "We all have our pretenses," she said. "That was his."

There was a sound of movement in the hall. Carina came in with Ted, her brother-in-law and his wife, Elinor. There were other Gibsons behind them and Hugh Paulen, Ralph Gibson's attorney. He was a gray-haired, affable man with shrewd eyes who was friendly in meeting people and who did not overdo the affability. There was a desk arranged for him, facing the grouped chairs. An attorney from his firm sat on his right, a well-groomed, impersonal young man named Kevin Ridgeway.

Greg was seated beside Pamela. She rested her hand upon his as Hugh Paulen began his short preliminary discourse. Her hand was as cold as if she had kept it in the refrigerator all morning. Hugh Paulen was explaining that Mr. Gibson's financial position in the brokerage firm of Gibson, Paskert and Rowe, and in the Gibson Tool Company, was protected through arrangements made in a document other than his will. The arrangements, including insurance, were too complicated for Greg Lind to follow and he was obviously not expected to follow them because the attorney was briefing an involved matter which seemingly concerned only Ted Gibson and several other Gibsons.

There was a noticeable tensing in the small library group when Hugh Paulen handed the document to his assistant and accepted another in its place. This was the last will and testament of Ralph Gibson and the respect accorded to it by the attorney was an indicator of its importance. This was a document which concerned the disposal of a tremendous sum of money. The attorney read, pausing for explanatory comment when he considered comment necessary.

Carina and her welfare were, of course, the first concern. There was an affectionate, complimentary paragraph and then the bequest. This, too, was involved beyond the understanding of Greg Lind. This house was already Carina's through past deeds of gift, as were the furnishings. The will established a trust for the maintenance of house and grounds, the provision of a suitable staff, the payment of taxes, et cetera and et cetera. Carina would not be called upon to handle money or accounts in connection with her home. All bills would be paid for her. There was then a complicated series of paragraphs that dealt with the transfer of stocks, bonds and real estate. Greg listened, dazed by it.

Hugh Paulen paused, turned a page and opened a new chapter: "To my beloved daughter, Pamela—"

Pamela's hand tightened and it was still cold. She sat stiffly straight and the attorney read the identity of a trust established in her name when she was a child and built over a period of years. Under the terms of the will she was to receive the interest from this trust over a period of ten years and, at her own option, continue the arrangement or draw upon principal after that. At least, that was how Greg understood the central thread. He did not understand the details at all.

"As of this morning, Mrs. Lind," the attorney said, "the capital sum in this trust is in excess of one half million dollars."

Greg heard Pamela's breath catch and then the attorney was reading again. The precise wording slipped by too swiftly but on the delayed register of a brain that was taken by surprise, the paragraph read:

"Because I cannot foresee the future, and because I do not believe that any man should be dependent upon his wife's income or capital, I bequeath to the husband of my daughter, Pamela, if she is married at the time of my death, the sum of one hundred thousand dollars."

It was a stunning paragraph. Gregory Lind stared at the attorney and he felt that everyone was staring at him. Hugh Paulen nodded to him in friendly fashion and then continued to read.

There was a bewildering array of bequests to people whom Gregory did not know. An incredible amount of wealth flowed on a man's voice across a desk top and it was impossible to calculate its amount because so much of it was expressed in terms of holdings, trusts, foundations, or identified merely by real estate code numbers. Ultimately the reading came to an end and people rose from chairs. There was polite visiting in the room but it was the lunch hour and various groups were eager for a chance to discuss the will, so the visiting did not last long. Greg, too, wanted to get away. He wanted to talk to Pam. Ted Gibson crossed the room to him.

"I'm happy that my brother did as he did in your behalf," he said. "If you have any problems, or if I can assist you, call on me please."

"Thank you. I will."

It was pleasant to have such a greeting from the senior member of the Gibson family, but Ted Gibson's words, like all of the other words that had been released in the room, were difficult to accept as reality. The feeling that he was part of a phantasy did not end for Greg even when he reached the bright blue room with Pamela. As soon as they had closed the door, she threw her arms around him and wept. She clung tightly to him and he could only pat her shoulder.

"Don't cry, Pam," he said. "Don't cry."

It sounded asinine to his own ears and Pam paid no attention to it. He drew the breath deep into his lungs and lifted her in his arms. He carried her across the room and sat on the chaise lounge with Pam on his lap.

"Talk it out," he said. "Don't cry it."

"I can't help it." She had her head against his shoulder and her voice came up to him, muffled. "He was so damned wonderful," she said. "I should have known. I was small and narrow and unpleasant and stupid. I was still his 'beloved daughter' even when I didn't deserve to be. He wanted to take care of me, no matter what I did."

Greg looked across the room. He did not like the pale blue effect. It got on his nerves but he did not think about it. He was thinking that Ralph Gibson in taking care of his daughter had not left anything for another man to do. In a material sense she had more as the daughter of Ralph Gibson than she would ever have as the wife of Gregory Lind. Her father had assured that. It, of course, was a thought that must be forever left unexpressed. Pamela stirred in his arms.

"And you!" she said. "What man ever did that? He thought of everything. Now you will never have to worry because I have money. You won't have to give it a thought. You have money of your own. Quite a lot of money."

"It isn't my money, Pam," he said.

She straightened her body and her face was inches from his own. There were tear stains on her cheeks and her eyes were red. "What do you mean?"

"It's an old will, Pam, written before you knew me. He wasn't leaving anything to me. He was leaving it to someone in his own world, someone accustomed to money."

Pam had drawn back. Her eyes widened. "You mean Rodney? He wouldn't. He didn't like Rodney for a minute. He wouldn't have left him a dime."

"He certainly didn't like me and he wouldn't have left me a penny. All that is academic. That will was written before he knew that I was on earth, before you did."

Pamela slid off his lap. She walked across the room and walked back. As always, she came to focus when she was challenged.

"Look," she said. "That will was written before I married Rodney Keller. My father was leaving money to my husband, no matter who. Do you understand? He could have taken that paragraph out when I married Rodney. He could have taken it out when I married you. He didn't. He wanted to be certain that my husband, whoever he was, had money of his own. It was an idea he had. He was leaving me a lot of money. He didn't want my husband outgunned."

Greg watched her. She was particularly lovely always when she moved around, stirred by something, talking about it. There was some inner fire that sparked her gestures, her expression, the toss of her head. She was tear-streaked and her hair was a bit wild, but she was beautiful.

"All right," he said. "Maybe I'm not outgunned, but what does all this money do to us, Pam, to you and me?"

"What do you mean?"

"I think you know."

She sank into a chair, leaning forward. Her eyes met his and she looked bewildered. He did not believe that she was bewildered.

"That money is ours," she said. "It will buy things. We do not have to live, ever again, in horrible places like the ones we had in Albuquerque and Hollister, or count nickels and dimes the way we did."

"We were happy in those horrible places."

"Of course. We're us. We'll be happy in lovely places, too."

"Pam," he said. "Do you mean that you're not going back to Hollister, that you want to stay here?"

"Of course. What else can we do?"

He stared at her. "You know that I can't. You know what I am. You know that I could never live in this town again."

"No. I don't know that." Pam shook her head slowly. "People accept facts accomplished, Greg. You will live well. You will find something interesting to do. A divorce seems like the end of everything, but it isn't. A person gets up out of the mud of it and walks again, and people forget. Leaving the priesthood isn't the end of everything, either."

"I can't live here as something else, Pam. Not in Culverton."

"You can't go back to Hollister and drive an ambulance, either. Or go to another strange town to look for work. Think about that." Pam rose. "Think, darling. I'll be out in a few minutes. We're having lunch with Carina."

He hadn't heard about lunch with Carina before. His life seemed to be arranged for him, he thought, like the life of a puppet, a pulling of strings here and there. He tried to think of Hollister. He had liked his job on the ambulance. He was, he supposed, more like that youngster, Jerry, than he had ever acknowledged to himself. He could not remember exactly how Jerry had phrased his thought, but the general idea was that he never wanted to hurt anybody but that when someone was hurt, he wanted to be present, to do what he could. There was something mystical in the way Jerry had phrased it, or maybe in the way that it had registered in his own mind. At any rate, that was how he felt, too, and ambulance work had had meaning for him.

He sat in the room that he shared with Pamela, surrounded by soft and filmy blue, and he realized that he was very far from Hollister. He could never return. A woman with a half a million dollars could not live on the edge of nothing in a mediocre Texas city. He could not, himself, ride an ambulance for long, ignoring the fact that he had one hundred thousand dollars of his own. A man's thought processes changed, inevitably, with changed circumstances in his life.

One hundred thousand dollars! It was as unreal as the overwhelming baby blue of this room. He wondered how, in any chapter of her life, it had been possible for Pamela to want such an insipid setting as this, or possible for her to endure it as a personal frame. He could, at least, see the blue; he had never seen anywhere, even from a distance, one hundred thousand dollars all in one place. He could not remember having seen a thousand dollars. Not at any time. There had been the collections at the cathedral but he had never counted the money or handled it; and no collection at Saint Anselm's had run over a few hundred dollars.

Pamela returned and she had erased the tears. Her coppery hair caught the sunlight and it was precisely combed, soft around her face. Her lips were vividly red, the upper and lower lips seemingly identical in shape and size. She was as simply dressed as he in her blazer-like navy jacket with the gold buttons.

"I've tried to tell you about Carina," she said. "I'm happy that you will have a chance to know her yourself."

He did not answer but he was thinking that if knowing Carina involved living in this house, he would not know Carina. He thought, too, that Pamela had a technique for handling difficult discussions; she found an excuse to break off and then came back with a lead into another topic. She put her arm through his now as they walked to the staircase but he was feeling detached from her; a little defensive, perhaps, a little hostile, definitely detached.

The snow had started to drift down. Snow had been a good bet with all of the cloud overhead. He could see the snow in a series of pictures as they passed windows. When they reached the sun room, the snow was all around them, but there was warmth in the sun room and comfortable chairs and soft colors. One could look in any direction and see snow through glass but, in effect, it was far away.

Carina Gibson was wearing black. She looked tired, a little washed out. She was, Greg thought, a woman who needed color. Color was a part of Pam, too. There were circles under Carina's eyes but there was nothing lacking in her smile. It was a faint smile but it lighted her face. She addressed herself to Greg rather than to Pamela.

"I hope that you do not object to a drink at noon."

"No. I wouldn't make a habit of it."

"Nor I. But today, thus far, has been an ordeal. We ought to relax." She smiled again. "Will you bartend, Greg."

"Gladly."

In the absence of any other instruction, he mixed three Scotches with water. His mood had lifted in the face of Carina's friendliness. There had been warmth in her, in her voice, in the way she looked at him. He had the fleeting thought, as he served the drinks, that he was one man and that these were two women who knew each other very well. He dismissed the thought with the reflection that, unless he watched himself, he would be as bad as Bart about women. Carina dipped her glass to him when he seated himself.

"I imagine that today was harder on you than on any of us," she said.

"In what way?"

"Oh, come now. That's unworthy of you."

"All right. I did know what you meant. The money was a shock. It is still a shock. I had not anticipated anything like that."

"No, of course not. Frankly, I did not anticipate it either and I thought that I knew my husband's mind."

Carina took a cigarette from a box and he crossed the room to light it for her. "Thank you," she said, "but don't do that again. I smoke them all of the time and you'll make me nervous jumping up." She blew a stream of smoke toward the ceiling. "Greg, you have an idea that you do not want that money, haven't you?"

"Yes."

"I knew you would. And I haven't talked to Pamela, as you know. It hit me that way when I heard Hugh read that paragraph."

She was relaxed against the cushioned back of the chair on which she was seated, but her head was lifted slightly and tilted back. She resembled Pam, or Pam resembled her, but Carina's face was rounder, not so strongly sculpted. Greg did not try to answer her. He sipped his drink, waiting.

"Tell me," she said, "so I can check how straight I think, why don't you want that money?"

He looked past her rather than at her, watching the snow. It was not falling lazily now; it was blotting out the earth and sky and all things.

"It is not mine," he said. "I have no connection with it, no relationship in effort or risk or work accomplished. The man who indicated that I should have that money was a man who did not know me. He left it to a symbol, a code figure."

"Ah, yes," Carina said. "I will give myself a perfect grade. That is exactly what I expected of you." She took a swallow of her drink. "You know, Greg, I like you. I like you tremendously. I did not believe that I would ever like you, but I do."

"Thank you."

"Don't thank me for what I cannot help. I started liking you when I read between the lines of Pamela's letters. You have been good to her and good for her. You are the only son I'll ever have and, as they say in the Navy—" She smiled a faint flickering smile. "I'm glad to have you aboard."

"I'm glad to be aboard."

The statement sounded banal, silly, inadequate to Greg's own ears but the words fell and he had to let them lie. Carina shook her ice in the glass, rotating it.

"Speaking of the Navy," she said, "there is no sun today and we do not have a yardarm, so do you suppose we could have another drink."

"I would suppose so."

Greg was surprised to discover that his own glass was empty. He did not remember having taken more than a sip. He looked at Pam. She was smiling at him, holding her glass to show him that there was nothing in it but a little ice. The sun room was a friendly spot surrounded by whirling snow. He enjoyed being here at this moment of time and Pam had been very right. He did like Carina. He crossed the room to the portable bar and mixed three drinks. He was aware as he seated himself again that Pam had not spoken a word. This was Carina's hour and Pam was leaving it to her.

"About money," Carina said. "I hope you will listen to me, Greg. I know a great deal about it."

"Certainly I will listen. Nobody could know less about it than I."

"In the first place," Carina said, "people have ancestry, money has none. Provided that you take care of your taxes, the money in your pocket is yours and nobody asks whether it came from day labor, professional services, investments or inheritance. It is money and it is yours. You can put it in a bank or buy an automobile or do any damned thing and nobody questions you. It makes no difference where it was before it ended up in your pocket. In that pocket, it is yours—the advantage of it and the responsibility."

She was leaning forward, intent, her eyes fixed on his face. "What are you trying to tell me?" he said.

"You know what I am telling you. It makes no difference on earth that you did not earn that one hundred thousand dollars. You'll earn it before you get through with it, and it gets through with you. People who have money, sizable amounts of money, know that they have to keep earning that money although they already have it; if they don't, they lose it."

"I have no feeling for, or about, money. I can't keep earning what I could not have earned in the first place."

"You'll be surprised. The money will teach you. Trust me on that. You'll discover it is true. Provided you have character, and you do have, you'll find it impossible to abuse money, to waste it, to use it foolishly. The money won't let you. You may gamble and lose some of it but you won't lose it all and maybe you'll learn from the gamble how you can win your losses back."

"I'd rather just turn it back to the estate. Not take it at all."

There was silence in the room. Carina lighted a cigarette and the flash of the match was measurable sound. The snow was a quiet constant beyond the windows.

"You could do that," Carina said slowly. "You heard some figures today if you listened to Hugh Paulen but, for one reason or another, they were not a true measure of my husband's estate which is much larger than it appears. If you turned that hundred thousand back, the books would absorb it, accountants would make entries, the money would be money still but diverted into various channels of sheer bookkeeping. Why should you do that?"

"I can't add to what I've said."

"Maybe not. Well, we'll have lunch in five minutes. Ring and tell them so, Pamela. I'm feeling those drinks. I'm not trying to convince you of anything against your will, Gregory. My husband was a wise man, a farseeing man. When he wrote that will he didn't see you. He saw Pamela. For Pamela's sake as well as her husband's sake, he wanted that husband to be in a position to oppose her if he wanted, to say 'No' to her, to walk out on her. There is no happiness in slavery and a man married to a woman with money is a slave if he has no money of his own. That is true, no matter how hard the woman may try to be a decent human being. If you have that hundred thousand, Greg, Pamela will still have more than you have, but she can't crack any whips."

"She hasn't ever. She wouldn't."

"I'm sorry. She's my daughter, but she would. She couldn't help herself."

He looked at Pamela who laughed. "I'll try not," she said, "but don't bring me into this. I'm enjoying myself as a spectator."

Carina rose. "It is time we had lunch," she said. "I'll only add one statement and a question. That money is all yours, Greg, and absolutely yours. No one, including Pamela, can tell you how to spend it or use it—and there is only one thing that you cannot decently do with it. Do you know what that is?"

He stood straight and met her eyes. "Yes. I cannot give it away."

Carina nodded. "I was not mistaken in you. I was positive that you would see that."

They walked into a little breakfast alcove for lunch and it was still snowing beyond the windows. Greg thought that there was nothing remarkable about his knowing that he could not give the hundred thousand dollars away. Ralph Gibson had bequeathed it for a reason if not a purpose and he, Greg, had the option of refusing it. If he did not exercise that option, then he was committed to the effort of justifying the Gibson reason for giving it to him. All of which might sound complicated if one put it in words but it was, actually, quite simple.

He did not know, or could not remember later, what they had for lunch: fish, flesh, fowl or vegetable.

They were back in the gay and frivolous blue room eventually, he and Pamela. It was still snowing.

"You did not have much to say," he said. "I don't know how you feel about anything."

"You can't have much doubt of how I feel about things," Pam said. "I did not want to interrupt when you and Carina were doing so beautifully. I have always wanted you to know Carina."

He walked around the room, aware that Pam was watching him intently. He did not look at her.

"Pam," he said, "I can understand how you feel about Hollister. You didn't have much there and you have everything here; but what we had there was ours, peculiarly ours."

"What we have here will be ours, too."

"Not in the same way. We won't be living in our own pattern; we will be living in another man's pattern, one that has been handed to us."

"You forget, Greg, that I was not a poor girl when you met me."

"I did not know what you were."

"You could have guessed. And I was a Gibson when you married me."

"Disinherited."

"So we believed. You saw this house before you married me. It didn't deter you."

"The other side of the coin is the fact that I was poor and you married me."

"That's right. I'd do it again."

He stopped pacing. "Would you, Pam?"

"Any day of any week."

He stood looking at her and her eyes did not waver. He turned away. "I can't stay in Culverton, Pam," he said. "I was a priest here. I'll be always meeting people who remember. I'll be meeting priests who know me. They despise me, of course."

"Maybe not. Maybe you could be surprised."

"No."

"Well, what did you have in Albuquerque or Hollister? Was life wonderful for you?"

He walked to the window and stood looking out. Life had not been wonderful for him in New Mexico or Texas. He had met people who despised him, many of them. He had shrunk from the filling out of application forms and from the expressions on the faces of those who read the forms. The ambulance work had meant something to him but Pam had been embarrassed by the fact that he worked on a hurry wagon, and he would never have been able to provide for Pam as she deserved while he worked there; never.

"Let's go out walking in that stuff," he said. "I want to see if it's blue."

"Wonderful," Pam said. "Let's do it."

They walked in the snow, and against it, wallowing at times in the fall. It was impossible to carry on a conversation and they did not try. They walked for an hour and Pam never suggested quitting or voiced a complaint. Something restless and unhappy in Greg found a level of quiet and acceptance in that hour. When they were back in their own quarters, he gripped Pam's shoulders hard.

"Thanks," he said.

Her eyes smiled up at him. "Want to do it again?"

They laughed together and they did not discuss a problem until they were in bed and suspended on the edge of sleep. He rolled over and enclosed her within his arm.

"There's a parable, Pam," he said. "The Lord told a rich young man to give his wealth away and to become a follower. The young man couldn't do it. I could do it once. I didn't have much but I gave up what I had and I became a follower. Some priests are going to remember that if they see me with money. They will think, and I will know they are thinking, that I gave up following for money."

"You didn't," Pam said sleepily. "I'll make a bet."

"What bet?"

"I'll bet that when you do something with that hundred thousand, when you score a success with it, whatever you do, some of those priests who know you are going to ask you for donations when they stage big drives. I'll bet you."

Greg did not answer her and within two minutes he could tell from her breathing that she was asleep. He lay on his back staring upward. He would not, he admitted silently, have had an answer for Pam if she had stayed awake demanding it. He was afraid that she was right.

– III –

There was no direct air service between Culverton and Hollister. One had to take the morning plane, or the early afternoon plane, to St. Louis and make connections with the Hollister plane there. Greg Lind took the morning plane. He was flying alone because Pamela felt that Carina needed her for a while and that he would not need her help on the few details that needed attending in Hollister.

"If you have any trouble packing my things," she said, "give Carol a ring and she'll take care of them."

He had no intention of calling Carol Dane. Packing the things that Pamela had in Hollister would not be a major problem. He had a window seat on the plane and he could see the snow-coated earth through a series of holes in the cloud design. He watched the changing pattern of cloud without any real interest in it. This trip to Hollister depressed him. As he had planned it in his mind, he and Pam would fly back together and it would be a matter of flying home; as it turned out, he was flying alone and Hollister was a stop on the round trip that would return him ultimately to Culverton.

There had been no violent changing of plans, no grim argument or debate. The picture had changed gradually, imperceptibly, and what he was doing now had become the logical, inevitable, reasonable thing to do. He could not place a finger on any moment and identify that moment as the one of decision; the decision had been reached by a sort of gradual conversion, or a growing of one thing into another. The same process had evolved other simpler decisions between Pam and himself in the past.

Bart, of course, had seemed fairly certain that he, Greg, had returned to Culverton to stay, that he would not return to Hollister. Bart had not hammered the point, had not tried to drive it home, but he had had an obvious conviction. Bart was a cynic, particularly where women were concerned. Bart's basic belief about women was that a woman, any woman, knew what she wanted and was undeviating in the getting of what she wanted. A woman might, of course, want an utterly silly thing, a ridiculous or a dangerous or an unworthy thing: whatever it was, she moved relentlessly to it.

Greg had been amused at Bart's cynicism but he had wondered a few times and he was wondering now. Pamela had been courageous and generous in her acceptance of his humble way of life and she had taken Hollister for hers as he had done. She had not wanted Culverton, but the Culverton of her not-wanting had been the Culverton of no money and of her father's displeasure. She wanted Culverton now and she could dismiss lightly the fact that he wanted it not. She seemed convinced that he would be better off there in the long run, that prejudice against him would subside, that he would make friends on another level; all of which might be merely the implementing of what she wanted; or it might be some deep wisdom in her, a wisdom deeper than his own.

Sitting in an airplane, riding now over unbroken fields of cloud, he faced the fact that he had been without a strong alternative to anything Pam proposed because he did not know what he wanted. He had no long-term want, no goal ahead of him to be attained. He had known what he wanted once. He had wanted to be a priest. Once a priest, he had wanted little more. He had not pressed for preferment or advancement; he had not even been a driving editor, fighting for his own concept of what the *Catholic Star* should be. He had looked at himself often with impatience when he worked on the *Star*, deriding his own lack of combativeness while, at the same time, maintaining a conviction that combativeness was not a priestly function. He was impatient with himself again, now.

"If I were piloting this airplane," he thought, "I would not know where I wanted to go. Instead of St. Louis I might end up in Chicago, or Tulsa."

The pilot had no such confusion in his mind. He brought the ship down through the cloud and there was a frost fog over St. Louis, icicles suspended from hangar roofs at Lambert Field. Greg walked off the plane with the other passengers and he had two hours before the plane to Hollister would leave; too little time for a trip to town but enough time in which to get bored at an airport.

He mailed a postcard to Pamela, then, on an impulse, one to Carina. It didn't seem right to neglect his own family so he sent a card to his mother, one to Janet, and to Bart. He hesitated and then wrote one for Barbara. It was time to board his plane.

"I am glad that the wait wasn't longer," he thought. "I'd be sending cards to perfect strangers."

Hollister, when he reached it, was bright and mild although there was a wind with an edge to it. Greg Lind had traveled very little and he experienced a sense of lift, coming into a city that he knew and recognizing the landmarks. He rode the airline bus to downtown and a taxi to the apartment. He missed Pamela when he stood for a moment on the sidewalk after he had dismissed the cab. This was a street on which the clicking heels of her shoes had left an imprint.

The apartment was silent, empty, airless, without warmth or light. When he snapped the wall switch, the orange-colored bulbs in the chandelier sent pale light down over the furniture, competing with, rather than complementing, the light which spilled in through the windows. The furniture looked drab and tired, the colors faded. He had been able to accept the apartment and the furniture without thinking about it while he had Pamela with him; he could see it now as she must have seen it. An apartment like this did not deserve Pamela.

He looked in the closets and the drawers. They had left a few possessions here, mostly Pamela's, but they had left no imprint of themselves. He had no feeling that this was, or had been, home; it was merely a run-down, shabby habitation which had sheltered too many people, forgetting them all.

"And that is a nice poetical thought," he said.

He walked three blocks to the garage where they had left Pamela's car. He paid the storage fees on it and drove out on the streets. Under the wheel, watching the traffic, aware of the Texas license plates, he developed again the sense of belonging. These were his streets. He had done a lot of driving on them.

There was one hour's time difference between Culverton and Hollister. It was earlier here. He checked his watch. He could catch Tracy Welton before he left and that seemed like a logical first move. He drove into the emergency space beside the hospital and mounted the familiar steps. Tracy Welton was seated behind his desk. He was wearing a gray shirt and a dark blue necktie with a multitude of white dots. There was a cigarette hanging from the corner of his mouth. His eyes narrowed when he recognized Greg.

"What in hell do you want?" he said.

"Nothing much. I landed in Hollister a little while ago and stopped in to say hello."

"You can trot right back to your airplane if that's where you were. I never give a bum two chances. You've had yours."

"Thanks. I did phone you. As I told you, my wife's father died suddenly and we had to go back to Culverton. There wasn't anything else that I could do."

"I didn't believe a word of it. You were hung over. That's what was the matter with you. I don't even know if you have a wife." Tracy crushed out his cigarette in the ashtray, twisting it. His head came up. "Now, get the hell out of here!"

Greg shrugged, amazed at himself that he had offered any explanation. There was certainly nothing to be gained by argument. He could neither win nor lose anything in Tracy Welton's office. He walked out and turned right in the hall. Both ambulances were in and there were half a dozen men in the bullpen, two of them early birds reporting for the three to eleven tour. He knew all of them except one, a tall young man with rolled sleeves who had flowers tattooed on his forearms. This, of course, would be the new driver on his old buggy. Jerry, presumably, had moved into his job.

Greg Lind felt at ease and at home in this environment; it was his. He raised his hand in a gesture of greeting and voiced his hello without a response. Jerry Kagat dropped his cigarette and ground it out with his heel.

"Are you coming back?" he said.

The eyes of the other men asked the same question. If Greg Lind was coming back, one of these men would be out of work and one of them would move from the job that he had to a lesser one. Groups like this resisted change though constantly experiencing it. Greg shrugged.

"No," he said.

"Wouldn't he take you on?"

"He wouldn't even talk to me."

"Tough."

Jerry's sympathy lacked substance and, once they had heard the verdict, the other men were no longer even interested. Greg looked at them and he thought that they were, actually, compassionate people, gentle in their handling of the injured, patient with the frightened and the hysterical, willing to accept hard, dirty work in behalf of others. Jerry was probably the best of them in identifying with the hurt and the maimed, so selfless in his identification that Greg had seen him as potentially a mystic. Jerry's sense of compassion, however, did not extend into the world beyond the injured; it did not extend outward to include a man looking for a job, particularly if that man's search threatened his own. It was the human limitation upon kindness and concern that one would not imagine; that one had to see.

"It's O.K.," Greg said. "I'm not even staying in town."

He walked out without waiting to see if his sign-off had any effect on the men in the bullpen. He slid in under the wheel of the car again and not until the engine was turning over did he face the fact that he had nowhere to go. He had not realized until this moment, because he had never given the subject any thought, that he did not have a friend in the city of Hollister. He had had men with whom he worked and he had had Pamela. He could see now the need that she had felt and he could understand the many protests she had voiced against their way of life, protests that he had taken lightly at the time that they were uttered.

He drove aimlessly but he headed away from the old section. He had had his picture in the paper after the incident of the murder in the hippie house, but he had no desire to see the house again, nor to visit the neighborhood. He stopped finally at a restaurant where he had never dined with Pam, and he ate a dinner to which he paid little attention. He remembered that he and Pam had passed a Catholic church on Christmas Eve, one they did not know, and they had not gone in. It seemed to be a matter demanding rectification. He drove to the church and there was a meeting in progress, twenty people in the pews and a layman on his feet talking about Vatican Two. He returned to the car.

He had nothing more to do in Hollister save to pack and get out. The packing when he returned to the apartment took him an hour and ten minutes.

"Take your time," Pam had told him when he was leaving. "Try to have a good time. You have certainly earned a vacation and I will be all right. Carina and I have so many things to go over. Dad, like anyone else, had a lot of personal things he prized. She couldn't face them alone. I'll be busy, so take your time."

He had taken his time and he had finished Hollister in a few hours. He was missing Pam. This was the first time that they had been apart since their marriage. He had thought often that it would be good to get away occasionally, that he would think more clearly, that his mind would discover great thoughts in solitude. It didn't work. He had the solitude and no thought came to him. There was nothing that he wanted to do. He was astonished that he had not realized earlier that there had never been anything in Hollister except Pam; nothing at all.

The morning was bright and he felt better with a new day. The day belonged to the car and he no longer thought of the car as belonging to Pam. "Sell it down there and come home on the plane if you can haul the stuff," Pam had said. "That poor old car has seen its best days." He did not sell it. He bought it four new tires, a wash job and an engine tune-up. Carina had offered him one of her husband's two cars but he preferred this small, slightly shabby car to anything pretentious; particularly if he were to live in Culverton. After he had cared for it and spent money on it, he regarded it as his. It was the first automobile he had ever owned.

He drove out of Hollister before dawn on the second morning. He liked early day and he had always associated himself with the people who were at work when the rest of the world still slept. The light in the sky was pale and uncertain when he crossed the boundary line into Louisiana, and turned north. He kept no track of time and only vague general track of direction. It was good to be driving.

He reached the church around a bend in the road. It was set back in a wide space of its own, with trees around it; a plain brick church with a bell tower and a spire with a Cross above it. Beyond the clearing there was water, green-blue in the early light. There was a sign before the church which identified it as Saint Mary of the River and its pastor as Reverend Jean Marc De Varennes.

"Saint Mary of the River."

Gregory Lind repeated the name of the church, liking the sound of it. He parked at the edge of the clearing and this, he assured himself, was his idea of a church; simple, perfectly proportioned, obviously old but not shabby, definitely not shabby. The door of the church opened and one man stood in the doorway momentarily, then stepped out. Other people followed him, four men and seven women. One of the men was young, a tall, athletic man who went off, striding. One of the old men and two of the women were colored. Greg looked at his watch. It was six thirty-five. This was the six o'clock Mass. He sat there remembering. The people were gone and he pulled into the lot, parking his car.

"Why not?" he said.

He walked into the church and genuflected. It was an old church but the interior had been remodeled. He rarely saw a remodeled church that he approved, or liked. He liked this one. Again, there was stark simplicity. There was a low plain altar, the altar of the Latin Mass and behind it a larger-than-life Christ hung on the Cross against a background of crimson and black stripes, floor to ceiling. To the right of the Crucifix, standing against the striped background, a solitary angel blew on an upraised trumpet. There was a modern altar immediately behind the altar rail from which the celebrant of the Mass could face the people. On the epistle side, to the extreme right of a man standing in the aisle, there was a statue of Saint Joseph and on the gospel side a statue of the Blessed Mother. There were stations of the Cross but no other statuary. The church was empty and it was beautiful; smelling vaguely of flowers and incense.

Gregory Lind knelt in a pew halfway down the aisle. He had a vantage point from which he could look over the facing altar of the vernacular Mass and project himself mentally and spiritually, imaginatively perhaps, to the main altar. He had missed the saying of the Mass and he had found little in the Masses of other priests, said in English, which satisfied him. Here, in the quiet, in this lovely little church, he could say his Mass even if he could no longer approach the altar.

He imagined himself vested, walking out, with one altar boy. He made the sign of the Cross and then uttered the "Introibo ad altare Dei." His mind supplied the voice of an altar boy: "Ad Deum qui laetificat juventutem meam." There was no hesitation in him. He did not have a missal or a Mass book, so he had to improvise in many places where he would have read, but he moved in his Mass, his hands physically clasped before him but moving in the projection as the hands of a priest moved. He consecrated the Host and the Chalice of wine and he took the priest's communion, his body motionless in the pew. At last he raised his hand over the congregation and blessed them, and after that, the "Ite, missa est."

It was over and he relaxed in the pew. There was sweat on his hands and his body ached. A haze seemed to float before his eyes. He did not see the priest who walked quietly down the aisle until he had all but reached his pew. The priest was not tall, not impressive physically, but he had a mane of white hair, thick white hair, that was brushed straight back. His face was long and thin, his features irregular and his

275

eyes dark. He wore the black soutane. He was a man of perhaps fifty. Greg rose when the priest stopped beside him.

"You will pardon me," the priest said. "I am Father De Varennes. I have been watching you for twenty minutes or twenty-five. I have never seen a man pray with such utter concentration."

"I was saying a Mass."

"Ah! You said it well, I am certain. You accepted no distraction. How long have you been away from us?"

"Over a year."

"A pity. There was a woman, no doubt."

"Yes. I am married. She has been divorced, so there is no reconciliation with the church possible."

"No. And now you are alone?"

"Oh, no. I am on a business trip. My wife is in Culverton. It has been a very happy marriage. She attends Mass with me every Sunday."

"How unusual. I would like to know you, if only briefly. I was about to have my breakfast when I saw you praying. I could not tear myself away. Will you share breakfast with me?"

"I would like that."

Greg followed the priest down the aisle. There had been a faint French accent in the man's speech which was not surprising when one remembered his name. The rectory was behind the church, a two story brick building that was surprisingly narrow. The dining room had a dark portrait on the wall which reminded Greg of the dining room at Saint Anselm's.

"The first pastor of this parish," Father De Varennes said, "or at least, the pastor who is reputedly the first. It is all a long time ago. His name was Father Godreau." He paused a moment. "You will pardon me. I do not know your name."

"Apologies. That is my fault. I am Gregory Lind."

"Gregory Lind." The priest repeated the name thoughtfully. "I shall call you Father Lind if you do not mind. I will be more comfortable."

"By all means, then. I was Father Lind for nearly ten years."

"It must be difficult not to be Father Lind still."

"At times it is very difficult."

"A pity indeed. Seat yourself at my table. I will return in a minute." Father De Varennes left the room, obviously to instruct his housekeeper. He was back within his minute. "One reads much in this day about the ordeal of celibacy," he said. "It weighs heavily on the priest who is young, and one never grows away from it although one may look back and, in his comparative safety, minimize it. Not so?"

"That is very well put. As is obvious, I did not minimize it."

"No. One does not know how you were tested, or why. There is a pain worse than celibacy. One does not anticipate it and, looking back, one does not minimize it."

"What is that?"

A smiling, middle-aged colored woman brought two glasses of orange juice. Father De Varennes dipped his glass in passing salute. "It is thwarted parenthood," he said. "One feels the need of children, of offspring. It is worse, in its way, than the need of a woman. It is a fundamental thing, a great want. You are too young. You have not felt it yet."

"No. Children have always been rather unreal to me, at least in relation to myself."

The face of the priest across the table was sad but there was something in his eyes that suggested a weighing, a measuring, an appraising. He did not listen idly. He had a strong face. There were deep lines in it and hollows. His lips still suggested fullness and once they might have been sensual. He had a firm chin.

"I sought them," he said, "the young lives I could touch with my own. One touches the young so briefly if they are not one's own. I had one, an orphan, a handsome boy. I educated him, or had him educated, I should say. He was brilliant. He could have done well at anything."

The priest paused. He finished his orange juice. "Actually, he did well at nothing," he said. "There was no loyalty in him. He deserted the faith, everything. I do not know where he is." He made a fatalistic gesture, a spreading of hands. "That happens, too, to those who are actual parents."

"Yes, it does."

"Maybe it is sadder for them. I do not know how." Father De Varennes made a sweeping gesture of dismissal. "I wax garrulous," he said. "I have never had breakfast before with a priest who had left us."

The woman brought in orders of scrambled eggs, biscuits, butter, a perculator full of coffee. Father De Varennes smiled. "Observe!" he said. "One lives like a monarch in this small place."

"One does indeed. I did not anticipate such a breakfast as this one. And I know very little about small places, I am afraid. I have spent my life in cities."

"Cities are exciting; rather frightening, also. I find them so. Here in my humble parish, we have the same problems that you have, the same sins, the same generosities, the same strengths and weaknesses of people."

"You are spared the innovations, such as guitars at your Masses."

"Yes." The lean face looked thoughtful. "I have read of them. Actu-

277

ally, the guitar is not a bad instrument if one understands it. To use it in church one should select the music carefully, most carefully."

The dark eyes lighted and the man's long lips curled in a half smile. "We change, do we not, we priests? The great Beethoven wrote the *Missa Solemnis* and found no friends in the Church for it. They said that it was profane music. Profane! Imagine that." The priest laid down his fork for the sake of a gesture, shrugging his shoulders and spreading his hands apart.

"One of his profanities was at the consecration," he said softly. "He expressed the consecration through a solo violin. I heard the *Missa Solemnis* once in New Orleans. God, it was wonderful!"

Greg Lind had noticed a stereo record player as he walked through the house. "You do not have it, the *Missa Solemnis,* on a record?" he said.

"No."

"I will send it to you when I reach Culverton."

The dark eyes lighted. "You can afford it?"

"Yes."

Greg had considered burdening this thoughtful man with his problem of a hundred thousand dollars, his problem of learning to live as he had never been trained to live, his problem of trying to find wants in himself apart from the two which cancelled each other out; Pam and the priesthood. He knew now that the man could not help him, that the problem always came back to himself, and always would. They had reached the coffee and it was nearly time to go.

Father De Varennes had his eyes fixed on his coffee cup. "I will never forget how you prayed," he said. "It was a privilege to watch you, Father Lind. I did not know you were saying a Mass."

His eyes came up and met Gregory's. "Do you say many of those Masses? For your own good, do not say them in your mind like that, Father Lind. That is a Trappist thing and it will not fit into the life you lead."

Greg stared at him. "You are probably right. I would not have thought of Trappists—"

"Think of them and stay in your own life. Theirs is not a half-discipline."

"No."

The two men walked to Greg's car. Father Jean Marc De Varennes was short and thin, but he was wrapped in an impressive mantle of dignity. There was no doubt that he would run his parish, that he would command it, that he would face unflinchingly any problem that it presented to him.

"I can pray for you, Father Lind," he said, "and I will. Beyond that I cannot help you. I could not wish you unhappiness in your marriage although that marriage denies to you the sacraments of the Church. God can weigh great intangibles of which we, perhaps, are unaware." He straightened and his brief, half-smile moved across his thin face. "I hope that you will say a Mass with your life, and all the acts great and small that make it," he said, "a few great prayers and many small ones. God bless you."

He turned then and walked slowly across the clearing to his church.

– IV –

There is a distinction and a difference between the fact of being lonely and the fact of being alone. Gregory Lind had been lonely through the greater part of his life. He had experienced the peculiar loneliness of the seminarian and of the priest, but his life had been set among people, no matter how lightly the people touched him; other seminarians and priests, parishioners, workers on the paper. He had served people and felt their need of him. Driving through Louisiana into Arkansas, facing the states beyond, he was alone. His only contact with people was casual and momentary, a stop at a filling station or a restaurant or a motel. He did not affect the people he met, or the people to whom he spoke. He knew nothing about any of them personally and they knew nothing of him; he paid them for a service they rendered, moved on and was forgotten, forgetting them.

His life, from this point onward, could easily be alone if he did not return to Culverton. Jack Serkle on the ambulance had been a man alone and, to a major degree, so was Tracy Welton. Being alone was intolerable even in the thought of it. To attain to any purpose, one's life had to be linked to people, involved with people, serving people. The brief human experiences of an ambulance man, so often on the thin line of life and death, were not enough because, in actuality, they were as unsubstantial as those of a filling station attendant, with no links to the past or to the future.

He, Gregory Lind, was fortunate enough when he was alone. He was returning to Culverton. That return had not been an easy decision to make. There were unpleasant experiences awaiting him in Culverton and there would be unpleasant experiences as long as he lived. He had been a Catholic priest in Culverton and many people would reject him utterly when he tried to live among them as a married man. He had been humbly poor in Culverton and, more than any other place, it would be embarrassing to live there with money, money in obviously sufficient amounts. He had faced all of that in his mind and the only weight in the scales against it had been Pamela. It had been enough.

No one else would ever understand what existed between himself and Pamela. They would say, as they would say of any priest who moved from celibacy to a woman, "Sex." That did not explain anything. There was a strong sex pull, an overwhelming need of each other, and that belonged in their story, the essential human fulfillment that men and women brought to one another; but the first ingredient had been companionship and it was still the electricity in the magnet. He could not explain to anyone else the magic of Pam as she moved in his memory when he was away from her.

He loved walking a street with Pam, stopping suddenly to admire a house, or a tree in blossom, a cluster of brightly growing flowers. Pam brought a newspaper to life, perhaps merely by slamming it down impatiently when the news displeased her. She could be stormy but she had humor; her gift of mimicry delighted him. She was hundreds of books ahead of him in reading and he would never catch up, but many books had entered his life when she was reminded of them, or when she quoted from them. He had learned to share living with Pamela and that was something that he could not unlearn. When others had found employment only for his muscles, Pam had kept him aware that he had a mind.

He called Pam from Memphis. Her voice, when she came on the line, was above her normal register. "Where have you been?" she said. "I've been worried to death."

"I'm sorry, Pam," he said slowly. "I should have called sooner. No excuse. I've been wandering around."

"Doing what?"

"Looking for my soul mainly."

"I didn't know that it was lost."

"Merely mislaid. I am all right now."

"Greg," she said, "we are fencing with each other. Are you really all right? Not hurt or drunk or anything?"

"I'm fine, really. And the car is fine. I haven't had a drink since I left home."

"Honestly? What are you doing in Memphis?"

"It's an old bromide, but the perfect answer—Memphis was here."

"Cute. When are you coming home?"

"Another week. O.K.?"

"I suppose so. But I can't imagine. You haven't got another woman with you, have you?"

"I haven't even talked to one."

"In that case, take your week if you need it. But I'd like more information. Can I help you in any way?"

"Not right now. I'm not wasting my time. And look, Pam—"

"I'm looking."

"I love you and I'm missing you terribly."

"That is the first interesting thing you've told me," Pamela said, "and you didn't put any conviction in it."

"I'm no good on a telephone, but I'm thinking the conviction."

He hung up eventually, feeling inadequate. He had never been comfortable with telephones. He had to see a person in order to talk with any feeling of ease, any sense of reality. He had a thousand things to say to Pamela but not over a telephone.

A week! He did not know why he had told Pam that he needed a week. It was a definite measurement of time, so precise that it was meaningless, like the measurement of a small boy in the confessional who said: "I had dirty thoughts seven times, Father."

A conviction was building in him. How long did it take for a conviction to build? His destiny, somehow, seemed to be linked to construction if he lived in Culverton. That was where his family name was rooted. Bart might not want him in his business, money or no money. He, an ex-priest, might be too heavily an embarrassment to Bart. The whole idea would have to be explored, but the important point at the moment was that he had an idea. It was a triumph having it, a moving back into the world in which he would have to live. He had drifted for a long time, in jobs and out of jobs, without an idea, with no target, no place to go.

He had had only one conversation with Ralph Gibson. Pam's father had praised Bart and had deplored that fact that Bart did not have the capital to build fine homes and churches and schools. What an irony it would be if Ralph Gibson, through that blind bequest of his, had supplied the capital that Bart needed. Ralph Gibson might be amused by that if he could know.

It would be, of course, all daydreaming, his poking around among the building materials out of which his memories were built, but he had told Pamela the truth when he said that he had been seeking his soul in unlikely places.

Some day, perhaps, if he could become a useful member of Bart's firm, or if he could earn money of his own in some other way, he could be a patron of Guadalupe House. He had never forgotten it. He could never again work there, but he could, perhaps, help those who worked. That, too, might be a daydream, or it might be another idea, a minor idea or a major one.

He did not take the week. He called Pam long distance from Cincinnati to tell her that he was on his way. At four forty-five he slowed the car momentarily before the stone pillars at the entrance to the Gibson place. He looked up at the griffons who seemed friendly. He had always liked those griffons. He did not like the house. It overwhelmed him as it always had. Pamela was in his arms before he reached the steps. She was soft and warm and a delicate scent surrounded her. He held her tightly against him and he could feel her heart beating.

"Lord!" he said. "How did I ever stay away from you?"

"I don't know. I didn't think that you were ever coming back."

"You should have known."

"I didn't. I never know."

Pamela was walking with her head down. They were heading toward the sun room and there was a certain inevitability about that. It was difficult to talk, to face the necessity for talking. He sensed a reality in that not-knowing of Pam's but he did not have any words that would reassure her, that would have meaning for her. She lifted her head suddenly.

"You weren't in a monastery or some place like that, were you?"

He laughed. "Not near one."

They walked again and he was not laughing inwardly. Pam was afraid of the Church. He had realized that when he was away from her, looking back and recalling the many times she had revealed that fear. He could understand perfectly. He had that fear himself. It seemed to him often, with Pamela or away from Pamela, that he was merely on an extended leave of absence from the priesthood, that a bell would ring some time and that he would be back when it rang. That was nonsense and he knew that it was nonsense, but he never got far away from the thought; wherever he was, he was always encountering the Church.

Carina was in the sun room. She was almost as he first remembered her; vivid, astonishingly young in the image that she projected. She was wearing a brown dress that had trimmings of red and she was wearing a vivid defiant shade of lip rouge.

"Your timing is perfect, Greg," she said. "The sun, this very instant, crossed the yardarm, I'm sure. How was your trip?"

"The trip was interesting. Were you hinting me into tending bar?"

"A hint would be ruined by an explanation. I have always admired men with intuition."

He crossed to the portable bar. It was, he thought, easier to pick up life again with Carina than it was with Pamela. He had been tense meeting Pamela, relaxed meeting Carina. Strange! He mixed the drinks and served them. He had no sense of wanting a drink or needing one. He tasted the Scotch and it was strange in his mouth.

"This is good Scotch," Pamela said. "What's the matter with it?"

He looked at her, startled. "Nothing."

"You looked like someone drinking iodine."

"Sorry. I'm out of practice. This is the first drink that I've had since I left here."

He was looking at Carina. She lifted her eyebrows. "Why?"

"No company. No occasion." He was aware of the questioning eyes of the two women. He had a thought about liquor. It was going to be difficult to express. He groped for it. "I don't believe any of us really like this stuff, or need it," he said, "but there are so many of us in the world that we can't seem to communicate without it."

"A dull theory, that," Carina said. "It might sound better at ten o'clock or eleven, never at five."

"I don't understand the 'No company' bit," Pam said. "Surely you knew people in Hollister. And where were you for weeks if not with people?"

"I was alone. I discovered that I didn't know anyone in Hollister, so I traveled. I looked at places, not people."

He could tell from their eyes that both Pamela and Carina doubted him. "What places?" Carina said tentatively.

"Louisiana, Arkansas, Tennessee."

He tried to make the travelogue interesting but his audience wasn't with him on the journey. Later in the bright blue bedroom, Pam stood before a mirror, smoothing eyebrows which did not need smoothing, pressing them down with one finger.

"I don't see how you could travel alone all of that time," she said.

"I couldn't."

"I had long training in self-sufficiency, Pam, and in the art of living alone."

She whirled away from the mirror, facing him. "And you missed it," she said. "Do you want to go back to it? Do you?"

"You know that I don't."

"Stop saying that I know this and that I know that! I don't know a damned thing about you. I only thought that I did."

She was wearing a white robe with a wide belt and an oversized buckle. She looked hurt and on the verge of tears. Despite the flamboyant lipstick, her mouth looked vulnerable. He took two steps and lifted her in his arms.

"You know everything about me worth knowing," he said. "I have no big secrets, Beautiful. I've been playing with an idea. It isn't ready yet. I'll tell you later."

"And you'll tell me where you were, what you were doing?"

"I will."

She sighed. "I have a surprise for you, too. You came home just one day too soon. It will be ready tomorrow evening."

She relaxed into his arms and he held her close to him, feeling whole again, feeling that he was home, dismissing all of the doubts and fears, telling himself that everything was all right, very much all right.

Friday was a day on which to face things, to clear decks, to seek answers. Greg was glad that Pam's mysterious project would keep her occupied. He wanted to talk to Bart but that would have to wait. He wasn't ready. It was a clear, cold day. He drove to Janet's house without a preliminary phone call. Janet herself opened the door. She stood for a wide-eyed second staring at him, then she threw her arms around him, her head against his chest.

"I never expected to see you again," she said.

"Foolish."

"No. You look wonderful. It will be hard to get used to the suit. Are you staying in Culverton?"

"Yes."

"Come see Mother. I don't know how she'll act."

"We'll risk it."

He walked in and, at sight of him, his mother rose from her big chair. She stood there, swaying slightly, and she looked older, feebler. He no longer felt that she acted older than she actually was. Her lips moved soundlessly and she took one step toward him. He crossed the room in three strides, swept her up and kissed her.

"It is good to see you again," he said.

"I've missed you, son, missed you. You'll never know." She plucked at his jacket. "You don't look like my boy in these things. Won't they take you back, son?"

"I won't ever ask that. I'm married."

"Married? No, you're not. You know that better than I do. The woman knows it, too. A priest can't be married."

He sat beside her and she kept patting his hand. She talked to him as she always had but she did not mention Joe and Janet. She paid little attention to anything he said. At the end of an hour he left and he knew that he would return and be welcome, in the collar or out of it, but that there would never be room for Pam in his mother's heart or Janet's. There was nothing that he could do about it.

He drove home and Pamela was waiting for him. She was wearing her light coat, the one with the big, black buttons. Her voice had the slightly breathless quality that it always had when she was excited.

"I'll drive," she said. "I wish that I could blindfold you."

"Can't you?"

"It wouldn't do any good." She bit her lip. "Just promise me that you won't say a word until I tell you that you can. Not even an exclamation."

"I promise."

She drove to Steuben Drive and parked three doors away from 751. She did not look at him and she was out of the car before he was. She walked ahead of him in the old prideful arrogant way that she had. He followed her up the well-remembered white curving staircase and he waited, silent, while she unlocked the door and stepped into the foyer. She crossed it and touched the light switch which illuminated the long room with the cream walls and the high ceilings. The Spanish dancer was reflected in the mirror above the fireplace mantel. One new thing had been added; Pam's concert grand piano at the far end of the room.

Pam did not speak to him. She walked to the arch, beyond which the credenza with the swan lamps stood, and vanished off to the right. She returned with a tray which had a bottle of twelve year old Scotch, a bucket of ice, a pitcher of water and two glasses. Behind her there was music playing, Vaughan Williams' *Thomas Tallis Fantasy*, two rooms away. It was all too perfect. She set the tray on the coffee table between the two small facing sofas.

"That gives the place a lived-in look," she said.

She seated herself on her usual sofa, hugged her knees and looked up at him with laughter in her eyes.

"Speak!" she said.

"I can't. I'm speechless. How did you do it? You moved all the furniture out. Someone else rented the place."

"Fix us a drink."

He fixed the drinks and sat facing her across the coffee table. It seemed a long time ago since they had faced each other across this table. Everything was the same; or, well, not quite the same.

"I bought the place," Pam said. "Lock, stock and barrel. The whole shebang."

"You didn't!"

"I had to do it. I wanted this apartment. It took a lot of doing. I didn't have much time."

"It cost you a lot of money."

"Some. I had it. As it turned out, it may be a buy. It's rental property. We have two tenants."

She was delighted, with the purchase and with herself. He was touched that she had had the thought. She had done it for him, of course. She knew that he could not live in the big house. She knew that he had always loved this apartment. Time had rolled over them. Maybe it would have been better to have kept it as a memory. It was a woman's apartment. She hadn't given a thought to the fact that he had to establish himself with a hundred thousand dollars, that he was the man of the house. She liked to arrange things.

Pamela was watching his face. She set her drink down. Her eyes looked frightened. "You don't like it," she said. "What is the matter with it, Greg?"

"Nothing. It's perfect. I always loved it."

"You did, but you don't. If the apartment is all right, it's us." She was leaning forward. "Have we run it all out in a year or so, Greg? Do you want to go back to being a priest again?"

He crossed to her and knelt at her feet. "Don't be silly, darling," he said. "I was too moved to talk about it. All the thought, the work, the planning—"

"It missed," she said. "I know it missed." She moved over and patted the sofa beside her. "Sit here, please."

He sat beside her and her body felt rigid when he put his arm around her. She gripped the fingers of his right hand and pressed hard.

"I'll give you the rest. I was going to hold it." She looked up at him. "I'm pregnant again, Greg."

After that first glance upward, she looked away from him, moving his hand up and down with the pumping motion of her own.

"I am not going to lose this one. I have time and money and I'll do what the best doctors tell me—and it will be a boy. I feel it."

He sat beside her, seeking desperately in his brain for words. He had never been able to imagine himself as a parent. He had felt no link between himself and the baby she had lost. He thought of Father De Varennes. It might be that the need for children, for the fulfillment of parental function, came late to some people. He tried to imagine a son of his own and he knew suddenly why he had escaped from the thought, fleeing it in cowardice. He would want the boy to be a Catholic. He would want him to go to Catholic schools. If Pam did not want that, the matter would be very difficult. He had been fleeing from the prospect, the certain prospect, of conflict. If there was a boy, a son of his, that boy would have to be told sometime that his father had been a Catholic priest.

Pam's hand pumped up and down. "You probably do not like that any better than you like the apartment," she said. "I'm afraid to look at your face. But I'm going to have that baby, Greg, even if you don't want him. I'm going to have him for him if I can't have him for you."

His arm tightened around her and he had a great fear that Pam was slipping away from him, slipping away in the words that she uttered and in the thought that she held. If she gave herself to the child she would never come back to him again, never belong to him again. If he lost Pam he would have nothing, nothing at all.

"I love you, Pam," he said, "and I will love the baby because it is ours."

She raised her eyes slowly and he was not afraid any longer. This, too, was a vocation. He could not go back. In Pam and in his child lay his only possible approach to ultimate peace of soul. He kissed her gently and then her arms came up and they clung together.